Stood Up

Stood Up

E Chapman

The
Book
Guild

First published in Great Britain in 2025 by
The Book Guild Ltd
Unit E2 Airfield Business Park,
Harrison Road, Market Harborough,
Leicestershire. LE16 7UL
Tel: 0116 2792299
www.bookguild.co.uk
Email: info@bookguild.co.uk

The manufacturer's authorised representative in the EU
for product safety is Authorised Rep Compliance Ltd,
71 Lower Baggot Street, Dublin D02 P593 Ireland (www.arccompliance.com)

This work is entirely fictitious and bears no resemblance to any persons living or dead.

Typeset in 11pt Minion Pro

Printed and bound by CPI Group (UK) Ltd, Croydon, CR0 4YY

ISBN 9781835742815

British Library Cataloguing in Publication Data.
A catalogue record for this book is available from the British Library.

Prologue

I take another sip of wine, scanning the room for what feels like the hundredth time. Claire's done a fantastic job with the decorations – fairy lights draped over the mantel, candles flickering in every corner, and that citrusy scent she loves so much lingering in the air. But even with all the warmth and chatter around me, I still feel like a bit of an outsider. Most of the faces here are unfamiliar, and the few I do recognise are deep in conversation.

I tug my cardigan tighter around me. It's late March, and inside it's stuffy and warm, but the second I step outside, I know the chill will hit me hard. Typical British weather – forever indecisive.

I lean against the kitchen island, swirling the last drops of wine in my glass, debating if it's too soon for a refill, or to leave. That's when *he* shows up again. Lewis. The overly confident insurance broker I was making polite conversation with twenty minutes ago and have been avoiding ever since. He's been hovering since I arrived, looking at me like I'm some sort of challenge. At first, I thought I was imagining it – maybe the wine had gone to my head – but no, Lewis has that air about him. The slick hair, the shiny watch he keeps adjusting to make sure I notice it's an expensive one, the practised grin. I've seen his type a hundred times.

"Another drink?" he asks, with that smooth tone of his, as if I've been eagerly awaiting the offer.

I smile, but it's forced. "I'm fine, thanks."

He leans in, too close, and the overpowering scent of his aftershave reaches me. "Come on, Nikki. Let me get you something. You're too lovely to be standing here all by yourself."

I resist the urge to roll my eyes. He's not awful to talk to, just a little too smug. But truth be told, I'm grateful for the distraction.

"I'm really fine," I say again, but he acts like he doesn't hear me.

"So," he says, inching closer, "how about dinner next week? I know a fantastic little spot by the river."

I blink, caught off guard. "Dinner?"

"Yeah," he says, with a grin that's a little too self-assured. "I'll pick you up, say, Friday?"

I shake my head, trying to be polite but firm. "Thanks, but I don't think I can." I'm desperately trying to think up a reason not to.

He doesn't miss a beat, still smiling. "Come on, it's just dinner. No harm in it, right?"

I pause, considering. Is it worth the hassle of saying no again? He's persistent, I'll give him that. Maybe one dinner will make him back off. Besides, it's not like I have other plans.

"Okay," I say, meeting his gaze, "but I'll choose the place, and I'll meet you there. Montrose in Mayfair – do you know it?"

His grin widens, triumphant. "Oh, classy. Yes, I know it. Okay, I'll let you book it and I'll meet you there."

I nod, giving a small smile, hoping it comes off as polite but not too encouraging. He finally steps back, looking like he's just won some kind of prize. We exchange details and I exhale in relief as he wanders off. I stare at my empty glass, already regretting the decision.

What on earth have I just agreed to?

One

I let out a big sigh as I lean back in my chair, closing my laptop with a satisfying click. My last meeting of the day is finally wrapped up, and I'm officially done for the weekend. The world of law can be relentless, and today was one of those days where every email felt like a mini-crisis, every call a debate. Even working from home didn't soften the blow – it's been mentally draining from start to finish. Now, instead of relaxing into the evening, I'm faced with the prospect of getting ready for a date. A date I'm not exactly enthusiastic about.

Lewis. The persistent insurance broker from Claire's party. I groan inwardly just thinking about him. Part of me is tempted to send him a message, claiming I've come down with some mysterious illness or found myself suddenly swamped with work. But I know if I were going to cancel, I should have done it hours ago. Now, it feels too late. No, I'll go. I'll get dressed up, show up at Montrose, and hope the food is as good as I remember. Maybe I'll surprise myself and actually enjoy the evening. Though I'm not holding my breath.

Dinner isn't for another two hours, and I'm already feeling peckish. My stomach growls in agreement.

I wander into the kitchen and open the fridge, eyeing its nearly empty shelves. I hadn't bothered to stock up much this week, knowing tonight I'd be eating out, and tomorrow I'd be crashing at Lizzie's. I grab some cream cheese and a pack of crackers from the cupboard – my go-to lazy snack – and perch myself on the stool at the kitchen island.

As I nibble on the crackers, I let my mind drift to the weekend ahead. Staying at Lizzie's should be fun, as it always is. I can already picture us curled up on her sofa, wine in hand, dissecting every detail of my date with Lewis. Lizzie will probably get a kick out of it, but I'm not expecting any romantic sparks tonight.

Just as I start thinking about what to wear, my phone beeps, cutting through the quiet of the room.

'Hi Darling, are you ready for your date tonight? xxx.' It's Lizzie, my sister.

I smirk, tapping out a reply. 'I just need to locate the frumpiest dress I can find, and I'll be ready!' She knows exactly how I feel about tonight.

Her response is quick. 'Ha Ha, I'm sure you'll still look stunning! Why did you agree to go if you don't want to?'

Good question. 'Soft touch? Drunk when I agreed?' I text back, cringing at the memory of Claire's party.

'No offence Darling, but you're not a soft touch, you did say you were quite drunk though!' A string of laugh-out-loud emojis follows. Lizzie loves her emojis.

I roll my eyes and type back, 'Well unfortunately I did agree and as you know, I'm not the type to go back on my word so I will put on my nicest underwear and my sexiest little black dress, slap a smile on my face and go!'

'Okay, well try and have a good time and we will catch up tomorrow, love you xxx.'

'Thanks, Hun, looking forward to seeing you, love you too xxx.' I hit send, put the phone face down on the counter and finish my crackers.

I live alone in Richmond, not far from the river, in one of those new gated developments that people associate with affluence. I co-own my apartment with the bank, but I'm proud to say I own a higher percentage. It's a two-bed, three-bath apartment on the third floor – the top floor – which adds a little more exclusivity, or so I tell myself.

The entrance hall opens into a large open-plan living area, the golden wood flooring stretching out beneath me, making everything feel light and spacious. Sash windows with white venetian blinds and luxurious champagne velvet curtains let in just enough natural light, while still giving me privacy. My office is nestled by the windows, with a view of the park across the road – an ideal spot for when I need to escape into my work.

The lounge is cosy, with two plush mocha-coloured sofas facing a black French-style coffee table. I keep a stack of property magazines on the table, my little guilty pleasure for interior inspiration. On the wall, a large TV is mounted above a glass-enclosed gas fire set into a stone-effect wall. It's a little indulgence, but I love being able to add instant warmth with the touch of a button.

The kitchen spans the width of the space, minimalist

navy units framing a light grey marble island, under a low-hanging chandelier. Two velvet grey 'cuddle' bar chairs are tucked under the island, and there's always a vase of fresh flowers sitting in the centre, adding a pop of colour. I miss having a garden – my little patch of green – but I've adapted, making sure there's always something blooming indoors.

Despite its masculine undertones, the apartment is my sanctuary. It's modern, it's stylish, and most importantly, it's mine.

It's now 6:15pm and I need to leave in an hour if I am to get to London on time. I call a local cab company and book my taxi before I jump into the shower. Both bedrooms are en suite; the master has a freestanding roll-top bath, which is just gorgeous, and a large shower equipped with double jets that caress you from top to bottom. After my shower, I barrel roll my long chocolate brown hair to soften it and lather on a scented moisturiser and a spritz of perfume.

Sitting at my vanity table, I pull on a headband to keep my hair out of my face and study my reflection in the mirror. Defined cheekbones, blue eyes staring back at me. My skin is clear – I'm lucky that way. Hormones are behaving today, so no need for heavy foundation. Instead, I add a sheer primer that gives me just enough glow.

I darken my eyebrows slightly, nothing too heavy, and add a layer of brown mascara – black seems too much these days – and choose a rose shade lipstick that has staying power, even through a night of eating, drinking and kissing. I will not be kissing tonight, though!

My eyes drift to my walk-in wardrobe, packed with clothes, mostly stylish. I like to make an effort, even when dressed casually. True to my word to Lizzie, I pull out a sleek, three-quarter-length black dress with a subtle glittery sheen. The crew neck is simple, but the deep V-back adds a bit of drama, and short wing sleeves give it a chic touch. The dress hugs me in all the right places, showing off my toned back. I lay it on the bed and rummage for a black lace thong – no bra needed tonight, thanks to the daring back of the dress.

I'm five foot six with a slim frame. I eat well and work out and it pays dividends. Lewis is taller than me, so I grab my classic black peep-toe Christian Louboutins. Rarely did I wear heels with my ex-husband; he was the same height as me and didn't like me towering over him. I slip into the dress, add a gold bracelet and a watch, not a Rolex but it's on the list, pin my hair up in a loose elegant bun and stand in front of my full-length mirror. Despite my lack of enthusiasm, I like what I see and I feel good.

The weather's been unusually warm for this time of year, at least during the day, and even though I don't plan to be out late, I throw on my favourite jacket, a tan faux leather one, short and chic. At 7:12pm, my phone rings.

"Hello?"

"Taxi for Nikki!" comes a reply.

"Great, I'm first on the right. I'm coming down now." I hang up, grab a clutch and head out of the door.

Two

The taxi drops me at the door of Montrose. I settle my fare, thank the driver and step out.

Immediately, I notice a small crowd lingering around the entrance – people with cameras, a few bystanders huddled together. Something's going on, or someone's in there. I chose this restaurant, not for the paparazzi appeal, but because of its good reputation and atmosphere. Oh, and a friend of mine works behind the bar, which could prove useful if this evening turns into something I need to escape from.

As I step inside, there's an air of sophistication. The place is styled like an old library, with dark oak wood panelled walls that remind me of my parents' lounge growing up. The overhead lighting is dim, giving the restaurant a cosy, intimate glow. Antique tables are dotted throughout, each topped with extravagant white feather shades and breathtaking floral arrangements. There's a soft hum of conversation around me, and the sound of a pianist playing something elegant on the sleek, black Steinway in the centre of the room adds to the atmosphere. The restaurant isn't huge, maybe fifty or sixty diners max; it feels exclusive. Towards the back, I spot the more secluded dining areas – booths with high backs, curved around tables to offer privacy, perfect for those wanting a quiet meal or something more romantic.

I make my way to the maître d's podium, where I'm greeted with a polite nod.

"Reservation for Harper," I say, "8pm." I'm early as usual. I am never late; it's a rule I live by.

"Certainly," he says, offering to take my coat. "Your fellow diner has not arrived yet. Would you like to be seated at the table, or would you prefer to wait at the bar?"

"The bar, please," I say without hesitation. He graciously takes my coat and hands it to a colleague, guiding me down a couple of steps to the bar where I see the familiar face of my friend Mike, who is mixing drinks.

"Hi! Long time no see!" He smiles warmly at me. The maître d' nods and retreats back to the front of the house. I pull out a bar stool and take a seat. Mike and I go way back. We met at the gym, where Lizzie and I used to spend many Friday evenings working out, only to undo our efforts at the local pub during our student days. "How are you? What brings you here tonight?"

"A date," I reply flatly. He looks at me curiously while wiping the bar down.

"A date, huh? I heard that you and Karl had split. You don't sound too thrilled to be going on this date, though?"

"I'm not really, not sure why I agreed to it."

7

He chuckles knowingly. "Drunk?" He winks. "So, what can I get you to drink, sweetheart?"

I laugh, shaking my head. "You sound just like Lizzie. I'll have a small house white, please."

"How is Lizzie these days? Still pursuing the starving artist life?"

"Yep, same old Liz."

Mike pours me a small wine and busies himself preparing drinks for the diners. We chat briefly about our student days, catching up, when my phone vibrates on the bar. I glance at the screen and see a text from Lewis: 'Can no longer make it.'

"Wow," I exclaim, half laughing in disbelief.

"What's up?" Mike asks, glancing over.

"He's stood me up," I say, shaking my head with a mix of irritation and amusement. "No explanation, no apology, just 'can no longer make it'. I mean, I wasn't keen on the date, but that's just rude!"

Mike lets out a low chuckle. "Well, I'd call that a blessing, wouldn't you?" He winks again before turning to another guest who's just approached the bar. "What can I get you, sir?" he asks, leaving me alone to digest the sudden change of plans.

I stare down at my phone, re-reading the curt message from Lewis, a wave of annoyance creeping in. I wasn't thrilled about the date, but still, getting stood up like this stings a little. As I stew over the message, the man next to me steps forwards and orders his drink, his presence now impossible to ignore.

"I'll have a Bud, please," he says with a smooth American accent.

"Coming right up. I just need to pop to the back to get some more. Would you like me to bring it over to your table?" Mike offers.

"No, no, it's okay, I'll wait," the American replies, and with that Mike momentarily disappears, leaving me alone with the American as he leans casually against the bar.

There's something familiar about that voice. I glance up, not expecting much, but when my eyes lock on his face – *holy shit*. I freeze for a second, trying to wrap my head around what I'm seeing. It's him. James Keller. One of the most famous actors in the world, standing right here, mere feet away from me. Not just an A-list celebrity, but treble A-list, the kind of star whose name makes headlines just for being seen at the airport.

A thrill runs through me, that frisson of excitement when you realise you're in the presence of someone truly iconic. I vaguely recall a recent headline calling him 'One of the most powerful men in Hollywood', and it's easy to see why. He's got that aura – magnetic, mysterious, larger than life. Even Hollywood royalty talk about him with a sense of awe, like they still can't quite believe they're in his orbit.

I remember a clip from an interview where one of his co-stars admitted he still got star-struck whenever he received a text from James Keller! And now here he is, casually standing at the bar, waiting for his drink like it's the most normal thing in the world. It's surreal, and I have to remind myself to breathe as I watch this man who, only moments ago, was just a name in the tabloids.

I compose myself and subtly take in his appearance. He's every bit as striking in person as he is on the silver screen – short, neatly styled dark brown hair, those piercing hazel-green eyes, and a perfectly chiselled jawline. He's tall, toned with broad shoulders that I imagine would make you feel safe if he wrapped you up in his arms. Casually dressed in dark blue jeans, a light grey V-neck jumper layered over a black shirt, and smart black loafers. He leans against the bar, his gaze locking onto mine.

"Hey!" he says casually. "How are you?"

I'm never quite sure if that's a rhetorical question or not, but I answer anyway. "Hi, fine thanks, you?"

"Good thanks," he replies, flashing that famous Hollywood smile. My heart skips a beat, and I feel myself melting, like wax under the heat of his gaze. I manage a polite smile and try to shift my focus back to my nearly empty glass, though I can't help but sneak glances.

He leans in slightly, lowering his voice. "I'm sorry but I couldn't help but overhear you just now."

"Sorry?" I say, slightly startled, wondering if I've done something embarrassing.

"That message you just received." He nods towards my phone on the bar.

"Oh that," I say, feeling the flush of embarrassment creeping up.

"Well, that's a real shame. For him, I mean," he says with a sympathetic smile. "He doesn't know what he's missing." There's something sincere in his tone that makes the line land perfectly, where it could've easily sounded cheesy.

"Thank you," I murmur, my cheeks warming further. *Stay calm*, I think, *stay calm*.

"To be perfectly truthful, I'm not that bothered," I

add, surprising myself with my honesty. "I wasn't exactly excited about the date."

"No?"

"No." I shake my head. "No chemistry."

"Fair enough. So, what will you do now? Did you travel far to get here?"

"No, not far, I'm about ten minutes south of the river, near Richmond."

"Oh yes, I know it," he says, nodding.

"I think I'll finish my drink, grab a microwave meal for one, and head home to watch a movie. Any recommendations?" I joke, a grin tugging at my lips.

He smiles with amusement. "I can recommend plenty, but it seems a shame to waste an evening on a microwave meal when you look so beautiful."

Be still my beating heart.

"Thank you," I say softly. "But you win some, you lose some, right?"

His eyes stay locked on mine. "This is true. But for the record, I think he has definitely lost this one." He pauses. "Well, I'd best get to my table. Can I buy you another drink before I go?"

"Oh, no, you don't have to do that," I say, feigning nonchalance while inside I'm hoping he doesn't leave yet. I want this moment to last just a bit longer.

"I'd like to," he insists, his smile warm.

"Okay," I agree, feeling the heat rise in my chest. "That's very kind of you, thank you."

As Mike returns, placing a bottle of Bud in front of James, James turns back to me, that smile still on his lips. "Sorry, I didn't catch your name?"

"Nikki. Nikki Harper," I say, offering my hand.

He shakes it, and the moment our hands touch, a shiver runs through me. "Pleasure to meet you, Nikki. I'm James," he says, like I didn't already know. "Please put whatever Nikki here would like on my tab," he adds, addressing Mike.

"Sure thing!" Mike replies.

James's gaze lingers on mine for a moment longer, and I feel like he's looking right into my soul, leaving me completely mesmerised. "It was really nice meeting you. I hope you have a great evening, whatever you decide to do."

"You too," I say, trying to sound casual, "and thanks for the drink."

"Pleasure." He flashes that brilliant smile one last time before turning and heading into the restaurant.

I watch him walk away, my heart still racing as I process what just happened. James Keller – one of the most famous men on the planet – just bought me a drink and called me beautiful. I take a deep breath, trying to compose myself, but it's impossible to ignore the flutter of excitement in my chest.

Mike's eyebrows raise in amusement. "Well, that was something, huh?"

I laugh softly, shaking my head. "You could say that."

"Hollywood royalty buying you a drink? Not bad for a night that started with a date cancelling on you," he teases, sliding the glass of wine over to me.

"Not bad at all," I say, still feeling a little dazed. I glance over to where James is seated, but his table is tucked away in one of those discreet private booths, completely out of sight. For a moment, I wonder if I imagined the whole thing, like it was some bizarre daydream.

Mike's voice snaps me back to reality. "Don't look now, but he's coming back," he whispers, eyes wide.

"What?" I mouth, trying to play it cool as my heart skips a beat. I turn around just in time to see James Keller walking towards me again.

"Hi there, sorry to bother you – again," he says with that same easy charm.

"No bother at all," I reply, doing my best to sound casual despite the butterflies wreaking havoc inside. *You can disturb me anytime*, I think.

"I was just wondering…" he pauses, flashing that grin again, "if you'd like to join me for dinner tonight instead?"

"Sorry, what?" I ask, caught off guard.

He chuckles and repeats himself. "Would you like to join me for dinner? Well, me and Mark Layton and his wife, Julia. Do you know Mark?"

Of course I know who Mark Layton is – he's a British TV host with a prime-time talk show, *The Mark Layton Show*. Interviewing celebrities every week, and he's hilarious. His wife, Julia, isn't in the public eye, so I don't know much about her. But I like Mark. At least, on TV.

I stare at James, utterly speechless. It feels like time stands still. "It seems a shame to waste that gorgeous dress on a microwave meal," he adds, with a playful tone.

I take a deep breath, trying to read his expression. He seems genuine, standing there with that open, relaxed posture, waiting for my answer. I promised myself I'd say yes to new opportunities this year. And this is *James Keller*. Sure, he's a stranger, but he's offering me a glimpse into his world, if only for one night.

I sit up a little straighter, feeling my confidence return.

"I know who Mark is," I say with a smile, "but I don't want to intrude on your evening."

"You won't be. I'd really like you to join us," he insists. Then, lowering his voice with a cheeky grin, he adds, "Plus, I'm kind of a third wheel over there, so it'd be nice to balance things out."

"Well," I say teasingly, "when you put it like that... I'd love to."

Three

*J*ames extends a hand to help me down off the bar stool, and I notice again how tall he is, even with my heels on. His height, presence – it's all a bit intoxicating.

"Here, let me take your drink," he offers, effortlessly taking my wine glass.

"Thanks," I say, my voice almost too casual, as he places a hand gently on my waist and guides me through the restaurant towards his table. His touch is firm, yet light enough to make me feel completely at ease.

"Don't worry, I already told Mark and Julia that I was going to invite you," he adds with a wink. My heart does a somersault. *Thank God*, I think. Otherwise, this would have been incredibly awkward – me walking up as 'Nikki, the girl who got stood up and James Keller has taken pity on'.

"I'm not worried," I reply, trying to match his casual

tone as I smile up at him. "But I do need to cancel my reservation."

"I'll take care of that for you," he says confidently, and in that moment, I get the distinct feeling that James Keller is the kind of person who always takes care of things.

As we pass the other diners, heads turn, and eyes follow us. Some people smile, while others just stare. I catch a whisper from a young couple: "That was James Keller!" My stomach flips. Is this really happening?

James leads me to a private booth at the back, beautifully set with fine silverware, crystal wine glasses, and a lit candle surrounded by delicate flowers in the centre. A vintage brass light hangs low over the table, casting a soft glow, and the table is only set for three people!

He gestures for me to slide in, introducing me to Mark and Julia. As I settle into the plush seat, he slides in beside me, close enough that I can catch the subtle, sweet scent of him, causing the fine hairs on my arms to prickle. I smile warmly at Mark and Julia, doing my best to appear composed.

"Hi, Nikki!" Mark stands awkwardly, ducking slightly to avoid the hanging light as he extends his hand. "I'm Mark. Lovely to meet you." He's probably mid-thirties, shorter than James, with short, fair hair and a softer build. His face is round, as is his frame, but he's got a certain charm.

"And this is my lovely wife, Julia," he adds. Julia leans across the table to shake my hand. She's petite and slim, with shoulder-length blonde hair and a friendly, open expression.

"Hi," she says with a warm smile. "Please, call me Jules."

So far, so good, I think. They seem welcoming, though this whole situation feels completely surreal.

"So, what are we drinking, guys?" Mark asks, leaning back in his seat. "I see you've already got yourself a beer, James!" he jokes. "Nikki, what do you prefer? White, red, or maybe some fizz with dinner?"

"I usually go for white or rosé," I say politely, "but I'm happy to go with whatever everyone else is having."

The waiter arrives, gracefully placing four menus on the table. James, without hesitation, orders a bottle of white wine, nearly £100 per bottle. He then asks the waiter to set an extra place and leans in to whisper something – likely cancelling my previous reservation.

"Right away, sir," replies the waiter, hurrying off to fulfil the requests.

"So, James says you've been stood up?" Mark asks, straight to the point. Hearing it spoken out loud makes the embarrassment hit a little harder, and I feel a twinge of discomfort creep onto my face.

"Yep, sad but true." I shrug, trying to laugh it off as I take a sip of wine.

"What's the excuse?" he presses.

"I've no idea," I admit. "He just texted saying he couldn't make it. Honestly, though, I'm really not that bothered." I hope my casual tone hides the lingering sting.

"Where did you meet him?" Julia asks gently.

"At a mutual friend's party last week," I explain. "We were both there solo, started chatting, had a few drinks. He seemed nice enough at first, but I wasn't really feeling it. He had this… confident vibe. Might've just been the alcohol talking, but still." I roll my eyes, feeling more at ease as I recount the story. "Despite my reservations, he was pretty insistent about dinner, so I eventually gave in."

Julia gives me a knowing smile. "So, didn't fancy him, then?"

"No, sadly not," I say, smiling.

"Well, that's just ridiculous. Who in their right mind would stand you up?" Mark says with a friendly smile, making me feel more comfortable.

"I agree. His loss, our gain," Julia adds kindly, sending me a warm look.

James nods along, locking eyes with me. "That's exactly what I said," he says softly, and I'm momentarily lost in his eyes again.

The waiter reappears, now with the wine, pouring a glass for each of us before quietly setting the extra place. We all raise our glasses as James holds his in the centre of the table.

"A toast," he says, his eyes smiling. "To good company and new friends."

"Cheers!" we echo, and the clink of glasses rings through the air. I take a sip – it's smooth, far better than the house wine I'd had earlier. The light, fruity aroma lingers pleasantly, and maybe it's the wine talking, or the fact that this is my third glass, but everything feels a bit more surreal. James gives me a small nod, lifting his glass to clink mine again. There's a quiet moment between us, and I can't help but wonder – why? Why did he ask me to dinner?

I open the dark red leather-bound menu in front of me and browse through the starters. Initially, I'd planned to keep it simple – a quick one course, maybe two to be polite – but now, with the way the night has shifted, I decide to indulge a little. Three courses might be the way to go: I'm not in any hurry to end this evening.

We place our orders. I choose the crispy duck salad to start and the grilled sea bass for my main. James opts for a prawn and avocado salad, followed by a steak, cooked medium. As the waiter leaves, the conversation naturally drifts to work – my work, specifically.

"What do you do for work, Nikki?" Jules asks in her warm, curious way.

"I work at a law firm," I reply, trying not to make it sound too heavy.

"Ooh," she says with genuine enthusiasm. "You're a lawyer?"

"Yes. I practise law. Employment law to be precise. I head up the employment law division – it's a busy role for sure."

"Sounds fascinating! Do you have a team?" she continues.

"Yes, I've got three direct reports, seven indirect, and my PA. They're a great team," I say, feeling proud.

"Do you go to court and wear one of those wigs?" she asks with a laugh.

I chuckle. "No wigs for me. It's usually barristers and judges who wear them, and they're becoming less common now. I do go to court, but in a suit."

"Got your own corner office?" Mark jumps in.

"I've got my own office, but it's not a corner one," I say with a smile. "We're based in London, but I work from home a lot unless I've got court or client meetings. We also have a New York office, though no private office there – just a hot desk."

"Any high-profile cases?" James asks, looking intrigued.

"One that made the press last year – Burleigh Limited versus MT Technology," I mention casually. I notice his curiosity deepen. "Look me up, you'll see."

James picks up his phone and begins to search. "It was a pretty big case, involving flexible working and discrimination," I explain as he finds the firm's site. I point him to the 'About Us' page, where my professional headshot and CV are neatly displayed. A small part of me relishes this moment – I'm leaving a door open: he now knows where I work, for future reference. Lizzie would insert a winking emoji right about now.

At thirty-three, I'm a senior director, which I know is young for a director, but I've worked hard to get here, sacrificing along the way – maybe even my marriage. As James reads through the details, he shows Mark and Jules, both of whom nod approvingly. Then, he reads aloud one of my client testimonials:

"Ooh, a senior director!" he says, shooting an impressed look at me. "*A brilliant lawyer who excels at identifying key issues in complex cases, personable and extremely knowledgeable in her field.*" Even I can't help but feel a bit impressed as I hear the words.

Then, James smirks, his eyes glinting with mischief. "Hang on, it says here you're a bit of a ball-breaker!" He winks at the others, flashing me a playful grin.

I raise an eyebrow, meeting his playful energy. "Hmm, sometimes. But I've heard the same thing about you!"

Mark bursts into laughter. "Ah, she got you there, mate!"

James grins widely, clearly enjoying the banter. "Touché," he says, his smile lingering.

Four

The first course arrives, and it's as delicious as expected – each bite cooked to perfection. As we eat, the conversation flows easily, and I learn that James is in the UK to promote an upcoming film due to release next month. He's set to appear on Mark's show, which is being filmed on Wednesday and airs Thursday night. Clearly, this dinner is a warm-up for that interview.

But as I listen, a small twinge of disappointment creeps in when I hear he'll be leaving in just over a week for Norway, where he'll be on location for his next film. Just when I'm starting to feel a little more comfortable in his presence, that reminder of the gap between our worlds hits.

Still, I keep the conversation going, asking questions without slipping into 'interview mode'. I don't want to be too familiar, even though it feels surreal sitting next to someone I've seen on the big screen so many times. He's in his early forties, maybe eight or nine years older than me, and has been in the business for over two decades. His range is impressive, from rom-com heartthrob to action hero, villain, and even a zombie in a horror film. There are probably movies he's been in that I've never seen.

Thinking about it now, I don't recall seeing him in any particularly racy scenes – he's done sex scenes, but nothing explicit. It's always been tasteful. But he does always kiss the girl. There's even one film where he played a villainous drug dealer, and he looked nothing like his usual charming self. But sitting next to him now, seeing him in the flesh, I realise how attractive he really is. There's something about him – a calm authority that draws me in, like a moth to a flame. I feel safe beside him, yet more alive than I've felt in a while.

He doesn't do TV, just films, and his rare interviews only seem to add to his mystique. In an industry full of egos and where unreasonable demands are par for the course, it's refreshing to meet someone like him who seems genuine. All of them do, really, and I like to think I'm a good judge of character. Hopefully, the Hollywood love mist hasn't clouded my vision.

As the conversation flows, I recall that James was once married to Melinda Stratford, a famous actress. They were together for several years before divorcing a few years ago. Since then, he's been linked to plenty of beautiful women, but only one relationship stands out – a brief, high-profile fling with Sarah Watts, another Hollywood star. I must be delusional to think someone like him could be interested in someone like me – ordinary me. He's just being kind, generous, that's all. But then again… what if? Dare to dream, Nikki. Dare to dream.

I snap out of my daydream as our starters are whisked away, replaced by a refreshing sorbet to cleanse the palate. A new bottle of wine arrives with the main course, and I can feel the warmth in the restaurant as the soft hum of conversation and the gentle melodies from the pianist fill the air. The lighting seems to have dimmed, casting a romantic glow over our little corner, and I can't help but get swept up in the moment. There's something intimate about being tucked away in this secluded cove, surrounded by good food, wine, and company.

Mark and James keep the conversation lively over dinner. Their chemistry is undeniable; they bounce off each other beautifully, with humour and ease. It's like watching a well-rehearsed comedy duo – they share funny stories from movie sets, and recount embarrassing interview questions with such vividness that we're all in stitches. At one point, I laugh so hard tears stream down my cheeks.

As I relax, I feel myself gravitating towards him. I feel a subtle energy between us, or maybe that's just the wine. The gentle brush of our legs beneath the table feels charged. Normally, I'd pull away or create some distance, but I don't. Neither does he. Instead, I find myself leaning in slightly, laughing a little more freely, and allowing my hand to rest on his arm when he makes me laugh. He doesn't pull back. In fact, he leans closer, and I can almost feel the heat between us. As he speaks, I catch myself gazing at his lips, wondering how they would feel if I dared to lean just a little further. It feels like we're flirting.

"Tell me," James says, swirling his wine glass slowly between his fingers, "what if this guy calls tomorrow with a sob story? Or maybe a genuine one. Tries to ask you out again?"

I lean in slightly, meeting his gaze. "That would be a hard no," I reply with a small smirk tugging at the corners of my lips. "I wasn't feeling it anyway, so it doesn't matter what he says now – it's still a no."

"Good to hear," James says, his voice dropping a notch, quieter now. "So… anyone else on the radar?"

I shake my head with a light laugh. "Nope. I'm not exactly winning at dating." I give a self-deprecating chuckle and dive into the story of how I once went on a date without even realising it.

"We met up at a local pub to watch rugby, with his friends and some of his family. That, in my mind, is firmly 'friend zone', right? He never said it was a date! A few days later, he calls me to say things were 'moving faster' with someone else." I shake my head, and they laugh along with me.

"Apparently, I need things spelled out."

"Tonight's guy at least made it clear it was a date, right?" Mark jumps in, earning an eye-roll from Julia.

"Oh, he was *very* clear," I say, giving him a look. Mark raises his hands in surrender and nods.

"All right, then. What about any serious relationships? You know, ones where you *know* what's going on?" Mark teases, and Julia swats his arm.

"Stop being so nosy!" she scolds him, offering me an apologetic smile.

I wave it off. "No worries," I say, smiling back. "I was married for six years." I pause, throwing a playful glance at Mark. "We've been divorced for a couple of years now."

"Sorry to hear that," he says, more gently. "Kids?"

I shake my head. "No, thankfully. He wasn't exactly cut out for kids – could barely take care of himself, to be honest. We just grew apart. Met young, married young… it happens."

James leans forwards slightly, his tone softer, empathetic. "That sounds familiar."

Mark, undeterred, jumps in again. "Would you do it again? Marriage, I mean."

Julia playfully slaps his arm, shaking her head at him with mock disapproval. They're sweet, comfortable in their affection, the kind of couple that doesn't make you feel like a third wheel.

"Yeah, absolutely," I reply, laughing lightly. "I'm not cynical about love – yet. I still believe in it, but next time…" I pause for emphasis. "I've got to love and be *in* love. That's what was missing the first time around. I loved him, sure, but I wasn't *in* love with him, if that makes sense."

They nod in understanding, the conversation growing a bit more serious. I swirl the last of the wine in my glass as the warmth of it loosens my tongue, and I feel myself becoming more animated as I continue.

"My next relationship has to have passion – *real* passion," I say, feeling the conviction in my words. "I want the kind of love that others envy. Affection, laughter, friendship. When he walks into a room, I want to go weak at the knees. And when we're out together, I want it to feel like no one else exists, just us. I refuse to settle for some predictable routine, where it's Friday night, so we order takeaway and have boring sex." I take another sip of wine, feeling a little emboldened. "He's got to know what he wants. I like a strong man who goes after what he wants."

As I say this, I notice Mark glancing at James. Their eyes flicker between each other for a second before both sets of eyes are back on me. I suddenly feel exposed, my heart beating a little faster, wondering if I've gotten too carried away. The room seems quieter for a moment, the wine's warmth no longer comforting, and I wonder if I've said too much.

I shift gears, deflecting with a smile. "You two seem really in love," I say, turning the focus back on Mark and Jules. "You're sweet together. How long have you been married?"

"Oh, we're not married," Jules quips, grinning at me. "He's just my sex slave!" Her laughter is infectious, and I can't help but smile. Mark pulls her into a playful embrace, planting a kiss on her forehead.

"She wishes!" Mark fires back with a grin as she nestles into him. They have that easy, comfortable affection that makes their connection obvious.

I glance sideways at James, catching his eye. He's already looking at me, a quiet smile on his lips. It lingers, soft, and I find myself smiling back before I can stop it.

Five

We finish the main course, and I glance at my watch, surprised to see it's nearly 10pm. Time flies when you're having fun. Just then, my phone vibrates on the seat beside me, and the name *Lewis* flashes across the screen. My smile falters. James notices.

"Call?" he asks, his voice curious.

"It's him. The date that never showed," I say, trying to keep the disappointment from seeping into my tone.

"Answer if you want. I don't mind," he offers casually.

"It's too late, he's rung off. And like I said, I'm not interested." I brush it off with a dismissive shrug.

James grins. "If he calls again, get Mark to answer. That could be fun."

Mark puffs up his chest theatrically. "Absolutely. I'll set him straight. Anyone up for dessert?" He shifts the topic, lightening the mood.

The food has been exquisite, but we're all full. "No thanks," and "Not for me," ripple around the table as we pass on the dessert. The conversation drifts to hobbies while we finish off the wine. I tell them about my love for hiking, the gym, and how I used to have a small garden at my old house. I miss having a garden and dream of having another one, a larger one someday. But dancing is my real passion, which turns out to be a hot topic.

"Mark, you were on that dancing show a few years back, weren't you?" James asks, glancing over.

Mark nods enthusiastically. "Yeah, I was! Loved every minute. Exhausting, but exhilarating. When it goes right, it's a great feeling." Considering Mark's heavier frame, I have to say that he glided across that floor when he danced. For a bigger guy, he was very light on his feet.

I smile. "You were brilliant! I remember your samba – it's a tough one, the changes in rhythm can catch you out, but it's so much fun. You were so light on your feet!" I say, surprising myself with how much I remember.

"Thanks." He beams at me. "Do you take lessons? Are you any good?" Mark teases.

"I do, most Tuesday evenings. I'm not bad," I say modestly. I'm Gold Bar two for both my ballroom and Latin, which is reasonable, not professional by any means but not bad. "My teacher knows your old teacher!"

"Ooh, small world." Mark nods approvingly. Then he turns to James with a smirk. "James did a bit of Latin, didn't you?"

James chuckles. "Yeah, I had to learn rhumba for a role. Just the basics, though."

Mark grins. "Made it look easy."

James shrugs with a smile. "It's all in the camera angles. But it's a hard dance – very sensual." His gaze locks onto mine, and I feel a flutter in my stomach.

"Speaking of hobbies," James continues, "next Saturday, I'm taking Mark skydiving before I leave." Mark visibly recoils at the mention.

"You are?" I ask eagerly. "That's exciting! I love skydiving. Have you done it before, Mark? Jules, are you going?"

Jules laughs. "Not a bloody chance. My feet are staying firmly on the ground, thank you!"

Mark groans. "It's terrifying. I've done it once before, and it was horrific."

"You loved it once you were back on solid ground," Jules teases.

"I found the first jump terrifying too," I say, smiling. "But after the initial fear, I loved it. By the second jump, I was still scared, but it turned to excitement. By the third and fourth, I just went for it and enjoyed every second!"

"How many times have you jumped?" James asks, sounding surprised.

"Only four. Nowhere near as many as you – you jump solo, right?"

He nods in agreement. "I've done a lot, yeah. Again, I trained for a role years ago, but I still do it for fun." He pauses for a moment, then asks, "If you're free next Saturday, why don't you come with us?"

Mark jumps in eagerly. "Yes! Please say yes, you can take some of the attention off me!" He gives me a pleading look.

I turn to James, trying to gauge if he's serious. "Are you sure?"

"Absolutely," he says, his voice sincere. "It'll be fun."

"I'd need someone to tandem with," I say cautiously.

"No problem. I can get that arranged," James reassures me. "So, how about it?"

The idea of skydiving with James feels thrilling and nerve-wracking all at once. He looks at me with that same intense gaze, and I know I can't resist. "Okay," I say, smiling. "I'd love to."

Jules beams. "You should come back to ours afterward! We can have a barbecue and a movie night. The weather's meant to be beautiful next weekend, and I think you'll love our garden. Only if you're free, of course," she adds quickly, as if realising she's being presumptuous.

I glance at James, feeling a little unsure. I want to, but I don't want to impose. "I don't want to overstay my welcome. You've all been so gracious tonight."

James smiles softly. "I'm up for it if you are."

Sensing my hesitation, Jules chimes in, "No pressure. Just decide on the day. It's no trouble, really."

I nod. "Thanks, Julia. It sounds lovely. I'll let you know."

My phone rings again – a video call from Lewis. I glance at James, who gestures, with a grin, for me to hand the phone to Mark. Without hesitation, Mark takes it and answers in his most professional tone.

"Hello, Nikki's phone," he says, smiling into the camera like he's my personal assistant. I hear Lewis, sounding a bit confused and surprised. "Oh, hi… is Nikki there?"

"She is, but she's a little busy at the moment," Mark replies, winking at me across the table.

There's a brief pause before Lewis speaks again, his voice filled with excitement. "Hold on… Are you…?

Whoa!" he exclaims, his voice loud and slightly slurred. Mark adjusts the volume down.

"Hi!" Mark says jovially. He turns the camera towards Jules, who waves. "Me and my wife here are having dinner with Nikki and James. That's James Keller, by the way."

"No way!" Lewis exclaims, clearly in disbelief.

"Yes, way," Mark continues, with a playful grin. "Hang on a second." He flicks the camera round to bring both James and me into view as James casually slides his arm around my back, sending an electric jolt through me.

"There they are!" Mark announces cheerfully. James raises his glass in a suave toast towards the camera.

Mark hands my phone over to James. "Hey." James greets him with an easy smile. "How's it going?"

"Shit me!" Lewis finally seems to believe him. "What the…?" He's slurring. From the background, it looks like he's standing outside a pub. "Um, okay, I think… Man, I'm a big fan! Loved you in that film… um, the one with the car chase… What was it called again? *Driver's Fury*! Oh man, this is unreal!" Lewis stumbles over his words. He seems unfocused, not fully paying attention. "Hang on…" he slurs. "*Ben? Ben!* Come here, mate!" he shouts to someone behind him, and within seconds, another equally intoxicated guy appears on the screen next to him, squinting and moving closer to the phone.

"Holy shit, that's James Keller! *Whoa*, all right, mate?" Ben holds up a pint, slurring even more than Lewis, and then falls out of view.

Lewis finally comes back to reality. "So… uh… can I chat with Nikki?"

James, still with his arm around me, looks at me. "Do

you want to chat with him, baby?" he asks, teasingly. He called me 'baby'. I almost go into meltdown, but I manage to hold it together. I shake my head nonchalantly, looking at James.

"No thanks, darling." I play along, flirting.

"There's your answer, buddy," James replies with a playful smirk. He adopts a Southern American accent and adds, "She don't wanna talk to you!"

"Wait, hold on… I just wanted to… I mean, Nikki, are you okay?" he asks, his voice faltering. Clearly, he's trying to salvage the situation but failing miserably.

James grins and shrugs. "She's fine, mate. But it's been a long night."

"Okay, I get it. I'll try and call you tomorrow," Lewis says.

"Please don't bother." I reply quickly, not wanting him to call. I didn't really like him in the first place, and seeing him now, drunk, only reinforces that sentiment. He makes me cringe. To be fair, after tonight, I'm not sure I want to see anyone else ever again. I'm on cloud nine! I reach across and abruptly end the call. James hands me back my phone, and I quickly check to ensure the call has disconnected.

"You okay?" James asks, his voice soft and concerned, his arm still resting comfortably around my waist. "He sounded pretty drunk."

I take a deep breath. "You know, I said earlier that you win some, you lose some? Well, I've definitely won tonight," I confess, looking up at him with a smile. It's cheesy, but the wine has loosened me up. Our faces are closer than they've been all evening, and my pulse races. Sitting next to this incredibly handsome Hollywood A-lister has definitely raised the stakes. His quiet confidence and easy charm are magnetic. I wonder if he feels it too, or if he's just being nice, or acting. Then again, maybe I just need a wee! My trail of thought breaks off. I don't want to move away from him; I'm enjoying being this close to him, wondering what could happen next, but I'm desperate.

"I must use the ladies," I say as I lean into his body a bit more and place my hand lightly on his chest, just to test his reaction. The alcohol is making me brave. He doesn't seem to mind me touching him. He holds my stare as I feel the rise and fall of his chest.

"Ooh, I need the ladies too!" Jules exclaims, standing up and grabbing her bag. "I'll come with you."

James stands and offers his hand to help me up. For just a moment, as our eyes lock, it feels like the rest of the room fades away. It's just the two of us.

Six

ules and I make our way across the restaurant, but no one seems to stare or even look up as we pass by. We head into the bathroom, where there are two cubicles, both empty.

"See you in a minute," I say to her as I enter one of them.

A few minutes later, we're at the mirror, both reapplying lipstick. Mine's mostly intact, but I want to freshen it up and add some gloss. Jules looks over at me through the mirror.

"That shade suits your skin tone," she remarks.

"Thanks," I say, still focused on perfecting my lips.

"I can see why he likes you, you're his type to a T." She raises her eyebrows at me. I must look a bit confused.

"James," she confirms. "He has a twinkle in his eye tonight." I feel myself blush and I brush off her comment.

"I'm sure he just felt a bit sorry for me for being stood up. He's just being kind, that's all," I reply, downplaying it.

Jules continues as if I hadn't said a thing. "To the outside world, he's known as being pretty fierce, especially with work, but he's a lovely guy. I've known him for about four or five years now, and he's always been warm. But there's something different about him tonight. I must admit, we were a bit shocked when he suddenly announced he was inviting you to join us for dinner – it's totally out of character, but…" She trails off, eyeing me up and down with a smile. "I can see why. You two look good together."

She's smiling warmly at me, and her words make me feel both flattered and a little nervous. I want to ask her a million things about him, about their friendship, about who he really is beyond the public persona. I'm envious of her, because after tonight, she'll still see him, know him, be a part of his life. For me, this might be a one-time thing.

We return to the table, and James stands to offer me my previous spot, but I gesture for him to stay, taking a seat at the end.

"You're back!" he says cheerfully. "Mark and I have decided we're all going to a club he knows."

"We are?" says Jules, slightly surprised.

"We are," answers Mark, snuggling up to Julia in an attempt to be seductive. "And you and I are going to have a little smooch on the dance floor," he adds with a smile, putting his hand on hers and giving her a tender kiss on the lips. They are so cute.

"Great!" I say, deciding to roll with the evening, no more second-guessing.

"Is that okay? Do you need to be up early tomorrow?" James asks me.

"It's fine," I say to him, "and no, I don't need to be up early tomorrow."

"Good." He smiles.

The waiter arrives with the bill, placing it in the centre of the table. James instantly pulls it in front of him.

"Let me know what I owe?" I say quietly. I have no idea how much the bill is, but given the wine we've had, it will be in the hundreds. My eyes water at the thought.

"You owe absolutely nothing. You're my guest tonight and it's my treat." He smiles at me, and I see that twinkle in his eye.

"Okay, that's very kind of you, I appreciate it. I was quite prepared to go Dutch tonight," I respond.

"Don't worry about it, I've got it covered." And with that he pulls out a sleek black Amex card from his wallet.

The waiter leaves us four shot glasses on the table filled with clear liquid. "On the house," says the waiter. We each take a glass and raise it. "Cheers," we say, as we down our drinks in one. The liquid burns as it goes down, and I grimace, placing the empty glass back on the table. James does the same, his face scrunching up for a moment. Julia makes a funny expression, sticking her tongue out in a way that makes me laugh, while Mark, ever the character, smacks his lips, grins and asks for another one.

James makes a quick call to arrange the car, and within five minutes, we're ready to leave. We head towards the front door where the maître d' retrieves our coats. As he hands me mine, James looks it over, smiling.

"Nice jacket," he compliments. Before I can respond, a tall, stocky guy with a sharp black suit and a very serious look on his face, strides over to us.

"Car's outside waiting," he says to James in a no-nonsense American accent.

"Great. This is Nikki, she's coming with us." James introduces me to the man. "Nikki, this is Sean, head of my security team."

Sean gives me a brief nod, no words, just a nod, making his presence felt without the need for small talk.

"What's it like out there?" he asks.

"There's a few," Sean replies.

"Okay." James shifts his tone. "Sean is going to escort us to the car. If you go out with Mark and Julia, and I will follow. Maybe keep your head down and get straight in." He breaks into a smile to soften the seriousness.

"Got it." I nod, fully aware of the chaos I might be stepping into. Just hours ago, I could have easily been a fan myself, standing outside waiting for a glimpse of someone like James. It's surreal. I pinch myself slightly, reminding myself that this is real.

"Ready?" he asks, checking in.

"Ready," I confirm.

As Sean opens the restaurant door, I spot a sleek, black people carrier with dark windows waiting for us. Mark and Julia step out ahead of me, and I follow closely behind. There are a few shouts of Mark's name and some camera flashes, but the attention doesn't seem overwhelming – yet. A smartly dressed man with grey hair, who I later learn is called Nigel, stands by the car and offers me a hand stepping up into the vehicle, giving me a warm smile and saying "Hello," with a very British middle-class accent.

Mark and Julia settle into the back seat, immediately leaning into each other for a quiet cuddle. I take a seat in front of them, glancing out through the darkened window as James leaves the restaurant with Sean by his side and the 'few' flashes quickly escalate into what feels like hundreds. The once quiet street is now filled with the sound of camera clicks and excited shouts of "James! James!" from fans trying to catch his attention. Camera phones are held high in the air, and I spot a few professional photographers zooming in, aiming for that perfect shot. I can see now why he needs security.

Sean stands close by, his eyes sweeping the crowd as James stops to shake hands and pose for a few selfies, effortlessly charming the small mob that's gathered.

After a few more photos and exchanges, James makes his way to the car, saying his goodbyes. He climbs in with Sean, who takes his place next to him in the row in front of me. I can't help but feel a slight disappointment – James is no longer sitting next to me.

He turns around, looking at me with a soft expression. "Okay?" he asks.

"Okay." I nod, managing a smile.

"You handled that like a pro!" he says, a hint of admiration in his voice. Sean presses a button, and the door slides seamlessly to a close.

Seven

Mark calls ahead to the club to give them a heads-up that we're on the way. As the car weaves through the streets of London, he keeps the party alive, dubbing our ride the 'fun bus'. Though the alcohol is working its magic on him, even his playful banter can't get a smile out of Sean, who remains stoically professional.

After a short drive, we pull up into another affluent part of London. As I look around, I wonder where the club could be. The area is lined with grand beige townhouses, each with towering sash windows and elegant black railings. As the car comes to a stop, Nigel kills the engine and steps out first, quickly joined by Sean, who exchanges a few words with him on the pavement – probably going over the next steps for our entrance.

Sean opens the door for us, and James steps out first, offering his hand to help me out of the car. We follow Mark and Julia as they approach a set of stairs leading to a large black door, guarded by two burly bouncers. They step aside immediately, allowing us access, and an immaculately dressed woman in her forties, wearing a sharp black trouser suit, a flamboyant white ruffled shirt, and red kitten heels, opens the door.

"Darlings!" She greets Mark and Julia with a kiss on each cheek and waves us in. "Come in."

As we step inside, Sean and Nigel fall in behind us, always keeping a careful eye on things. Mark quickly introduces me and James to the woman, and she gives us each a handshake. I notice she lingers on James's hand a little longer than necessary.

I hear the low thud of music getting louder as she escorts us down a hallway lit with crystal chandeliers that throw flickering reflections onto the dark wood floors and pop art of iconic women lines the walls.

The woman chats casually with Mark as we walk. "I've cordoned off the VIP area for you guys and got you two of our best security for the evening," she says as the bass from the music grows more intense, vibrating through the walls.

She finally opens a door, and we step into the heart of the club. The music pulses through me, a perfect mix of dance and R&B – exactly my kind of vibe. We descend a few steps and are led to a private, circular balcony that overlooks the buzzing dance floor below.

The club is a wash of crimson, its dark, sultry ambiance amplified by a red glow that seems to permeate everything. The smell of sweat, mingled with musty perfume, clings to the air. Our VIP area is intimate, with a standing table surrounded by red bar stools and a black leather sofa for two, accompanied by a low coffee table. It feels like we've been transported to the red-light district of Amsterdam.

An iron spiral staircase, roped off at the bottom, leads down to a raised dance floor, which is glowing red from underneath, giving it a surreal, floating effect. The dance floor isn't huge, but it's enough to create a vibrant pulse. Barrel stools and booths line the edge, while a bar gleams on the far side. From where we are, the view of the DJ, with strobe lights dancing around him, is perfect.

Despite the club not being overly crowded, there's an undeniable buzz to the place – a great vibe that hit me the moment we walked in. The woman who greeted us takes Mark's drink order and disappears, while James's security heads downstairs to confer with the club's team.

Mark wastes no time, pulling Julia in and grinding up against her, as she loops her arms around his neck. I'm left standing beside James, unsure of what the etiquette is here. Should we dance, stay up here, and chat and drink? If we do dance, do we stick to this secluded space, or can we join the others on the floor below? I can't help but wonder if James would get mobbed if we ventured down.

He steps closer to me, his hand resting lightly on my back as he leans in. "I think those two are going to continue their party at home." He nods towards Mark and Julia, who are fully absorbed in each other.

I laugh. "Maybe, or he'll just pass out! They're a nice couple, very in love."

"They are," he agrees. "They're also some of my best friends, one of the few genuine ones I have. I always make time for them when I'm in the UK." His words hit me like a jolt. *He lives in America. I live here.* The reality of our separate lives suddenly stings.

Before I can dwell on it, a waitress arrives with a tray carrying a bottle of champagne and four glasses. She expertly pops the cork without spilling a drop. James calls Mark and Julia over, and we gather around the table. I glance at the label – 2008, a vintage I know to be expensive.

She fills our glasses and leaves. James raises a toast again before Mark resumes his position with his wife. I take a sip, and the bubbles hit the back of my throat. It's exquisite! James turns to me again, pulling me closer this time, his arm wrapped snugly around my waist, our hips brushing together as I rest a hand on his shoulder. "Are you having a good time?" he asks, his voice rising just enough to be heard over the music.

I meet his gaze. "I'm having an amazing time."

"Better than a microwave meal for one?"

I chuckle, feeling lightheaded. "So much better."

He grins at me with a glint in his eye. "Better than a date with that guy?"

I lower my voice, looking at his lips for a brief moment. "Yes, much better," I say. "Although, I do have a question for you."

"Go on," he prompts, curious.

"Why did you invite me to join you for dinner, given you don't know me at all?" I ask, half-jokingly. "And why were you at the bar in the first place?"

His brows rise in amusement. "That's two questions."

I nudge him playfully. "Smart arse."

He laughs, then grows more thoughtful. "Honestly? When I walked into the restaurant tonight, I saw you sitting at the bar – well, I saw the back of you in that dress – and I just… I felt compelled to go over. So, I left the other two and made my way over to the bar just in time to hear you'd been stood up. And when we spoke…" He pauses, locking eyes with me. "I thought you were gorgeous. As I walked back to my table, I made an impulsive decision to ask you to join us. And here we are."

His words send a thrill through me, and for a moment, I'm lost in the feeling of his body against mine, the warmth of his arm around my waist, the curve of his pectoral muscle under my hand. I feel an overwhelming urge to kiss him.

"I want to dance with you," he murmurs into my ear, his breath warm against my skin.

"What?" I ask, the music drowning him out.

"I want to dance with you," he repeats, louder this time, pointing towards the glowing dance floor below.

"Won't you get mobbed?" I ask, a little apprehensive.

"Maybe. Maybe not. Do you want to?"

I nod and with that he takes my hand and calls out to Mark that we're heading downstairs, and they follow us down. The security team unhooks the rope, and we slide through, my fingers resting lightly in his hand. He keeps me close and leads me onto the dance floor; so far, no one has noticed. Sean stands near the edge watching everyone closely while Nigel stays on the balcony hovering like a meerkat. We begin to move, a simple two step at first but I can feel the energy between us building as the seductive bass reverberates through the floor. His hands glide over my waist, sending shivers down my spine, and I wrap my arms around his neck, pulling him closer but not too close.

It's not long before I spot them – three women dancing nearby, their eyes fixed on us. They're good-looking, well-dressed. Rich. The type of women used to getting attention. Early forties, I'd guess. I try to ignore them, but I can feel their gaze on us, on him. They keep glancing over, whispering to one another, and inching closer.

"You've been spotted," I say to him quietly. He doesn't react, just shrugs and keeps his focus on me. He's used to it. As the ladies move closer, I start to feel a little uneasy. But just as I'm about to suggest we move somewhere else, one of the women taps him on the shoulder. She's tall, taller than me, with a fantastic figure and short blonde bobbed hair. She's wearing a sparkling vest top that shows off her tanned neckline and skin-tight faux leather trousers… she looks great.

We stop dancing, and James turns to face her.

"Excuse me," she says coyly, completely ignoring me. "I'm so sorry to interrupt, but I absolutely love you! I'm such a fan!"

James smiles politely. "Thank you."

"Would you mind if I got a picture with you?"

He glances at me briefly. "Er, yeah sure. Excuse me one second," he says to me, then turns back to her. He lets go of me and stands next to her, draping his arm lightly round her shoulder while she leans in close. She beams at the camera while her friend snaps the picture, but even when the photo's done, she doesn't move. I stand there awkwardly, feeling my stomach twist.

Julia, noticing what's happening, moves closer to me. Sensing my discomfort, she leans in and whispers, "Unfortunately, this is what happens when you're with James Keller. People think he's public property."

I manage a small smile, trying to shrug it off.

"I absolutely loved *Driver's Fury*," the woman gushes, her coyness slipping away as her fingers lightly touch his chest. "It's not every day a girl gets to meet someone as talented and charming as you."

He smiles at her and glances in my direction, a hint of amusement in his eyes. "That's very kind of you to say."

"I bet you hear this all the time, but there's something about you that just draws people in."

He remains courteous, but I see he takes hold of her hand to release himself from her grip.

"It's a shame we have to part ways so soon. Maybe we could chat a little more? I'd love to spend some time with you."

"That would be lovely, but I'm afraid I need to get back to my friends, but it was nice meeting you."

"Hey, James!" shouts Mark, trying to help him out. The woman glances up, and James disentangles himself from her and walks back to me. His polite smile has faded, replaced with a look of genuine apology.

"Sorry about that, it comes with the territory," he says, looking at me intensely.

"It's no problem," I reply, doing my best to sound nonchalant.

"Where were we?" he asks, sliding his hands around my waist, pulling me close again, wanting to pick up where we left off. But unfortunately, our bubble has burst. The murmurs from the crowd are growing louder as more people realise James Keller and Mark Layton are in the room. Camera phones flash to life, and excited shouts of "James! James! Mark!" start to fill the air.

It's time to retreat.

Sean and the club's security team move in like clockwork, parting the sea of people and carving out an escape route for us. As we make our way off the dance floor, a few determined fans manage to stop James, requesting selfies. Ever the gentleman, he obliges, flashing a quick smile before Sean gently nudges us along.

Soon, we're back upstairs, tucked away in the calm of the VIP area. The atmosphere up here feels worlds apart from the chaos below. James keeps his arm wrapped around me, his thumb tracing gentle circles on my shoulder as we chat casually with Mark and Jules. Slowly, I let myself relax again, sinking into the warmth of him, allowing the evening to sweep me away once more.

Eight

The people carrier is waiting outside the club when we finally emerge. Sean ushers us in and this time we manage to avoid the crowds entirely. Mark and Jules settle at the back, her head resting gently on his shoulder, their fingers intertwined. James takes a seat by the window and pats the spot next to him, inviting me to join him. I do, sinking into the seat with a happy sigh. We are all exhausted. The radio is on quietly and it seems it's 'love song' hour, which is a welcome change as my ears are still ringing from the club's music. I give Nigel my postcode and we pull away down the road.

After a moment, James turns to me. "Take out your phone," he says. "I want you to add a number."

I do as he asks, and he gives me a US mobile number. "If something comes up and you can't make Saturday, call this number. I hope you can make it, but just in case."

I don't ask if it's his number. Instead, I enter it under 'J' and give him a smile. "You should take my number too, just in case you change your mind."

"That won't happen." He grins. "But I'll take it anyway." He punches my number into his phone, giving me a playful wink as he saves it.

It's about twenty minutes to my place from the club at this hour, and as we drive, James takes my hand, resting it on his warm thigh. He leans his head back, eyes closing in quiet relaxation, and I feel myself sinking into the moment, laying my head gently on his shoulder. Everything feels easy, like we've been doing this for ages.

When we arrive at my building, I gently lift my head to buzz the gates open. The car glides up the driveway, and I direct Nigel to the first building on the right. "You can turn around just past that corner," I add as we pull up alongside my place.

James opens the sliding door for me. I stand, turning to Mark and Jules. "Thanks for a wonderful evening. It was so nice meeting you both," I say, waving them goodbye. James steps out and offers his hand to help me down.

"Thanks," I say, taking his hand. The car pulls away behind us as we walk hand in hand towards the front of my building. Wide white steps lead up to an imposing black front door, flanked by large, matching white pillars. The night is quiet, and no one is around. The night air is crisp now, with a chill that wasn't there before. The sky is clear, and though it's nearly 1:30am, it feels almost light because of the bright full moon above us.

We stop at the bottom of the stairs. I gesture towards the building. "This is me. I'm on the top floor."

He looks up, taking in the place, then turns back to me. I can feel adrenaline coursing through me, the night playing over in my mind like a dream. "Thank you for an

49

amazing evening," I say, feeling giddy.

"You're welcome. I've really enjoyed your company," he says, his voice soft but steady. "I'm glad that guy stood you up." His eyes lock onto mine, serious, intense.

"I am too," I whisper, holding his gaze. His eyes flick to my lips, and I feel my heart speed up. He leans in, and for a second, I'm unsure if he's going for my cheek or my lips. The corners of our mouths brush lightly, a hesitant touch that sends a jolt through me. His breath is warm, carrying the faint scent of champagne. There's a moment of pause, both of us caught in the same hesitation, before he tilts his head and our lips meet fully. It's electric, soft but sensual, sending waves of heat through my entire body. I close my eyes and lean into him, feeling his hand slide into my hair, pulling me closer. The kiss deepens for a brief second before we part, our bodies still close, our breaths mingling in the cool night air. I open my eyes to find him gazing at me, his expression a mix of desire and tenderness.

James Keller has just kissed me – it was brief but incredibly sensual.

Before I can say anything, I hear the low hum of the car approaching again. He steps back slightly, his hand still holding mine for a moment longer. "Goodnight," he whispers. "I'll see you on Saturday." He leans in once more, kissing me lightly on the cheek, the lingering warmth of his lips leaving my skin tingling. Then, with a smile, he turns and makes his way to the car.

"Goodnight," I manage to say, feeling both elated and dazed. I turn, walking up the steps to the front door, and slip inside.

What has just happened?

Nine

*a*s dawn breaks, sunlight streams through the bedroom window, casting a warm glow across the room. I squint, my head pounding slightly, and my mouth dry like sandpaper. I fumble through the drawer beside my bed, searching for the paracetamol. After downing a pill with a sip of stale water from the night before, I sink back into the pillows with a contented smile despite the hangover.

For the next hour or so I doze, drifting in and out of slumber, replaying the previous night in my mind over and over. Did it really happen? Was it all some vivid dream? The kiss, oh my God, the kiss!

When I finally surface from the haze of my half-sleep, it's already 10am. I rarely sleep this late, but today feels different. I've missed my 9am Pilates class – not that I'd have been able to focus anyway.

I pull myself out of bed and into the shower, letting the

warm water fall over my face, wondering what he's doing now. Is he also thinking about last night and that kiss we shared? Or is he too busy, too caught up in his famous life to even give me a second thought? The thought nags at me, leaving a trace of disappointment in its wake.

After towelling off, I throw on my favourite pair of dark blue skinny jeans and a dark green V-neck top that hugs me just right, and makes my boobs look fabulous; it shows just enough cleavage. I've got a couple of hours before I head to Lizzie's place for the night, but I can't seem to settle. My stomach is in knots, and I feel like I'm in some sort of limbo, unable to focus on anything else. I didn't have this problem yesterday morning.

I manage a slice of toast and butter and pour myself a cup of Earl Grey, but my mind keeps wandering back to him. The temptation to search his name on the net becomes overwhelming. There's a battle raging inside my head: one half of my brain says, *Do it!* while the other half shouts at me, *No, don't.*

I give in.

After opening my iPad, I type his name in the search bar. Instantly, a flood of websites appears – fan pages, gossip columns, interviews, all there, right at my fingertips, and I can't help but scroll.

'James Keller, one of Hollywood's most enigmatic and resilient stars. He's an institution. He continues to deliver hit after hit whilst maintaining his mystique.'
'Power mad but anyone who has worked with him or knows him personally attests to his kindness, dedication and humility.'

'The lightning speed with which the internet spreads news about him is a testament to Keller's monumental celebrity status.'

I scroll through the search results, my heart doing a little flip at the sight of his name. Pictures of him on the red carpet, dashing modelling shots, and candid photos of him caught in moments with various women, including his ex-wife and ex-girlfriend. As I click through, studying his smile, the easy confidence and the way he carries himself with effortless charm, a few things leap out at me:

Hollywood's most influential actor.

Hollywood's most eligible bachelor.

Ranked in the top five of highest-grossing actors for lead roles.

A formidable force.

Net worth is estimated at $750 million.

Owns houses in NY and Beverly Hills.

Owns Falcon 900EX private jet.

That last one catches my eye. A private jet? Curious, I tap on it. It's a twelve-seater, sleek and luxurious, and flies transatlantic. I skim through the photos – soft leather seats, polished wood interiors. It looks like it's more comfortable than my living room.

I avoid diving into the endless gossip about his personal life. It's tempting, but it's not something I'm ready to face just yet. I close the tab and decide to log on to my work emails instead. Work never fails to distract me. A couple of hours pass and I'm just thinking about getting myself ready to go to Lizzie's when the door buzzes. I answer, curious as I'm not expecting anything.

"Delivery for Nikki," comes a cheerful female voice through the intercom.

"Okay, third floor," I tell her, buzzing her in. Moments later, there's a knock at the door, and when I open it, she's standing there, smiling brightly.

"Nikki?" she asks, and I nod.

"These are for you," she says, handing over the most stunning bouquet of red roses I've ever seen. The open blooms are as big as my palm, and they smell divine. "Two dozen," she adds, grinning. "You're a lucky lady." With a wink, she turns and heads back down the stairs, leaving me standing on the doorstep, still a little stunned, holding these beautiful but surprisingly heavy roses.

Inside, I carefully place them in the sink and detach the small card nestled between the stems. My heart skips a beat, and a moment of dread flickers through my mind – what if they're from Lewis, by way of apology? As gorgeous as they are, the idea fills me with disappointment. I take a deep breath and open the card. It's handwritten, neat writing.

'*Looking forward to seeing you again on Saturday. J x.*'

I get goosebumps as I read the message. A smile spreads across my face, and I can feel my cheeks flushing with warmth. The anticipation of seeing him again fills me with a sense of nervous excitement. After finding the biggest vase I have, I arrange them as best I can. I'm no florist, but they look fabulous – vibrant, the brightest red I've ever seen. I place the vase in the centre of my kitchen island, admiring how the sunlight makes the petals almost glow. With a satisfied smile, I move the flowers I bought for myself earlier this week to the coffee table. Then, I snap a picture of the roses.

I grab my overnight bag and head down to my car. After the divorce, I treated myself to a convertible Porsche 911 Carrera S. It's two years old, with a sleek black exterior and a matching interior. I love the feeling of the wind whipping through my hair as I drive. My ex-husband would have called it 'garish', which, if I'm honest, is exactly why I bought it. It's a symbol of my newfound independence; I can be who I want to be without apology. I lower the soft top, letting the warm sun flood into the car, and pull away.

Two hours later, I pull into Lizzie's driveway and give the horn a quick beep, though the purr of the engine is probably enough to let them know I've arrived. Her home sits just on the outskirts of Brighton – a pretty, white, cottage-style house with pale blue garage doors and matching shutters. It's picture-perfect, like something out of a storybook. The front is mostly tarmac, spacious enough for a few cars, but the little lawn with its bed of bright red tulips and delicate blue forget-me-nots adds a lovely pop of colour. The daffodils are starting to fade now, but there's still a hint of yellow left.

Lizzie appears at the door with a huge smile on her face. She's eighteen months younger than me, a bit shorter but with the same slim frame. Her hair was light brown, but for some reason, she decided to go peroxide blonde a while back, and even though you can see dark roots, it looks good on her. She married well, settling into family life with two children, which, in some ways, took the pressure off me. She was always the creative one, whereas I was more studious. We've always been very close, and thankfully have different taste in men.

"Well, look who's finally arrived in her fancy Porsche!" Lizzie teases. "Hi, darling! Good to see you!" She rushes forwards, wrapping me in a tight hug. "You look amazing!"

I hug her back, returning the compliment, though she brushes it off with a wave. I grab my bag from the boot of the car, and I'm greeted by Bella, the fox red Labrador, bounding over with pure puppy energy. At just eight months old, she's all wagging tail and clumsy enthusiasm. From up the stairs, I can hear the splashing and laughter of Poppy and Rose, my four- and two-year-old nieces, clearly enjoying their bath time.

Lizzie's home is vastly different to mine. Mine is very minimalist and tidy, and hers... is not. There's clutter everywhere, paintings stuck to the fridge door, shoes scattered across the floor – chaos, everywhere. But it's the best kind of chaos from a home filled with love and fun.

"Mind the mess," she says, picking up toys from the floor as we make our way towards the kitchen. "How've you been?" she asks, wiping something sticky – jam, I think – from the counter and clearing away the kids' dinner plates. She sighs dramatically, her hands on her hips. "I love my kids, but I *cannot* wait for a grown-up night out." Her eyes light up suddenly, and she grins at me. "Oooh, how was your date?"

I hesitate, unsure how to answer. "It was... um, not as expected, let's just say." I trail off. I'm not quite sure how to tell her – do I just blurt it out? Or maybe I don't tell her at all? I *must* tell someone, though; I can't keep it in.

Just as I'm about to say more, my phone rings from inside my bag. Saved by the bell. "One sec," I say, reaching into my bag. I glance at the screen: no caller ID. Without thinking, I hit the green button and answer.

"Hello, Nikki speaking," I say in my usual professional tone when I don't know who is on the other end.

"Hi, Nikki, it's James," comes that smooth American accent, sending a shockwave through me; so much so, I nearly drop my phone. As I fumble to get it back to my ear, Lizzie looks at me curiously, her ears pricked. I give her a quick wave and retreat to the lounge and out of earshot.

"Hi," I reply, trying to sound casual, like hearing from him is no big deal, even though my heart is racing. I'm extremely pleased, of course, but I don't want to come across *too* eager. "How are you?" I ask, my mind racing. When we swapped numbers, it was only in case one of us needed to change our plans for Saturday. A wave of panic rises – what if he's calling to cancel? My heart plummets for a moment before I remember the roses sitting at home with the note from him. That restores some hope, but still – why is he calling?

"Hey, I'm great, thanks. Did you manage to sleep well after our night out?"

"I slept okay, thanks," I reply, trying to sound breezy. "How about you? And by the way, thank you for the roses. I assume 'J' is you?"

"Yes, it's me. I hope you like them."

"They are gorgeous, thank you," I say sincerely, feeling a warmth spread through me. We exchange some pleasantries, a bit of small talk that does little to calm the growing tension in my chest.

"So, I was thinking…" He pauses, and my heart skips a beat. *Here it comes*, I think. "Saturday seems kind of far away, so I was wondering if you'd like to have dinner with me before then?"

I'm momentarily stunned. "I'd love to," I manage to say, excitement bubbling up. "When?"

"Are you free Wednesday evening?" he asks. "I'm filming until about 6:30pm, but I'm free after that. And just to be clear, I mean like a *date*," he adds, with a light laugh, making my stomach do a little flip.

I laugh. "Very funny! I'd love to have a dinner *date* with you," I reply, emphasising the word. "Did you have somewhere in mind?"

"Well," he says, his tone softening slightly, "if you're comfortable with it, I was thinking we could have dinner at my hotel." He pauses, and I hear a hint of caution in his voice. "You saw what it was like last night, and that was pretty tame. I thought it might be easier, you know, to keep things a little more… private."

I pause for a split second, processing the suggestion. He's not wrong. Last night had been chaotic, and I can only imagine what it would be like if we were seen out together somewhere even more public, on our own.

"Okay," I say. "That sounds good."

"Great, I can swing by and pick you up on my way back from filming, about seven?" he offers, his tone lightening again.

"Yes, perfect. You remember where I live?" I ask.

"I sure do," he replies, and just the way he says it sends shivers down my spine.

We say our goodbyes, and I hang up the phone, feeling like I'm floating. James Keller just asked me on a date. His voice is still ringing in my ears, so smooth, so sexy. I could listen to him all night. I wonder if things will feel different now that we've kissed, if watching him on my TV screen will evoke new emotions.

I wander back into the kitchen, where Duncan, Lizzie's husband, is with Poppy and Rose and their infectious laughter.

"Hi, Duncs!" I say with more enthusiasm than I meant to, planting kisses on both his cheeks. At six foot two, Duncan towers over me – something I've always been a little envious of. Lizzie lucked out with her tall husband, especially since my ex was nowhere near that height, but despite his height, he has a gentle demeanour that perfectly complements her bubbly personality. With his slim build, short wavy brown hair, and easy-going smile, it's no wonder everyone likes him.

"She's just taken a call," Lizzie chimes in, with a mischievous glint in her eye. "From a man…!"

I didn't tell her who was on the phone, but judging by my grin, she's managed to figure it out on her own.

"Ooh, how exciting!" Duncan adds, clearly picking up on Lizzie's teasing tone. "He's put a smile on your face, that's for sure!" He doesn't pry further, just flashes a knowing smile – typical Duncan, letting me share when I'm ready. Still, I feel my cheeks flush a little.

"Aunty *Nik Nik*!" Rose shouts excitedly, her little legs pumping as she and Poppy race towards me. I crouch down, arms open wide, bracing myself as they throw themselves at me, nearly toppling me over in their enthusiasm. Bella, not wanting to miss out on the fun, bounds over too, her big paws landing on my back. Duncan steps in, trying to calm the excitable puppy down, though it takes a few commands and some gentle tugging of her collar before she gets the hint. Training Bella is definitely still a work in progress.

"All right, girls, calm down slightly." Lizzie laughs, trying to restore a bit of order.

"Aunty Nik Nik? Are you staying? Will you take us to bed tonight? Can you read me a story? Are you having breakfast with us?" Poppy fires off questions so quickly it's a wonder I manage to catch them all.

"Yes, sweetheart, I'm staying, and I'd love to take you up and read you a story," I reply, my heart warmed by their excitement.

Ten

The taxi pulls up outside, ready to take Lizzie and me to the local Indian restaurant, Bombay Spice. It's only a five-minute drive – easily walkable, but we decide to give our feet a rest tonight. Being a Saturday evening, the place is buzzing with life, and we're shown to a small table for two tucked away at the far end.

The decor is… well, let's just say it's like stepping into someone's 1970s living room. Brown swirly carpets, pale pink tablecloths, and those amber light fittings that give the whole place a warm, nostalgic glow. I'd like to call it retro, but the reality is, the place just hasn't been redecorated in decades. Still, it has its charm, and more importantly, the food is always top-notch.

Lizzie raises an eyebrow at the surroundings, smiling. "Nothing's changed, has it?"

"Nope." I laugh. "But I wouldn't want it to."

We order a bottle of the house white wine and skim through the menu, even though we both know exactly what we're having: tikka masala for me, and chicken korma for Lizzie. As I absently browse through the options, considering whether I should try something different for a change, my thoughts inevitably drift to James.

What's he doing tonight? Is he having dinner with someone else? Dancing with someone else? But then my mind wanders to a different scenario – James sitting next to me here, in this very restaurant. I imagine us on a double date with Lizzie and Duncan, all of us laughing over naan bread and sharing curries. The idea makes me smile.

The waiter approaches our table, snapping me back to reality.

"Hello, Miss Lizzie! How are you?" He greets her with a familiarity that suggests she's quite the regular.

"Hi, Sammi," she replies with a friendly smile. "I'm good, thank you. Hmm, I think I'll have the chicken korma, please, with pilau rice."

"Good choice," he says, turning to me with a kind smile. "And for you, lady?"

"I'll go for a chicken tikka masala with coconut rice, please. Oh, and can we have some Peshwari naan and saag aloo as well?"

"Of course, ladies," he replies, before heading off to the bar to place our order. Lizzie settles back into her seat and takes a sip of wine.

"So, tell me about the date, then. My life is as dull as dishwater at the moment, so I need to live vicariously through you!"

"Is it?" I reply with a hint of concern. Lizzie usually seems content as a full-time mum, unlike me, who was always restless, always wanting more.

"Oh, you know." She shrugs off her comment. "It's just hard being home with the kids. I have managed to produce a few pieces of art recently."

"That's fantastic!" I say, my enthusiasm genuine. "You love drawing, and you're so talented at it!" She's always been the creative one. I think back to when we were pre-teens and our parents were redecorating our rooms. Lizzie got to paint huge murals on the walls – Garfield the cat on my wall and Snoopy the dog on hers. I loved it so much that I was heartbroken when they eventually wallpapered over it. It's probably still there underneath the layers of wallpaper in our childhood home, where Mum and Dad still live. They've been in that house for at least thirty-five years now!

"There's a local artist exhibition being held in the church hall down the road next Sunday. I've secured a stall," she says with cautious excitement.

"Wow, that's great news, I'm so pleased for you." I reach across the table and give her hand a little squeeze. "Have you told the folks?"

"No, not yet. I'll give them the good news tomorrow when we see them for lunch. Anyway… tell me about this date. Not as expected, you said – better or worse than expected?"

I shuffle in my seat, unsure how to answer. "He stood me up," I say flatly.

Lizzie's jaw drops. "What? Why? Did he bail before you got to the restaurant, or did he just leave you hanging?"

"Hanging," I reply, and the look of disbelief on her face almost makes me laugh. "And I have no idea why."

"Well, that's bloody awful! What an arsehole!" She

shakes her head in disgust. "Where did you say you met him again?"

"At Claire's husband's party last week," I remind her, leaning back in my chair. "You remember Claire, right?" She nods. Claire and I met years ago at one of my first jobs – we trained together. Even after I left, we stayed close. "Lewis, the guy, is a friend of her husband's, and he was there alone too. We ended up chatting for a while. He wasn't bad company, but there wasn't really a spark. Still, he seemed keen, and after a few drinks, he asked me out. I guess the wine clouded my judgement, because I agreed."

"So, this Lewis, he left you alone in a London restaurant?" she asks, sounding concerned. "You deserve better than that. Honestly, I can't believe he had the nerve. Men!"

"Yep, Mike was there, though, behind the bar," I reassure her.

"Oh good, but how embarrassing! So, what did you do after that, then? Just go home?"

I pause, considering my next answer. "No, I stayed and had dinner."

"On your own?" She sounds like Mum!

"No…"

"With Mike?"

"No…"

"Then who?" I sense a little frustration in her voice.

"James Keller," I say quickly.

"Who?" she questions, not expecting me to say I had dinner with a major movie star!

"James Keller," I repeat, more slowly this time. "*Driver's Fury*? *Hibernation*? *Stranger in Paris*?" I reel off just a few of his films. She furrows her brow, and I can see the cogs turning as she looks at me quizzically. I nod at her when I think the penny has finally dropped.

"Shut the front door!" She laughs. "No you didn't!"

"I did," I say, trying to suppress a grin. "He overheard me at the bar telling Mike that I'd been stood up and, well, long story short, he invited me to join him for dinner. He was there having dinner with Mark Layton."

"Are you serious? James Keller? Mark Layton? No way!" Her voice rises, catching the attention of a couple of diners two tables away.

"Shhh!" I hush her, trying to downplay it. "Yes, James Keller and Mark Layton, plus Julia, Mark's wife."

"Holy shit!" she whispers, eyes wide. Funny, that's exactly what I said when I saw him.

"So, you had dinner with him?" Her question is rhetorical; she's still processing. "What was he like? Did you get a selfie or an autograph?"

"No, it wasn't that kind of night. He was lovely." I feel myself swooning for a second before reeling it in. "They were all very friendly. I had the best time!" I can't help but grin widely.

"What kind of night was it, then?" she asks, scrutinising my face.

"Bloody fantastic!" I reply. My smile is getting wider, if at all possible.

"What's he like?"

"Debonair, as you'd expect. Charming, engaging, funny – just nice! Down to earth." I recount the evening in detail, feeling butterflies all over again. It dominates our conversation for the rest of the meal.

"So, let me get this straight." She leans forwards, elbows on the table. "You have dinner with him, which he pays for, like a date, then whisks you off to a nightclub where you dance together. Then what happened?" Her tone turns suspicious.

"He drove me home, well, his driver did."

"And he came with you? In the car, back to yours?"

"Yes, we were all in the car together. He dropped me home," I reply coyly.

"Like a true gent, and that was it? You went home, and nothing else happened?" She raises an eyebrow.

I hesitate, then take a sip of wine. "We kissed," I say quietly.

"*What?*" she shrieks, drawing more attention. She quickly lowers her voice. "Fucking hell, Nik, you kissed James Keller?"

"I did!" I grin.

Lizzie sits quietly for a moment, trying to process what I've just told her.

"Hang on a minute. Who was that on the phone tonight?" She suddenly remembers the call I took earlier.

"That was him. He asked if I wanted to have dinner with him again before Saturday, just the two of us."

"And you said yes, of course. *Oh my God*, you're dating James Keller!" Her voice rises again in excitement.

"Shh!" I press a finger to my lips. "I did say yes, and no, I'm not dating him," I reply as casually as I can manage. Lizzie raises an eyebrow at me. "I don't think so, I don't know!" I start to ramble. Am I dating him? He said 'a date', but does that mean we're dating? God, why isn't there a textbook for this?

"Sounds like you're dating him to me!" she states.

"He sent me roses today – two dozen red roses."

"Dating!" She bursts out laughing.

"I took a picture of them. Let me show you," I say, reaching into my handbag for my phone. I scroll to the Photos app and pull up the last picture I took of the beautiful roses, proudly displayed on my kitchen island, before handing the phone to Lizzie.

"Oh wow!" She gasps. "They're gorgeous! Better than anything Karl ever sent you," she adds with a smirk. Then, as she swipes through the photos, her eyes widen. "Oh my God, there's a picture here of you and James!"

"What?" I grab the phone back and see it for myself – a picture of me and James Keller, both looking straight at the camera. James is raising his wine glass in a toast, and we're both smiling. My heart skips a beat as I stare at the photo. Mark must've taken it when Lewis called. Then I notice something in the bottom right of the picture… Lewis. He's there, slightly blurred but clearly visible. I can't help but let out a small laugh.

"Well," Lizzie says, still studying my expression, "if that's not the most surreal love triangle ever…"

Eleven

fter dinner, we move on to a cocktail bar a few doors down from the restaurant for a nightcap. The place is bathed in neon light and buzzing with energy. It's noisy, vibrant, and alive.

We order our cocktails at the bar – me a classic Martini, Lizzie a colourful cosmopolitan – and find ourselves a table by the window.

"I still can't believe you're dating James Keller!" Lizzie teases as she takes a sip of her cosmo. "I mean, I might not have believed it if I hadn't seen that picture! Show me again?"

"I'm not dating him!" I protest with a smile, rummaging through my bag to find my phone. I pull up the picture and hand it over to her, still unsure what to make of it myself.

"You do look good together." She winks as she examines the photo. "Does he live here, then?"

An obvious question, but it hits me like a sharp blow. "I think he lives in the US – California, maybe."

"Oh," Lizzie says, her voice tinged with concern. "How long is he here for?"

"Just until Sunday." The thought lands hard again. Am I just a fleeting romance, something to pass the time while he's here? "I'm trying to take it at face value and not get carried away. He's gorgeous, but you're right – he lives in a different country, and he's in a completely different world. Am I out of my depth, Liz?"

"No, of course you're not, babe! Don't be silly. He's just a man, at the end of the day, and you're as beautiful as any of those Hollywood women. If you look at his previous loves – including his ex-wife – you're his type. But," she adds, leaning in slightly, "the woman who dates him will have to be really confident, you know? Comfortable in her own skin. There'll be attention, from other women – and maybe some men" – she winks – "trying to steal him from under your feet. I don't know, Nik. Just relax and enjoy it. If it's a fling, make it a fantastic one. And if it's more, great. Just promise me you won't move to the States without me."

Ah, the classic Lizzie pep talk.

"Promise," I say, grinning as we clink our glasses.

We spend the next hour talking about James, dissecting every moment from last night. Lizzie asks if I'll tell Mum and Dad about him. Does Mum even know who he is? Probably not. But Dad? Definitely. He's a massive film buff and never misses an opportunity to rave about *Driver's Fury*, where James played a racing driver pushed to his limits both on and off the track.

"His driving skills are incredible!" Dad always says whenever that film comes up.

We decide it's best not to mention James to them just yet – not until I know what's really going on. I make Lizzie swear to secrecy, too. Not a word to anyone. Not even Duncan.

The next morning, I wake to the sound of the girls already up and running around, which means Lizzie's already awake too. We didn't get in until around 12:30am last night. It was nice to have some real sister time, especially since I don't get to see her as often as I'd like, with me living near London. I shower, dress, and head downstairs to join them.

"Morning, all," I say cheerfully.

"Aunty Nik Nik!" Poppy yells.

"Shhh, sweetheart, Mummy has hurt her head!"

I laugh at Lizzie's explanation for her hangover.

Duncan is cooking a fry-up, and the smell of sizzling bacon fills the kitchen. It smells tempting, but I help myself to some fruit and yoghurt, knowing we're having a big lunch with Mum and Dad later. After breakfast, Duncan takes the girls swimming, and I help Lizzie clear up the kitchen while she brews us some tea.

"I searched him last night," she says, turning to me with wide eyes. "Do you know how many followers he has on social media?"

I shake my head.

"Forty-five million! *Forty-five million!*" she repeats, her voice full of disbelief.

"Wow! Is that forty-five million and one now?" I laugh, though Lizzie scowls, undeterred.

"He doesn't post anything personal. It's just work, work, work. Perfect for you!" She chuckles. "And there's no gossip! No affairs, no bitter exes spilling the beans."

"Maybe they all had to sign NDAs?" I suggest, imagining what it must be like to be in his world. "I'd probably do the same if I were him."

"Would you sign one? I bet his people have already done a full background check on you!" she says, handing me my tea.

I take a sip, trying to sound casual. "I'll cross that bridge when I come to it." I glance out at the garden, admiring the lush green lawn. "Duncs is really doing a fab job with the grass. I miss having a garden."

"The gardener does the lawn," Lizzie says dismissively, already engrossed in her phone. "Oh my God, he's got so many fan pages! 'Always James Keller', 'James Keller Lovers', 'James Keller Fans'… someone's posted an old modelling shot with the caption 'My love is forbidden to James Keller, but I'll love him forever'. These people are obsessed!" She laughs, scrolling through the madness, taking a sip of her tea.

Suddenly, her face freezes. "Holy shit!" she shrieks, almost making me spill my drink. "It's you! Or, at least, I think it's you… taken on Friday night." Her eyes are wide as she examines her phone.

"What's me?" I ask, a nervous knot forming in my stomach. She looks up, then reads the headline to me.

"'James Keller spotted dancing with pretty brunette in London nightclub.'"

I jump up from my seat and lean over Lizzie, scanning the article with her. My heart races. She's right – it is me. The picture is grainy, the lighting dim, and if you didn't know I was there, you wouldn't necessarily recognise me, but I do.

'James Keller was spotted dancing with a pretty brunette on Friday night in a London nightclub. Has the Driver's Fury *star found love again? No details are known about the lady in question, but an eyewitness said they looked very close. James is in town promoting his new action film, due to be released next month –* Driver's Fury: Downforce.'

I slump back into my chair, completely stunned. Lizzie looks up at me, her eyes wide with excitement.

"Well," she says, unable to contain her grin, "it's official. You've gone public!" Lizzie's eyes are wide as she continues scrolling. "There's already so many comments. People are speculating who you are, some are saying you're his new girlfriend! This is insane!"

I reach for her phone and look closer at the image. "I had no idea we were being photographed. It was a private member club."

"Well, you are dating a massive movie star," she says with a cheeky grin. "This is your life now, babe. The fans, the gossip, the headlines."

"I don't know if I'm ready for this," I admit, feeling a little overwhelmed. "I didn't expect to become some 'mystery brunette' overnight."

Lizzie shrugs, handing me back my tea. "Well, if you're gonna be with James Keller, you're gonna have to get used to it. The world's watching now."

Twelve

We arrive at the pub in convoy, me in my sleek little two-seater, while Dunc and Lizzie roll up in their much more practical seven-seater. As we pull into the car park, I spot Mum and Dad already waiting for us outside, waving, with big smiles on their faces.

The pub is quintessentially English, with low-beamed ceilings, cosy little corners, and the warm, welcoming smell of ale and woodsmoke from the open fire. It's packed, families gathering for their traditional Sunday lunch.

"Hi, Mum. Hi, Dad," I say, giving them both a kiss on the cheek, Dad pulling me in for one of his signature bear hugs that always feel like home.

"Hi, Nik, how are you doing, love?" Dad asks, squeezing me a little tighter before letting go. "Hi, darling," Mum adds.

Mum and Dad only live about twenty-five minutes away from Lizzie's place, so they're very involved with

Rose and Poppy – code for they babysit a lot. Duncan's parents, on the other hand, live all the way down in the New Forest, so they don't get to see the girls as much. As soon as we step inside, Mum and Dad turn their attention to the grandkids with the usual "Aren't you getting so big!" comments, and Rose and Poppy beam under the attention. We all settle down at a large wooden table, the kind that's been worn smooth by years of use, and the chatter starts up almost immediately.

"How's the world of law, then?" Mum asks, her voice filled with a mix of curiosity and concern.

"It's good, busy but good," I reply.

"You work so hard," she says, her brow furrowing slightly, as if hard work were a personal affront.

"You do," Dad chimes in, nodding approvingly. "How is it being a senior director, then?" he asks, his pride visible.

"It's great, going really well so far, but yes the hours can be long."

"You have no time to yourself!" Mum exclaims, her concern ramping up a notch.

"I enjoy the pressure," I say, my eyes lighting up at the challenge. "I get time to myself, but my plan is to work my backside off now and retire early!" I wink at Dad, knowing he'll understand. He retired in his mid-fifties and always says it was the best decision he ever made. Now, he spends his days at the golf club, perfectly content with his decision.

"For what, though?" Mum retorts, her voice sharp. "You have no one to go home to." Ouch. Christ, she stings like a wasp.

I try not to wince at the jab, but it lands harder than

I'd like. Typical Mum, always cutting right to the bone without even realising.

"Actually, she had a date on Friday," Lizzie pipes up, coming to my defence.

"You did?" Mum asks, sounding more surprised than pleased. "Who with?"

"He didn't show up," I admit, trying to sound nonchalant. But instead of her offering any sympathy, I catch Mum rolling her eyes.

"What?" Dad exclaims, leaning forwards, looking genuinely concerned. "Why ever not?"

Before Lizzie can jump in, I manage to answer. "I don't know," I say, shaking my head.

Dad's face twists into an expression of utter disgust. "Well, I assume you won't be entertaining him again if he asks!" he declares, more statement than question.

"Oh, I don't think she will, Dad. You've nothing to worry about there!" Lizzie chimes in with a knowing smirk, shooting me a mischievous glance. I glare at her, silently telling her to zip it.

"I hope not," Dad adds, shaking his head. "If he lets you down on date number one, he's not someone you want in your life." He gives me a kind, fatherly smile, the sort that's meant to reassure, and I can't help but feel a pang of guilt for keeping James from them. Dad has always been supportive, a steady presence in my life. He was firm with us growing up, but never overbearing.

When I first told them I was getting a divorce, I went to Dad first. He softened the blow for Mum, who was devastated. Mum adored Karl, my ex-husband. He could do no wrong in her eyes. She never said it outright, but I always sensed that she thought I didn't try hard enough to save my marriage.

Even though she knew how unhappy I'd been, she still believed that I should've fought harder for it.

My relationship with Mum has always been close, but ever since the divorce, there's been this unspoken rift between us. I know she only wants what's best for me, but what she thought was best wasn't what I needed. I never told her the full story. To this day, neither she nor Dad knows the truth about what Karl did. Only Lizzie and Duncan know that secret.

A couple of hours later, full from our Sunday lunch, I leave the restaurant with a wave to Mum and Dad, promising to visit more often. "You're always working," they remind me, and I know they're right. I need to make more of an effort. But for now, I'm content, the roof of my Porsche down, the wind in my hair, and a smile on my face despite Mum's little digs. I'm halfway home when my phone rings – Claire flashes up on the screen. I press to answer the call.

"Hi, Claire, I'm driving, with the roof down!" I tell her, the rush of air in the background making the call feel carefree.

"Ooh, I can hear! Lucky you, it's a beautiful day. Where are you off to?" she asks, her voice light.

"Heading home, just had lunch with Lizzie and my parents," I say.

"Sounds lovely. How's Lizzie?"

"She's good," I reply, then quickly add, "How about you? What's up?"

There's a pause on the other end before Claire speaks,

a little hesitant. "Well, I wanted to call and apologise…"

"Apologise? For what, hun?" I frown, taken aback. What could she be sorry for?

"Lewis… it turns out he has a girlfriend. I had no idea!" she blurts out.

"Oh!" I say, fighting back a laugh. Well, this just keeps getting better.

"Did you meet him for that date?" she asks, her voice full of concern.

"I did," I say.

"Oh no, I'm so sorry! I only found out this morning! I would've told you straight away if I'd known and stopped you from going." Her words tumble out in a rush, her guilt palpable. *Thank goodness she didn't know*, I think, *because that date-that-never-was turned into the best night of my life*. I listen as she explains that her husband, Richard, was away on business until yesterday. When she mentioned my date with Lewis in passing, Richard casually dropped the bombshell that Lewis has a long-term girlfriend.

"Honestly, don't worry about it," I reassure her. "It's fine. He didn't show up anyway."

"What? He stood you up? I'm not sure what's worse – setting up a date while having a girlfriend or not showing up at all. What a prick!"

I laugh. "Maybe he grew a conscience at the last minute. Either way, no harm done. I ended up having a great night." I stop short of telling her just how great it was – dancing with James Keller wasn't something I wanted to casually mention just yet.

"Well, I'm glad you had fun regardless. Still, I'm fuming on your behalf!" Claire huffs.

"It's sweet of you to worry, but honestly, it worked out perfectly," I say, my smile widening, and I know she can probably hear it in my voice.

"Are you sure? I feel awful!" Claire insists, still sounding guilty.

"I promise, it's all fine. Really, don't worry about it," I reply, trying to put her mind at ease.

"All right, if you say so. But you know I'm here if you ever need to vent."

"Thanks, Claire. I'll talk to you soon, okay?"

"Okay. Take care, hun," she says before we hang up.

Thirteen

I work from home on the day of *the date*, which is a small blessing – it means I don't have to rush. I'm not entirely sure which hotel he's staying in, but I decide it must be a very plush one. After all, James Keller wouldn't be staying just anywhere. I try on at least six different outfits, tossing each one aside for being too formal, too casual, or just not right. Finally, I settle on a three-quarter-length satin wrap dress in teal with a soft cream floral print and long sleeves, and the delicate gold necklace and matching bracelet I choose complement it perfectly. Yesterday's fake tan has left me with a subtle glow, and I sweep my hair into a low ponytail for a more sophisticated look. For the shoes, I choose classic beige stilettos. I feel good, feminine. As I catch my reflection in the mirror, I allow myself a small smile of approval.

It's nearly 6:45pm. I head into the kitchen and pour myself a glass of chilled white wine, hoping it will take the edge off my nerves. Never in my life have I felt this nervous about seeing a man. The nerves are there, fluttering away in my stomach, but so is the excitement – there's something exhilarating about it. I keep checking my phone, making sure it's not on silent and that I haven't somehow missed a call. It's ridiculous how jittery I feel. I've already been to the loo three times in the last hour! In an attempt to distract myself, I switch on the TV, but the news is on, and it's too depressing. I flick through a few channels and land on some quiz show. That'll do, at least for now.

Then, my phone rings. I practically leap off the sofa, nearly tripping over in my rush to grab it before it goes to voicemail. My hands are shaking as I glance at the screen – no caller ID.

"Hello, Nikki speaking," I say, trying to keep my voice steady.

"Hi, Nikki, it's James" comes the smooth male voice down the line. "You okay?"

"I'm good, thanks, you?"

"Very good. I'm looking forward to our date," he replies, and I grip the edge of the kitchen island to stop myself from wobbling. "I'm about five minutes away. Will the gates open automatically?"

"Yes, they will open as you drive up. I'm also looking forward to our date," I manage to say, feeling like my voice could give away just how excited – and nervous – I really am.

"Great, I'll see you soon, then."

"See you soon," I reply, and we hang up.

I down the rest of my wine and pour myself another small glass, just enough to calm the nerves a bit more. I give myself another mist of perfume and start pacing back and forth. After a few minutes of anxious waiting, I take another sip and make my way to the window, where I have a perfect view of the gates.

It's still light outside, so no one can see me standing there, curtain twitching. Then, right on time, a sleek black Mercedes with dark windows pulls up to the gates. My heart is thudding in my chest. The gates swing open slowly, and I feel like I'm holding my breath. It's him.

My phone rings again, with no caller ID. "Hi," I answer, more softly this time.

"Hi, I'm outside," he says, even though I'm already well aware.

"Okay, coming down now." I hang up, grab my knee-length royal blue wool coat, and slip it on. Bag in hand, I take a deep breath before heading outside to meet him.

Nigel is waiting outside the car for me, his usual polite and friendly manner on full display as he opens the back door. I step in as gracefully as I can, my heart racing, and there he is. It's like a dream – a surreal, pinch-me moment that I can't quite believe is happening. I'm completely star-struck and smitten all at once, trying my absolute hardest not to show it.

His smile lights up the car as his eyes meet mine – a genuine, heart-stopping smile that makes me feel like the only person in the world. He leans over, and we exchange a kiss on the cheek. His scent – warm, woodsy, and intoxicating – fills the small space between us. My pulse quickens as those dark, intense, yet kind eyes hold my gaze, and in that moment, all I want is for him to pull me in for a proper kiss.

But instead, I smile back, attempting to play it cool,

even though everything inside me is screaming otherwise.

"Hi," he says.

"Hi," I reply, not breaking eye contact, like we are in our own little bubble. It's only when Sean, sitting in the front seat, turns and nods in my direction that I realise he's even there. Well, that's a step up from the weekend! Progress.

Nigel climbs in, and we set off. It's quiet in the car, and Sean and Nigel don't say much, which makes the atmosphere feel... well, a bit formal. His gaze keeps drifting back to me, and I swear every time our eyes meet, my stomach does a little flip.

"James? It appears there are no paparazzi – do you want to stop outside the hotel?" Nigel asks.

"Not tonight. Let's use the side entrance," James replies, sounding calm but decisive.

As we approach the hotel, we bypass the grand front entrance entirely. Instead, Nigel steers the car towards a quiet, tucked-away side door. There's no regal doorman in sight here – just a discreet entrance for those who prefer to slip in unnoticed. Sean and Nigel move like clockwork, both stepping out and opening the doors for us. I step out, heart racing a little, as Sean gestures towards the nondescript side door. We enter a small, tastefully designed lobby, far quieter than the bustling main entrance, and go to a private lift. Sean uses a key card to swipe us in, and the lift ascends smoothly without a sound.

As the lift doors slide open, a gold-plated plaque on the wall reads *Hyde Park Suite*. James pushes the door open and gestures for me to follow him into the penthouse suite.

"Wow!" I breathe, my eyes roaming over the elegantly styled room.

He smiles, clearly pleased by my reaction, and with a quick nod, he sends Sean off to… well, to do whatever it is Sean does.

The room is everything you'd expect: beautiful dark wood floors, a mixture of dark wood furniture, and soft beige sofas that look far too comfortable to resist. The walls are covered with thick striped wallpaper in tan and cappuccino colours. Long beige drapes hang by the windows, complemented by simple white nets from ceiling to floor. A massive TV dominates one wall, and nearby, a chaise lounge sits beside an open fire, with flames flickering and dancing around each other.

Across the room, French doors open onto a balcony with a breathtaking view of Hyde Park. It's still light out, and in the distance, I can see joggers, dog walkers, and people enjoying the spring weather.

Right in front of the doors is a dining table perfectly set for two. A single rose stands tall in the centre, with a lit candle and a bottle of something nice on ice.

"Make yourself at home," he says, smiling at me. "Here, let me take your coat." He steps behind me, gently sliding my coat off my shoulders before hanging it in the hallway. I glance back and notice how well he's dressed – a dark grey suit, and a light purple shirt with shiny black shoes. As he removes his suit coat and hangs it next to mine, I notice it's a three-piece suit. God he is sexy! He casually removes the undercoat, loosens the dark purple tie, and unbuttons the top button of his shirt. I feel a wave of dizziness sweep over me.

"Champagne?" he asks, walking over to the dining table.

"A glass of champagne would be lovely," I reply, still in awe of my surroundings and, truth be told, him.

James pours us both a glass, and as the bubbles rise to the surface, I catch a glimpse of the view from the balcony. "That view is stunning!" I comment, trying to focus on something other than the heat rising in my cheeks.

"Yeah, it's pretty amazing. Here you go," he says, handing me my glass, his eyes locking on mine a second longer than necessary, and I get the feeling he's not just talking about the view. "To a wonderful evening," he adds, raising his glass. "I'm glad you agreed to have dinner with me tonight. I really enjoyed Friday night."

"Me too," I reply. "Thanks for rescuing me from what otherwise would have been a very dull night."

We clink glasses and sip the champagne, but before I can think about taking a second sip, James gently takes the glass from my hand, setting it down beside his on the table, leaving me feeling exposed with nothing to hold. As he looks at me with those intense eyes, I swear the temperature in the room has just shot up about ten degrees. My pulse quickens, and my mind is racing. Does my hair still look all right? Is there lipstick on my teeth?

He steps closer, and just like that, the nervous energy is replaced by something... electric. I barely have time to process it before he leans in, his lips brushing mine. It's soft, tentative, like he's testing the waters, but it sets off a spark in me. He pulls back slightly, his eyes searching mine, and I can see the hint of a smile at the corner of his mouth. Before I know it, we're in a full embrace, holding nothing back.

And wow. He's good at this.

I wrap my arms around his neck, my fingers tangling in his hair. His hands slide around my waist, pulling me closer, as our tongues explore every inch. His kiss is deep, his touch firm, and everything about it is sending little shivers down my spine. I can feel the warmth of his body pressed against mine, and it's all so... swoon-worthy.

Just as I'm getting lost in the moment, he pulls back and trails light kisses along my jaw, working his way down to my neck. I tip my head back, offering him more skin to explore, and his lips are like feathers, brushing just enough to drive me completely mad. My heart's thudding away like I've run a marathon, but in the best possible way.

Then, almost too soon, he moves back up, his lips finding mine again for one last tender kiss. He pulls away, just far enough to look down at me, a glint in his expression that tells me he's enjoying this just as much as I am.

"You look beautiful," he says.

"Thank you. You look pretty hot too!" I flirt, giving him a playful smile, and he gives me that famous smile again, the one that makes you forget how to breathe for a second.

"Are you hungry?" he asks, handing me a menu.

"Yes," I reply, trying to keep my cool while I flip open the menu. My eyes quickly scan the options before landing on the Chateaubriand.

"Ooh, Chateaubriand," I say out loud.

"You like that? Feel like sharing one?" he asks, giving me a cheeky wink.

"Mmm, absolutely, if you're up for it." I nod enthusiastically.

"Perfect. I'll order it," he says, standing up and making his way over to the telephone on the desk. He glances back at me as he asks, "How do you like it cooked?"

"Medium rare," I answer, and he nods approvingly, placing the order with a side of vegetables. When he hangs up, he grabs the champagne bottle from the table, refills our glasses, and slides onto the sofa next to me, so close our knees are almost touching.

"Dinner will be here in about thirty minutes," he says, setting the bottle down in front of us. "Fancy some music while we wait?"

"Sure," I say, starting to feel more relaxed.

"Anything in particular you like?" he asks.

"I like all sorts; I'm always keen to hear what other people have in their music collection."

"Okay then," he says, picking up his phone and connecting it to the sleek speaker system. He sets it to shuffle and smirks. "Let's see what we've got."

The first track is some indie song I don't recognise. He glances at me expectantly, but I shake my head, pulling a face that says, *next!* He chuckles and skips to the next song, and I'm pleasantly surprised when a dance track I love fills the room.

I raise an eyebrow. "Didn't peg you for a dance music fan," I tease.

He shrugs, grinning. "I'm full of surprises."

We spend the next few minutes playing a fun little game of name that tune as the playlist shuffles between rock, pop, and some old-school hip-hop. I have to admit, his taste is more eclectic than I imagined, and most of it we actually agree on. After a while, we finally settle on something mellow – some Bob Marley – filling the room with a soft, relaxed vibe.

"Not bad, Mr Keller, not bad at all," I say, giving him a playful nudge.

"I aim to please," he replies with a wink, and I can't help but smile.

"So, how was the interview with Mark?"

"Yeah, it was good. Airs tomorrow night, I think. Will you watch it?" He shoots me a sideways glance.

"I might do," I say, playing it coy.

"Oh, only might?" he teases.

I give him a cheeky smile. "When does the film come out?"

"It premieres in the States on 27th May, then two weeks later in the UK."

"I'm looking forward to seeing it."

"You'll have to let me know what you think."

Before I can respond, there's a knock at the door. James answers it, and in walks a butler – yes, an actual butler – dressed in full tails and white gloves. *This room comes with a personal butler!* Of course it does! Dinner is ready. He wheels in a silver cart as James pulls out my dining chair for me like an absolute gentleman and I take my seat. The butler pours us another glass of champagne and removes the silver cloche, revealing the feast. He carves the meat, placing generous slices on our plates, along with thick-cut chips and vegetables, and leaves a delicate gravy boat of sauce in the centre of the table before stepping back.

"Is there anything else I can get you, sir?" he asks James.

"No thank you, we are good for now," James responds, still in his effortlessly cool mode.

"Very good, sir. Please press the buzzer when you're ready for the plates to be cleared." With that, he hands James a small device, almost like we're in some secret club, and takes his leave, gliding out of the room.

James raises his glass to me.

"Thank you, again, for agreeing to have dinner with me. Here's to a nice evening," he says, clinking his glass to mine.

"Pleasure. And thank *you* for inviting me. Is champagne usually your drink of choice?" I ask, curious.

"Depends on the occasion. Normally, I'm more of a cold beer kind of guy." He smiles.

"Ooh me too."

"You like beer?" He looks genuinely surprised.

"I do, but only when the sun's shining. Something about a beer on a warm day, right?"

He nods, amused. Bob plays quietly in the background; the conversation is easy and there's a fair amount of flirty eye contact. He teases me just the right amount – enough to keep me on my toes but not too much. We get into a playful debate about whether it's a 'cell phone' or a 'mobile phone', which has us both laughing. Then we dive into the 'chips' versus 'fries' discussion, and it only escalates when we debate the pronunciation of 'route' – is it *root* or *rowt*?

He shakes his head, grinning. "The English language is ridiculous."

I grin back. "Or maybe Americans are just simple."

He laughs heartily, enjoying my cheeky comeback.

The banter between us feels natural, and when he asks about my work, I can tell he's genuinely interested, not just asking to be polite. For someone who's mastered the art of acting, he seems refreshingly real.

"Do you enjoy your work?"

"I do," I reply with a nod.

"Do you get to travel much?" he continues.

"Our head office is in New York, so I go there occasionally for big meetings or training events. Sometimes they hold them in other countries. Last year, for example, they sent me to Rome for what they called a 'training event.'" I roll my eyes with a smile. "It was more of a jolly, to be honest."

"Rome is beautiful. Where in New York is your office?" he asks, clearly interested.

"Upper East," I reply casually, and his eyes light up.

"No way! My apartment's on the Upper East Side too!"

"Really? What a coincidence!" I say, feeling a sudden thrill of connection. "Maybe next time I'm over, we can grab a coffee. Or, you know... whatever it is glamorous Hollywood types drink," I tease with a wink. But the reality of him living in the States tugs at the back of my mind, so I quickly push the thought aside.

James chuckles. "I'll take you up on that. And for the record, I'm very partial to a good cup of coffee. So, is it a typical nine-to-five for you?" he asks, sounding slightly horrified at the idea.

"More like 8am to 7pm most days," I say, trying not to laugh at his reaction.

"In the office?" He looks genuinely surprised, and I can't help but chuckle. I suppose for someone who travels and works on sets, the idea of being stuck in one place seems a bit alien.

"Not always. I'm often out for client meetings, in court, or working from home. But I like to go into the office at least twice a week, just to show my face."

"Where's your office?" he asks, still trying to piece together my day-to-day life.

"Canary Wharf," I tell him.

"Yeah, I know it," he says, nodding, clearly familiar with the area.

We chat about family, and I tell him about mine – my parents, my sister Lizzie, and her husband Duncan. He listens intently, nodding along, and when it's his turn, he tells me about his younger sister, Louise, who, to my surprise, lives quite close to my parents in a small village near Tonbridge. What are the chances?

James reveals, as I already suspected, that he has a house in Beverly Hills, but he primarily lives in his New York apartment. He was born in Sacramento, California, but his family moved to New York when he was ten. I always imagined he was more of an LA guy – Beverly Hills and all that – but New York seems to suit him better. Part of me isn't sure if I'm disappointed or relieved about that; I had this tiny dream of living that Beverly Hills life, but New York has its own allure, too.

His parents are still in New York, and he has another sister, Dianne, who lives nearby. Apparently, he's the only one in the family who pursued a career in acting. Listening to him talk about his family, it sounds like he had a lovely upbringing – solid and stable. None of the typical celebrity sob stories of troubled childhoods or issues with substance abuse. The more I learn about him, the more genuine he seems.

The rest of the evening is nice and relaxed. He's open, not guarded at all, which is a relief. We laugh, share anecdotes, and the conversation flows effortlessly – except, of course, we've yet to touch on past relationships. And I wonder if that's a topic he's deliberately avoiding or if it'll come up naturally in time. For now, I'm content to let it lie and simply enjoy the night.

After dinner, we move to the sofa with our champagne, the fire still gently crackling from when the butler last stoked it.

We talk about our favourite films and books – turns out he's an avid reader, both novels and a lot of scripts! I feel perfectly comfortable in his company. And, judging by the way he's leaning in just a little closer, I think he feels the same. As he refills our glasses, I notice how he's now sitting subtly closer to me on the sofa. Not that I'm complaining. The bubbles are starting to work their magic again.

"So, tell me, did you ever hear from that guy again after we gave him a little shock on Friday night?"

I laugh, remembering the video call. "No, funnily enough, I didn't hear from him."

James raises an eyebrow. "So, you never found out why he stood you up?"

"Oh, I did, actually." I explain how Lewis has a girlfriend, and how Claire, my friend, only found out after the fact. "She would've stopped me from going if she'd known."

"Well." He grins. "If she had stopped you, you wouldn't

be here now. Here's to her not telling you!" He raises his glass, and I can't help but laugh.

"True," I say, clinking glasses with him.

His tone shifts just slightly, teasing but curious. "So, why did you agree to go on a date with him if you weren't that into him? Just trying to figure out if we have a similar situation going on here." He flashes that mischievous smile, but there's a genuine question behind it.

I smile back and gently place my hand on his thigh. "We definitely don't have the same situation here," I reassure him. He takes a light hold of my hand and smiles at me. "It's been a challenging couple of years after the divorce, trying to find myself again. Towards the end of last year, I made a promise that this year, I'd say yes to as many things as I could. Not just dating – everything. I figured good things happen when you're open to them. If you keep saying no, nothing changes, right?"

He nods thoughtfully. "That's a good mindset."

"And because of that," I continue, "I got a fantastic promotion, moved into a nice apartment, got myself a nice car. All material things, but I feel like I'm more myself again. Happier." I pause, debating whether to say what's on my mind. And then, with a deep breath, I decide to go for it. "And… it's led me to you."

The second the words leave my lips, I feel a rush of vulnerability. Did I just say that? I quickly switch to a more upbeat tone, trying to cover my nerves. "And now I'm going skydiving with you, which is insane! Never in a million years did I think I'd be doing that."

He stares at me for a moment, and I can't quite read his expression. Did I just blow it by being too forward?

But then, without a word, he leans in and kisses me. It's different from earlier – softer, more tender.

Our lips part, but our faces stay close, the warmth of the moment lingering between us.

"I'm looking forward to skydiving," he says, his voice soft but teasing as he stays right there, inches from me. "So, if you're saying yes to everything, how about dinner with me again on Friday evening?" His eyes never leave mine.

I smirk, trying to play it cool despite the butterflies fluttering in my stomach. "You do eat a lot of dinner!" I joke, raising an eyebrow. "And I didn't say I was saying yes to *everything*," I tease, dragging out the pause just long enough to make him wonder. Then, with a smile, I add, "But yes, I'd like that."

His grin widens, and I feel that familiar rush of excitement wash over me again.

Fourteen

*J*ust as I sit down at my desk on Thursday morning, Lizzie rings. I close the door to my office, knowing full well she'll want all the juicy details.

"Did you stay with him?" she blurts out before I can even say hello.

"No!" I exclaim, rolling my eyes, even though she can't see me. "I left around 11pm. He had his driver take me home. It was a nice evening."

"So, no sex, then?" Typical Lizzie, so brazen!

"No!" I say, pretending to be offended that that thought would even enter her head. I share a lot with Lizzie, she's my sister and my best friend, there's not much she doesn't know about me, and she can read me like a book.

"But you wanted to, right?" she teases, and we both burst out laughing.

"*Hell yes!*" I admit, barely containing my excitement. "I mean, he's gorgeous on screen, but off screen, he's something else! And he's so nice – proper gentleman, really down to earth."

"Sounds like you're falling in love!" she sings down the phone, clearly enjoying herself.

"I'm not!" I laugh. "Maybe a little star-struck still. I keep pinching myself!"

"Ooh, I can't wait to meet him!" Lizzie squeals.

"Easy there," I warn her. "He's leaving on Sunday to go film something somewhere, so you might have to rein in that excitement for a bit."

"Oh yeah, I forgot about that," she says, her tone dropping slightly. "Sorry, babe. How are you feeling about it?"

"I'm trying not to feel anything at the moment." I decide not to mention Friday night – not enough time to dissect it.

"I guess you just have to go with it and see what happens."

"Yep, you're right. Listen, I've got a client meeting in an hour that I need to prep for. I need to head off. I'll fill you in more on Sunday, okay?"

We say our goodbyes, and I promise her more updates later.

The rest of my day flies by in a blur of client meetings, staff catch-ups, and endless to-do lists. By the time I look up, it's already 6pm. I pack up and head straight to my gym class, grateful for the distraction. Once I get home, I jump in the shower, quickly rustle up something to eat, and collapse on the sofa. I'm flicking through the TV guide absentmindedly when something catches my eye – *The Mark Layton Show.*

I select the channel, hoping I haven't missed James's appearance. The live music segment is just finishing. Agh, if I've missed him, I'll have to catch it on replay later.

"Ladies and gentlemen," Mark says from behind his desk, "our next guest is quite simply the one, the only Mr *James Keller!*"

The audience goes wild – cheers, whistles, even a few screams – as James walks into the studio, looking effortlessly charming. He pauses for a moment, soaking in the applause with that humble smile of his. He's wearing the same suit he wore last night. My heart races, thinking about how surreal this all is. Yesterday, he was sitting there, knowing full well he'd be having dinner with me in just a few hours. Me. Dinner. With James Keller.

I sink back into the sofa, my feet up, unable to stop the flood of memories from last night and Friday. The excitement from watching him on TV is nothing compared to the realisation that I was with him, just last night. My mind is half on the interview, half on replaying every little detail from our evening together.

The next day follows a similar pattern – back-to-back meetings, endless emails, and, to my disappointment, I'm needed in the office. Tonight, James is coming over for dinner. We've agreed to stay in, preferring the quiet and privacy, which suits me just fine. I like to think I'm a decent cook, but knowing he is going to be sitting at my table adds a whole new level of pressure. I decide to play it safe and throw together my go-to Thai curry in the slow cooker before heading out the door.

As I step off the Tube into the hustle and bustle of the busy London streets, I weave through the crowds like everyone else, keeping pace with the city's rush. Then, out of the corner of my eye, I spot a big red bus passing by, and there, splashed across its side, is a huge picture of

James promoting his new film. I stop in my tracks for a second, grinning like a fool. A week ago, I wouldn't have given it a second glance. But now? Now I know him, it feels personal, and I can't help but smile as it drives past, and I get an extra spring in my step.

My last meeting ran over, of course – don't these people realise I'm having dinner with *James Keller*? The Tube was packed as usual, and I'm doing my best to stay calm, knowing I won't have time to shower before he arrives. Fortunately, I live just a five-minute walk from the station, so I should make it home before he arrives. Kicking off my black stilettos, I slip into my pumps for the walk home.

As I open the front door, the aroma of coconut and spices from the slow cooker greets me. At least the curry looks good. I toss my bag and coat on one of the bar stools and dash into the bathroom, still in my work clothes: a black pencil skirt with a cream blouse adorned with black spots. A quick top-up of deodorant, a swift brush of my teeth, and I'm back out in no time. It's 7pm. Two minutes later, my phone buzzes – no caller ID. He's here. I quickly shove my coat away, slip my heels back on, and buzz him up.

"Hi, gorgeous!" he says as he steps through the door, holding a square bag in one hand and a six-pack of beer in the other. His accent is still enough to make my knees go weak. "I've brought supplies," he declares, flashing that famous smile before giving me a quick kiss on the lips. I usher him down the hall and into the open-plan living space.

"This is a great space," he says, taking in the room. "Reminds me of my place in New York."

"It does?" I ask, feeling a little chuffed.

"Yeah, I've got a similar open-plan layout. I like it," he says, his eyes sweeping over my place with approval.

He hands me the bag and gestures for me to take a peek inside. There's a beautifully wrapped box of chocolates and a nice bottle of white wine. I place the beer and wine in the fridge and set the chocolates on the island. "Thank you!" I smile.

"You look a bit stressed," he observes. "Have you just got in?"

"Yes, sorry. I got held up at work," I say, feeling a little flustered.

"You should have called; we could have pushed it back a little bit."

"No need, really," I assure him. "I just haven't had time to change out of my work clothes yet."

He looks me up and down with a grin, clearly not bothered. "Well, I think you look very sexy in your work clothes," he says, pulling me in for a real kiss. Thank goodness I freshened up earlier! "You go get changed," he says, his lips lingering near mine. "I'll pour us some drinks. Anything that needs doing?"

"No, just the rice. I made us a Thai coconut curry," I tell him, feeling a bit more relaxed now.

"I can smell it, and it smells amazing. I'll cook the rice," he says confidently, and I raise an eyebrow.

"Wait, you can cook?" I tease.

He laughs. "Of course I can! Just show me where the stuff is."

He's too good to be true, surely. But I point out where I keep everything and thank him again before heading off to change.

When I come back out fifteen minutes later, barefoot and in my casual light jeans and a half-tucked white shirt – casually sexy is the look I'm going for – I find him standing by the cooker, stirring the rice like a pro. There's a glass of wine waiting for me, and he's already halfway through his.

"You look great," he says with that easy smile of his as I walk over and wrap my arm around his waist, watching him work at the stove.

We work well together in the kitchen, like we've done this a hundred times before – he rinses the rice while I warm the plates. We put some music on, and I serve up the dinner. Even though we've known each other for only a few days, it feels so natural with him. *This is how couples act*, I think.

After dinner, we move the few feet to my lounge. I flick the fire on as we cuddle up on the sofa and open the chocolates.

"Have you told anyone about me?" he asks, glancing at me.

"My PA knows I went on a date last Friday. I can't keep much from her, but I didn't give her details, and I didn't tell her he didn't show. I just said I had a really good time."

I pause for a moment before continuing. "My sister does know." I shift slightly in my seat, wondering if I've broken some unspoken rule. "We're really close. If you want to know anything about me, she's the go-to person."

I feel the tension lift as he just smiles. "That's fine," he says. "I like that you're close with your sister. Family's important."

"She was there when I got the call from you on Saturday,"

I explain, leaning back into the sofa. "She knew I'd been stood up, so naturally, she questioned me. Honestly, I can't hide anything from her, no matter how hard I try."

He laughs, and I find myself relaxing even more.

"And… she also saw this." I pull up the online article from Friday night – the one with that blurry photo of him and the 'mysterious brunette' – and hand my phone over for him to see. He skims it without much of a reaction, his face unreadable.

"How did she react?" he asks, handing the phone back.

"Well," I start, chuckling, "once I picked her up off the floor, she was more excited than anything. She's sworn to secrecy, though, and she's good with that. She's kept a couple of my secrets over the years."

"Oh yeah?" He raises an eyebrow, his curiosity piqued.

"Nothing major." I shrug. "She did tease me about being completely star-struck, and she can't wait to meet you." I watch his expression carefully, but there's no noticeable change.

"What did you say to that?"

"That she needs to hold her horses!" I grin.

"Ah," he says, still unreadable. There's a brief moment of silence between us, but it's comfortable, like we're both just letting the conversation settle.

"So." He breaks the quiet. "Are you looking forward to tomorrow?"

"I am," I reply, feeling the excitement bubble up again. "I'm really looking forward to it."

"Good," he says, a smile tugging at his lips. "Me too. Weather looks promising. What about going to Mark's in the evening? Do you want to come?" His voice is casual, but I hesitate for a second, unsure if he genuinely wants me there or if he's just being polite. "I'd like you to come," he adds, as if reading my mind. That makes me smile, warmth spreading through me.

"I'd love to," I say, my hesitation gone.

"Great, I'll let him know," James says, taking out his phone and firing off a quick text to Mark. It doesn't take long for his phone to buzz with a reply.

"They're looking forward to seeing us." He smiles, placing his phone down on the coffee table. He reaches for my hand, placing it gently on his thigh. "I've got an early meeting tomorrow," he says, "but how about I pick you up around eleven?"

"Yeah, that works. I've got a Pilates class in the morning at nine, but why don't I drive us tomorrow?" I suggest. "I can drive us there and bring us back here. We can hang here until we go to Mark's?"

"Yeah, we can do that, saves me going back into the centre of London. You sure you don't mind?"

"Not at all."

"Okay, I'll let Nigel know to pick us up from here in the evening."

I hesitate, feeling awkward about discussing money, but I don't want to take advantage. "Please let me know what I owe you for the tandem," I say.

"You owe me nothing, it's my treat," he says, smiling at me.

Before I can argue, he leans in and kisses me, and what starts as a sweet, soft kiss quickly ignites into something deeper, more passionate. His lips press against mine with an urgency that makes my heart race. We shift on the sofa, our bodies adjusting naturally, until we're lying down. His body hovers just above mine, the weight of him grounding me as his kisses trail from my lips down to my neck, sending shivers down my spine. His hand wanders over my breast as my fingers caress his back, pulling his T-shirt out from his jeans, craving the touch of his skin. He doesn't object. He lifts my knee, drawing me close as his hand slips to the small of my back, pressing me against him. I grasp his solid frame, feeling the strength in his shoulders, the heat radiating between us.

His arousal only heightens my own, each nerve in my body alive with longing. For the next half-hour, we're wrapped up in each other like two teenagers, swept up in a heady rush of kisses and touches, exploring each other's warmth with a mix of curiosity and intensity. We're utterly lost in our own world, oblivious to everything else. Then his phone buzzes on the table, breaking the spell. He ignores it, but it buzzes again, insistent. With a sigh and a hint of reluctance, he reaches over, still keeping one hand on me, and checks the message.

"It's Sean, checking in on me," he says with a sigh, glancing at his phone. "I'd better get him to come and pick me up – I've got an early start tomorrow."

"What time is it?" I ask.

"Ten fifteen," he replies, giving me an apologetic smile. I don't want him to leave but I'm too chicken to ask him to stay, so I let him reply to Sean to come and get him.

We manage to fit in another few lingering kisses, and just when I think I might lose my nerve and ask him to skip the early start, he straightens up, tucking his shirt back in, looking all dashing and deliciously rumpled. We make our way to the door, where he pauses, holding me close one last time.

"See you tomorrow. Thanks for dinner," he says, flashing me that smile that could melt steel.

"You're welcome," I reply, trying to keep my tone light and breezy as he steps out and disappears into the hall. The door clicks shut, and suddenly, my apartment feels far too big and far too empty. I flick off the lights and wander to the window, watching his car ease through the gates, and he's gone.

Fifteen

*T*rue to his word, James arrives at my place the following morning. We hop into my car and drive the forty-five minutes it takes to get to the airfield. I can't resist double-checking with him about insurance. "You're sure I don't need some special Hollywood insurance to drive you around?" I ask, half joking.

He laughs, shaking his head. "I think you're safe."

With his baseball cap pulled low and sunglasses on, he's nearly unrecognisable. No one notices him when we stop at traffic lights – you know, that casual glance you give the person next to you when sitting waiting for the lights to change.

When we arrive, Mark's already there. He greets me with a warm hug and a kiss on the cheek.

"Nikki! Great to see you again. How've you been?" He's got that same warm, laid-back charm as his wife – a natural, genuine friendliness that makes you feel like you've known him for years.

Next, I'm introduced to Scott, my tandem partner, who seems calm and reassuring, exactly what you want in someone you're about to jump out of a plane with.

Mark and I are then escorted to a training room for our safety briefing. As we step in, I notice it's just the two of us; there's usually a full group for these sessions, so I'm beginning to suspect that James might have arranged an exclusive day. The room itself is a throwback, with brown plastic chairs that look like they are from a school classroom, all lined up to face a whiteboard and a TV screen ready to roll out the safety video.

I glance over at Mark, who's looking a bit pale. "Have you eaten?" I whisper.

"Yes, I had a big breakfast," he mutters back, trying to sound upbeat but clearly wishing he'd skipped the extra sausage.

"You'll be fine." I smile, trying to reassure him. He squeezes my hand, giving me a brave smile.

After the training session, we're directed into a locker room to be fitted with our bright blue jumpsuits, which, let's just say, won't be winning any fashion awards. We look like either we've escaped from a high-security institution or we are gearing up to join the circus. Mark catches my eye, chuckling. "You still look good," he says. "I, on the other hand…" He gestures down at himself, all snug in his jumpsuit, and I can't help but laugh. The straps are fitted and tightened, and we are off outside to begin our adventure.

I feel slightly embarrassed with my new look as we head out to the tarmac where James is waiting, parachute strapped to his back, looking effortlessly stylish in his black combat trousers and a crew-neck jumper. While we're channelling 'prison escapees in goggles', he's rocking a matte black helmet and an air of calm confidence like he's about to film the next action blockbuster.

"Look at you two!" He grins, giving me a quick kiss on the cheek and pulling Mark into a manly hug. "Ready?"

I muster up what I hope is a confident smile, despite my nerves. "Ready!" I say, while Mark glances around for a possible escape route.

"I think I left my, erm, bravery… in the car," he mutters, backing up a step.

James claps him on the shoulder. "No backing out now, mate!"

Thirty minutes later, we're soaring high above the countryside in a clunky, bare-bones plane that leaves much to be desired. There's no service trolley or reclining seats here – just Mark trying to lighten the mood with one-liners, clearly masking his own case of the jitters. I make a mental note to never complain about economy class again.

Soon enough, we're at the edge of the jump zone. Mark and I, strapped up to our tandem partners, shuffle towards the open door, going over our final checks while the wind whips through the plane.

Outside, the sky seems both thrilling and terrifying, stretching out forever. Then, we get the countdown: "*Three, two, one…*" And there goes Mark, arms flailing as he plunges into the vast blue. My heart races, but with a quick breath, I jump too, plunging into the rush of free-fall as the world opens up around me.

The sensation is electric – pure freedom, pure exhilaration. I spot Mark just below, doing his best 'starfish in the sky' impression. And then, there he is – James, cool as anything, gliding through the air beside me. He shoots me a thumbs-up and an 'okay?' signal. I grin back, returning the gesture. With a cheeky grin, he flips onto his back, free-falling just beneath me for a moment before gracefully rolling over and diving down towards Mark, making it all look as natural as breathing.

Below, I see Mark's parachute open, his descent slowing as he glides gracefully (or so I hope) towards the ground. Suddenly, there's a firm tap on my shoulder, the rustling of straps – and whoosh! A tug pulls me upright, and my own parachute blooms open above me. We glide through the air, the noise of free-fall replaced by a serene quiet. I have the biggest smile on my face. The view stretches out endlessly, and I search for James, eventually spotting his bright blue chute floating below us. Scott, my tandem partner, leans in, shouting, "All okay?"

"Amazing!" I shout back, laughter bubbling up as we gently sail through the sky.

As we near the airfield, Scott points down to our landing spot. I watch as James touches down first, landing with perfect precision as his parachute drifts gracefully to the ground behind him. Then there's Mark, coming in with… well, let's just say 'enthusiasm'. He hits the ground with a bit of a thud, skidding in, and I can't help but wince – hopefully, only his pride's been bruised!

Now it's my turn. I brace myself, mentally chanting, *Don't fall, don't fall*. With the ground rushing up, I concentrate on Scott's signal to extend my legs. Tap – there it is! I stretch out, knees slightly bent, toes up, and… we land smoothly, right on my feet! No awkward bum slide, no tumble. I'm grinning like a Cheshire cat. Scott gives me a congratulatory clap on the shoulder, clearly as thrilled as I am.

Mark and James come jogging over as Scott unhooks me from the parachute. "Wow, that was a fantastic landing," Mark says, clearly impressed.

James reaches out to shake Scott's hand in thanks, then turns to me, sweeping me into a hug that nearly lifts me off the ground.

"You were amazing! Well done!" He beams, planting a quick kiss on the side of my head. I can't help but grin, my cheeks flushed with pride and excitement.

I help Scott scrunch up the parachute, feeling exhilarated – and maybe just a bit smug.

As we stroll back across the tarmac towards the locker room, Mark looks both elated and just a bit relieved that it's over. Ah, normal clothes, here we come! Once we've finally shed the oh-so-flattering jumpsuits, we make our way to the canteen for a well-earned late lunch. James lingers to chat with a few instructors he knows, while Mark and I settle down at a table, armed with a couple of sandwiches. I sink into the seat opposite him, still buzzing from the jump.

"So, that was fun, right?" I say, giving him a cheeky grin. He glares at me, trying to be serious. I smile, waiting for him to break. "Go on, admit it, you enjoyed it!"

"All right, all right," he finally admits with a reluctant grin. "You were right – it was good. It's just that first part... you know, the actual jumping!"

Just then, James slides into the seat beside me, slipping an arm around my shoulder. I lean into him, cosy and content, managing to resist the urge to rest my hand on his thigh – barely. I catch Mark eyeing us curiously, his gaze darting between the two of us. I can see him debating whether to make a cheeky remark but wisely holding off... for now.

"You okay, buddy?" James grins at him. "You've got a bit of colour back in those cheeks."

"I'm good," Mark replies, shaking his head in mock disbelief. "I still can't believe you talked me into that!"

"It was fun, right?" James presses, clearly enjoying himself.

Mark rolls his eyes. "You sound just like Nikki!"

"I *loved* it!" I chime in, still buzzing, and James gives me a warm smile. Mark gives us both a mock glare, trying to look serious.

"You two are absolutely nuts!" he declares, before breaking into laughter himself.

We make our way back to the cars after lunch, and Mark makes a beeline straight to a gorgeous dark gunmetal grey Aston Martin, clicking the fob as he approaches.

"Is that a Vantage?" I ask, admiringly, as the lights flash. "It's stunning!"

"It is," he replies with a grin. "You into cars, then? Your Porsche is pretty nice too!"

"Oh, definitely. I get that from my dad; he's a proper car enthusiast."

Mark chuckles. "Then maybe next time, we'll go for a track day instead – keep my feet on solid ground!"

I laugh, and James nods in agreement. "See you at yours around seven?"

"Seven it is!" Mark gives us a wave as he slides into the Aston, looking every bit the part.

"See you, Mark!" I call out, still grinning as James and I settle into my car and drive away.

Sixteen

We arrive back at mine after an exhilarating few hours, still riding the high, and dump our bags on the sofa. We have a few hours to kill before we need to leave to go for dinner at Mark and Julia's house.

"I'm going to have a shower; do you want one?" I say to James. As soon as the words leave my mouth, I realise how they sound. He raises an eyebrow at me and gives me a cheeky grin. "There's a shower in that room if you want one." I point to the door of the spare room, quickly backtracking and laughing at my faux pas. "I'll get you a towel."

I grab a spare towel from the airing cupboard, choosing the softest one available, and hand it to him before heading to my bedroom.

"Let me know if you need your back washed," he calls after me. I turn my head and smile at him, catching that twinkle in his eye again. The temptation is strong.

"I will," I say softly as I walk into my bedroom. I leave the sliding doors slightly open; the frosted glass allows only a silhouette to be seen. I'm willing him to come in and seduce me.

I run the water in my walk-in shower to warm it up, then return to my bedroom to undress, knowing he might be watching. I drape my clothes over a chair, tie my hair back in a messy bun, and wrap a towel around myself. It's now or never. Lizzie's comment runs through my mind: *The woman who dates him needs to be very confident and comfortable in her own skin.*

I walk over to the gap in the door and see him sitting in the chair, scrolling on his phone, the towel still beside him.

"So, are you coming or what?" I say to him as seductively as I can while keeping my nerves under control and praying he doesn't rebuff me. "There's room for two." He looks up at me, but I don't wait for a reply. I go into the bathroom, hang my towel on the hook and walk into the shower, letting the water rush over me. A few minutes pass and I'm starting to think he's not coming, then the door opens.

I glance over my shoulder as he enters the bathroom with just the towel wrapped around his waist. His body is beautiful, muscular – broad shoulders and golden skin. His dark hair shines in the light. His chest is smooth, and his abs are defined; he takes care of himself. My eyes subtly trace the lines of his Adonis belt. As he removes the towel, I inhale sharply. He places it by the sink and steps into the shower, saying nothing. After reaching past me for the shower gel, he squeezes some into his palm and lathers it.

With a light touch, he places his hands on my shoulders and massages the soap over my shoulder blades.

Then he moves lower down my back, covering every inch with his hands until he glides them back up and over my shoulders, down my arms to my fingertips. He stops with his hands covering mine. Our fingers entwine as he moves closer, his naked body pressing against me. He kisses my neck, sending shivers down my spine.

I turn my head, and he kisses my mouth. Our hands part and I let him touch my stomach and caress my breasts, as I reach behind me and pull him closer to me. He drops one hand down over my stomach, going further down until he's touching me between my legs. I gasp with pleasure. He turns me round to face him, his touch igniting a fiery sensation that courses through my veins. My hands instinctively find their way to his firm backside, fingers teasingly squeezing as our lips meet, his kiss consuming me entirely, his tongue exploring every corner of my mouth.

With a gentle pressure, his hand finds its place lightly against my throat as he guides me backward. My back meets the cool, tiled wall, and with effortless strength, he lifts my leg to his hip, the water flowing over us. Breathing heavily, I feel the heat of his body pressed against mine as he rubs against me, making me very sensitive. He teases me with just the tip. I can't keep still; the anticipation is driving me wild. He looks me straight in the eye and pushes himself inside me fully. I groan with pleasure, a sense of euphoria rushes over me, and then he's out. My God, I've never felt so turned on in all my life; I've never wanted someone as badly as I want him now.

"I want you," he whispers in my ear. "Wanna get out of the shower?"

We spend a blissful hour together, rolling between the sheets. He's a generous lover, truly attentive. He pleased me not just once, but twice! Time, however, has a habit of slipping away, and before we know it, we're hopping back into the shower. This time, he washes me all over and I return the favour. I quietly watch as he gets dressed in my bedroom. He brushes his teeth, adds some gel to his wet hair, and *et voilà*! He is ready. It feels good having him around. I put on a pair of skinny white jeans with a tan belt and black sleeved top. Simple tonight. No heels, just white trainer pumps.

Seventeen

Nigel picks us up right on time at 6:45pm, and we head off to Mark and Julia's, holding hands in the back of the car, as the endorphins still pulse through my veins. It's a short fifteen-minute drive, and soon we're pulling up to a grand, dark wood gate that swings open as we approach.

The house is stunning. Red brick, built within the last decade at a guess, double fronted with a huge front door, cream pillars on either side and sash windows. There's a triple garage to the left of the house with what looks to be an annexe above. The kind of place that says 'we've made it!'

Mark arrives at the front door to greet us.

"Hey!" he exclaims in his usual chirpy manner, kissing my cheek and shaking James's hand. "Great to see you both again, come on in!"

James takes my hand as we walk inside into a grand, double-height hallway that exudes modern elegance. The light grey tiled floor contrasts beautifully with the duck-egg-coloured walls adorned with abstract art. On the right, a staircase with a sleek glass banister leads up to a galleried landing, creating a sense of openness.

Directly in front of us, the dining room extends from the hallway, with a large table illuminated by funky-coloured pendant lights hanging overhead. Mark leads us into an expansive, state-of-the-art kitchen with a cosy family TV area at the far end. The walls are pristine white, and the shiny grey units gleam under the natural light flooding in through floor-to-ceiling sliding glass doors.

Jules is in the kitchen, preparing food for dinner. She looks up as we enter, her face lighting up.

"Hello, you two!" she says warmly, wiping her hands on a tea towel. "Glad you could make it!" She walks over and greets us with a hug. She is the sort of person you feel instantly at ease with. She laughs, giving Mark an affectionate nudge. "How was the skydive? I don't think Mark's quite recovered yet!"

He grins sheepishly as James gives him a playful hug and a hearty slap on the chest. "It was fantastic!" James says, still buzzing. "Sorry, mate, didn't mean to traumatise you."

Mark laughs, waving it off.

"Where are the kids tonight?" James asks, looking around as if half expecting them to jump out.

"Safely with the grandparents – all night!" Jules replies, looking thoroughly pleased with the rare adult-only evening.

James raises an eyebrow, giving Mark a knowing wink. "Oh, a free night, eh? We'd best not stay too late, then!"

Mark chuckles, glancing at me. "The kids adore him, you know. Anyway, let's get you a drink. Wine? Beer? Soft drink?"

"I'll have a beer, please," I reply.

Mark hands us each a cold beer, and we step out into the garden, which, if possible, is even more stunning than the house itself. The patio area is a design marvel, divided into perfect sections, each laid with the same light grey porcelain tiles that give everything a chic, seamless look. The main patio, just outside the kitchen, has large dark grey sofas surrounded by topiary, with a spacious light grey canopy overhead. A little further along, there's a beautiful swimming pool with light blue tiles and a sleek chrome fountain at the far end. A summer house, which houses a gym, stands on the far side of the pool. The garden is huge and is lined with tall fir trees at the back, rhododendrons starting to bud, and cottage-style flowers in the borders. I'm eager to explore.

We settle onto the comfy sofa under the canopy as the evening sun sets. It's a cool evening, and I'm grateful for the tall pyramid patio heater beside us, its flames providing extra warmth. As we all get comfortable, I catch Jules's eye as she notices James holding my hand. She gives me a knowing smile, one that says, *I see what's going on here*. James is openly affectionate, which I love; in my last relationship, affection in public was practically illegal, but James? Not a second thought, not in private anyway.

"This garden is stunning," I say, breathing in the fresh scent of cut grass – one of those little pleasures I adore. Jules beams with pride.

"Thank you! I thought you'd like it – I remember you mentioning how much you enjoy gardens," she says. "I'll take you around in a bit; it's even lovelier at dusk."

James and Mark are in full grill-master mode, and I must admit, I'm pleasantly surprised – they know their way around a BBQ. Each burger and skewer is cooked to perfection, and between the sizzle of the grill and the laughter, it feels easy and familiar. It's like we're old friends instead of people who just met a week ago. James is just James now, not James Keller the movie star, especially after this afternoon.

As I glance at the oversized clock on the wall, a wave of reality crashes over me. It's nearly 9pm, and every passing minute feels like sand slipping through my fingers. Tomorrow, James flies out, and this dreamlike bubble we're in might just pop. I've felt so at ease with him, so… normal, like we're just two people enjoying a barbecue with friends. But then I think, *What happens next?*

James's voice pulls me from my thoughts. "Another beer?"

"Er, yeah, go on then," I say. He detaches himself from me and goes inside with Mark to get some more drinks.

"Nikki, let's go around the garden before it gets too dark," Julia suggests with a smile. I follow her onto the lawn, taking in the lovely, secluded space, where the borders rise in perfect layers. There's a pink clematis trailing up a trellis, roses just beginning to peek open, and giant rhododendrons promising a colourful display soon. A mature magnolia has just finished its show, leaving a scattering of delicate pink petals on the grass. It's like spring herself decided to throw a party, and I'm completely here for it – fresh-cut grass, fragrant blooms, birds singing their evening chorus.

"This border's for wildlife," she says, gesturing proudly. "Another few weeks, and it'll be bursting with life."

"Wildflowers?" I ask, intrigued.

"Yes, I just threw some seeds down and crossed my fingers. Any tips?"

I laugh. "No, sounds perfect as it is! Jules, this garden is just glorious! I love it."

"Ah, thanks, hun." She beams.

As we reach the top of the garden, I glance back and spot the boys on the patio, drinks in hand, deep in conversation.

"I see you and James are getting along quite well," Julia says, giving me a knowing, sideways glance. I feel my cheeks warm. "I'm pleased for you both; you look good together."

I can't help myself. "We've had dinner twice this week since we met last Friday."

"Twice? And skydiving today! You've been busy!" She laughs.

"Yep, Wednesday, last night, and today." I grin, deciding to keep details from this afternoon to myself.

"Wednesday after the show?" She raises an eyebrow. "That explains it. Mark said James vanished straight after. He normally stays for a drink. He said James had 'somewhere important' to be, and I think he suspected it might've been you." She winks.

"Guilty," I admit, and then, feeling bolder, add, "And he sent me two dozen red roses last Saturday after our night out."

"Oh wow! I bet they're gorgeous! That's really sweet." She gives me a smile. "So, are you guys planning to see each other again?"

I feel my smile falter. "I don't know; we haven't really talked about it."

She pauses, noticing the change in my expression. "You know he leaves tomorrow?"

I nod, my heart sinking just a little.

"Do you want to see him again?" she asks gently. I nod again, and she squeezes my arm reassuringly. "Well, if it's anything to go by, you two have chemistry. I saw that spark between you both last week."

"I don't know how it would work. Can I cope with his level of fame? He's James Keller, for Christ's sake! I'm not anyone special." Suddenly, a wave of impostor syndrome washes over me, and my confidence dips. Why would someone like him want to be with me? What do I even bring to the table?

Julia gives me a reassuring look. "Yes, he's James Keller, and you're not a nobody," she says warmly. "He's also just James, you know? And trust me, he doesn't let just anyone into his circle, but he's let you in. It can be intense at times, sure. James gets a lot of attention from the media and fans, but if you like him – and you clearly do – then go with it. He'll look after you, and you can work out the details as they come."

I go quiet, letting her words sink in. She's giving me hope.

"He likes you, that's obvious," she adds, giving my arm a light touch. "If you both want it enough, you'll find a way. Get on that train and enjoy the ride, love. See where it takes you!"

I let out a small laugh, feeling more positive. "Okay," I say, nodding.

"Go talk to him," she encourages, with a smile.

"Thanks, I will," I reply, smiling back at her.

We wander back over to the boys, and James opens his arms, inviting me to cuddle up beside him. I happily oblige, nestling into him as he wraps us up in a blanket and kisses the side of my head. I feel warm, cosy, and just… safe.

Julia nudges Mark with a playful grin. "Darling, why don't you go set up the cinema room? I'll grab us some more drinks and popcorn." She gives him another nudge, and he finally gets the hint.

"What? Oh right, yeah… So, what film are we watching, then?" He looks around with a mischievous smile. "I'm in the mood for a horror or a thriller. What do you reckon?"

James shrugs. "Suits me."

"Very romantic," Julia quips, rolling her eyes with a smirk.

"As long as it's not gory," I say. "I can't handle gore or zombies!" I glance at James. "Sorry, I haven't watched *Hibernation* for that exact reason!" He puts on his best hurt face, which only makes me laugh.

Julia gives Mark another prod, and they head inside, leaving James and me alone for a moment.

The night has fully set in, and we only have the light from the house and the flicker of the flame from the patio heater to illuminate our surroundings. It feels incredibly romantic snuggled under the blanket together. James looks at me, his eyes softening as he leans in and kisses me briefly on the lips.

"Enjoy the garden tour?" he murmurs.

"I did! Although it makes me miss my garden even more!" I admit, feeling a pang of longing for my own green space.

"You'll get another garden one day," he assures me. "I'm glad we've got a few moments alone." He looks at me with that intense gaze that always sets my heart racing.

"Mmm?" I respond, a mix of anticipation and nerves swirling inside me.

"I wanted to talk to you this afternoon… but you distracted me," he teases, stealing another quick kiss. Is this the moment where he asks for a repeat performance, a one-night stand? My mind starts to race with questions and doubts. "You know I leave tomorrow?" he says gently, and my heart dips. I hold my breath, waiting for what comes next. "I've really enjoyed spending time with you this week," he says, and I feel a glimmer of hope rising.

"I've enjoyed it too," I reply honestly, my heart drumming in my chest as he holds my hand.

"My life can get a little… chaotic," he admits, his eyes turning thoughtful. "Don't get me wrong, I love what I do, but it's not exactly normal, and the media… it can be overwhelming." He pauses, searching for the words. "Not everyone can handle it, and I wouldn't blame you if you said it's not for you."

"I understand," I say, trying to mask the pinch of fear that he's about to say goodbye.

He continues, "I've never dated anyone outside the industry, and I wouldn't blame you if you wanted to say no, but…" His gaze locks onto mine, and the nerves in his eyes mirror my own. "I'd like to see you again, to see where this could go."

"Really?" I ask, caught off guard but filled with excitement.

"Really," he says, his tone sure. "Would you like to see me again?"

"Yes, I would," I say, a smile spreading across my face. Relief floods through me as I realise that he wants this as much as I do.

"Let's make it work, then," he says, his face lighting up with a smile. We look at each other, the air charged with excitement. This is really happening; we're going to give it a shot. My heart swells with happiness, the doubts and uncertainties fade away. Before I can stop myself, the words tumble out:

"Stay with me tonight?"

He smiles, eyebrows raised. "I'd love to. Your place or mine?"

"Mine? We've already messed up the sheets there," I joke.

"Yours it is, then," he agrees, his smile widening. We share a passionate kiss, lost in the moment until Mark appears at the door, clearing his throat loudly.

"Put her down, James!" he calls, grinning. James raises a dismissive hand, keeping our moment intact a little longer. We break apart, laughing like we've just been caught sneaking around, and tidy up the empty bottles from the table.

As we walk back into the house, Julia gives me a knowing glance, whispering, "Everything good?"

"I got on the train!" I whisper back, grinning from ear to ear. Julia does a little jig of excitement as we all head into the movie theatre.

The film scared the living daylights out of me, and I lost count of how many times I nearly crushed poor James's hand in fright. I kept telling myself it was only a movie, but honestly, I was grateful for the company tonight.

Afterward, I offer to help clear things away, but Julia waves me off with a tired smile. "Honestly, we'll sort it tomorrow," she assures me. There's a look in her eyes that says she's ready for a quiet night with Mark, and I can't blame her one bit – I know that feeling all too well.

As we say our goodbyes at the door, Julia squeezes my hand. "Let's do that yoga class next Thursday?" she says.

"Yes, I'd love that," I reply, already looking forward to it. Somehow, I feel like Julia and I are going to be good friends.

Eighteen

I wake the next morning at 7am. I turn to see James lying next to me on his back, his eyes closed. He's as naked as I am under the duvet. James Keller is naked in my bed; the thought sends a wave of excitement over me. We were awake until the small hours talking, among other things. I place my hand lightly on his chest, not wanting to disturb him but desperate to touch him. He opens his eyes, turns his head, and smiles at me.

"Morning, baby," he says in a deep morning voice.

"Hi."

He pulls me in for a cuddle and I lay my head on his chest, drape my leg over his and hold his waist as he kisses my head.

"Sleep okay?" I ask him as he holds me a little tighter.

"Yeah, I did, did you?"

"Mmm hmm," I reply, feeling warm and cosy. We lie there for a while just dozing, saying nothing. I reflect on the previous night. We chatted a lot when we got back. His schedule is as expected: pretty packed for the next couple of months. He flies to Norway this afternoon for ten days, then he's off to the Cannes film festival, and then back to Norway, then he's in LA for the premiere of his new film, then Canada, and finally in about six weeks he's due back in the UK for the London premiere. We decided that I will try to fly out to him as often as I can, starting with a trip to Norway next weekend.

James gets out of bed and makes his way to the bathroom; I watch him as he goes. I get up and put my gown on, purposefully finding my black satin one, and make my way to the bathroom in the spare room where I clean my teeth and use the loo. As I leave the spare room, I find James in his boxers in the kitchen. He's found the coffee. I'm pleased he seems handy around the kitchen but disappointed he's no longer in my bed.

"Tea? Coffee?" he asks.

"Hmmm, coffee please, black, one sugar."

"No way, that's exactly how I have my coffee." He laughs.

"Really?" I say sarcastically.

"Yes." He pecks my lips gently. He takes the stovetop coffee maker, unscrews it, adds the coffee and water, then places it on the heat.

"How are you feeling?" he enquires, wrapping his arms around my waist. "After our chat last night?"

"I'm feeling good," I say, draping my arms around his neck.

"Good," he murmurs, pressing a brief kiss against my lips. "I know it's not ideal, but I promise I'll do all I can to see you as often as possible," he reassures me.

"I know you will," I say, and I believe him. He switches

off the cooker before the coffee is ready and takes my hand.

"Coffee can wait," he says, leading me back into the bedroom. Three times in less than twenty-four hours, I am a lucky girl.

A few hours later, we are up, dressed, and James is getting ready to leave for Norway. Standing in my hallway, he brushes my hair away from my face.

"I'll give your number to Allison."

"Who's Allison?"

"She looks after things for me. She's London based, quite a character but I'm sure you'll like her, eventually. Anyway, I'll get her to contact you to make arrangements for next weekend, that okay?"

"Yeah, sure."

"I'm going to be on set a lot this week, long days, so I'll call you when I can. Feel free to call me whenever you want. If I can't answer, I'll call you back."

"I don't have your number," I state.

"Yes, you do." He smirks at me and I look at him, puzzled. "I gave it to you the first night I met you." I retrieve my phone from my back pocket and search for 'J' in the contacts. Showing him my phone, "Is this you?" I ask, sounding surprised. I assumed it would be the phone number of his PA or agent, not his direct dial!

"Yep, that's me," he confirms. I'm speechless; I've had his number this whole time and I didn't know it. His phone buzzes. Nigel and Sean are here waiting for him. The time has come to say goodbye. We share a passionate kiss, one that's hard to break away from. I revel in the pleasure of kissing him, and he assures me the feeling is mutual.

He leaves, and I immediately call Lizzie.

Nineteen

The week flies by, filled with the usual whirlwind of work, dance classes, and gym sessions. On Thursday, I join Jules for yoga, and she beams with excitement when I mention that I'm heading to Norway to see him this weekend.

"Oh, that's so exciting! Let me know how it went when you get back. I'm sure he'll have something nice planned for you," she gushes, her enthusiasm infectious.

Allison emails me during the week, a rather formal email asking me to call her during office hours. When I do, she maintains the same level of formality on the phone. She has arranged a flight for me to Bergen airport on Friday evening, arriving just before 10pm and returning to London on Sunday afternoon. She's also arranged a car to pick me up from home and take me to the airport and bring me home on Sunday. I've not paid for a thing; James has covered it all. He's called a couple of times during the week, not withholding his number, and we've exchanged texts daily. Filming is going well; he's looking forward to seeing me. To think that just two weeks ago I was getting ready to go on a date with Lewis and now I'm travelling to Norway to spend the weekend with James Keller – what a turn of events.

I text James to let him know my flight is on time. When I arrive, Sean is waiting at the airport for me. He nods when he sees me, and mumbles something that sounds like "Hi," before taking my case and leading the way to the car. Unlike Nigel, who is super friendly, Sean is very odd, not attempting to engage in conversation at all.

I have huge butterflies dancing around my tummy as we drive into the hotel's secure underground car park. I see some paparazzi lurking outside; they know he's in town. We enter the hotel via a back entrance and take the lift up to the fourth floor. Sean still hasn't said a word, giving me plenty of time to think about spending thirty-six hours solid with James. We've seen each other naked but this feels different; it's only our second night together. There's no hiding from the realities of just being human. There is no bathroom conveniently two rooms away.

Sean knocks on the door of room 420, and James answers. The butterflies grow wild. It's like they have taken a dose of amphetamines. James smiles widely when he sees me, takes my case from Sean, thanks him, and then closes the door behind him.

"Hi, gorgeous," he says once we are alone, enveloping me in his arms and kissing me hard. "I've been so looking forward to seeing you."

"Me too," I reply, feeling the warmth of his embrace.

"Come on in," he says, gesturing me inside. "Make

yourself at home. Drink?" he asks, holding up a bottle of gin.

"Yes please," I say, slipping off my shoes and placing them neatly in the hallway. His corner suite is luxurious, less grand than Hyde Park but still very elegant, with a grey and white decor. Windows on two walls are covered by drawn curtains, likely because we're in the city centre, surrounded by other buildings. He pours drinks for us, then sits next to me on the sofa, lifting his arm for me to snuggle into him. I lean against his body while we sip our drinks. I can smell the sweet aroma from his aftershave. It feels so good to be next to him again: warm, cosy, and sensual. Just being in his presence, feeling him and hearing him breathe sends my pulse racing. I place my hand on his thigh and rub my thumb back and forth over his leg. The anticipation of the night ahead excites me and I wonder if he feels the same way.

"How was your flight?" he asks, taking a sip of gin.

"It was good, non-eventful, which is just how I like it," I say with a smile.

"You hungry?" he asks.

"No, I'm fine, thanks. There was food on the flight," I reply. There's a brief pause in the conversation. I turn to look at him.

"Tired?" he asks, holding my gaze.

"Not really." I flutter a smile at him.

"Wanna go to bed?" he suggests, his eyes glinting with anticipation.

"Yes," I whisper.

"Let's go, then." He stands, holding out a hand to help me up, and leads me into the bedroom.

Twenty

 wake in the morning curled up next to him. I don't think we lost body contact all night. My ex and I used to sleep back to back, barely touching each other at all. I didn't want to touch him. I want to touch James. I really want to touch him, and it seems that feeling is mutual. He orders room service for breakfast, though given our late night, it's more like brunch. I was told to dress for hiking during the day and have smart casual wear for the evening. I slip into some skinny black jeans, with long grey socks scrunched around the ankle, a black T-shirt and a khaki fleece zipped jumper. James is equally casual in black combat trousers and a navy fleece jumper. The weather here is cooler than London but it's not raining at least.

Sean arrives to pick us up. We put on our walking boots and James grabs a rucksack. We leave via the same entrance I used last night. As we drive off, I see a couple of hardcore paparazzi still waiting outside, hoping for a shot they didn't get. Sean drives us to a coastal area not far from the hotel. As we approach, I spot a dark grey helicopter in the distance.

"Are we going in that?" I ask, feeling a mix of nerves and excitement. I've never flown in a helicopter before.

"Yep," says James, very excited at the prospect.

"Are you flying it?" I ask, half joking.

"I am. Zach and I will be flying it. Are you okay flying in a helicopter?" he asks, suddenly realising he hadn't checked.

"I've never been in one before," I admit.

"You'll love it! If you can jump out of a plane, you'll be fine on this."

I hope I like it; it will be rather embarrassing if I don't.

He introduces me to Zach, the other pilot, whom he seems to know quite well. We climb in, put on our headphones, and away we go. I need not have worried; it was an amazing experience. Once I got over the take-off, which is so very different from a plane, I was captivated. We flew thirty minutes north up the coastline. The views were breathtaking, with the green, rugged landscape stretching out beneath us.

We land between two mountains, next to a vast lake that stretches far into the distance, its dark waters reflecting the surrounding peaks. As the helicopter's motor shuts off and the blades slow to a stop, the deafening noise fades into serene silence. Apart from Zach and Sean, we are alone in the wilderness, with no other soul around for miles. The skies above are a brilliant blue, though the air feels slightly chilly.

"We've got a couple of hours here to explore and

have a picnic," James tells me. I barely hear him, I'm so mesmerised by the view.

"You okay, Nikki?" he asks, gently bringing me back to the present.

"This is absolutely stunning," I reply, still taking in the breathtaking scenery.

"It is beautiful," he agrees, glancing around at the majestic landscape. "Come on, let's walk." He takes my hand, and we stroll for a while, leaving Sean and Zach at the helicopter. We chat about everything and nothing, absorbing the views until we find a sunny, grassy spot on slightly higher ground that overlooks the lake with a distant mountain backdrop.

James lays out a blanket, and we enjoy a feast of smoked salmon and cream cheese sandwiches, olives, fresh fruit, some classic sausage rolls, and a couple of cans of gin and tonic. It's perfect.

"Are you okay?" he asks, looking at me with concern. "I wanted to take you somewhere where I can be with just you, no interruptions from anyone else. Next time, maybe I'll take you on set with me," he adds with a wink.

"Ooh, that would be exciting!" I say. "But this is perfect here." I lean forwards and kiss him. He pauses, and I can see a slightly more serious expression cross his face.

"So, tell me about your ex-husband. How long were you married?" he asks. I had been wondering when this topic would come up.

"I was married for six years. We got divorced two years ago," I begin, and he listens intently without interrupting. "We met at uni. His name is Karl."

"Are you still in touch?" he asks.

"No, I cut ties once the divorce was final."

"Why did you break up? You said you weren't in love with him," he recalls, from our previous conversation.

"You've got a good memory," I point out. "That's right. He was a nice enough guy but didn't have enough ambition for me. He's a history teacher – sixth form," I explain, realising James might not be familiar with the UK education system. "Ages seventeen and eighteen." James nods, understanding. "There was no spark between us in the end," I continue. "He used to go to the gym a lot, but eventually, he'd either work late or come home and just sit in front of the TV. I like to veg in front of the TV as much as the next person, especially in the winter, but this was every night. He stopped making the effort with pretty much everything. He was happy just to exist. I, on the other hand, wasn't. I wanted someone I could come home to and have a conversation with, someone to go out to dinner with, to the cinema, to see friends. He just wasn't interested, so I threw myself into my work and climbed the ladder, which I think bothered him because I was earning a lot more than he was. I then started to build my own life, without him. I just outgrew him, I think."

James looks at me with sensitive eyes. "Has there been anyone since?"

"Nothing serious. A few dates, including the date I didn't realise was a date," I say, and he laughs. "Oh, and the date that never showed up, of course. Let's not forget him."

"Hmmm, and now me."

"And now you," I repeat. James looks thoughtful.

"Are you ready for another relationship?" he asks tentatively.

"Yeah, I am." There's a moment of silence. I desperately want to tell him I'm ready for him. He breaks the silence.

"Would you marry again?"

"Yeah, if it felt right, I would. Would you?"

"Yeah, I would," he replies. "What about kids? Or are you too set on your career?" he asks.

"Same as marriage. If it felt right, I would. My career is important to me, but I wouldn't let it stop me if I was with the right person. My ex wasn't the right person, hence ex." I pause, feeling the weight of our conversation. The urge to ask him about his past relationships bubbles up, a topic I've avoided until now to respect his privacy. But it seems he's just given me permission to cross that line. "What about you? You were married, right?"

"Yeah, I was, very publicly. It was also very public when we split too."

"That must have been hard. I know you're used to having things written about you but when it's that personal, it can't have been easy," I say sympathetically.

He nods. "Yeah, it wasn't easy, but like you say, it's part and parcel of it, you take the rough with the smooth."

"What happened?" The words come out before I can stop them.

"We were young, met on the set of a film, our chemistry was good on and off screen," he says, and I feel a pang of jealousy, "but ultimately, we wanted different things back then. She wanted a family and at the time I didn't. My career came first. We made the mistake of not communicating; we were apart a lot, which didn't help. I was a bit of a shit to her sometimes because I was still climbing the ladder, and no one was going to get in my way. Anyway, between my career and not wanting children, it broke us eventually."

"Oh," I say, processing his words. "How long were you married?"

"Eight years. It obviously wasn't meant to be. I also think she might have had an affair."

"You never found out for sure?"

He looks down solemnly. "Nope. If she did, I think it ended before we divorced. Anyway, it was a long time ago, all water under the bridge as they say."

"Did she divorce you, or you her?" Now I've started, I can't stop asking questions.

"She divorced me. It was a bit of a shock, but I didn't try and challenge it," he says quietly, looking at the grass.

"Are you still in touch with her?" I ask, not sure I want to hear the answer.

"No, we haven't spoken for years. There's no animosity between us but our paths haven't crossed." I feel only slight relief hearing that. I get the impression he was hurt badly by her and would still be with her if she hadn't asked for a divorce. The thought tugs at me, but I push it aside, trying to focus on the here and now.

"Anyone else since?"

He looks at me curiously, surprised I don't already know.

"I don't read the gossips," I tell him. Of course, I know he dated someone else, but not the details.

"Oh. Yeah, I've dated a few but the only other serious one was Sarah Watts?" He looks at me to see if I know who he means, which I do. "I was with her for a couple of years, but it just fizzled out between us. Our schedules were too busy, it wasn't right, so we ended it."

"And are you in touch with her?" I ask as casually as I can.

"No." He smiles at me. "You've no need to worry. That's dead and buried and there's no one else," he reassures me, before giving me a long, lingering kiss on the lips.

We finish our picnic and start the walk back to the helicopter. We talk less on the return, a comfortable silence, enjoying the presence of each other and admiring the views.

Twenty-One

ack at the hotel, we shower and change ready for dinner. I brought with me a classy royal blue dress in a satin material that is tapered in at the waist, knee length and sleeveless. As it's cooler here, I add a plain black cardigan with puffed shoulders, Christian Louboutin shiny black heels and a black purse.

I let my hair tumble down and spray the roots to give it a bit of volume. My makeup is subtle again, apart from the lips. This time I opt for a classic red lipstick – quite brave for dinner but it will stay, unless I kiss him, then I'm in trouble. I put on some jewellery, spray some perfume, and I'm ready. James is in the lounge, ready and waiting for me with a gin and tonic. He's in his classic dark blue jeans with a navy blue shirt, untucked. He is sexy; he wears casual as well as he wears smart.

"Wow!" he says, admiring me as I enter. "That colour is stunning on you. You look beautiful." He kisses my cheek, and I feel on top of the world.

"Thank you," I say, trying to be coy. "You look handsome, and you smell so good," I tell him as I get a waft of his spicy aftershave. A different guy arrives to escort us to the restaurant. He's quite a lot younger than Sean and Nigel, maybe in his late thirties, tall and stocky, with slightly long wavy blond hair, dressed in a dark blue suit. I'm not given his name; he just discreetly gets us out of the hotel and drives us to a restaurant on the outskirts of town by a river. It's still light out when we pull up outside a long row of timber-framed buildings that look like houses, all with pitched roofs. They are painted different colours; some are red, some yellow, and there is a blue one in the middle. The evening sun is shining brightly on them. We enter the restaurant. There are diners already in there, but we are immediately escorted upstairs by a member of staff, where there are no other diners. It's just us. It's not a big space and there is a table for two on the far side, near the window overlooking the river.

The restaurant is traditional and bursting with character, with very old slanting floors and low ceilings. The walls are decorated in dark red, with mounted animal heads, and old paintings with fancy gold frames. Old-fashioned display cabinets with china and glass are on show. It's quirky and over four hundred years old, so our waiter informs us. Even though there are no other diners with us, it doesn't feel awkward, possibly because I feel like I'm in my grandmother's dining room. Music is playing quietly in the background, instrumental music. I like it; it matches the atmosphere perfectly.

We chat about his work, as the first of our four-course menu arrives. Scallop carpaccio in dill oil. I'm learning fast about the film industry. We talk about all the famous people he knows; he knows many but wouldn't call many of them his friends. He asks me more about my work and actually listens to my reply. I like to talk about my work; I enjoy it, it gets me fired up, and I think he sees that. Maybe he's just humouring me, but he seems genuinely interested.

The second course of fish soup is cleared, and the main course arrives, venison, and the subject turns to my other favourite, dance.

"How's the dancing going?" he asks me. "Did you go last week?"

"I did."

"I can tell you really like it. Your two passions are your work and your dancing – your eyes light up when we talk about them," he observes. I won't mention that he's one of my favourite passions too!

"It is. Would you ever learn properly? Someone that can glide you around the floor is very sexy to me," I tell him. Too much wine again.

"It is, is it? Well in that case…" He reaches for his phone, jesting that he will make an immediate call to arrange lessons. I laugh.

"I did enjoy it," he says. "It's not something I've thought of doing as a hobby. I prefer more adventurous things," he winks at me, "but I can see the attraction, so yeah, I might learn. Why? Do you want to have lessons with me, then?"

"Ooh, that would be good." I swoon.

"Okay." He smiles at me. "When I've finished filming this movie, let's do it!" He raises his glass and clinks with mine. I decide not to ruin the moment by thinking too much about how that would work and just go with it. One thing Lizzie always said to me was it's always good to have something in the diary to look forward to. Sound advice. "Do you want to dance now?" he asks. I feel my heart rate increase.

"Sorry?"

"Dance with me now. What's a good rhumba song?"

"Are you serious?"

"Yes!" he says, and I suddenly feel very self-conscious.

"Um." I think hard for a few moments then reach for my phone and open the music app. "This song, a song called 'So Beautiful' by Darren Hayes?" I say, handing him my phone.

"Okay, let me see what I can do." He gestures for the waiter to come over. "Can you play this song for us?" He shows my phone to the waiter, who frantically scribbles on his pad and promptly disappears downstairs. A few minutes later the instrumental music stops, and our song starts. James stands and takes a large swig of his wine, and offers me a hand, which I shyly take. I love dancing, but this is taking me well out of my comfort zone. He leads me out to the centre of the room. There are no other tables in here, so there's space. He takes me in hold.

"Mind the rugs, let's not trip over them!" He laughs. "Let's see what I can remember." He starts with the basic step. This feels very different to dancing with the old boys in my class; it feels sensual, not clunky. I can tell he was being modest about it being all camera angles making him look like a good dancer; he's had a few more lessons than he's let on! He does an underarm turn, then sends me out into a fan and brings me back, followed by another basic and then we turn together in close hold, a natural top.

Our rhumba soon turns into a good old-fashioned slow dance, which leads to a good old-fashioned smooch on the makeshift dance floor.

"That was pretty good," I compliment him as the song finishes. "You're a good lead."

"Either that or you're very good at humouring me!"

"I don't dance like that with anyone in my class."

"I'm glad to hear it," he says as we take a seat again.

"Who was your teacher?" I ask, curious.

"Lisa Waugh."

I think for a moment before the penny drops.

"Lisa Waugh," I repeat. "The Lisa Waugh? Five times world champion Lisa Waugh?" I ask.

"That's the one!" He smiles at me.

"Wow! She's incredible!"

He holds my hand across the table as the dessert arrives, brown cheese ice cream or 'brunost', which sounds awful but is a taste sensation!

"So, I'm off to Cannes next week, Tuesday I think."

"I've never been, what's it like?"

"I don't get to see too much of it but the bits I have seen are beautiful. You should add it to your bucket list."

"What's it like for you when you go there?" I ask inquisitively.

"Busy, loads of promo work, lots of films, parties, small talk, you know."

"Do you enjoy it?"

"I do, but it's tiring. Anyway, so I'm there next week, then I'm back here. I thought I would stop in London on my way through?" he says as more of a question than a statement.

"Could you do that?" I ask keenly.

"Sure I can. I can leave Cannes Saturday morning; I can maybe even sneak off on Friday and I don't have to be back here until late on Sunday."

"Okay, do you want to stay at mine? We can hide away in my apartment," I tease.

"Sounds good, if you don't mind. I'd like that."

"I absolutely do not mind," I tell him. I love the thought of spending time with him in a more natural environment rather than a hotel.

"I have one other question for you." He looks at me across the table. "I'm in LA and then Canada for the premiere of the new movie in a few weeks, then it's the premiere in London the week after. I wondered if you wanted to come, to the London one." I think my face drains of colour.

"Don't worry, I won't throw you to the lion's den that is the media and the public. We will be discreet," he says, noticing, and I feel slight relief. I need time to get my head around being with him first before I deal with that side of things. He continues.

"Mark and Julia are attending, so what if I arrange for you to arrive at the premiere with them and Allison and you'll sit with them? I'll get there before you guys to do the media stuff and I'll probably need to sit with the crew for the film, but they will be with you and make sure you're okay. Then spend the night with me?" There he goes again, flashing that irresistible smile. "It's on a Wednesday evening."

"Okay," I say. "So will I see you at all?" I try not to sound too disappointed.

"I hope so," he reassures me. "I'll make sure I see you in the movie theatre, but I might not be able to sit with you. I'm staying in the Hyde Park suite again. I'd really like it if you were there with me, the premiere, and the hotel." Damn it! The Hollywood love mist does it again.

"Okay," I agree.

Twenty-Two

I arrive back in London with no delays and call James to let him know I got back okay. When I get to my apartment, I crash in my bed for an hour. A bit later and feeling much more refreshed, I head out to my hot yoga class. Later that evening I get dinner from the freezer; I'm still full from the cooked breakfast we had this morning. I flick through the TV channels, but there's nothing much on. My phone beeps; it's Jules.

'Hi, are you back? How did it go and do you fancy yoga again on Thursday? xxx' reads the message.

'Hi, yes got back this afternoon, had the most amazing time and definitely yes to yoga! xxx.'

'Really pleased to hear it went well, look forward to hearing about it on Thursday, see you then xxx.'

I'm about to get ready for bed when Lizzie calls me. It's 9pm so the girls must be in bed.

"Hi!" I answer.

"Hi, darling, how's things? How was Norway?" Typical Lizzie, straight to the point.

"It was short and very sweet." I tell her about the trip, about the helicopter, the romantic picnic, and about the dinner and the dance.

"Nikki," she interrupts me, "you're gushing."

"I'm not!" I protest.

"Oh, you most definitely are! To be fair, I'd be gushing as well. It sounds amazing."

"That's not the end of it either. He's invited me to the London premiere of the new film in a few weeks," I tell her.

"Shut up! The new *Driver's Fury* film? Dad will go nuts!" She laughs. "That's amazing. How lucky are you – what will you wear?"

"I hadn't thought of that! I've no idea, but it will be understated. Maybe I'll seek advice from Jules when I see her." One of Lizzie's girls starts crying; I can hear it through the monitor. We arrange that she'll come up to me the week after next for some shopping. We hang up and I head to bed, happy and exhausted.

Thursday night comes around quickly, and work is busy, which is perfect. I head to the private members' club and meet Jules at reception. She signs me in as her guest.

"You should consider joining here," she suggests. "It's really close to you and you never know but you might need something a bit more… exclusive soon," she says, raising her eyebrows at me.

I consider her words. "You mean if I start getting recognised as being with James?"

"Exactly," she confirms.

"I've got no idea what that will be like, if it ever gets to that. Maybe people just won't be that interested," I say.

"I think it will come to that and people are always interested in his love life!"

We walk into the beautiful changing rooms. Everything is light oak wood and immaculately clean, with tall wooden lockers, and vanity stations with hair dryers, straighteners, lotions, and perfumes all available to you. The white towels given to us are beautifully fluffy, unlike the rough whitish towels at my gym. It's clear that this place is a lot more upmarket.

We change into our yoga gear and head for the studio, grab our mats and lay them near the front.

"So, Norway was good?" she asks with a friendly smile, while tying her blonde hair back in a low pony. It's quiet in the studio but a few people are starting to file in and sit around us, so I keep my voice low.

"Yeah, it was fantastic. That reminds me: I need your help. Apparently you and Mark are going to the London premiere in a few weeks?"

"Yes," she confirms.

"He's invited me to attend. He said he'd arrange for me to go with you guys and Allison." Jules rubs her hands together excitedly; she reminds me a lot of Lizzie.

"You're coming?" she asks hopefully.

"I am," I say, getting a little excited myself.

"Fantastic, I'm so glad. Yes, of course we can all go together. I'm not sure what Mark has arranged but between them they'll sort it out. All we have to do is turn up and look gorgeous!"

"Well, that's the thing," I start. "I need help with what to wear. I've not done the red carpet before. Also I'm there as his guest but I'm not going *with* him, so I want to look glam but not over the top, if you know what I mean. I don't want to look like mutton."

"You could never look like that, but yep, I get it. I can absolutely help you find something."

"My sister is coming up not this weekend, but next. We are going to hit the shops – fancy joining us?"

"Oh my God, yes, I'd love to."

"Great, I think you'll like Lizzie, you're like two peas in a pod!" I wink at her.

Our yoga teacher walks in and greets us all with "Namaste," and an hour later I can bend myself in half again. I feel longer, leaner, and lighter on my feet.

"Are you guys busy on Saturday evening?" I ask as we make our way back to the changing room.

"I don't think so."

"James is over this weekend. The weather is not meant to be great. Do you fancy coming to mine and having dinner with us?"

"We'd love to, as long as we're not intruding. I guess your time with him is precious."

"It is, but he arrives tomorrow sometime, so I'll have some 'precious' time with him then. I know James will be pleased to see you both."

"Fab, I'll see if Mark's parents can have the kids and we will come over. You're sure?"

"Absolutely. You can bring the kids if you want?" I smile at her.

She dips her chin and looks up at me; that'll be a 'no' to the kids, then. I laugh.

Twenty-Three

riday afternoon, and my phone beeps. James is just pulling up outside. From my desk, I can see the black car driving up. I'm still on a Teams call with some colleagues. I briefly step away from my laptop to press the buzzer, allowing him up. I leave the door on the latch and hurry back to my call.

He walks in with his case. He can see I'm at my desk on a call, so he quietly closes the door and makes himself comfy on the sofa, the sofa facing me. He casually sits back and observes me work. I find myself struggling to concentrate on what's being said. I can see he realises the effect he's having on me because he just smiles knowingly at me. I snap back my focus, and put on my usual professional no-nonsense voice.

"What are these guys playing at?" I say exasperated. "I've told them before, they cannot do that because it could lead to a constructive dismissal case. She'd be perfectly within her rights to take them to court and would probably win!"

"I know," replies Liz, my colleague. "What do you need me to do?" She pauses, waiting for my instructions. I take a deep breath.

"Okay, can you review the file again, in particular their absence management procedures? Can you get that done by Monday lunchtime?"

"Yes, I can do that."

"Ivy, can you set up a meeting with them on Monday afternoon, after 3pm to give Liz and me a chance to review her findings."

"Yep, on it."

"Okay, I think that's it for now. Luke, do you have anything you want to add?"

"No, I think we've covered everything," he replies.

"Great, thanks, guys. I appreciate your support on this," I say gratefully. "Have a great weekend, all. Chat on Monday." The team call ends. I close my laptop, sit back, and swivel my chair to face James.

"I was just about to get the popcorn out!" he jokes.

"Agh, this particular client is a pain in the arse," I say to him. "They haven't a clue what they're doing. I'm half tempted to let them hang themselves!" I stand and make my way over to him on the sofa, but I don't sit down. His eyes wander over me, wondering what my next move will be. He looks hopeful. I hitch up my skirt and place myself on his lap, straddling him.

"I find your authoritarian side quite a turn-on," he says, pulling me in closer.

"You do, do you?" I lower my head and kiss him deeply.

"I've missed you," he tells me as we break apart, and my heart flips.

"I've missed you too," I reply. He smiles. "By the way, did I tell you? I've invited Mark and Jules over for dinner tomorrow night."

"Oh, you have, have you? So now you're arranging double dates?" he teases. "That's fine by me. Are we cooking for them or going out? Do I need Sean?"

"No Sean. I was planning on cooking something – you like to cook, right?"

"I do, do you?"

"I do indeed."

"We can do it together, then. Let's plan it tomorrow because right now I've got other ideas for you." He moves forwards to the edge of the sofa, takes a tight hold of me, and in one swift move stands and takes me with him. He's holding me, my legs wrapped around him. I know I'm not heavy but, wow, he's strong! Still holding me, he walks into my bedroom.

The next morning, I'm getting ready to do my Pilates class online in my room while James takes a shower. I'm careful to tell him that I'm on video and can be seen by the instructor.

"That's okay, I can just pretend it's my bum double," he says, laughing.

"You have a bum double?"

"No, I don't, but I'm thinking of holding auditions and I want you there to help me select the right one!" He grins mischievously.

I flick him with my towel. "You're impossible!"

We decide to get a little adventurous with the meal and cook beef Wellington – from scratch – something neither of us have cooked before, eaten plenty of times but not cooked. The recipe says level 'challenge', and it has sixteen steps in the method and takes two hours, which means, in reality, it will take three!

I head off to the supermarket to get the ingredients, leaving James alone to do some work; he works more than I do! An hour later, I arrive back home to find him pacing the lounge having a heated discussion on the phone. I leave him to it and unpack the shopping as quietly as I can. He finishes his call and comes over and helps me with the last few bits of unpacking.

"Everything okay?" I ask as I only caught the tail end of the conversation.

"Yep, that was Martin, the director I'm working with on this project, creative disagreement," he says.

"Resolved?"

"No but it will be next week," he says, and I can tell by his tone that he will probably win this one.

I turn to him and put my arms around him. "I like this authoritarian side of you!" I jest, and I do, I really do. To have someone who can take charge is a huge turn-on, although I do wonder if we will ever clash, both being so strong-willed.

James smiles, pulling me closer. "Is that so?" he teases.

"Yes, it is," I reply, leaning in for a kiss.

It was fun working side by side in the kitchen with him. We drank probably more wine than we should have and had quite a lot of mess to clear up before getting ourselves ready for our guests. The Wellington is chilling in the fridge when Mark and Jules arrive at 7pm. The buzzer goes and I let them up. James is putting the oven on when they walk in.

"Bloody hell!" Mark says as he sees James in the kitchen. "I didn't have you down as a sous chef!" He laughs and hands some beers and red wine to James.

"I'm a man of many talents! How are you, buddy?" he says, giving him a hearty handshake and a man hug.

"Hi, Jules, good to see you, you look lovely," James compliments her.

"Hi, darling," she replies, handing me a lovely bouquet of flowers, which I cut and arrange in a vase. They make themselves comfy on the bar chairs and we have a drink while we get the rest of the dinner going: new potatoes and green veg.

"This is a lovely place you have here, Nikki," Jules observes, looking around.

"Thanks," I say. "It's not huge but it suits me perfectly. Easy access to London and easy to get out into more rural areas if I need to escape." I smile.

"Yeah, it's great and I see James has made himself at home!" Mark teases him.

We sit down to eat the beautifully cooked beef Wellington, which was a hit all around, compliments to both chefs.

As we finish the main course, Mark turns to me with a curious look. "Nikki," he begins, "I hear you're coming to the premiere with us?"

I nod, trying to sound casual. "I am, if that's okay?"

"Yeah, of course it is. We're all staying in the same hotel that night, right?" he checks.

"Yep," James confirms.

"Oh, by the way, Mark." Jules turns to her husband. "Next Saturday, can you look after the kids? I'm going shopping with Nik and her sister to help her find something to wear."

"Er, yeah, I can do that, no problem," he replies, smiling affectionately at his wife.

"Jules, come and see what I've got," I say, beckoning her to come and look at my wardrobe.

"We'll clear up here and get dessert out," James says, being helpful.

"Thanks," I say, lightly touching his shoulder as Jules and I leave them to it.

In my room, I open the wardrobe, or closet as James calls it. It's a nice size walk-in with open hanging space on two walls and shelves on the other wall for my folded items, shoes, and handbags.

"Wow," says Jules, admiring my collection.

"And you've got nothing to wear out of this?" she says, spreading her arms wide. My wardrobe is organised: shirts, tees and jumpers hang above the skirts; trousers and jeans and dresses hang the other side. I try to keep it in colour order. Jules takes a seat on my chair while I sift through.

"I think you'll marry him," she blurts out suddenly, catching me off guard.

"Sorry?" I laugh, a little embarrassed.

"I think you two will get married. I'm convinced of it. You're so well suited."

"I've not known him that long!" I protest, though her words make my heart race.

"I know, but when you know, you know!" She smiles at me and points to a dress. "Show me that one, the pink one." I pull out a hot pink shift dress and hold it up against my frame; it sits just above the knees, a bold statement piece.

"Too bright, I think," I say to her, shaking my head. "I don't want to draw attention to myself."

"Yeah, probably, shame, it's a nice dress!"

"What about this?" I pull out a black slip cocktail dress with lace over – elegant, yet understated.

"Nice, but you don't want all black either!"

"Good point. You know I just want an excuse to buy a new outfit," I admit.

Jules laughs. "Fair point!" she says as I hang my clothes back in their rightful place.

"You really think we're good together? I can't get anyone else's opinion as no one else sees us together apart from Sean, who says nothing."

She nods thoughtfully. "I know what you mean about Sean. Yeah, I do. I genuinely think you two have something good going. I can tell you're really into each other by the way you look at each other, and I've got good judgement on these things!"

"I really like him," I admit. "And not just because he's mega famous!" I tease.

"And mega rich!" she teases back, laughing. "I know you do, and I also know that the feeling is mutual, my friend!"

Just then, James pops his head around the door of 'the closet'.

"Any luck with the dresses?" he asks.

"She's got loads of fab clothes but actually we just want an excuse to go shopping," Jules replies with a wink.

"Fair enough. Are you coming back? Dessert is ready."

Jules stands and walks past James, smiling at him as she goes back out to the lounge. As I follow, he takes hold of my arm and gives me a tender kiss. I feel a flutter in my chest. Is it too soon to be catching feelings? I wonder.

We drink some more and play a quiz for the remainder of the evening, a quiz Mark brought round. He plays a song, and we have to guess the movie it's from. One point for the film, another for the name of the song and a bonus point for the artist. Ten songs, thirty points available. I'm one point ahead of James with one song to go; the other two are way behind. I sit forwards on the sofa, concentrating hard.

"Ooh, she's competitive." Mark laughs.

"I'm competing against people in the business. I have to prove my worth, and yes, I'm competitive!" I laugh. If James gets this correct, he beats me!

"Ready?" asks Mark and he plays the song. Almost immediately, I shout out the name of the song. Julia laughs out loud.

"She's good!" says Mark. I'm deep in thought, desperately trying to remember the name of the artist before James does. James shouts out the film title. If he gets the artist, it's a tie. I'm thinking hard. I've got it! I shout it out and jump up from the sofa!

"Yes!" I say with excitement. James falls back on the sofa, defeated.

"She won fair and square, mate," says Mark. James smiles at me.

"She did," he concedes. I regain my composure, sit back down next to him and cuddle into him.

"I'll make it up to you later," I whisper to him.

"I look forward to it. You've got a lot of making up to do. I don't lose, ever!"

"Well, on that note." Mark shuffles in his seat. "We'd better order our taxi and be going, leave you guys to it." He winks at James.

Their taxi arrives and James and I walk them both downstairs to the door. It's absolutely chucking it down outside.

"Glorious British weather!" says Mark as they wave goodbye and rush into the cab. We head back inside and up the stairs. It feels cosy indoors, the rain pelting against the windows. We shut the blinds, do the bare minimum in the kitchen and head to bed.

Twenty-Four

A week later Lizzie and Julia meet at my house for our much-anticipated shopping trip. The three of us take the short walk to the train station and head to Bond Street first. It's shoppers' paradise, so many famous designers on one road, and Union Jacks flying high. My first stop is Rolex. I drag the girls in there as watches are my thing. We are immediately approached by a member of staff who offers to assist us; this is good because it means we look like we can afford their prices! And so we should; we all made an effort to look very chic for our shopping spree. I catch a glimpse of our reflections in the polished glass display cases: three stylish women, poised and ready to indulge, but not in a Rolex!

"She loves watches," Lizzie tells Jules as we admire the glamour. "Every time we go shopping, we need to look at watches, and if it's Rolex, even better." It turns out Jules owns a Rolex and happens to be wearing it today. Hers is a dainty gold one with a pearl face and a diamond-set dial.

It looks elegant and expensive, glinting under the shop lights.

"Yes, and I typically have an eye for the most expensive ones," I admit, eyeing up a slightly chunkier platinum watch with a pale-yellow face and a diamond-set dial. The price is listed as 'on request'.

"Try it," says Jules, her eyes sparkling with encouragement.

"Go on." Lizzie nudges me playfully. The assistant asks if I'd like to see what it is like on. I agree, just for fun. She retrieves a set of keys and unlocks the cabinet. After donning white gloves, she carefully removes the watch from its display and drapes it over her gloved hand under a brilliant white light for me to view.

"It's stunning," I say, slightly mesmerised by the intricate design and sparkle. The assistant indicates for me to hold out my arm and she places the watch on my wrist, turning my arm gently to fasten the clasp. It's gorgeous and fits perfectly. I can't help but ask how much it is.

"It's fifteen thousand pounds." She smiles at me. I smile back, through gritted teeth. *£15k?*

"Well, it's absolutely beautiful," I say, stalling. "How many diamonds on the dial?"

"Twenty-four," she immediately replies.

"Ah, well, thank you very much for letting me try it on. I will give it some thought," I say. She smiles graciously and removes the watch from my arm. We exit the shop and crack on with some real shopping!

For the next two hours, I try on what feels like twenty different dresses in various shops until we finally find the one. It's sexy, classy, and understated. We all agree it's perfect. The price is £400. Though I earn a six-figure salary and have a small mortgage thanks to an inheritance from my grandparents, I'm usually frugal. James obviously lives a certain lifestyle, a lifestyle I can only dream of, which worries me slightly. But so far, he's been extremely generous.

I decide to buy him a little gift, a token gesture if you like, but what do you get the man who has everything? With Julia's help, I decide on a silk tie, a very expensive jacquard silk tie in navy blue with gold dots, almost as expensive as my dress. It's subtle but distinctive, something he's not likely to already own. I also buy a gold tie pin to go with it. Jules finds a new dress for herself, and Duncan, unbeknownst to him, treats Lizzie to a bracelet.

Exhausted after our expedition, we head into a hotel for a champagne afternoon tea. "That was good," I say, placing my bag on the chair next to me.

"It was. I've not had a marathon shop like that for ages," agrees Jules, settling into her seat. She turns to Lizzie. "So, you've not met James yet?"

"No! And I'm dying to meet him, see what he's like in real life!" she says enthusiastically.

"I will introduce you as soon as the time is right and when he's here for longer than a day or two!" I promise her.

"Yes, that's the downside to him, he travels a lot, but he's a really lovely guy, considering his fame. He's very down to earth. When are you next seeing him, Nik?"

"I've managed to sneak in a day next week to travel to Norway. I'm really excited because I think he's taking me on set!"

"Ooh, exciting!" She shares my enthusiasm.

"Thank goodness the flight time is short," I reply.

"Can you fly there and back in a day and still manage to get quality time there?" Lizzie asks, curious.

"I'm flying private jet, his plane I think," I tell her. She sits up straighter, her eyes wide.

"You're flying in his own private jet? Oh my God!" she exclaims. I'm not sure if she's pissed at me or pleased.

"Well, you're right. If I fly commercial, I barely get any time there. This way I get a full day there. I won't see him after that until the film premiere."

"Gosh, of all the flying Mum did, I don't think she ever flew in a private jet!" remarks Lizzie. Jules looks curiously at her. "Our mum was cabin crew, senior cabin crew. She flew a lot. That's how she met our dad. He used to fly for business and, well— Hey, do you think they joined the mile-high club?" Lizzie lets out a loud laugh.

"Lizzie!" I exclaim, acting shocked but finding it funny.

"Don't laugh, Nikki, you'll be a member soon enough!" says Jules.

"Julia!" I gasp. "Are you a member?" I ask her, leaning forwards in my chair, keen to know. She looks at me, smiles mischievously, and raises her champagne glass.

Twenty-Five

*a*fter a short flight, I am back in Norway. That private jet was something else – pure luxury, so much space and none of the usual annoyances, like someone kicking the seat behind you. Still, it felt a bit surreal to have no other passengers around, just a few discreet crew members. A far cry from my usual commercial flights.

Sean picks me up from the airport and drives me to 'location', which isn't far. We drive up to a Portakabin where he flashes his ID card, and I have to sign a stack of secrecy documents before being issued a pass. We drive on to what looks to be an airfield with a couple of hangars big enough to house aircraft. He steers the car towards the area with trailers, parks, and leads me to James's trailer. I half expected to see a big, flashy gold star with his name on it, but there's just a small, unassuming magnetic nameplate reading 'James Keller'.

Inside, the trailer is predictably nice, a well-laid-out

posh caravan with all the comforts you'd expect. Sean points out a large marquee not far away.

"That's where you can get tea, coffee, some food. Otherwise, make yourself at home here until James gets back. He's filming right now but should be done soon. You can't go anywhere else on site without security or James." That is the most Sean has ever said to me; I feel quite honoured. He leaves me alone in the trailer, and I kick off my shoes and have a little look around. There's a beige leather sofa, a dining table, a TV, and a small kitchen area – though no tea or coffee supplies in sight – a compact bathroom with a toilet and shower, a vanity area likely for hair and makeup, and a bed – not our usual size, but still, plenty of room to roll. I settle on the sofa, sinking into its softness. It feels surreal to be here. I glance around. Everything is meticulously arranged, typical of James. After a few moments, curiosity gets the better of me, and I wander into the bedroom. The bed is neatly made. I run my fingers over the crisp white linen and imagine myself lying here with him, wrapped in his warmth. A flutter flows over me at the thought. Next, I wander over to the vanity area. It's simple but practical, with a large mirror and plenty of lights. I can see him here, preparing for a scene, going over his lines with that intense focus he has.

Half an hour passes and no sign of James yet, so I decide to take myself over to the marquee and get a coffee. I slip my shoes back on and step outside to see a flurry of activity – crew members bustling about, equipment being moved, and the general controlled chaos of a film set.

As I enter the large white tent, there are a few people scattered around, no one I recognise. Some are grabbing a quick bite at long picnic-style tables, others engaged in animated discussions. I'm standing at the counter, pondering over which coffee to order, when a woman cuts in front of me.

"Coffee, black," she snaps at the lady serving behind the counter. I turn to see who is being so rude and I'm met with a frosty stare. "Runners are needed down on set one," she snaps at me too. Amanda Harrington, actress and wife of director Martin Harrington, was in *Driver's Fury: Downforce* with James and is now co-starring in this film with him too. She has a reputation for being a diva. I've seen her in a couple of films but never had an opinion on her until now. I know I'm dressed casually today, but even so!

"Excuse me?" I reply, feeling slightly agitated by her tone.

"Runners, on set one," she repeats.

"Thank you. If I see a runner, I'll be sure to let them know." I smile sweetly at her. She glares at me. It appears we are having a standoff. Her eyes flick to look at someone approaching behind me and her face changes in an instant to a sweet smile. It's James.

"Hey, James!" Her tone is light.

"Hey!" he replies. "Hey, Gladys." He greets the lady behind the counter. He slides his arm around my shoulder and smiles at me. "I wondered where you'd got to. You've met Amanda, I see." I reach forwards and offer a hand for her to shake.

"Nikki," I say as pleasantly as I can. She shakes my hand and smiles that sweet smile, but her eyes are steely.

"Yes, we were just getting a coffee. Yours was black, right? Same as mine," I say, determined to get in there first.

"Yes please," she replies.

"You want a coffee, babe?" I ask James. He glances at us both briefly, like he can sense something in the air.

"Yeah, I'll have one, please."

"Can we have three black coffees, please?" I ask Gladys, who has been standing there, watching this whole encounter unfold. She hands us our drinks; James tells Amanda he will see her on set later that evening and leads me over to a corner table to drink our coffee.

"Did I sense an atmosphere between you two?"

"No, no, she got her wires crossed that's all – didn't realise I was with you and assumed I was a runner."

"Oh, and you corrected her?"

"Kind of."

"Good for you, I wouldn't expect any less from you." He smiles at me. "How was your flight?"

"My flight was fantastic, thank you. That's a pretty amazing plane you have there."

"Good, isn't it?" He beams. "Do you want a quick tour of the set?"

"Ooh, yes please!"

"Come on, then. I'll give you a tour," he says, taking my hand.

He leads me through the set, introducing me to various crew members and showing me some of the intricacies of the production. It's fascinating to see some of the behind-the-scenes magic that goes into creating a movie.

"So, what do you think?" he asks as we step up into his trailer some time later.

"It's amazing, James. I'm in awe of how much work goes into this."

He smiles, reaching for two wine glasses from the cupboard and pouring us both a glass. "I'm glad you're here. It means a lot to me. How long have we got until your flight home?"

"You should know, given you organised it." He raises an eyebrow while handing me my wine. "Ah, Allison organised it!" I roll my eyes and get comfy on the sofa again. "We have a few hours before I need to leave."

"Hmm?" he says, locking the door. "What *shall* we do with those hours? Maybe we can say hello properly? I won't be missed on set for a while."

"Maybe we can."

He kneels on the sofa, with a mischievous glint in his eyes, and closes the blinds behind me. The room suddenly feels charged with electricity as he leans in, his lips brushing against mine in a tantalisingly slow kiss. His hands are gentle yet insistent, drawing me closer until there's no space left between us. I melt into him, savouring the warmth of his touch and the intoxicating mix of his aftershave and the faint scent of the wine. His kisses grow deeper, more urgent, as he traces the line of my jaw and moves down to my neck. Each touch sends a shiver through me, a delicious anticipation building with every second. My hands find their way to his hair, tangling in the soft strands as I pull him even closer.

He pauses for a moment, looking into my eyes with a mix of affection and desire. "You know," he murmurs, "I've been looking forward to this all day."

"Me too," I whisper, my heart pounding.

He smiles, a slow, sexy grin that makes my heart skip a beat. "Good. Because I don't plan on letting you go anytime soon."

Twenty-Six

I arrive at the hotel at 6pm. I couldn't get away from work earlier because of a late lunch out with clients and a meeting that overran slightly. As I step into the reception, I immediately spot Allison. James described her perfectly: a short lady, in her mid-forties but looks older, with mid-length mousy hair, and will probably be wearing a black skirt suit with frumpy shoes! Looks like she'd eat you alive but is extremely efficient. I walk up to her.

"Allison?" I approach her with a warm smile. She scans me from head to toe, the Manhattan once-over, I believe it's called, even though she's British. He was right: she does look like she'd eat you alive! "Hi, I'm Nikki, so nice to finally put a face to the emails," I say, trying to be as friendly as possible.

"Hello, Nikki," she replies flatly. "Please, follow me. I'll take you up to the suite so you can get ready." She escorts me through reception to a door I'm familiar with – the same hotel, the same room we had our first date in, the

166

Hyde Park suite. She opens the door for me. "James has left for the premiere already. I will come by and collect you at 7:15pm. Please be ready by then," she instructs and with that she leaves. She's certainly efficient. I wonder how she gets on with Sean! I already know James has left for the premiere because he messaged me earlier to let me know and to tell me to order any room service I'd like.

I'm alone in his suite. I put my bag down and look out of the window at Hyde Park, such a beautiful green space in the centre of busy London. I spend a few moments just looking around, remembering. The dining table where we had dinner and he kissed me; the sofa where we listened to music and he kissed me again. Sweet memories. I wheel my overnight bag into the bedroom and realise there must be a second bedroom; this bed is untouched. I open another door. This looks better; it's lived in. I can see his belongings here, tidy as always. I've not seen him for just over two weeks since Norway. He briefly went back to the States, and we decided this time it wasn't worth me travelling that far when he was back here so soon, plus it would have been a struggle with work. He arrived in London yesterday and we spent the night apart, which felt strange. He attended a private cocktail party for cast, crew, and people in the industry that he invited me to, but unfortunately, I had a client dinner to attend.

I open the zip on my dress cover bag and hang the dress that Jules and Lizzie helped me choose on the wardrobe door. We went for sexy but understated. A pure white bodycon that sits just above the knee with black ruffle detail down one side, it shows off my figure nicely. Classy enough for the red carpet without being over-the-top 'look at me everyone' red carpet. I team it with open-toed ankle strap heels in gold. It's warm out, so I don't need a coat, but Jules has lent me a black cashmere shawl to drape over my shoulders to add a touch of elegance.

I take a shower in the en suite; I thought my shower at home was nice, but this is just divine. After my shower, I unpack a few things from my overnight bag. James and I have naturally fallen into a habit where he sleeps on the right of the bed, and I sleep on the left, so I place my water bottle on the left bedside table and take out the gift box containing the tie and pin that I bought him and place it beside the bed. The shop assistant packaged it beautifully for me in a black box with 'GIORGIO ARMANI' embossed in gold on the front.

I sit at the dresser and apply my makeup, opting for subtle shades again, and slick my hair back in a low ponytail, and put on my black feather dangly earrings. I mist some perfume over myself before slipping into a white lace thong and matching bra and then into my dress. It fits perfectly. Taking a seat on the high bed, I just about manage to strap up my shoes and grab my clutch out of my overnight bag.

Right on time, there's a knock at the door. I go to the peephole just to check it is Allison. It is. I open it and say "Hi."

She gives me a curt nod, approval maybe. "Hello, are you ready?" she asks very matter-of-factly.

"I am," I reply in an equal tone. I step out and close the door, then it occurs to me: how do I get back in?

"Do I need a room key?" I say in a bit of a panic. She looks at me like I'm the stupidest person in the world.

"No. I have one and I can let you in, if necessary. Do you need to go back in?"

"No," I reply sheepishly, feeling about one inch tall! She escorts me back down to reception, and Mark and Julia are already there.

"Hi, darling!" Julia greets me with a hug. "You look gorgeous, it fits you perfectly!" she compliments me, standing back to admire the dress.

"Thanks," I reply, starting to feel a little taller again. "So do you."

"Hi, Nik." Mark greets me with a double kiss. "Gorgeous as always," he compliments me, boosting my ego.

"The car is ready," Allison announces. We walk out onto the pavement. There are a few fans lingering about. Mark and Jules give them a polite wave and we get into a black limousine; wow, I really travel in style these days. The bar is fully stocked. Mark pours us a glass of champagne. Allison opts for water. She doesn't say much on the way there; she leaves the chatting to us.

The weather is kind tonight, warm, and dry. The driver pulls into a private area for VIPs where we can exit the car discreetly without the risk of the photographer seeing your knickers if you're not very graceful! Jules and I step out and smooth out our dresses.

"If we get separated on the red carpet, we will meet you inside," Jules says to me. I'm absolutely bricking it, I can't lie. The four of us walk around the corner and I get my first glimpse of the red carpet. The atmosphere is electric; the crowds are about ten deep and cheering. There are barriers between the public and those on the red carpet, security staff manning each one each with earpieces and walkie talkies. Immediately Mark gets called over by a media person, leaving me with just Allison.

Of the cast and crew, the gents are mostly in suits, and the ladies in beautiful and some quite flamboyant dresses. I see a huge poster of the film, probably about twenty-foot wide, on the far side of the red carpet near the entrance to the cinema. I guess this is where the official photos are taken. James's face is right in the centre of the poster.

'DRIVER'S FURY: Downforce, *starring JAMES KELLER, Jeremy Conor, Blake Simmons, Suzanne Lindt and Amanda Harrington.*'

Allison walks slightly ahead of me, escorting me along the red carpet, not saying a word. Her demeanour calm and composed, as if she's done this a thousand times. I try to emulate her confidence, straightening my posture and taking a deep breath, but I have major impostor syndrome going on. The carpet is long. I'm looking for James as we walk; he's easy to spot, because I hear his name being shouted by fans. He's surrounded by people and appears to be giving a press interview as he chats with someone holding a microphone. Sean and other security members are working hard behind him as fans lean over the barriers, trying to get his attention and shoving camera phones in his face. He seems to take it all in his stride. He doesn't see me; it's too busy and I'm certainly not going to shout his name. He's wearing a well-tailored black suit with a white shirt, unbuttoned at the top, and no tie. Tall, dark and extremely handsome.

Allison ushers me through the doors of the cinema

and into the foyer. It's quite crowded in here too but a little less noisy, no screaming or shouting, just the rumble of conversation.

"We need to wait here a minute," she informs me. We stand awkwardly at the side, saying nothing to each other. Thankfully, Mark and Jules walk in and rescue me.

"Sorry about that," says Jules. "You okay? It's a bit crazy, isn't it?" I nod in agreement. Then the noise level rises again as the doors open and in walks James with Sean close by. He's still surrounded by people, and he's chatting away, clearly in his element! He pauses and looks around; he sees us standing at the edge. He breaks free from the groupies and makes his way over, followed by Sean and another lady, a tall blonde lady, classy, mid-fifties at a guess. He greets Allison with a light touch on her arm.

"Everything okay?" he asks her. She smiles at him. I'm amazed. She can smile?

"All good here, James," she informs him. He kisses Jules on the cheek and compliments her dress, then shakes Mark's hand.

"Good to see you, buddy," he says to Mark, then he turns his attention to me and smiles. I feel I could melt into the ground. He gently places his arm around my waist and leans into my ear.

"Hi, darling, I missed you last night. You look beautiful," he whispers.

I so badly want to wrap my arms around him, but I can't. He has a knack of making you feel like the most important person in the room.

"Hello," I say coyly. "Thank you. You look good too,

very handsome, almost good enough to eat," I whisper back playfully.

James smiles, his eyes twinkling with amusement. "Later," he murmurs, his voice low and intimate, sending a shiver down my spine.

He introduces me to the blonde lady with him, Rebecca, his agent. She's much more approachable than Allison. She greets me with a smile and a friendly handshake. We have a few minutes before we are due into the theatre. No photographs are allowed inside, only official ones, so James takes my hand and leads me to where his co-stars are standing to introduce me. Jeremy Conor, Blake Simmons, and Suzanne Lindt are all well-known actors, but Suzanne I am a big fan of; I think I might be more star-struck meeting her than I was James! She's also a fellow Brit, and lives in the UK. She was in the first *Driver's Fury* film with James, and she starred with him in a film called *Townhouse* years ago. They know each other quite well, I believe, and he speaks very highly of her.

"Nikki! Finally, we get to meet you!" says Suzanne in a very middle-class British accent, while holding out a delicate hand to shake and smiling warmly. I feel my cheeks flush a little. I guess he's told them about me. "It's a pleasure to meet you. James has mentioned you, quite a lot." She places her hand affectionately on his shoulder and winks at him. "It's all good, though. Is this the first time you've seen the film?" she enquires.

"Yes, first time, and first time at a premiere!"

"Oh, you'll love it!"

"I'm sure I will." I smile back at her. Someone starts to clap their hands, trying to get people's attention.

"I'll see you in there, darling." She kisses James's cheek. "So lovely to meet you, Nikki." She smiles warmly at me as we return to Allison and the others.

"Were you a little star-struck then?" he teases me. "Nothing when you meet me but meet Suzanne and you go weak at the knees…!"

I laugh. "That is not true. I always go weak at the knees when I see you."

"Are we ready?" he asks us all. With his arm still around my waist, he escorts us through the foyer to the screen. "I need to go and do my bit; Allison will take it from here," he tells me. He disappears off somewhere and Allison steps in, guiding me and the others to our seats. "This way, please," she says efficiently, leading us to a row reserved for close friends and family. I'm seated in the second seat in from the aisle. She and Sean walk past and sit a few seats further down with Rebecca, which I'm glad about. I'm good at making small talk, but I fear they may push my limits. Julia and Mark are next to me, leaving the seat on the end empty, but not for long; a middle-aged guy comes and sits in it, a media person I suspect. Thankfully, he doesn't seem interested in talking to me. The theatre is filling up as others take their seats, but I notice the three rows in front of us remain empty and a large white stage is set just to the right of the screen with a microphone in the centre.

The lights dim and the audience begins to clap. The stage lights up and people start to walk on, people I don't recognise. Then the applause gets louder as James appears with his co-stars. I feel so proud of him, I want to shout out 'That's my man!' but instead I just clap along with everyone else.

A man who introduces himself as the director gives a short speech about the film and thanks the cast and crew. Then James moves forwards to the microphone. He stands for a few moments to let the applause die down before he begins.

"Thank you." He raises his hand and flashes his famous smile to the audience in appreciation. "Thank you," he says again and goes on to talk briefly about the film, how it was made, and how long it was in the pipeline. Then he thanks the cast and crew for their dedication and hard work. "It's been a real pleasure for me to work with so many talented people, and to not only to star in the film but also to produce it. Everyone you see before you on this stage, and the team behind the scenes, has put in a tremendous amount of effort to bring this film to fruition. I'm so incredibly grateful to them all and so proud of them. We hope you enjoy the film as much as we enjoyed making it for you."

He finishes his speech, and they exit from the stage as the audience rises to their feet to applaud. The cast make their way up the stairs to the empty seats in front of us. James is in the row below me, almost in front. He sees me, pauses momentarily, leans in, and says something to his co-star Jeremy Conor, before giving him a pat on the back and then making his way up to the man next to me, who looks a little star-struck to see James Keller approaching him.

"Excuse me, sir, would you mind swapping seats with me? I'm just there," he points to the seat in the row below, "next to Jeremy Conor. If possible, I'd like to sit with my agent." He nods in my direction; I smile sweetly at the man next to me, playing along. The man fumbles. He can't get up quick enough; I think he might have sat on the floor if James had asked him. It's a great result for him, though. He now gets to be one of the first to see the film and sit next to one of its stars. Better result for me, though, as James slides into the seat next to me.

"Won't you get in trouble, leaving your co-stars like that?" I ask jokingly.

"No, it's not like they can fire me, is it? I've missed you!" He winks at me and I'm a happy bunny again.

Twenty-Seven

The film is a perfect mix of action and suspense with a light dusting of comedy and romance. Watching him on the big screen while he sits next to me is surreal; I don't know whether to look at the screen or to my right. A romantic scene starts to play out between James and Suzanne, or Jason and Scarlet as they are known on the screen. It's a typical scene: friends in denial about their feelings for each other, they've had an argument, he looks at her intensely, the same way he sometimes looks at me, he tells her he's in love with her and moves in for a passionate kiss.

The follow-up isn't shown, but you know what it leads to. I can feel his stare on my face as the scene plays out, his fingers brushing against mine in the dark. I keep my expression neutral, trying not to show any reaction. It's just acting, I remind myself; I've seen him kiss on the big screen many times before. The difference is I now know what it feels like to be with him, and I can't help but feel a tiny twinge of envy. Is it because he's kissing someone else or is it because it's public, on the screen for everyone to see? We only kiss in private; no one outside his circle knows about us.

As the film ends, the audience erupts in applause, the atmosphere electric. Chatter fills the air, handshakes and appreciative slaps on the back as people leave the theatre. We follow the crowd and make our way back to the foyer. It's chilly now, so I wrap my shawl around my shoulders.

"I'll see you soon," James whispers, kissing my cheek. He nods to Mark before moving off to mingle with the press. Allison escorts us out to the red carpet and to the car, where we wait for James and Sean. It's not long before they arrive, Rebecca in tow, and we head back to the hotel.

When we arrive, crowds are still gathered outside, shouting his name. "James! James! We love you, James!"

He stays outside for a few moments with Sean, greeting the fans, before joining us inside, where we move through the reception and into the lounge bar, which has been cordoned off for a private function.

"Did I mention, there's always an after-party?" he says, smiling at me.

"Um no, you failed to mention that!" I feel a slight panic rising within me; stupidly, I thought we'd just go back to his room.

"Don't worry." He puts an arm around my shoulder and escorts me in. About a hundred people are milling around in their little groups, a few cheering as he enters. Waiting staff weave between the guests, skilfully balancing trays of champagne. We are handed a glass, and quickly, he's surrounded by people. It's fascinating to watch how he commands the room, how people are drawn to him; everyone seems to want a piece of him. My two security blankets, Mark and Jules, are off chatting with a group of people not far away and I can feel the nerves kick in. I give myself a pep talk; treat it like a client meeting, I say to myself. He introduces me to everyone he talks to, making sure I'm okay.

Sometime later and a few drinks in, I'm standing with James, feeling more at ease while about five people all try to talk to him at once. The conversation drifts on to the success of the premiere when I feel a tap on my shoulder. I look to see who it is. It's Suzanne. She gestures for me to follow her, and as I do, James turns to see where I'm going.

"Don't worry, darling, I'll look after her!" She waves at him dismissively as we walk away. She's a similar height and build as me, with the glossiest shoulder-length auburn hair I've ever seen, slicked back to expose her fair-skinned face. She's probably in her mid-forties and looks fabulous in a full-length black gown.

"It's nuts being with James at times, isn't it?" She smiles sympathetically, linking arms with me as she escorts me to the bar where we take a seat. I have to help her arrange the folds of her dress so she can sit down on the bar stool.

"Thanks, darling. Let's get you a top-up – that champs is almost empty." She nods towards my glass and gets the attention of the bartender. With our glasses full again, she leans in towards me.

"So, James tells me you're a lawyer? Quite a successful one, by all accounts," she says enthusiastically. I smile, flattered.

"Yes, I am a lawyer and I'm reasonably successful, I guess."

"And modest. What area do you specialise in?"

"I work in employment law. It's quite interesting and useful," I tell her.

"Good for you! If I hadn't got into acting, I would have been a lawyer. The closest I got was playing one in a film once."

"I know the film. I was still studying when it was released, and I have to say, you played the role exceptionally well. I was inspired by you!"

"You were? Oh, that's sweet of you to say. Did you have an alternative career, or did you always want to be in law?"

"It was always law, but in years to come I might retrain as an interior designer."

"Really? Are you good at it?"

"I'm told I have a flair for it."

"Well, if you ever do, look me up. I'm useless at it!" She gives a little laugh.

I laugh with her, feeling a genuine connection forming. "I will. Maybe I can start with your place."

"Oh, you'd have your work cut out for you," she says with a playful roll of her eyes.

We chat generally about things for a while. I find her to be warm and down to earth; it's easy to see why she and James have such a good rapport. Thankfully, she doesn't ask me any probing questions about James or my relationship with him. We are joined at the bar by the director Adam and Jeremy Conor, quite the social circle. The bar buzzes with conversations and laughter. I glance at James, who is not far from me, still surrounded by people.

I look up to see Amanda Harrington striding towards us. She's a striking figure, her muscular legs accentuated by her black gown that sits above the knee and flows elegantly to the floor at the back, with a plunging neckline. Her sharp blonde bob and her piercing blue eyes, framed by dark makeup, survey the room with confidence. As she reaches us, I offer a friendly smile, but she looks right past me.

"Where's James?" she asks Suzanne, her tone brisk and direct.

Suzanne points to her left. "He's just over there," she says, gesturing towards the cluster of people surrounding James.

"Thanks, doll," she says as she turns on her heels and saunters towards him without acknowledging my presence. Maybe she doesn't remember me.

As the conversation with Suzanne, Adam, and Jeremy continues, I can't help but keep an eye on Amanda and James. There's a certain familiarity in the way she interacts with him, and it makes me uneasy. She leans into him, her arm around his neck, and whispers something in his ear. It reminds me of the woman in the club who tried to lure him away from me the first night I met him. James smiles to whatever she says as she leans in closer. Her laughter carries across the room, and she lightly touches him on the chest. Part of me wants to stride over there, but another part hesitates. I trust James, I really do, but these situations stir up insecurities. It's the nature of his world, the constant attention, the flirtations that come with fame. He takes it in his stride, but it's still unsettling for me to witness. I've been used to having him all to myself.

Suzanne, noticing my distraction, leans in slightly. "Don't worry about Amanda," she says softly, her voice reassuring. "She's always been a bit... intense. But James knows how to handle her."

I smile and take a sip of my champagne, trying to refocus on the engaging stories Jeremy is sharing about the film's production.

About fifteen minutes pass when Suzanne excuses herself to go to the loo, leaving me with Adam and Jeremy. As I sip my drink and engage in small talk, I glance around the crowded room, looking for James, but neither James nor Amanda is anywhere in sight. A few moments later, Suzanne returns and takes her seat again at the bar; she laughs as I help with the folds of her dress again.

"How did you manage on the loo?" I jest.

"With great difficulty, darling," she replies with a wink.

"Have you seen James?" I enquire.

Her eyes flicker, a hint of something that I can't quite place. "No, I've not seen him," she says, but then glances over my shoulder as someone approaches. "Ah, scrap that, here he is, the man of the hour!" she says as James appears by my side and slides his arm around my waist. I smile at him and look around the room to see where Amanda is. She's chatting with another group of people, but I spot her glancing over in our direction a few times, with that steely look in her eyes again.

James leans in and whispers, "Missed me?"

"Of course!"

"Hey, I hope you're not getting Nikki drunk and filling her head with terrible stories about me, Suz?" James jokes with her.

"Oh, darling, as if I would do that! She's a bright lady – shc can figure these things out by herself!" She winks at him.

"Are you ready to leave?" he asks. "Or do you want to stay and let Suzanne here lead you astray some more?"

"I'm quite enjoying myself; I think I might stay." I smile at Suzanne, who in turn raises her glass to me. James rolls his eyes at us.

"Okay, let's go," I say, stepping down off the stool and holding on to the bar to steady myself. Suzanne bursts out laughing as James steadies me with a reassuring grip on my waist.

"You okay?" he asks with a teasing grin.

"Yes, yes, I'm okay," I reply, regaining composure and waving off his concern with a playful smile. "Just a bit wobbly in these heels, that's all."

Twenty-Eight

We relax back onto the sofa in his suite with a small nightcap, very small for me, and I can hear the faint rumble of thunder outside.

"How was your night, then?" James asks, putting his feet up on the footstool.

"Amazing, I loved it," I say, removing my shoes and putting my feet next to his.

"I've been thinking." He hands me my drink.

"What about?"

"I think we should go public; I want to be out in the open with you. I want to show you off to the world and let everyone know I'm officially off the market."

"Say again?" I say, slightly taken aback. "What does that mean exactly, 'go public'?"

"I don't mean a front page spread in *Vogue*." He smiles at me. "I'm thinking dinner out, holding hands, being seen together out and about as a couple."

I take a sip of my drink to steady my nerves.

"I've got some downtime coming up in a couple of weeks, I thought I'd come over and we could go out for dinner, publicly. I also wondered if you wanted to go away with me during that time, just the two of us. Spend some quality time together without rushing around. I was thinking of hiring a cottage in Wales, doing a bit of hiking, relaxing – what do you think?"

I look him straight in the eyes. "I'd love that, but, before we go public as you put it, I should tell my parents."

"You've not told them yet?" he says, sounding surprised.

"No, I've not told anyone apart from Lizzie."

"Oh. Okay, sure, I thought you would have told them by now. Does that mean I can meet them?" he asks, with a glint of amusement in his eye.

"My dad would be absolutely thrilled to meet you!"

"And your mum?"

"Oh, she'll be pleased, I'm sure."

He looks thoughtful. "I am slightly apprehensive about going public with you, though."

"Why?" I ask.

"Because I don't want it to change things between us, I don't want it to scare you off. Media intrusion can be intense."

"How do you suggest I handle work once we are 'public'? I've had some media training but only for work purposes, not how to handle my private life, never been an issue before," I tease.

"Let's chat with Allison and Rebecca about it and see what they suggest. Bedtime?" He looks at me with those come-to-bed eyes that I can't resist.

"Bedtime," I agree.

We turn everything off in the lounge, go into the bedroom and get ready for bed, the rumbles of thunder getting louder, and every now and then I see a flash of lightning. James removes his suit jacket and hangs it neatly in the wardrobe.

"Babe?" I say, watching him unbutton his shirt to reveal his toned body. Damn he's fine. I walk over to him and hand him the gift box.

"I got you a gift," I say, feeling both excited and nervous.

"You did? You didn't have to do that." He smiles warmly as he takes the box and opens it.

"I hope you don't have one like it already?"

"No, I don't think I do," he replies, holding the tie in his hand, letting the smooth silk slide through his fingers.

"I just wanted to say thank you. From the moment we met, you've been so kind and generous, you've taken care of me, and I want you to know that I'm not taking you for granted. I appreciate it. I appreciate you." I might be a bit drunk but I'm feeling genuine love for him.

He puts the tie back in the box and places it on his bedside table.

"It's just a small gift," I say, starting to feel a little embarrassed that it might not be grand enough for him. He moves to stand in front of me with a serious look in his eyes, cups my face in his hands, lifting my head to meet his gaze.

"It's a gift from you and I love it," he says softly. "Thank you, baby." He pulls me in for a hug.

His arms hold tightly around my waist, and I wrap my arms around his neck. I brush my cheek up against his. It feels good; it feels sensual. It reminds me of the first night we met, the anticipation of the first kiss. We stand for a few moments, both of us enjoying the closeness of each other. He moves his hands down over the contour of my lower body, caressing me. He kisses me and I can feel the sexual energy soaring around my body.

Swaying gently as we kiss, I untuck his shirt fully – as he unbuttons the cuffs – and move my hands up over his torso to his shoulders to remove the shirt, down over his beautiful, toned arms, letting it drop to the floor, where it stays. I undo his belt and slide it out from the loops; he holds his arms out, allowing me access, and I throw it onto the chair. I unbutton his trousers, lower the zip and glide my fingers over the material of his boxers, stroking his manhood. He groans with pleasure.

My body is completely open to him as I lean my head back and he kisses my neck. His lips are warm and soft, sending shivers down my spine. His hands roam over my body, exploring every curve until he reaches the zip on my dress and lowers it. I step out of it and, like the shirt, it drops to the floor, where it stays. As I stand there, feeling vulnerable, he removes his suit trousers and flings them onto the chair. His hands wander over my body, admiring the white lace of my lingerie. With a skilful move, he undoes my bra with one hand. He kisses me again, holding the back of my neck. It's a deep kiss, our tongues exploring every inch of each other. I feel his fingers trace the straps of my bra as it slides off my shoulders and falls to the floor. His touch is electric. He cups my breasts, his thumbs brushing over my nipples, eliciting a gasp from me. Our kisses grow hungrier, more urgent, as if we can't get enough of each other.

He lowers me onto the bed, and lies between my legs, continuing to trail kisses down my neck, over my collarbone, and to the sensitive skin of my breasts while rocking his pelvis up against mine, arousing me. I arch my back, offering myself to him. His mouth finds my nipples, sucking and teasing, sending waves of pleasure coursing through me. I moan softly, my hands tangling in his hair, urging him on.

He moves lower, his lips following a path down my stomach, his hands caressing my hips. He hooks his fingers into the waistband of my panties and slowly slides them down, discarding them carelessly. He pauses for a moment, taking in the sight of me completely exposed before him.

"You're so beautiful," he whispers, his voice husky with desire as his fingers enter me. I moan with pleasure, so aroused that I find it hard to keep still. He's enjoying me, enjoying him. When he senses I'm on the edge, he removes himself from inside me and sits up on his knees. He takes off his shorts, so I can see him in all his glory.

He kneels on the floor and parts my legs, lightly kissing up my thighs until he reaches my groin. I moan louder and louder; he's sending me into a frenzy. I squirm, my hands gripping the sheets as waves of pleasure wash over me. I look down to see his head moving up and down between my legs, his tongue and lips expertly working their magic. The pleasure is insane, an overwhelming surge that has me teetering on the brink of ecstasy.

Every flick of his tongue, every gentle suck, sends shockwaves through my body. My breathing quickens, and my hips instinctively lift towards him, seeking more of his touch. He responds with even greater fervour, his hands gripping my thighs to hold me steady. I feel the tension building. My moans turn into cries of pure pleasure as the intensity of his movements drives me closer to the edge. And then, with a final, exquisite flick of his tongue, I reach a powerful orgasm. My body arches, my fingers clutching the sheets, as I am consumed by the overwhelming sensation. He moves back up to me, his eyes filled with satisfaction, and kisses me deeply so I can taste myself on his lips. I can feel his arousal pressing against me. He enters me slowly, filling me completely, and we both let out a sigh of pleasure. We move together, our rhythm steady for a while.

He turns me over onto my front, spreads my legs, and enters me again, spreadeagle style. I lift my pelvis, allowing him to go deeper. He's very aroused – I can feel it, I can hear it – and I'm more aroused than I've ever been with anyone else.

He slides himself out and allows me to take charge. I climb on top and feather his chest with kisses, teasing his lips with mine before working my way down to his Adonis belt and beyond. I take as much of him as I can in my mouth, playfully biting, sucking, licking, and rubbing my finger over his perineum, which he likes.

His breathing becomes ragged, and I can tell he's struggling to maintain control. His hands grip the sheets tightly, knuckles white. The combination of my mouth and fingers drives him wild, and I feel a surge of power and connection between us. I look up at him, meeting his eyes with a mischievous smile, as he groans, thrusting gently into my mouth.

"God, you're amazing," he murmurs, his voice thick with desire.

Encouraged, I increase the intensity, my tongue swirling and teasing, my fingers applying just the right amount of pressure. His moans grow louder, more urgent, and I can sense he's nearing the edge. I slow my pace slightly, wanting to prolong the moment, to keep him teetering on the brink for as long as possible. I turn him over onto all fours; I can sense he feels vulnerable in this position as I kneel behind him, reach between his legs and take hold of his throbbing penis, and rub my hand up and down his shaft while tonguing his anus. We've had lots of sex, but this is the first time we've done this. It is so erotic. I bring him to the edge and stop abruptly, asking him to turn over, and I climb on top, putting him inside me again. I ride him hard until I reach orgasm, the sweetest orgasm that seems to go on and on. Seeing me climax has the same effect on him; he starts to moan louder and thrusts himself up into me, harder, faster, deeper until he climaxes as well. I collapse onto him and kiss him, both of us sweating.

"That was so good," he says, catching his breath.

"It was," I say as I feel the endorphins pumping hard around my body.

Twenty-Nine

"I hate saying goodbye to you." He strokes my hair.

"I hate it too." We spent the weekend after the premiere in my Richmond flat but now it's time for him to leave – again – back to the States for a couple of weeks.

"What are your plans for the next week or two whilst I'm out of town?" he asks.

"Oh, you know, I've got a few dates lined up with tall, dark, handsome strangers," I tease him.

"You'd better not be dating anyone other than me," he replies, kissing me.

"I'm just joking. I am exclusively yours," I tell him.

"Good, I don't want to share you with anyone."

"Work is going to be busy, but I'm going to a new salsa club on Friday night with a few of my dance friends."

"That reminds me, dance lessons," he says, tapping his finger on his head. His phone buzzes, meaning Sean and Nigel are here to take him away from me.

"Time to go. I'll call you when I land," he says, kissing me goodbye. "I'll miss you, see you very soon."

"Can't wait. I'll miss you too." I wave him goodbye, close the door, and I get a little lump in my throat.

The advice from Allison and Rebecca was to tell who I needed to and that was about it. I was disappointed not to get something more dramatic from them. I have decided I will tell my PA Ivy and my manager John when I get back from holiday, and everyone else can find out organically.

I wrap up work for the day and I'm just about to head for home when my dad calls me.

"Hi, Nikki, how are you, love?"

"Yeah, I'm great thanks, you?" I ask cheerfully.

"Hmm, great are you?" he teases. "Listen, I'm going to lunch in London with some old work people on Saturday. I wondered if I could park at yours and catch the train from there? Also maybe stop by for tea on my way back?"

"Yeah, sure, you can park here no problem. And yes, stop by for a cup of tea. Do you know roughly what time? I'm off out dancing that night."

"Oh right, that's nice, love. Glad you're still dancing. Probably about 4pm. I won't stop long as it takes a couple of hours to get home from yours and you know your mum will be missing me."

"I'm sure she will. That's fine; I'll see you on Saturday, then." We say our goodbyes and I head home. I text James while I'm on the train.

'Hi Babe, hope you're okay? Just heading home after a manic day! Miss you xxx'

I get a reply almost immediately. I look around the train at the other commuters. An older guy in a grey pinstripe suit, carrying a brown leather suitcase, sits opposite me reading a newspaper. Next to him sits a young girl. She's wearing flared jeans, a floral blouse and a denim jacket; she has headphones in and just stares out of the window. I look at the others. None of them know that the message I just received was from James Keller. I wonder if any of them are fans; it still feels so surreal to be dating James Keller.

'Hi Darling, I was just thinking about you. Busy here too, and just about to meet with Rebecca. Not long until Wales! I've hired a car for the trip by the way. I'll call you later before you head to bed, I miss you too. xxx'

After dinner I give Lizzie a call. I've not spoken to her since before the premiere. "I saw the pictures online – he looked good! Didn't see you, though."

"You really need to stop searching for him. There was none taken of me. I didn't meet up with him until we were inside the cinema, only official photos allowed in there."

"I can't help it, I'm excited. Was it good?"

I dread to think what she'll be like when she meets him! "Yes, it was brilliant. I've never seen a cinema so busy; it was buzzing."

"What was the red carpet like, did he like your dress?"

"The red carpet was non-eventful for me. I got ushered straight along it into the cinema. He seemed to like it – he liked taking it off." I laugh.

"Nikki, you little minx!"

"Listen, something else happened," I tell her. The silence tells me she's waiting to hear what. "He said he wants our relationship to be out in the open, go public is what he said."

"Oh." She sounds a little disappointed. "I thought you were going to tell me he asked you to move in or proposed."

I laugh out loud. "Don't be ridiculous," I tell her.

"That's a good thing, right? It shows he's serious about you. I don't think he would want to do that if he wasn't."

"True. I need to tell Mum and Dad, though, before we do that."

"Yes, you do. Can I be there when you do? I'm dying to see their faces, especially Dad's. How exactly do you go public, though?" she asks.

"Dinner out, just being out and about together, I think, instead of hiding out in my flat or a hotel. He did say media attention would be intense once we start down that road."

"You can handle it," she reassures me.

"I'm seeing Dad this weekend. I'll try to make a plan to meet up with them and I'll bring James. Don't worry, I'll make sure you're there too!" I can feel her excitement bubbling away.

"Fantastic, I can't wait," she says.

Dad arrives at my flat. I make him a nice cup of sweet tea as he takes a seat on my sofa. "How are you doing?" I ask.

"Oh, not bad, love, had a nice lunch with some old work colleagues," he says, rubbing his stomach and taking the tea from my hand. "Two sugars?"

"Two sugars," I confirm. Mum won't let him have sugar in his tea, so this is our little secret. We chat generally about things with work, what he and Mum have been up to, and the golf club gossip.

"So, you're off dancing tonight, are you?" he asks.

"Yep, dancing tonight."

"Are you going with anyone?" His eyes twinkle.

"No, not tonight, but, whilst we are on that subject…" I pause and think briefly about whether I will tell him who I am dating or just that I'm dating. "I have met someone."

"I knew it!" He sounds pleased with himself. "So, tell me all about him."

"Well, he's American for a start, lives in New York."

"Oh, did you meet him through work?" he questions, sounding a little confused.

"No, remember I said about the date that stood me up, a few months ago?"

"It's not him, is it?"

"No, but I did meet him that night. He overheard me saying I'd been stood up and he stepped in, and invited me to dine with him instead."

"Oh right, well, that was nice. You said he lives in New York, though?" I guess this is a question I'm going to face a lot.

"He travels, a lot. He works in the film industry; he was over here on business when we met." Dad looks at me, waiting for me to give more information. "His name is James. I'd like you to meet him; he's really nice and I think you'll like him," I say, hoping to avoid any more awkward questions.

"Okay, that'd be nice. When?"

"Well, we are, James and I that is, we are going to Wales for a holiday, week after next."

Dad raises his eyebrows at this nugget of information.

"His sister lives not far from you, and he wants to see her on Sunday before we leave, so I thought, as it looks like nice weather, you and Mum might like to have one of your fabulous barbecues on Saturday and I could bring him, get Lizzie and Duncan there too, just family though, no one else," I state firmly. Last time, they invited most of the golf club.

"Okay, just us," he confirms.

"We might want to stay the night too, or we could stay at Lizzie's?"

"Sounds like a great plan, and of course, you can stay with us. I imagine Lizzie will want to stay too; there's enough room for everyone. It will be fun. I shall look forward to meeting the man who is taking my daughter on holiday!" He raises his eyebrows again, trying to look disapproving, but breaks into a wide smile, pleased to see me happy again. "I'll tell your mum tonight and I'll tell her it's to be just us." I raise my eyebrows this time. "You know she only wants what's best for you," he says sympathetically.

"I know. It's just she can be very judgemental at times, that's all."

Dad gives me a hug. I always like a hug from my dad. I wonder how he will react when he realises which James I mean.

Later, when Dad has left, I send a text to Lizzie, so she doesn't let the cat out of the bag.

'Done, BBQ arranged for the Saturday before Wales, will firm up time later, told dad I'm bringing someone but not told him who!'

Immediately, I get back three laugh-out-loud emojis!

Thirty

onight is the night we 'go public'. We arrive at the upscale restaurant in Mayfair with Gina Rossi and her husband, Clive. Gina is another very well-known actress. She's been in many films; the last one was quite racy, very racy in fact. She's stunning. The epitome of Italian beauty, with long dark hair, deep brown eyes, full lips and chiselled cheekbones. Gorgeous, and lovely too. Gina and James co-starred in a film years ago and have remained close friends ever since. Her husband, Clive, an investment banker, typically avoids the spotlight, but tonight, we dine out publicly with them.

James steps out of the car first and turns to help me out. "Don't worry, I've got you," he reassures, his warm hand enveloping mine. Gina and Clive follow closely behind.

This part of London is always bustling, but tonight it seems even more alive. They are immediately spotted and out come the flashing camera phones. Someone moves in on me and James, wanting a selfie with him, until Sean steps in, keeping the man at arm's length.

"It's fine," James says, agreeing to have his photo taken with the man, and then another one with him and his friend. He keeps hold of my hand as the picture is taken – my arm will be in that picture, my famous arm! Gina is then required for a third photo.

With Sean's help, James manages to break free from the growing crowd, and we finally make it into the restaurant, the quiet a welcome contrast to the chaos starting to build outside.

The evening is a success. Gina and Clive are delightful, both very different people and both very interesting. Clive gave me a few tips on how to cope with the level of fame James has and dealing with the media. Advice from most people so far is the same: head down and say nothing.

"You can smile if you want. I know I'll be smiling." James kisses my shoulder. "At least look happy to be with me," he teases.

A large crowd has gathered outside the restaurant as we leave; word has obviously got out. People are standing on the pavement, spilling onto the road, and surrounding our car. Camera lights flash incessantly as we step outside, and a cacophony of voices call out for James and Gina. It's a frenzied scene. Sean and Nigel have their work cut out for them, keeping the crowd at bay. James and Gina pose for photographs and sign a few autographs, handling the chaos with practised ease. I don't keep my head down; instead, I wear the biggest smile. I can't help it. I feel like the luckiest girl alive.

Suddenly, someone in the crowd shouts, "Who's the date, James?" He keeps smiling, ignoring the question. We had agreed to be seen together but to try to keep my name quiet for a while longer. Sean creates a path for us, and James holds my hand firmly as we make our way to the car and drive off back to my apartment. He squeezes my hand.

"I'm proud of you," he says quietly. "You handled that like a pro."

The next afternoon, we pull up at my parents' house in the brand-new BMW X5 we hired for our trip to Wales. It's a beautiful, warm, sunny day, and I can see that my sister, Lizzie, is already there. I have keys, so I let myself in.

"Hi!" I shout out.

"Hi, darling! In the kitchen," Mum replies. We leave our overnight bags in the hallway and make our way through to the kitchen. My parents' house is in a sleepy village surrounded by fields. There's a post office, a shop selling essentials, a church, and a pub. The nearest town is a few miles away. The house itself is big and quite old, with six bedrooms, three of which are en suite. In its day, it boasted quality furniture and fittings, but now, though still in good condition, it's a bit dated.

Everyone is in the kitchen, except for the kids and the dog, who I can see playing in the back garden. Mum is busy preparing the salad, Dad is washing the BBQ grill, and Lizzie and Duncan are drinking wine at the kitchen table.

"Hi," I say again as we enter.

"Hi, love, be with you in a sec," says Dad, not turning around. Mum looks up, and it takes her a few seconds to register who is standing in front of her with her daughter. She screws up her forehead.

"Are you…?" She trails off.

"This is James!" I say, trying not to laugh. "This is my mum, Mandy, and my sister, Lizzie." Lizzie literally jumps off her chair to greet him in a fashion not too dissimilar to the greeting her Labrador gives people. She throws her arms around him and kisses him on the cheek, giving him no choice but to accept her enthusiastic greeting.

"So pleased to finally meet you!" she gushes.

Duncan, as chilled as ever, gets up and greets James the same way he would any of his mates at the pub. He holds out a hand to shake.

"Pleasure to meet you, mate!" he says and rolls his eyes at James and the effect he's had on the women. "They don't react like this when I walk in the room." He laughs. James appreciates his humour.

My dad finally turns around, drying his hands on a tea towel. "James! Lovely to meet… holy shit!"

"Keith!" Mum reprimands him for swearing.

"Nikki, when you said James and he works in the film industry, you failed to mention it was James Keller!"

"Did I?" I say casually, taking a crisp from the table. "Sorry about that." I smirk. James is amused by this but takes charge, offering a firm handshake to my dad.

"James Keller," he confirms with a smile. "Pleasure to meet you, sir. This is for you." He hands my dad a very nice bottle of whisky he bought as a gift.

"Oh, wow! This looks like a very expensive bottle of whisky!" Dad says, admiring the bottle with its navy label adorned with deer antlers.

"It's a thirty-year-old single malt. Nikki tells me you appreciate a good malt," James confirms, looking pleased that my dad looks pleased.

"I do indeed. Well, thank you, thank you very much. We shall have a glass later. Anyway, please, call me Keith, and this is my lovely wife, Mandy," he says, placing an arm around Mum's shoulder, and I notice she's turned a light shade of crimson.

"Hello," she says timidly.

"Hi," says James, stepping forwards and kissing her on the cheek. "And this is for you." He hands her a pretty paper bag containing a bouquet of flowers and a beautiful box of very expensive dark chocolates. That light shade of crimson deepens to a rich, dark hue.

"Thank you, James. These are lovely," she says.

Once introductions are over and everyone has recovered, we head outside into the garden with our drinks. James looks around and admires the lush surroundings.

"Wow. This is a beautiful garden," he compliments Mum while helping her bring some nibbles outside. "Do you look after it yourself?"

The back garden is large and quite formal, stretching far into the distance with a huge lawn. There's a tennis court with a summer house, and nearer the house is a play area that my parents built when Lizzie had her girls. It's bark-covered, with a couple of swings, a pretty wooden playhouse, a slide and a climbing frame.

"Well, we do have a gardener to help, but Keith and I do most of it ourselves. It's hard work," she tells him.

"Well, it's beautiful. I can see where Nikki gets her green fingers from." Mum smiles at him, clearly pleased.

"So, James," Dad starts, and I wonder what he's going to say. "The new film is out now, right? Mandy and I were planning on going to see it. I loved the first one!"

"Oh great, let me know what you think. Nikki and I were at the London premiere a couple of weeks ago, weren't we?" James looks at me and I glance at Dad.

"You were at the premiere?" Dad looks stunned. "You lucky thing. How was it?"

"It was very good," I tell him, smiling widely.

"I saw the pictures online of the red carpet," Lizzie pipes up.

"You were on the red carpet?" Now Mum looks stunned.

"No, I wasn't. I met James inside the cinema. He did the red carpet; I ran down it as quickly as I could and hid inside." I laugh.

"Well, hopefully, next time, you'll be on it with me."

"Why weren't you this time?" Duncan asks matter-of-factly.

"Because nobody knows about us. It's not public knowledge, or at least it wasn't until last night," I reply. Duncan looks confused. "We had dinner out last night with Gina Rossi and her husband, Clive."

"Gina Rossi!" exclaims Lizzie, taking a large gulp of wine.

"Yep." I smile at her. "There were quite a few people outside the restaurant when we left, so, Liz, you might see those photos online too." She reaches for her phone and starts searching, and I roll my eyes at her.

"Found them!" she announces a few minutes later. She shows Duncan, who just nods. Then she hands her phone to Mum and Dad, who examine the pictures.

"Very nice," says Dad. "You both look happy." James squeezes my hand again.

They pass the phone to me and James, and now I see it with my own eyes. I'm a little shocked to see myself on the internet and in a picture with him, but I think Lizzie and Dad are right – we do look good together. The headline reads:

'James Keller Steps Out with Mystery Woman—Is Romance in the Air for the Hollywood Heartthrob?'

"We do look good together," he says.
I nod, smiling. "Yes, we do."

'James Keller was all smiles as he stepped out for dinner with a mystery date in London on Friday night. James, currently in town for his latest film's promotion, dined out in the heart of Mayfair with actress Gina Rossi and her husband, Clive. The trio was joined by a stunning brunette, who appeared to be James's date for the evening.

'The group exited the restaurant together, with James and his date holding hands and smiling as they swiftly made their way to an awaiting car. This public appearance has sparked curiosity and speculation, especially since this mystery woman bears a striking resemblance to the brunette he was pictured with in a London nightclub back in April.'

A picture follows of James and me in the nightclub the night we first met; the same one Lizzie showed me back then.

'Keller hasn't publicly dated anyone since his

split with Watts three years ago. Has the Hollywood heartthrob found love again? James's team have not yet commented on the event.'

I chuckle as I read the rest of the article. "And here we are again, back to discussing your biceps."

James grins, flexing playfully. "Well, they do get a lot of attention."

Dad laughs, shaking his head. "It's good to see the media isn't too harsh. You both look great in that picture."

Lizzie, still scrolling through her phone, nods. "You two are definitely the new hot topic. Just look at the comments."

I take a peek at her screen, seeing a flood of comments from fans and curious onlookers, all speculating about our relationship. Some are supportive, while others are simply curious. It's a mixed bag, but I feel a strange sense of pride seeing us together like this.

Mum looks thoughtful. "You'll have to navigate this carefully, Nikki. The media can be relentless."

"I know, Mum," I reply.

James nods, his expression serious. "We've talked about it. I have a good team behind me, and I'll make sure she's looked after."

Mum looks at James, considering his words. "That's good to hear. Do you see the articles written online about you, James?" she asks.

He gives a small, self-assured smile. "I see some of them. Most of them I ignore. People are going to say what they are going to say. I know who I am and so do the people who matter. My agent or my sister alert me to things that might need my attention, but this doesn't need my attention." He gestures towards the article. "I like this one." He winks at me, and Mum seems satisfied with his answer and calm demeanour.

Dad, always keen on discussing his passions, seizes the opportunity to delve into car talk with James. Duncan was never really interested, so I can see he's really pleased to have someone to talk to about them. "You're into cars, aren't you?" he asks, with a gleam of excitement in his eyes.

James nods. "Absolutely. I've always had a fascination with them."

Dad's eyes light up. "Well, I've got something in the garage you might be interested in. It's a bit of a gem."

Lizzie and I exchange knowing smiles. We both know what's coming next. Dad's prized possession – a 1988 Ferrari 328 GTS in black – is his pride and joy, a car he adores more than anything, more than Mum, I think. It's pristine. Dad lures James off into the garage to admire it while Mum heads back inside and Duncan takes the girls off to play some tennis, leaving me and Lizzie to enjoy the sunshine.

"James and Dad are going to hit it off," Lizzie remarks, grinning. "They both love cars too much."

I laugh. "It's true. Dad talks non-stop about that Ferrari. He'll be in his element showing it off."

"He's nice." Lizzie swoons. "Gorgeous. Does he chew with his mouth open?" she asks, knowing this is one of my pet hates.

"No," I reply.

"Eat spaghetti with a knife and fork or spoon and fork?"

"Spoon and fork, and he can cook!"

"Shut the front door, I'd marry him in a heartbeat!" She laughs.

"Hmmm, he's hot," I say, not able to stop myself from grinning.

"Cheers to you and your hot man, darling." Lizzie raises her glass to mine. "Seriously, I hope he's everything you want, deserve, and more," she says, looking genuinely pleased for me.

"I hope so too."

There's always a risk that famous people never turn out how you expect them to be when you meet them – never meet your heroes, isn't that what they say? But so far, he's not disappointed me.

"He's so much more mature than Karl, which makes him very sexy in my eyes." I give her a little wink. "He knows what he wants, and he gets it. I could put him in any situation, and he'd handle it, unlike that stupid ex-husband of mine, who couldn't cope with anything. He couldn't organise a piss-up in a brewery. James is very different – he takes care of things, he gets things done, and I really like that."

So much with Karl was on my head. Anything that needed to be done had to be done by me. I don't get that feeling with James – he's proactive, which is a refreshing change. "He's so manly," I say, and we giggle like we used to when we were teenagers.

"That's what you need. Karl was a lazy arse. Does he know about Karl?" she asks.

"He knows about him, but not everything," I tell her. She nods sympathetically.

"How long before Dad takes James out for a drive in

that car, do you think?" She smiles. And right on cue, Dad pokes his head out from the garage door.

"Nik?" he calls out. "I'm just taking James for a spin!" Lizzie and I laugh.

"Sure thing, Dad," I shout back. "Have fun!"

Half an hour later and they are back. Duncan has warmed the BBQ for us, and Dad gets cracking with the cooking. James comes and sits next to me on the sofa. He looks like he's had a great time.

"Hey," he says, giving me a kiss, making me feel warm and fuzzy inside.

"You had fun?"

"Yeah, it was great, fantastic car!" He beams like a kid in a candy shop.

"I'm glad you enjoyed it. Dad looked over the moon to have someone appreciate it as much as he does."

"Yeh, we had a great chat about cars. He's really knowledgeable."

"That he is," I agree, glancing over at Dad, who is now engrossed in turning the burgers and sausages.

"You're officially in his good books now." Lizzie smiles at him.

"Well, that's a relief," James says with a mock sigh of relief.

The smell of the BBQ wafts over, and I can hear the sizzle of the meat. The girls come running over, their faces flushed from playing tennis, and Duncan follows behind, looking equally flushed.

"Food's almost ready," Dad announces.

"Great, I'm starving," Duncan says, rubbing his hands together.

The food is delicious as always; my parents know how to put on a good spread. The alcohol flows nicely and the sun is shining. It's a beautiful day, and everyone is relaxed. After food, Dad and Duncan get out the garden games, all sorts of games, from the very British middle-class croquet on the lawn to skittles with tin cans. It's a very enjoyable afternoon.

I relished seeing James interact with my family; he got on well with everyone, and Rose and Poppy loved him. He pushed them on the swings and even got involved in a game of tennis with them, Poppy and James versus Rose and Duncan; it melted my heart.

The sun is setting over the garden and Mum notes it's the girls' bedtime but Lizzie and Duncan are nowhere to be seen.

"Ganma?" asks Poppy. "Who is taking us to bed?"

"I don't know, sweetheart. Where's Mummy and Daddy?" she asks her, kneeling down to her height.

"They are in the kitchen…" Poppy wraps her arms around herself in a self-hug and starts wiggling and pouting her lips. "Kissing," she says finally and giggles. We all burst out with laughter.

"She's so dramatic!" Dad chuckles at her cuteness. "Watch out, James, she'll be after a role in one of your films!" James laughs and then Lizzie and Duncan appear from the house, and I'm sure I see Lizzie adjusting her blouse! James gives me a sideways glance; he's noticed too.

"Bedtime, girls! Say good night to everyone, please," Lizzie instructs them. They make their way around to each of us and give us a cuddle and kiss. They reach James and Poppy throws her arms around him, like mother like daughter, I think.

"Thank you for playing tennis with us," she says in her cute little voice.

"You are most welcome," he says, leaning forwards to embrace her hug. "It was fun."

"You speak funny!" she blurts out, and we laugh again, and with that, Lizzie ushers them both out of the room.

It's about 11pm when we retire to bed, having had a fair amount to drink over quite a long period of time. We're tired. We snuggle down under the duvet, skin on skin. I lay my head on his chest.

"Your family are nice," he says, stroking my arm.

"You were a hit with Dad," I tell him.

"You think?"

"I do, and Poppy and Lizzie obviously love you!"

James laughs. "I'm pleased. That's a nice car he's got there. I might have to get one myself. If I did, do you think he'd let me store it in his garage with his until I find somewhere more permanent to keep it?" I can't work out if he's joking or if he's serious. I assume joking; why would he store a car over here and not in the US?

"I'm sure he would."

He holds me closer and kisses me goodnight. We are just settling into slumber when I hear a faint noise coming from somewhere, the room next door.

"Can you hear that?" I whisper to James. He lifts his head off the pillow slightly to listen.

"Yes," he says, and a huge grin spreads across his face. Oh my word, Lizzie and Duncan are in the room next to us.

"I'm mortified," I say. "I hope it doesn't last long."

"Well, if they're anything like us…" he says, turning to face me with that twinkle in his eye I'm now familiar with.

I can't help but laugh. "You're incorrigible."

"Guilty as charged," he whispers, leaning in to kiss me again.

"Thank goodness Mum and Dad are on the other side of the house!" I whisper.

"They are? In that case, you want to give Lizzie and Duncan a run for their money?"

"We can't!" I protest, but only slightly as he runs his fingers up my thigh.

"You said your parents are on the other side of the house. This is a pretty big house." He kisses me and my body aches for him. I cannot resist the Hollywood love mist as he begins to move slowly and deliberately above me.

Thirty-One

The next morning, I head downstairs, leaving James to get dressed after his shower. Mum and Lizzie are bustling around in the kitchen making breakfast.

"Hi," I say as I walk in, trying to mask the remnants of a sleepless night.

"Morning, Nik, good night?" Lizzie's voice is tinged with a hint of sarcasm. I raise my eyebrows at her, and she lets out a quiet laugh.

"Did you sleep well?" asks Mum. "Where's James?"

"He's just getting dressed; he'll be down soon," I reply, and I can see Lizzie's eyes light up. "Stop it!" I tease her.

Mum's expression shifts, her concern turning into something more pointed. "He seems very lovely, Nikki, but are you sure you want this? I mean, this is not going to be a *normal* relationship, is it? And you failed at your last one—"

"Mum!" Lizzie interjects sharply, stepping in to defend me.

"It's fine, Liz," I say, trying to stay calm despite the sting in Mum's words. "Mum, I didn't fail at my marriage. Karl did." I pause, take a breath, and decide it's about time she knew he was an arse instead of the wonderful person she thought he was. "He cheated on me, with one of his students!" I watch as Mum's face drains of colour, disbelief etched across her. Lizzie nods in agreement.

"It's true, Mum," she says.

"You knew about this?" Mum's voice is strained. Her gaze flickers between Lizzie and me, the hurt evident in her eyes. "Does your dad know?"

"Dad doesn't know," I say, with a sharp edge to my voice. "Turns out you're not the best judge of character after all. I was trapped in a loveless marriage, Mum. There was no affection, no attention. It was like living with a ghost."

"You worked all the time!" she snaps, trying to deflect back at me.

"I worked because I had nothing at home. I wanted more, but Karl made no effort. He was lazy, uninterested. And then, to top it all off, he was unfaithful. His stupid student broadcast it on social media, and Lizzie happened to see it. That's when I finally had the courage to file for divorce."

"Why didn't you tell me?" she asks, sounding shocked.

"Because I knew you would have blamed me!" I retort, with another sting. Mum takes a seat at the table. "It wouldn't have changed anything. I wanted out before I even knew about the affair." I sigh and take a seat at the breakfast bar; it feels better to have it out in the open. "With James, it's different. He lights up my life."

Mum cuts me off, her voice a mix of scepticism and concern. "I'm sure he does. And he seems like a lovely man. But he's from a completely different world. How do you plan to fit in?"

"There you go again, trying to put doubt in my head!" I feel anger rising in me, but I'm determined not to let it show. "I don't have all the answers. I don't know how it's going to work, but I do know I care about him deeply. James has more emotional intelligence in his little finger than Karl had in his entire body. Karl could barely wipe his own fucking arse!"

"Nikki!" Mum scolds me like I'm ten years old again.

"And the sex is fantastic!" I snap, digging the knife a little further. Lizzie chokes on her coffee, and Mum's glare intensifies.

Just then, Dad walks in from the garden joyfully, completely oblivious to the tense atmosphere. Mum stands again, busying herself with wiping the countertop.

"Ah, my three favourite ladies, good morning! Where's Duncan and James?" he asks, getting himself a glass of water.

"Duncs is upstairs helping the girls get dressed," Lizzie informs him.

"Ah, he's a good man!" he says, gently placing a hand on Lizzie's shoulder. "And James? I still can't believe he's here!" Dad's eyes light up with excitement. "He's still here, isn't he?"

"He is, he'll be down in a minute," I say.

Dad puts his arm around my shoulder and pulls me in. "Well, I think he's a great guy, Nikki. You look happy with him, and that makes me happy," he says, planting a kiss on my forehead.

"Thanks, Dad," I say. The kitchen door opens and James strides in. "Good morning, James, did you sleep okay?" Dad asks him.

"I slept very well, thank you, Keith. Good morning, Mandy. Hi, Lizzie."

"Can I get you a drink, James?" Mum offers. "We've got coffee, tea, orange juice."

"An OJ would be great, thank you."

I really need a cuddle from him after my confrontation with Mum; he seems to sense this as he walks up behind me and envelops me in his arms. "Hi, baby," he says, kissing the side of my head. I melt into him. I'm in love, completely and utterly in love.

After breakfast, we gather our things, ready to leave to go and meet James's sister.

"Pleasure to meet you, Keith. I hope to see you again," he says to Dad, shaking his hand.

"Likewise, James, take care of my girl."

"I will." He kisses Mum on the cheek and thanks her for her hospitality and fantastic cooking; my mum smiles at him and wishes us a safe journey. Lizzie grabs both me and James in for a group hug.

"So lovely to finally meet you," she gushes.

"I'll message you later," I say, prising her off us.

Duncan casually shakes his hand. "Good to meet you, mate. Have a great trip to Wales – see you again."

"We will have a great trip. Good to meet you too, buddy!" replies James.

Thirty-Two

It takes thirty minutes to drive to his sister Louise's house from my parents'. I can tell they share a close bond straight away as he sweeps her up in a bear hug, lifting her off the ground.

"I've missed you, sis!" he says to her. They are close in age too; she is fifteen months younger than him, whereas Dianne, his other sister, is three years older than him. Louise and James went to the same school, different years but had the same circle of friends growing up. Her British husband, Robert, is also there and seems to get on well with James. Louise still has a soft American accent despite living here for the past ten years.

Rather than going out, Louise decides to make lunch at home. With James and their three young children – two girls and a boy – going out would be too chaotic. This way, we can chat without too many interruptions. She tells me how she's now a full-time mum. She used to teach children back in the States, but in her late twenties, she took a secondment to travel, which was when she met Robert, over here in the UK, and the rest, as they say, is history. They live in a nice, detached house, not unlike my sister's. Robert, I find out, is a highly sought-after paediatric surgeon.

We don't spend as long with Louise as she would like as we've got a long drive ahead of us. James gives the children a parting gift of noisy musical instruments, much to his sister's dismay.

"Maybe we will see more of you now you have another reason to be here," she says to him, nodding towards me.

"Maybe you will," he says, scooping her up in another hug.

She wraps her arms around me as we say our goodbyes. "So lovely to meet you," she says. "Please try and get him to come over more often," she pleads with me. I can see James smiling at us.

"I will do my best," I say, and of course I'd like nothing more than to have him here more often, permanently maybe.

When James said 'just the two of us' going away, what he actually meant was us two and Sean, oh and Allison as Nigel wasn't able to come. The place we've rented has a smaller annex for them to stay in, and James even hired a separate car for them with the promise that we wouldn't know they were there.

We share the drive to Wales with me taking the first half and James taking the second half and make a quick pit stop at the service station to use the facilities and grab a snack. James dons a baseball cap and sunglasses, keeping his head down to go undetected – it works! Sitting in the car, eating our fast food in the romantic setting of a motorway service station, James turns to me and tells me he overheard my discussion with my mum this morning.

"I didn't want to eavesdrop, but you sounded like you were having a moment," he says, apologetically.

"It's fine. What did you hear?" I ask, trying to think back to exactly what I said.

"I was just about to come into the kitchen when I heard you tell your mum about your ex having an affair. I'm guessing she didn't know?"

"No, she didn't. Seriously, I'm fed up with her thinking it was all my fault and that I didn't try hard enough. She doesn't believe in divorce. She thinks it's the easy option," I say, trying not to get frustrated again. He nods sympathetically.

"I'm sorry he did that to you," he says, taking hold of my hand.

"I must admit, I didn't think he would do something like that. I never pegged him as a cheater, and even though in my head it was over, it still wasn't nice."

"I know," he says, kissing my hand; of course he does. "Onwards and upwards?" He tries to cheer things up. "By the way, the sex is fantastic, is it?" He raises an eyebrow and smiles at me; I feel myself blush.

"It is," I state. I might as well own it!

"I can't argue with that!"

As we drive into Wales, we drive along a long winding road that seems to go on for miles, passing through picturesque villages. Finally, we arrive at the village we are staying in; it reminds me of where my parents live, only prettier: small stone houses, a village shop, and a pub. We drive over a little bridge that crosses a stream and turn in to a no-through road.

"I guess we are down here, then?" James says.

"I guess so," I reply, feeling excited. There are only a few houses on this road; it's surrounded by fields. We find ours and pull up to the wooden five-bar gate, which I get out at and open as James pulls onto the large sweeping drive. Sean's car is already there.

The house, named Aprils Cottage, is long and seemingly narrow, with at least three chimney breasts. It's white and looks like it should have a thatched roof, but it has a dark slate roof instead. The backdrop to the house is a mountain. The locals probably call it a hill – looks like a mountain to me!

The keys are in a key box tucked away at the side of the house; the owners gave us the code so we could let ourselves in. James gets our cases out of the car as I unlock the front door, and I step into a small hallway painted white with light grey carpeted stairs leading up to the first floor. I open the door on the left, which leads into a large but cosy country-style kitchen. There is a log burner on the far side, chimney number one. James comes in a few moments later.

"This is nice," he says.

"It is," I say, looking around and admiring; it's got a lovely country cottage feel about it. He stands behind me and puts his arm around my waist.

"Think we'll be okay here for a few days?" he asks.

"I think we will be fine," I say, leaning into him.

We explore the rest of the house. Downstairs there is a big lounge with a huge inglenook and a nice log burner –

chimney number two – a wooden coffee table and a couple of sofas. There's a nice dining room, a utility room, a large boot room and a downstairs bathroom. Upstairs there are four bedrooms, all nicely decorated in neutrals, with king beds in each. A modern family bathroom, and the master suite has an open fire with logs on ready to use, chimney number three. We take our cases upstairs and unpack a few bits, light the fire, and get ourselves ready to turn in for a snuggle; it's been a long day.

The following morning is grey and overcast, with rain in the forecast. We unpack the rest of our belongings and head to the local supermarket in the next town, about a ten-minute drive. It's mid- morning on a Monday, so we hope it will be quiet, and we're right. James dons his usual disguise of a baseball cap but skips the sunglasses today, too "super-star-ish," he says. Instead, he pulls the rim down lower over his face.

As we push a pound into the trolley and walk through the automatic doors, a thrill runs through me; I always find it exciting when he gets spotted. We stock up on fresh groceries, agreeing to eat in every night except the last, when we'll find a pub. If we get spotted, then at least we'll be leaving the next day.

We brought our own tea and coffee, so we grab pasta, tinned tomatoes, bread, yoghurts, fish from the counter, chicken, and a few other bits – anything we don't use can come home with us. But I don't want to think about home right now; I want to savour every second of this holiday.

James unloads the trolley while I organise the items on the conveyor belt. I pay, allowing him to walk straight through without interruption.

We get home and unpack the shopping, then explore the garden before the rain sets in too hard. There is about an acre of land with the property, part of which is a formal garden. The rest is wild. It's very private. We spend the afternoon playing board games and watching a film. James has a script to review, so he reads some of it to me. I find it fascinating, especially when he asks me to play the role of the female lead. My attempts at acting leave us in fits of laughter, as my skills are less than stellar. Finally, we indulge in a bit of fun in the hot tub outside. Despite the rain, the tub is undercover beneath a charming thatched roof adorned with fairy lights. The warm water and the enchanting atmosphere make it feel as if we are in the Caribbean.

Thirty-Three

The next four days are perfect for exploring as the weather improves: sunny and warm but not too hot, ideal for walking. We stay away from the more touristy areas and go off the beaten track. James has excellent orienteering skills; in fact, I'd love to see him team up with Bear Grylls. He decides the route each day, the difficulty level depending on how energetic we feel, which depends on how much we slept the night before!

We discover the most beautiful, picturesque views. The rugged terrain can be challenging, but the long U-shaped valleys are incredible. On the first day, we take a packed lunch and eat by the side of a serene lake, which is very romantic. It reminds me of Norway; the trees reflecting perfectly in the deep dark water against the backdrop of mountains is quite breathtaking. But then nature calls. That's not quite so romantic; thankfully there's no one around at that time!

We pass plenty of people on our walks. Everyone says

hello, and only one group stops us for a picture. An older couple chats with us for a good five minutes, sharing tips on places to visit. They either don't recognise James or simply don't care. Perhaps they don't know of him, but I find that unlikely.

The rest of the days, we opt to eat out for lunch. We stumble across charming cafés and country pubs, where we aren't quite so anonymous. Several people approach James, asking for pictures. Thankfully everyone is nice. I take lots of photos, more of James than the scenery, some of him alone and quite a few of both of us together with panoramic views behind us. I think about framing one for home, maybe another for James to take back to the States. Ping goes another heart string.

"I just love it here," I say as we start our descent back down a mountain on our last day of hiking. "It's so tranquil and there's so much more to explore." It's not my first time here. I have walked this part of the world once or twice before as a child on family holidays, but there's something magical about it this time. I appreciate it much more as an adult.

"It is, it's beautiful," he says thoughtfully. "I'm really glad we did this."

"Me too. You okay?" I ask him, noticing he seems quieter than normal.

"I'm fine." He smiles, pulling me close and putting his arm around my shoulder. "Look at that." He points at a bird of prey swooping in the distance. "Do you know what type of bird that is?"

"Hmm, Dad would know better than me. Maybe an osprey or buzzard?"

James laughs. "I love that you're a fountain of knowledge."

"Are you being sarcastic?" I laugh.

He leans into my ear and whispers seriously, "Not being sarcastic. I love it. I love you." My heart stops. His hand tightens around my shoulder. I turn to look at him, and he's gazing right at me.

The sky above us rumbles, like continuous thunder that's getting louder by the second, and the ground beneath begins to vibrate. I don't know what to do, look adoringly at him or run for cover. It's deafening! Louder and louder. I cover my ears. James does the same, but I see he's grinning, whereas I'm petrified! Two fighter jets fly right below us, low and fast, sweeping through the mountains. I watch, fingers in my ears, and in a nanosecond, they're gone.

"This is the Mach Loop!" he shouts over the echoing sound. "Are you okay?" He pulls me back in and wraps his arms around me.

"Holy shit! The what?" I catch my breath. "That scared the living daylights out of me!" I hold him tightly.

"Sorry, babe, I forgot to mention we might see one or two of those. The RAF training base is close by."

"My heart can't cope with another one!"

"Awesome bit of flying, and great timing." He looks down at me with his intense dark eyes, and my heart is in my mouth again. "I mean it, I love you," he says softly. I think I've known for a while that I was in love with him but to hear him say he feels it too is the most amazing feeling ever; I could cry.

"You do?" He nods at me and watches my expression,

waiting for my response. "That makes me very happy," I tell him.

"It does?"

"It does, because…" I pause; the flutters are kicking in hard. "I love you too."

Thirty-Four

That evening, we stroll down to the local pub, just us arm in arm. No chauffeur-driven car, no visible security. It's nice, it's normal. A few patrons sit outside enjoying the last of the evening sun, too engrossed in conversation to notice us.

Inside, we're greeted by an older chap with a bit of a beer belly and grey hair standing behind the bar.

"Hello," he says joyfully in his Welsh accent, his eyes widening as he does a double take. "James Keller?" I guess he doesn't get many Hollywood A-list celebrities walking into his pub like a regular customer that often.

James smiles his famous smile. "Hi."

"Well, I never, what brings you to my pub?" He grins.

"We've been on vacation around here," James replies.

"A holiday in lovely Wales? Well, *croeso i Gymru*," he says, offering a hand to James. "It means welcome to Wales!"

"Thank you!" James accepts his hand.

"I hope you're having a good time?"

James looks at me and smiles. "Yeah, we're having a great time."

"You are most welcome here. Are you dining with us tonight or just wanting a refreshing drink?"

"Dining, if we may?" I reply.

"Of course! There's a nice table over there, tucked away," he says, pointing to a table in an alcove in front of a window with views into the pretty beer garden. He escorts us, hands us menus, and takes our drinks order.

A few moments later, he brings over a chilled bottle of wine with two glasses, pours us each a glass, places the wine in a cooler, and leaves us to it. James raises his glass to mine.

"Cheers, baby," he says, his eyes locking onto mine. I love his eye contact. Whenever I raised a glass with Karl, he'd always look away.

"Cheers, darling," I say, clinking his glass.

"Have you enjoyed our vacation?" he asks, not breaking eye contact.

"I have enjoyed our *holiday* immensely," I tease, holding his gaze and smiling.

"Good. Me too," he says and picks up his menu.

"Are you okay?" I ask, noticing his distraction.

"Mmm hmm," he replies, seemingly in a world of his own. I wonder if he feels worried about being alone without security.

I browse through the menu – steak pie, haddock and chips, butternut risotto – but I quite fancy a curry tonight. Homemade fragrant Sri Lankan chicken curry or sweet potato massaman curry – oh, which to choose? James interrupts my serious decision-making.

"So, what do you fancy?"

"I think a curry, but not sure which one," I say. "What about you?"

"Maybe the same," he replies. He puts down his menu, his expression serious. "Actually, before we decide, there's something I want to talk to you about, something I want to ask you."

"What's that?" I ask casually while still trying to decide which curry to have.

He pauses before answering. "I wondered, if you wanted to move in with me?"

I look up from my menu, not sure I've heard him right. "I'm sorry, what?"

He looks at me intensely. "Move in together," he says. "Hear me out, my suggestion is we live here, in the UK, London."

I stare at him, trying to digest what he's asking; curry has long gone from my mind. "I know that moving to the States would not be ideal for you, and I've been considering a move out of the States for a while, and given I travel all over the world, it's not such a big deal to me. I have family and friends over here, I can do business as easily here as I can in the States, I like it here, and I spend a fair amount of time here anyway. I'd still travel a lot, though. That won't change anytime soon."

"What about your family in the US?" I ask, my heart pounding as I try to keep up with his words.

"They will be fine. I don't see that much of Dianne, and my parents are used to me not being around. Louise, on the other hand, would be over the moon if I was here."

"She certainly would," I agree.

"So, my suggestion is, if you're agreeable, that we find somewhere in London to rent short term, somewhere furnished, and we move into that for a few months to see how we go. You keep your apartment in Richmond. If, after a period of time, we're still happy, then we look for something more permanent, although… I'm not sure I'd want to be in London permanently. I think I'd rather be further south with easy access to London."

"Further south suits me. Are you serious?"

"Very," he states.

"You'd move to the UK for me?"

"I absolutely would." He smiles warmly at me and takes my hand over the table. "From the moment we met in London that night, I knew you were special, so what do you say?"

"I say yes! One thousand per cent yes!" My jaw aches from smiling so hard.

We enjoy our pub meal undisturbed. I chose the Sri Lankan curry, and it was delicious. The bar manager, who we find out is called Clive, approaches to check we are okay. We ask for the bill, and he hurries off to fetch it. He's been extremely attentive this evening; nothing has been too much trouble. We pay our bill and leave a generous tip. As we are about to leave, he asks for a photo of him with James, and me. I'm slightly taken aback that he wants me in it too. We stand either side of him in front of the bar, while another member of staff, a young lad, in his late teens, takes the picture. Then he asks for one with us and all the staff, of course. James, being James, agrees; I think he secretly likes it. The chef comes out to the bar to join us with two other bar staff, the young boy and Clive's wife. The next thing you know James is buying everyone, including the fifteen-odd punters, a round of drinks and we are behind the bar pulling the pints! It was hilarious. I can't pull a pint to save my life! The head on mine was almost the entire glass! James, of course, was much more skilled at it than I was. We drank a bit more and chatted with the staff and customers. Loads of photos were taken, James signed some beer mats, and everyone had a thoroughly good time, including me and James!

An hour later, Sean picks us up and drives us back to our holiday home. I can honestly say that this is the first time I've seen Sean all week. I'm impressed.

It's late. James is already in bed as I walk over. He opens the duvet for me to get in.

"That was a fun evening!" I say, snuggling into his chest.

"It was, I enjoyed it. Are you tired?" he asks.

"A little," I reply.

He moves his arm from around my shoulder and turns on his side to face me. "When we get back, I'll get Allison on the case to shortlist a few apartments, then you can pick which one you like."

"Do you not want to choose with me?"

"Yes, but Allison knows what I need in terms of security etcetera, so you can have the final decision. I want you to be happy there. By the way, you won't pay for it; I will sort it."

I prop myself up on one elbow. "James, I can't let you pay for everything. I want to contribute."

He takes hold of my hand. "Listen, I know you earn good money, but the kind of places we'll be looking at come with a hefty price tag. We need privacy and security. Please, let me handle this. It's important to me that you're safe and comfortable."

"I understand, but it feels unfair," I say, feeling a bit guilty. He looks at me. "Okay, if you're sure." I nod.

"I am," he says, kissing my hand.

"I'll buy the food, then?"

"Deal." I move a bit closer; he holds me tight and sighs a happy sigh. "I was nervous about asking you to move in with me," he says.

"You don't get nervous? Surely not!" I tease. "You needn't have been."

"I love you."

"I love you too."

I'm just drifting off to sleep when a thought suddenly occurs to me. "James?" I say quietly.

He murmurs.

"What about Sean?"

"Sean? What about him?"

"If you move over here, what will he do? The guy has barely said two words to me since we met but I feel a strange fondness towards him."

James gives a little laugh.

"He's a good guy, very loyal and trustworthy, but yes, he can be a little standoffish. I wouldn't take it personally. I strongly suspect he will come with me; I hope so anyway."

Thirty-Five

We return to London the next day and have an early dinner with Mark, Julia, and their children at their house. James and I share our news over a bottle of champagne, and they are delighted for us. I'm not sure who is more excited. Mark's face lights up as it dawns on him: he'll have his best mate in town.

"That's fantastic news, mate, be nice to have you around more," he says, clinking glasses with James.

Julia is beaming at the prospect. "Oh my God!" she squeals. "I'm so excited for you both!" I can almost see her planning her wedding outfit.

Mark leans back in his chair, a contented smile on his face. "So, when do you start looking for places?"

"Allison is already on it," James replies, squeezing my hand. "We'll be looking at a few options soon enough."

It's Sunday, and James has just left to return to the States. I dial my dad's mobile number. He answers on the second ring.

"Hi, love, are you back? Did you have a nice time?"

"I had an amazing time, Dad. It was brilliant. Is Mum there too?"

"Yes, she's here, let me put you on speaker, hold on… can you hear me?"

"Yes, I can. Hi, Mum."

"Hi, darling, how are you? How was Wales?"

I spend a few minutes filling them in on where we stayed, what we did, and what it's like being with James. Then I take a deep breath.

"He's asked me to move in with him." I let what I've just said sink in for a few moments.

"Do you mean move to New York?" Mum asks.

"No, he says he'd move here. He travels so much, it doesn't really make a difference where he's based, but he knows it would be harder for me to move there. So, he suggested we rent an apartment in London for a few months, test the waters and take it from there. Don't worry, I will keep my flat."

"Well, that sounds very sensible," says Dad.

"Have you agreed?" Mum sounds a little concerned.

"I have. It feels right, Mum. I feel totally different about him than I did about Karl, and no, before you ask, it's not just because he's James Keller. He's just James to me."

"Well, I'll admit, you both looked very happy when we met him. I didn't ever see that side of you when you were with Karl, so I'm pleased for you." I think that might be Mum's way of saying sorry.

"I'm bloody over the moon!" Dad announces over the phone. "And he's *the* James Keller to me!" We laugh. That wasn't as hard as I thought it might be.

Lizzie was beside herself with excitement when I rang her next. Now, I need to start telling some of my closest friends and my colleagues.

I agree to meet Claire for coffee that afternoon in Richmond. We find a cosy little coffee shop not far from where I live; it's busy, so I ask Claire to grab a quiet table in the corner while I order a cappuccino for us both. I decide to get straight to the point when I get back to the table with our drinks.

"So, I've some news for you," I start.

"Ooh sounds exciting, pray tell."

I scroll through my messages from Lizzie and find the link she sent of my first public outing with James and hand Claire the phone. She studies it for a moment, her brows furrowed in concentration.

"That's you," she says, looking slightly confused. "Isn't it?"

"It is," I confirm.

"With… James Keller?"

I've heard this quite a few times now. "Yep."

"You're holding his hand, what the… how, why, when?"

"I'm dating him… more than that, actually. This may be a bit of a shock, so I apologise, but we're moving in together."

She looks up at me with a serious expression. "Are you serious? That is a shock. How did you meet him?" She looks at the article again.

"Remember Lewis? Lewis who stood me up?"

"Yeah…"

"I met James that night. He very chivalrously stepped in and asked me to dine with him as I had been stood up."

"But that was months ago?"

"I know. I didn't say anything partly because of who he is, but also I didn't know back then what it was or if it would lead to anything other than just dinner. Lucky for me it did and here we are. We just got back from a hiking holiday in Wales yesterday."

"I'd say you're bloody lucky. James Keller! Where is he now?"

"On his way back to the States. He asked me this weekend to move in with him and I agreed."

Her eyes widen in shock. "Well, I am gobsmacked but pleased for you. Oh my God, my friend is dating James Keller!" she says excitedly. She leans over and places her hand on mine. "You deserve it after Karl. Where will you live? I mean, in which country?" She smiles.

"Thanks, hun, I'm really happy. He's moving to London. We are going to rent for a while and see how it goes."

"Bloody fantastic, I can't believe it... So, tell me all about him...?"

I walk through the swing doors into the office reception. The usual security guy is sitting behind the desk, waiting to clock off from the night shift. He gives me a nod as I walk past and into the main open-plan area towards my office on the ground floor. The office is quiet; no one is around, except, today, I notice Ivy, my PA, is at her desk already, which is unusual. She's not normally there until 8:30am, and it's just gone 7:45am. I walk over to her; she looks up suddenly from her screen when she hears me approaching.

"Good morning, Ivy, you're here early and looking

rather sheepish," I say, hovering over her desk. She spins her chair and looks at me.

"Good morning, Nikki," she says, leaning back in her chair, twiddling a biro between her fingers.

"What are you up to?" I ask. I have a very good relationship with Ivy. I've worked with her for eight years, and she's been my PA for two. She's seen me through my junior roles to where I am now, and I adore her. She's outspoken, not afraid to tell me or anyone, for that matter, what's what, and she swears like a trooper. Most people are afraid of her, but she has the biggest heart, and she's very efficient.

She's Nigerian-born but spent most of her life in Britain. Four years younger than me and has the most amazing wardrobe. I love clothes; I like to think I'm quite stylish, but she's another level, sexy and sassy. Today she's dressed in faux leather, which consists of a black pencil skirt that sits below the knee, which is a surprise, and a dark green faux leather bodice with black lace trim covering her shoulders, teamed with killer heels. She has a fantastic figure, perfectly balanced between bum and boobs, boobs she's not afraid to show. Her long afro hair is braided and highlighted blonde today; the last time I saw her, it was highlighted pink.

"I am not up to anything." She looks up at me knowingly. "The question is, what are *you* up to?" I smile at her because I know exactly where this is going.

"Come with me." I beckon her into my office. She follows and takes a seat in front of my desk, sitting bolt upright with her knees together and ankles crossed, very elegant, very regal. I close the door and take an equally upright position in my chair opposite her.

"You know, then?"

"What about?" she says, fluttering her eyelash extensions.

"Don't try and be coy. You know I'm dating, and you know who," I state. She leans forwards slightly.

"I knew you were dating; you've been smiling way too much lately! But James Keller? Was it him you went to Wales with?" I nod. "How the fuck did that happen?" she demands to know. I sit back in my chair and laugh as I proceed to tell her how we met. Her eyes are wide and glossy as I relay it. It's like she's five years old, and I'm telling the story of Cinderella for the first time.

"Oh my God, I'm in love with him! Who else knows? Has he met your family yet?"

"Well, it's all over the internet now! My family met him the day before we went to Wales."

"Ooh, how'd that go?" she asks keenly.

"It was good. My dad is a massive fan, so he was very excited once he got over the shock. Lizzie was beside herself."

"Understandably. Anyone else know?"

"I've told a couple of friends this weekend, and I was planning on telling you this morning, but you beat me to it." I smile at her.

"What about everyone else in the office? Oh, hold on, does this mean you'll be leaving us now that you're famous?" she teases but looks sad.

"I'm not famous!" I laugh. "And I have no plans to leave you." A look of relief crosses her face. "Everyone else can find out organically, although I will tell John this morning. I'm going to see if I can work from the New York office for a week or two over the next couple of months."

"Do you think he'll let you?"

"If you don't ask, you don't get, right? I think he'll be fine with it, and the company won't be paying for my travel or accommodation."

She nods and double taps her finger on her nose. She gets it.

"You want to come to New York with me?"

She sits up straighter, If that's even possible. "Oh my word, can I?" Her eyes light up. "All that shopping I can do!"

"If I can arrange it, I will. You're my girl here!"

"Oh, I love you!"

I let her know about Allison and Rebecca, so she knows not to lay into them if they call me. She immediately asks for James's mobile number.

"Just in case I might need him for something!" she pleads with me.

"If you need him, contact Allison." I smile, and she pouts her bottom lip.

Later that morning, I meet with my manager, John, and update him on what's been going on in my life. I've worked hard and earned his respect. I reassure him that my work will not be impacted, and luckily for me, he gives the go-ahead for me to spend some time in New York, and Ivy can come too. I walk back to my office via the kitchen and grab myself a coffee and one for Ivy, which I place on her desk as I walk past. She's not there; she's in my office, leaving a note on my desk.

"Good news," I say. She looks at me like an excited puppy. "We're on!"

"We are?"

"We are," I confirm. She punches the air. I smile and pick up my phone, ready to make a call. "Leave it with me," I say, dialling a number. She walks backward out of my office, her hands in prayer in front of her, mouthing over and over again, "Thank you."

Thirty-Six

Two weeks later, we find ourselves in the first-class lounge at the airport, sipping champagne while we wait to board our flight.

"I've never flown first class," Ivy admits.

"You'll love it. The problem is you won't want to go back to economy," I warn her.

We board the lunchtime flight, which gets us into JFK in the late afternoon. The flight is wonderful; nothing is too much trouble for the cabin crew. The pods are beautiful, the food is a far cry from the rubbery eggs of economy, and there's so much legroom. I settle into my pod, put on a film, and review some legal documents for the office while Ivy indulges in a massage.

One advantage of flying first class is you get through the airport so much quicker. No hour-long lines for passport checks. Within thirty minutes of getting off the plane, we are through and out the other side, and as a nice surprise, Nigel is there waiting for us.

"Nigel!" I say, giving him a kiss on the cheek. "How lovely to see you. I wasn't expecting you."

"Yes, you have me this week. Sean is on holiday catching up with family. I am at your disposal." He looks at Ivy and gives her one of his warm smiles. "Hello, you must be Ivy?" He offers his hand to shake.

"Hello," she replies, timidly, quite unlike her.

"Right, let's get you two where you need to be before James fires me," he jokes, giving me a cheeky smile as he takes both of our cases and leads us to the car. He drops Ivy off first at her hotel with instructions that she'll be picked up tomorrow morning at 8:30am and taken to the office, then we weave through the traffic to James's penthouse apartment.

I've not been to his place yet; I just know it's on the Upper East Side. We pull into a cobbled side street flanked by high red brick buildings on either side that look more like offices, not that inviting. I'm wondering where the plush houses are. On the left is a large black garage door that opens as we drive up and into a private underground car park where there are some very nice cars!

"We're here!" Nigel announces, pulling into a spot next to what looks like a classic Ford Mustang. He gets out, opens the back door for me, and grabs my luggage. We walk to an elevator where he beeps his ID tag to call it. It arrives quickly, and I step inside with Nigel. He beeps his ID tag again and steps out, sending me on my way up to the penthouse.

The elevator doors open, and there's James, casually leaning against the wall, barefoot, in light denim jeans and a white untucked V-neck T-shirt. He looks like he's just stepped out of a jeans commercial. I've missed him!

"I saw you coming," he says, smiling. He steps forwards, wraps his arms around me, and dives straight in for a full-on kiss. It feels so good. He takes my case and walks across the hallway to a black front door. Nothing out of the ordinary so far, although this hallway reminds me of a posh hotel with its light marble flooring, dark red walls, a beautiful gold French console table with a large vase of white flowers, and a stunning crystal chandelier overhead. There are no other doors leading from this hallway except for what appears to be a fire escape, so I'm guessing that was a private elevator.

James opens the door and invites me in. I nearly fall to the floor when I see his home.

"Wow!" I say, standing still next to the open door. "Just wow!"

"You like it?" he asks, gently steering me in and closing the door behind us.

"I love it!" I reply, taking in the open hallway. The double-height window offers a view of a retro red brick building opposite, but what really catches my eye is the black, shiny grand piano standing proudly in the centre of the hall. I walk over and run my fingers over the keys, the sound echoing and sending shivers through me.

"Do you play?" I ask, surprised I didn't already know this.

"No, sadly not. This," he says, patting the top, "is just for decoration. Do you play?"

My eyes light up as I nod. "Yes, I do."

"How do I not know this? Can you play well?"

"I reached grade eight, so yes, reasonably well. I've

always wanted a piano, a Steinway of course, but never had space for one."

"Well, we shall put one on our UK list, then. You can play for me later."

I follow him into the vast open-plan living area. Light oak wood floors flow throughout, and two large, light grey L-shaped sofas face each other, forming three quarters of a square. There's an open fire in front of them and a massive TV on the wall above. Beyond that is an eight-seater round dining table, and further on is the grey marble kitchen with an expansive island. It's minimalistic, modern, light, and airy, with floor-to-ceiling windows on the far side offering views over the East River and beyond. Considering we are in a very busy city, there is so much greenery.

"Let me show you around and we can take your case up," James says, pointing just beyond the kitchen. "Down there are two bedrooms, my office, and a gym."

He guides me back into the hall and up the stairs to the second floor. "Your room is up here, with me." He leads me up the open slatted wooden stairs with a glass banister to the first floor and into his bedroom. It's decorated much like downstairs, minimalist. An enormous bed with beige bedding sits on a light grey rug. The wooden floors continue, and there's a black coffee table with two snug chairs and a gas fireplace. The walls and drapes are cream. It's clean but not clinical. There is a walk-in wardrobe leading off the master, which is vast and organised, much like mine, but on a larger scale.

"I've made a space for you to hang your clothes," James says, pointing to a free area in the walk-in wardrobe. "Make yourself at home."

"This place is amazing!" I exclaim in awe. "Are you sure you want to leave it and come to the UK? I'm not sure I would!"

"Why? Are you considering coming to live here?" He smiles at me.

"I might! It's incredible!"

"Well, I'm sure we will find something in the UK that is equally impressive, but there's more to see here." He takes my hand and leads me out of the bedroom back onto the landing and out of an oversized frosted glass door that opens onto a rooftop terrace. You can instantly hear the hum of the streets below but it's not intrusive. From the silence inside, it's nice to get the atmosphere of people going about their business. The terrace is spacious, with a BBQ, a couple of sun loungers, a wooden dining table with eight reclining chairs and a hot tub. Despite it being September, the skies above are blue, and the air is pleasantly warm. We are not overlooked at all. It's just beautiful.

"Ah, so this is where you dry your washing?" I tease, walking to the edge to take in the view. "The view up here is spectacular!"

James stands beside me, smiling. "It is. I'm glad you like it. So, what's the plan, then? Do you want to unpack and freshen up and I'll meet you downstairs? I'll make you a tea, or coffee?"

"A tea would be great."

"Do you want it up here as it's nice out?"

"Sounds good. Can I take a quick shower?"

"Of course. Like I said, make yourself at home."

He directs me to the bathroom and goes back

downstairs. I unpack a few of my things, feeling a bit strange being on his turf rather than mine. I fumble around for the light switch in the wardrobe, only to realise the light comes on automatically when you enter.

It's quite dark in here, even with the light on. Dark wood wardrobes line the walls. Some have no doors, allowing you to see the contents, while others are closed. His shoe collection is neatly displayed on the far side. I open one of the doors; I can't resist a sneaky peek. Drawers, on top of which is a nice selection of sunglasses and watches. Hanging on the inside of the door are all his ties, all neatly displayed, and right in the centre is the tie I bought him. I smile, remembering the night I gave it to him, and close the door.

The bathroom is very similar to mine, only four times the size. The walk-in shower is huge and the dark grey marble floors with matching walls give it a luxurious feel. I switch on the backlight of the large mirror, turning off the overhead lights for a romantic glow, undress and lay my clothes over the freestanding white bath, take a towel from the cupboard, and place it by the sink. I step into the shower and let the water flow over me; it's bliss.

After my shower, I put on a pair of black leggings and a sweatshirt and head out onto the terrace, where James is relaxing at the table, letting the late afternoon rays hit his face.

"Thanks, babe," I say, sitting next to him and taking a sip of my tea. We sit quietly for a moment, holding hands and enjoying the last of the warmth of the sun and admiring the views. I think back to the night we met, and where we are now, where I am now. I feel like the luckiest girl in the world. I feel such a genuine love for James. I love being with him, from the mad moments when he's being bombarded by fans or paparazzi to the quiet moments like now. This is so different to what it was like with Karl.

"How was your shower?" he asks, breaking my thoughts.

"Heaven."

"So, the plan for the next few days is, tomorrow night, dinner here with Ivy."

"She's really looking forward to that!"

"So am I. She sounds like quite a character! The following night, dinner with your work colleagues?"

"Yep, you're still coming?"

"Yeah, of course. I'm still invited?"

"Absolutely, I'm looking forward to it."

"Me too. Remind me who's going?"

"My counterpart and his wife; his boss, the senior partner, and her wife; Ivy and us – seven in total."

"Two guys and five women? Sounds great!"

"Yes, but two of them are gay!" I add, nudging him playfully.

"Shame, and that's all booked for a restaurant downtown?"

"All booked."

"Then a night in, just the two of us, then I've got a couple of business dinners and a social dinner for us to go to, and then meet the rest of my family."

"Busy but perfect," I agree.

"Allison has shortlisted four properties for us, by the way; we should look at them later and set up a viewing when we are back in the UK."

"Okay great."

"And then your birthday is coming up."

"It is."

"I'm so sorry I can't be there on your actual birthday."

"That's okay," I say, feeling a little disappointed. Of course, I'd love nothing more than to spend my birthday with him, but I know the deal; I understand his commitments.

"At least Paris is almost in the same time zone. I promise I'll make it up to you." He lifts my hand and places a light kiss on it. "What are your plans for your birthday?"

"A spa afternoon and dinner, I think. Lizzie is organising it."

"That sounds nice. Who's going?"

"Girls only. Lizzie, Claire, Jules, Ivy, and I was thinking of inviting your sister Louise. Do you think she'd like to come?"

"I think she'd be really pleased. Want to call her later and ask?"

"Yes, let's do that."

Thirty-Seven

"Wow, this place is incredible!" Ivy says as she steps into the living room, taking in the floor-to-ceiling windows and the breathtaking view of the East River.

"Wait until you see the terrace. I can't wait for you to meet James," I say, leading her up the stairs and out onto the rooftop terrace.

"I'm not gonna lie, I'm nervous!" she admits.

"Don't be," I reassure her.

James is already there, busy at the BBQ as the sun begins to set, casting a warm glow over the city. She smooths her vibrant red dress down over her curvaceous hips and steps outside.

"Ivy, meet James, the chef for the evening," I say, introducing them.

"It's a pleasure to finally meet you, Ivy," James says, extending a hand and kissing her cheek. "Nikki has told me so much about you."

"All good things, I hope," Ivy replies with a coy smile. It's so funny to see her star-struck; she's normally the loudest in the room.

"Absolutely," James says, returning the smile. "Can I get you a drink? We have wine, beer, or a soft drink if you prefer?" he offers.

"A glass of wine would be nice." She flashes me a nervous look while James pours her a wine and mouths, "He's gorgeous!"

He hands her the drink, and she takes a small sip, savouring the taste, and then glances back at me, her eyes still wide with a mixture of excitement and disbelief.

"So, Ivy," James says, flipping a piece of perfectly grilled salmon, "Nikki tells me you're quite the fashionista. I have to say, that dress is stunning."

"Thank you," Ivy replies, running her hand over her dress again. "I've always believed that dressing well is a form of good manners."

"I couldn't agree more," he replies, turning back to the BBQ. "Nikki's mentioned how you've been a huge support for her, especially these past few years."

Ivy glances at me and smiles. "Well, she's more than just a boss to me. She's a friend."

Her words make me smile. James nods, his expression thoughtful. "It's good to hear that. It's not often you find such a strong bond at work."

We sit around the outdoor dining table, and James serves us a delicious spread of grilled vegetables, salmon, and a fresh salad.

"This looks amazing," Ivy says, her nerves settling.

He grins, setting the plates down. "I hope it tastes as

good as it looks. Dig in, everyone."

As we start to eat, the conversation and wine flowing, Ivy relaxes and starts sharing office stories with us in her usual animated tone, which makes James laugh out loud and me cringe slightly.

"Nikki, remember the time," she begins, with a mischievous glint in her eye, "when you had to give that big presentation to the board and walked in with two different shoes on?"

I groan, covering my face with my hands. "Oh God, Ivy, do you have to bring that up?" James chuckles, looking at me with amusement.

Ivy leans in, recounting the incident. "So, Nikki was super prepared for this presentation, had all her slides ready, notes in order, looking sharp in her suit. But in her rush to get out the door, she grabbed one black heel and one navy heel. She didn't notice until she was halfway through the presentation, when one of the board members pointed it out." Ivy lets out a raucous laugh. "I added his comment to the minutes!"

James laughs, shaking his head. "That was kind of them. How did you handle it?"

I sigh, smiling despite myself. "I had two options: pretend I didn't notice or own it. So, I said something like 'Well, I wanted to make sure you were all paying attention.' Everyone laughed, and we moved on... thankfully!"

"It was brilliant," Ivy adds, still laughing. "Turned a potentially awkward moment into a memorable one."

James looks at me with admiration. I shrug, feeling ever so slightly embarrassed but also proud. "You do what you have to do."

Ivy isn't done yet, though. "Huh, remember the Christmas party where we got kicked out of the restaurant for being drunk and disorderly?"

"I had already left," I say smugly. "So I didn't get kicked out. I left when the directors at the time left, if you remember?"

"Ah yes, so you did! Shame, you missed a good after-party!" She laughs.

"Sounds like you have had some fun!" James says.

As the night wears on, Ivy and James bond over their love of fashion and travel. Ivy shares stories of her childhood in Nigeria and her life in Britain, while James tells of his experiences filming in various exotic locations around the world. He shares stories from his last film shoot, giving us a behind-the-scenes look at the glamorous yet demanding life of a Hollywood actor. Ivy, ever curious, asks insightful questions, making James laugh with her candidness.

"So, what's the craziest thing that's happened to you on set?" Ivy asks.

James smiles, thinking for a moment. "Loads of crazy things happen but one springs to mind – there was this one time in Morocco. We were filming a desert scene, and a massive sandstorm hit. We had to halt production and take cover. The entire set was buried in sand by the time it was over. Took us days to get back on track."

Ivy gasps. "That sounds intense! How did you manage?"

"With a lot of patience and a great crew," James replies. "It's all part of the adventure."

By the end of the night, Ivy is completely at ease, and

it's clear she's charmed by James, just as I am. As we say our goodbyes, she pulls me aside.

"You've got a good one there, Nikki," she whispers, giving me a hug. "I'm so happy for you."

Over the next week, work goes well. He meets my New York colleagues for dinner, which is a success. He was very charming with them, although they were slightly taken aback by the paparazzi reception we received leaving the restaurant. I take a day off and hit the shops with Ivy before she leaves and heads back to the UK. After that I meet producers, directors, editors at informal business meetings he has at luxury private houses; this really is a different world, one I'm enjoying!

It's Sunday evening, and my trip is almost over. We've been invited to Martin and Amanda Hamilton's house for dinner. Given my previous two encounters with Amanda, this is an invitation I'm dreading. Amanda and Martin live on the west side of Manhattan in a lavish townhouse that practically screams privilege and exclusivity. We are in the back of a blacked-out Merc, weaving through the hazardous traffic of Manhattan, when I finally confess to James that this is one social event I'm not looking forward to.

"No? Why not?" he asks, eyebrows raised.

"I've met Amanda twice now, and she's not exactly been friendly. The first time, she spoke down to me because she thought I was a runner, which says a lot to me. Then, at the premiere, she completely ignored me!"

"Did she?"

"Yeah, I was sitting at the bar with Suzanne. She walked over, looked straight through me, and asked Suzanne where you were."

He considers this for a moment, his expression thoughtful. "Hmm, she's okay but, yes, she can be a little… frosty sometimes."

"She didn't seem frosty with you!"

James looks over at me, smiles, and squeezes my hand reassuringly. "You just have to get to know her, that's all. She'll be fine, I'm sure."

To my surprise, Amanda is quite pleasant towards me, friendly even. They cook us a nice meal, or should I say their chef cooks us a nice meal. She asks me questions about my work and my family. Maybe my judgement was wrong. We chat about the film industry, potential upcoming projects, who is who in Hollywood. It's a nice evening.

After dinner, I excuse myself to use the bathroom while the others move into the lounge for a nightcap. On my way back, I spot Amanda lingering in the kitchen. She catches my eye and waves me over.

"Hey, the boys are busy talking shop, so I'm taking a breather in here. Come on in, have a seat," she says, motioning towards a stool at the island. She places a champagne glass in front of me, the kitchen around us gleaming in light beige marble and stainless steel. The place is spotless, which makes me suspect this isn't where the real cooking happens.

"Top-up?" she offers, holding up a bottle of chilled champagne.

"Sure, thanks. You have a beautiful home," I say, taking a seat. I notice she doesn't sit down herself but leans casually against the counter, radiating a quiet sense of superiority.

"Oh, thank you, yes, we're rather fond of this place. We also have a home in Beverly Hills and one in London. I'm very fortunate. But so are you, landing James Keller, what a catch!" She raises her glass towards me, and I sense a slight undertone. "How's it going with Hollywood's most eligible bachelor?"

"Great, it's going great," I reply, careful to keep my tone light.

"Fantastic. I'm so pleased for you both. But I imagine it's not always easy, being with someone like James." She takes a sip of her drink, her gaze sharp as a knife. I give her a questioning look.

"Oh, you know, with all the attention he gets. He's never short of admirers, is he?"

"No, he's not."

"And with him being away so much, and you not being in the business." She pauses, letting her words hang in the air like a challenge. "I just think it must require a lot of trust. But you're a confident woman, I'm sure."

"I trust him," I reply, my voice steady.

"And why wouldn't you! He's an absolute darling, inside and out, which I'm sure you already know. Of course, I've known James for years. I remember when he was married to Melinda. She often mentioned how challenging it was, dealing with all the attention he attracted. She's such a lovely woman, beautiful too. It's a shame they couldn't make it work; they were so good together. But hey, life goes on, doesn't it?" Her smile is all sweetness, but her words have the sting of a well-aimed barb. "Oh, I love this colour on you!" She gently touches the fabric on my coral blouse. "Martin and I will be spending quite a bit of time in London and Paris filming over the next few months, so I'm sure we'll be seeing more of each other. Will you be visiting the set?"

"Yes, I hope so."

"Well, at least now I know you're not a runner!" She laughs. I try to laugh, but my acting skills aren't as good as hers.

She leans in a little closer, lowering her voice. "You know, James and I had a little thing once. Just a brief fling, nothing serious, but it was quite the whirlwind. He's such a passionate man, isn't he?"

My heart races, but I keep my face neutral. "Hmm."

"Oh, come on," she purrs. "A man like that, you must feel it every time he looks at you. Though, I suppose it's different for everyone. Melinda used to say the same thing before... well, you know. It's a shame, really. They were so perfect together. But then again, maybe perfection is overrated, don't you think?" Her eyes glint with something I can't place.

"And you know," she adds, her tone silky smooth, "the press can be absolutely relentless when it comes to James. I do hope you're ready for that."

"Oh, I can handle it," I say as confidently as I can muster, refusing to let her see that I'm rattled.

Amanda's lips curve into a smile, and she takes another sip of her champagne. "Good for you. That's the spirit. If anyone can handle it, I'm sure it's you."

Her demeanour shifts back to the gracious hostess. "Well," she says, "we should probably get back before the boys start wondering where we've disappeared to. They'll be talking films all night if we let them."

"Absolutely," I agree, eager to put some distance between us.

We return to the lounge, and James, as usual, lifts his arm for me to cuddle next to him. He gives me his warm, reassuring smile, but this time, I don't smile back. Amanda's words echo in my mind: *they were so good together*. She had a brief fling with James. A pang of jealousy hits me, sharp and unexpected.

"You okay, babe?" he asks as I sit next to him, while Amanda settles next to Martin, across from us. I can feel her eyes on me, watching.

"Yep," I reply, but even to my own ears, my voice sounds cold, distant.

"You sure?" He can sense it too clearly.

Determined not to let Amanda get to me, I place my hand on his thigh and force a smile, looking him in the eye. "Yes, all good," I say, leaning in to kiss him.

It's my last day in New York before we both head back to the UK, and finally, it's time to meet James's parents and his sister Dianne. His parents live in Brooklyn in what I'd describe as a quintessential New York home – a big three-storey townhouse with concrete steps and black railings leading up to the front door. As we pull up outside, the front door opens right on cue. There's no one on the street, so we slip inside unnoticed.

His parents, Joan and Peter, greet us warmly as we step in. James hugs his mum and shakes his dad's hand before introducing me.

"Well, Nikki, my love, it's a pleasure to meet you. If he's bringing you to meet us, it must be serious," his mum says with a warm smile, guiding us through to the kitchen. She puts the kettle on – very British for an American.

In the kitchen, we find his sister Dianne, already there with her husband, Chris, and their teenage son, Dan. Dianne is older than James, and while they seem to get on, there's definitely a different vibe with her. She's more aloof compared to Louise, who is super friendly.

His parents prepare an amazing roast dinner for lunch, and I genuinely enjoy my time with them.

Behind closed doors, they're just a normal family like any other. They share stories about what James was like as a child – adventurous and fearless, always getting into something. They tell me how they'd often find him sitting on the roof of their house back in California or doing crazy jumps on his bike, with Dianne usually the one to tattle on him. He gave them more than his fair share of stress, but for him, it was all in good fun. He had a happy childhood, and while he was studious, his passion for acting was evident early on. They never stood in the way of his dreams, and it paid off in the end.

They find it amusing when I recount how my family reacted when they first met him.

Over dinner, James tells his parents and sister that he's planning to move to the UK to live with me. He was right about their reaction – whatever makes him happy, they're on board. Louise will be thrilled, they say, and I'm relieved to hear them support the decision. I had worried they might not like me, thinking I was taking their son away, but I needn't have. They couldn't have been more welcoming. Their advice to me? Avoid reading anything about James in the tabloids because it's usually inaccurate.

Thirty-Eight

ack in the UK and it's the day of my birthday celebrations with the girls. James is in Paris with the promise that he will fly back tomorrow, albeit briefly, to see me, and I can't wait. Lizzie has gone all out, booking us a stay at a five-star spa hotel for all of us girls, including Louise, who was overjoyed to be invited. She planned everything – a luxurious treatment for each of us in the afternoon, followed by dinner in the hotel's main restaurant.

We arrive in convoy and check into our rooms. James treated me to the king's suite for the night as a birthday gift and it's every bit as extravagant as it sounds – it is contemporary and gorgeous, with a separate lounge, a bedroom featuring a large four-poster bed, and views over the perfectly manicured gardens and outdoor pool. The best room in the house. I try to video call James, but he doesn't pick up, so I send him a text instead:

'Room is gorgeous, wish you were here to share it with me. xxx.'

I choose a hot stone massage for my treatment followed by a manicure. After our treatments, we all meet in the indoor Roman bath pool. The space is breathtaking – massive Roman pillars at either end of the Olympic-sized pool, with large palm trees at the far end. The domed ceiling is painted a soft blue with fluffy white clouds – not quite Michelangelo, but impressive nonetheless. Exposed brick walls, arch windows, and several loungers complete the scene. We quickly claim six of them and order tea, coffee, and a slice of cake each, settling in to relax.

"Thanks so much for organising this, Liz. This is my favourite spa," I tell her.

"My pleasure."

"It's gorgeous. I've never been here before." Louise looks around, admiring the surroundings.

"There's more," Liz adds. "They have a sauna, steam room, another pool and hot tubs outside, but given the weather today, we'll probably give them a miss. The heated ceramic sun loungers are really nice."

"I'll be going to them soon!" Ivy declares.

"I'll join you. They also have a floatation tank, and a gym," I finish.

"So, yoga is on in forty-five minutes, then the hot ceramics and then get ready for dinner?" Lizzie confirms the plan.

"Sounds perfect," says Claire. "So, what did James get you for your birthday?"

I laugh a little. "He got me walking poles!"

"Walking poles?" Claire repeats, bemused.

"Yep, says they'll help keep me upright on our next hiking trip!"

"Romantic! How many times did you fall over?"

"Once. Maybe twice," I admit.

"And how many times did he fall over?"

"He didn't!" I say, rolling my eyes.

"Typical James!" Louise laughs.

"So anyway, have you found a place to move to yet, you and James? I still can't believe you're with him – I've not even met him yet!" Claire gives me a playful poke.

"He's so busy, he's hard to pin down. But he'll be here tomorrow, and if not, I'll invite you around to the penthouse we have in London."

"Oh nice!" says Jules.

"Wow", "oooh," they all say at once.

"It's very nice!" I coo.

"When do you move in?" asks Jules.

"In two weeks!" I say, the excitement bubbling up.

"I can't wait to see it," says Lizzie, then with her usual bluntness, she adds, "What's the rent on it?" I give her a look to let her know how uncouth the question is, but she just shrugs, unfazed.

"It's in the thousands," I reply, hoping to end the conversation there. She raises her eyebrows, clearly unsatisfied. Reluctantly, I give in. "Somewhere in the region of £30k."

"Wow! For London rent? That's good. Hang on, is that per year?" She eyes me with suspicion.

"Per week." I watch as her jaw drops in slow motion.

"Shut up!" announces Ivy a bit too loudly. Jules bursts out laughing.

"*Thirty grand*? Per week?" Lizzie repeats in shock. I nod.

"Well, it's got a rooftop terrace where you can see the London Eye!" I say, trying to justify it, but I am ignored. "It's short term, just to test the waters. If it works out, we find something more permanent. If it doesn't, well…"

"I think you'll be just fine," Jules says with a reassuring smile.

"I agree," Lizzie adds. "I bloody hope so anyway – thirty grand!"

"I love him! I'll have him if it doesn't work out!" Ivy jokes.

"You've got Tyrone," I remind her. "He's gorgeous!"

"He is," she gushes slightly. "But he can't cook!" She winks at me.

"I'm really pleased! And I'm praying you two work out because that means I've got my brother back living in the same time zone as me!" Louise says, her face lighting up with a huge grin. My heart melts a little at her words.

We head to the yoga class and then spend half an hour relaxing on the heated ceramic sun loungers. The room is warm and peaceful, filled only with the gentle trickle of water from a large fish fountain at the centre. Ivy dozes off beside me, and Claire nods off too. Somewhere in the room, someone starts snoring rather loudly, and the four of us who are still awake struggle to keep our giggles under control.

Later, back in my room, I check my phone and find a message from James.

'Sorry baby, service is not great! Glad you like it; wish I was there to share it with you. Have fun tonight, miss you, love you, J xxx.'

Ahh, he never fails to put a smile on my face.

I jump in the shower and start getting ready for dinner. We decide to make an occasion of it and dress up red carpet style – Julia's idea. I take it literally and slip into a dark red strapless fishtail dress; it's a lot more daring than I would usually wear but I figured I'd get some practice in. Gingerly, I make my way down the stairs to the lounge; I can only take small steps in this gown. We all arrive at the same time, and wow, everyone has really made an effort – we look fabulous, like we just stepped off the red carpet. I notice a few other guests in the lounge staring as we enter, clearly impressed.

We order some wine and spend some time admiring each other's dresses. "What's everyone's other half doing tonight, then?" I ask.

"Duncan has gone out with the boys. Mum and Dad are staying at mine tonight babysitting," says Lizzie.

"Same," says Jules.

"Yep, Rob has used the opportunity to get a sitter and head out too!" says Louise.

"We don't have children, so I'm not sure what Richard is doing. Enjoying some quiet time, maybe," says Claire.

"And Tyrone?" I ask, turning to Ivy.

"He's hiding in my room!" Ivy jokes.

"Is he?" I ask, half-believing her.

"No, but I wish he was. I'm feeling fruity!" she says, shaking her boobs at us, which has us in fits of laughter.

"And James is in Paris tonight, you say?" Claire asks.

"Yes, he is in Paris," I say, feeling a slight tug on my heart.

"Oh, very nice. Do you wish he was here?" Claire nudges me.

"I love you all, but yes, I do miss him," I admit.

"He'll be back tomorrow," Lizzie reassures me just as a waiter approaches.

"Excuse me, ladies, the dining room is ready for you." We follow the waiter, expecting to be led into the main dining room, but instead, we're taken into a private reception room.

"I thought we were in the main dining room?" I whisper to Jules.

"We were, but given your high profile now, I thought I'd organise for us to be in a private room instead," she teases me.

"She actually said it was so we could all get ridiculously drunk and no one could catch it on camera!" Ivy laughs.

Two waiting staff come into the room with some more drinks and some light canapés.

"We will be back in a few moments to take you through," one of the waiters tells us and they leave.

The room is light and cosy, with no chairs, just standing room and French doors that lead out to the patio and onto the garden lawn. It's a pretty space, with a beige patterned carpet and walls painted in baby blue. The high ceiling has white intricate coving, and a crystal chandelier hanging elegantly in the centre. There's art on the wall, portraits mounted in gold that look like they belong in a gallery. A glossy dark wood corner table holds a light blue vase filled with beautiful pale pink roses. Soft music plays quietly from speakers high up on the walls, and double doors on the far side of the room likely lead into the dining area. The ambiance is perfect.

I'm busy chatting with the girls when I hear the door

open again behind me and assume it's the staff finally coming to see us through, which is good because I'm starving. I'm about to turn around when I suddenly feel the presence of someone standing close. Before I can react, hands gently cover my eyes, and I jump.

"Guess who?" comes that smooth American accent I've come to know and love.

My heart races so fast that I think everyone in the room must hear it. "James!" I say, spinning round and flinging my arms around him. Over his shoulder, I see all the boys – Duncan, Mark, Richard, Rob, and Tyrone – have joined us. I'm absolutely gobsmacked.

"Surprise!" James beams, hugging me and lifting me off the ground. "You didn't really think I'd miss your birthday, did you?"

I feel my face flush as I wipe my eye and hope no one notices I'm overcome with emotion. "Are you staying?"

"Yep, all night, that okay?"

"Of course! How? When did you get here?"

"I conspired with Lizzie and Ivy," he admits. "I arrived at the hotel about half an hour ago." I hug him again and he holds me tightly.

"I'm so pleased to see you. I've missed you! You look gorgeous!" I whisper in his ear.

The boys are dressed in suits for the evening, and James is all in black, not funeral black, movie premiere black – black trousers with satin trim, a black shirt unbuttoned at the top, and a sleek black jacket. I should nickname him James Bond! I would if he were British.

I introduce James to Claire, the only one who hasn't met him yet. "She's been eager to meet you," I say.

"Pleasure to finally meet you, Claire. I've heard good things about you," he says, offering her a handshake.

She smiles weakly. "Likewise," she says, taking his hand, and I swear I see her blush a little.

He makes his way around all the ladies, charmer that he is, and says his hellos before making his way back to me with a small gift bag.

"I got you a gift for your birthday."

"You've got me enough already," I protest.

"Just take it, I think you'll like it. And no, it's not more walking poles," he teases as he hands me the gift bag. I untie the black ribbon, revealing a box. I pull it out and glance at the logo, 'ROLEX'. I look up at him in surprise. He gestures for me to open it. A small brilliant white light inserted into the lid of the box illuminates a royal blue velvet cushion holding a platinum watch with a pale-yellow face and a twenty-four-diamond-set dial. The exact one I tried on when shopping with Julia and Lizzie. I'm speechless.

"Do you like it?" he asks when he's met with stunned silence.

"I love it!" I finally manage. James looks pleased with himself.

"I had Jules's help with this one." He takes my arm and helps me put it on. "It suits you."

"I really love it. Are you sure? You really didn't have to get me anything!" I protest again, but only slightly this time.

"Nikki, let me spoil you, I want to."

"Okay, if you insist, thank you, baby!" I say, giving him a kiss. I catch Julia's eye and wave my wrist for her to see.

She rushes over, followed closely by Lizzie, Ivy, Claire, and Louise. Poor James gets pushed aside while they coo over the new 'baby'!

A few minutes later, we are called into the dining room where we take our seats at a beautiful mahogany table set for twelve and we're served a wonderful five-course dinner. The drinks flow, and there's plenty of conversation and laughter among us. I sit back, taking in the sight of my friends all getting along so well. The girls have been fantastic company today, and the boys are bantering with James about which football team – or should I say soccer team – he'll support now that he's moving to this side of the pond. I feel incredibly lucky to have such a great bunch of people around.

Thirty-Nine

wo weeks later and it's moving day! Since James asked me to move in with him, he's gradually been leaving some of his clothes here; my flat is pretty cramped now. All of our belongings are piled into a moving van and escorted by Nigel over to the new place with Allison and me following behind.

It's a new building, and we've got the penthouse on the top two floors. We pull up to the underground car park, the large dark grey doors looming in front of us. There's a keypad for access, and since we know the code, we let ourselves in. The car park is spacious and well-lit. The tyres squeak as I turn the wheel on my Porsche, manoeuvring it into one of the designated spaces.

"You have three spaces here," Allison says as I stop in front of the sign saying 'PRIVATE PARKING PH1'. To my right is another space, 'PRIVATE PARKING PH2', and a third space with 'PH3'. I guess 'PH' stands for 'penthouse'! To the right is a lift entrance, which can only be accessed with the code we have or a key card. We enter the lift and input the code to take us to the penthouse level. Guests must go through reception and be announced by security – just like in New York.

The lift pings to say we have reached the third floor, and the doors open into a sleek hallway with beautiful light marble floors. A stylish black side table stands against the wall, topped with a large silver figurine and a black lamp. The walls are cream, and the ceiling is adorned with simple ceiling lights.

Opposite the lift, a light oak front door is slightly ajar. We walk in, excitement buzzing as I step into my new home.

"Hello?" I call out.

"Hi" comes a cheerful voice. A young man, in his thirties and smartly dressed, joins us in the hallway. "You must be Miss Harper and you are Allison?"

"That's right," Allison confirms, her expression neutral.

"Great, I'm Daniel Crede," he says with a friendly smile. "Mr Keller is due to meet us here in about half an hour, correct?"

I nod to confirm. "Yes, that's right."

"Excellent! Come on in and let me show you around your new home," he says, extending his arm in an inviting gesture.

Daniel leads us through the apartment to complete the inventory. It's a four-bed, four-bathroom apartment covering nearly six thousand square feet. It's fully furnished, very modern, in neutral colours.

We enter a spacious reception hall that smells new, with everything crisp and untouched, like a show home.

To the left, there are stairs, the kitchen, a family room, and an office space. To the right is a large lounge, a hallway leading to a utility room, a TV room, and a gym – my very own gym!

Daniel takes us into the kitchen, which is immaculate. The papers are laid out on a large black marble island with light grey veining, surrounded by four dark grey barstools. The walls are a matching dark grey, while the units are a contrasting light grey. Three brass dome chandeliers hang above the island, and the large window makes the space surprisingly light and airy. There's an alcove by the window with a small white sofa and a TV, a cosy spot where I can relax while James cooks.

"Is everything satisfactory to you, Miss Harper?" asks Daniel formally.

"Yes," I reply in my most professional tone, though I'm already imagining jumping on the bed.

"Great, in that case it's just the contract to review and sign and then I will leave you to settle in."

I stand at the island and flip through the contract. It's standard stuff, and everything appears to be in order.

"Hello?" comes the American accent. James is here. Allison calls out from the kitchen to let him know where we are. He walks in with Sean.

"Mr Keller!" Daniel almost leaps towards him, extending his hand. "Daniel Crede," he says enthusiastically. "Pleasure to meet you, sir." I smile; I still find it amusing to see how people react around him. He politely shakes Daniel's hand.

"Hey, babe," he says to me. "Everything okay?"

"Hi, yes, all okay."

"Paperwork all in order?"

"Yes, all here and all as agreed," I confirm.

"Happy?"

"Very happy." I smile at him.

"Good, where do I sign?"

Daniel hands him the contract. He glances at it, but he trusts me, and that I've reviewed it properly with Allison, and signs without hesitation.

"Everything's set, then," Daniel says, taking the signed contract. "Congratulations on your new home! If you need anything else, don't hesitate to reach out."

"Thank you, Daniel," I say. "We'll be sure to let you know if we have any questions."

Allison and Sean escort Daniel out, leaving us alone in the apartment. James wraps his arms around me. "So, what do you think?"

"I love it!" I exclaim. "It's perfect."

"Good. I'm glad you're happy," he says, leaning in for a kiss. "Now, let's get settled and make this place our home."

Forty

The first two weeks of living together have been a whirlwind. I took a few days off work to organise our new home with my mum's help and to take delivery of a brand-new high-spec Range Rover. It's sleek and stylish, with an all-black exterior, including the alloys, darkened windows, and a chic beige interior. I have to admit, it's a gorgeous car. I wonder if that means he's staying permanently.

When I return to work, I'm thrust into fourteen-hour days on a high-stakes and complex case, while James has been spending an equal amount of time on set in London. He had to travel back to Paris last weekend to wrap up filming and attend an award ceremony. Unfortunately, because of the pressing deadline, I couldn't go with him. But at least he's been in London most of the time, so we managed to enjoy our nights together.

It's Saturday afternoon, and with the pressure of my deadline finally behind me, I decide to visit James on set as it's local. He's been here all week, and the shooting schedule suggests he should be finished late afternoon, but you never can tell. I've got my pass, and I'm sitting with the makeup team watching a scene unfold on a TV monitor. It's a reshoot of a romantic kiss scene between James, aka Dean, and a beautiful Dutch-American actress, Lucinda Brower. She's tall, blonde, with the most amazing legs! The intimacy director requires a closed set for this reshoot and although it was only a brief kiss, the director, Martin Hamilton, insists on three retakes, all because the lighting wasn't quite right. It was a little awkward to say the least.

Once it's complete and we are allowed back on set, I take a seat in one of those iconic directors' chairs near the back of the vast studio filled with scaffolding, camera tracks, and a hive of activity.

The warm overhead lights cast a glow over everything, and there's a musty smell lingering from the pyrotechnics. It's not often James is in a studio filming; often sets are outside, or 'on location', as it's called, but this particular scene is inside. They've constructed a detailed *Orient Express*-style train, the kind you'd expect to see in a classic film, not the typical commuter trains. The side of the train is exposed, revealing elegant dining tables with vintage table lamps with fringes. However, the far end of the set has been damaged in a fire, hence the musty smell.

On the other side of the set, the scene they are working on now, is a modern, masculine lounge. The movie is a light-hearted romantic action film, with plenty of action, and a sprinkling of romance.

James is playing the part of a former assassin, named

270

Dean, who teams up with the cops to bring down a notorious criminal gang. Along the way, he meets a captivating woman who brings both chaos and love into his life.

James spots me from across the set, and his face lights up with a smile. He makes his way through the maze of equipment and crew up to where I'm sitting.

"Hey, beautiful," he says, wrapping me in a warm hug. "You made it!"

"Yep, thought I'd come and see how the movie magic happens," I reply, looking around with curiosity. "How's it going?"

"Good," he says. "We're almost done with this scene. It's been a long week, but we're making progress. Shouldn't be too long."

"Positions please!" bellows the director, Martin.

"Gotta go, enjoy!" he says, and he runs back down onto set. The lighting shifts dramatically, surrounding me in darkness and illuminating the apartment on set. A cameraman manoeuvres into position, accompanied by a figure holding a grey fluffy microphone above them.

"Quiet on set! Roll cameras!" shouts a crew member.

"Camera one rolling," echoes another voice.

"Camera two rolling" follows another. A clapper board is hoisted into view, its sharp snap echoing as it's swiftly closed in front of a camera. Quiet murmurs sound among the director and some crew members, until Martin's voice resounds once more:

"And *action*!"

As James, sorry Dean, sits in the lounge, engrossed in his reading, the eerie silence of the apartment is shattered by the faintest of sounds. His senses sharpen, alerting him to imminent danger. He rises from his seat, turning off the lights as he positions himself behind the door, hidden from view. A camera zooms to the other side of the set.

In the darkness, an intruder is lurking. Dean braces himself as the doorknob twists and the door creaks open; the silhouette of the assailant looms in the doorway, oblivious to Dean's presence.

Even from back here in the rafters, I can feel the tension hanging thick in the air above the set as the intruder steps into the room, unaware of the trap that lies in wait just behind the door. Dean remains poised, ready to spring into action at the opportune moment.

As Dean steps forwards towards the attacker with calculated precision, he delivers a powerful punch from behind, sending the intruder crashing to the ground. The impact reverberates through the room, captured faintly on one of the cameras positioned in front of the director. The assailant grunts and attempts to rise, but Dean seizes the opportunity, delivering a swift kick while he's down. He retaliates, sweeping his leg under Dean's, causing him to tumble to the ground. Dean scrambles, trying to evade the incoming assault, but a punch strikes him squarely in the face. I grimace as the scene unfolds with startling realism. Dean, undeterred, retaliates with a well-aimed kick between the legs, incapacitating the attacker long enough for him to regain his footing. He grabs the intruder by the scruff of his neck and hurls him backward onto a glass coffee table that shatters by the force of the impact.

The director's voice cuts through the chaos, commanding, "*Cut!*"

As they step down from the set, James and his co-star make their way over to a TV screen where the director is seated. They huddle around, watching a playback of the scene, their expressions intent as they analyse each movement and gesture. There's animated discussion, accompanied by vigorous pointing at the screen, as they fine-tune the choreography of the fight sequence. Amidst the discussions, I feel a light tap on my shoulder. Amanda Hamilton. She settles into the chair beside me; I offer her a friendly nod and smile in acknowledgement. She's wearing a smart brown suit, which seems fitting for her role on set, although I can't quite picture her donning it on Rodeo Drive, definitely not her usual style.

"How are you doing?" she asks, her tone warm and genuine.

"Good, thanks. You?" I reply, reciprocating the friendly gesture.

"Great, just wrapped for the day. Planning to head home as soon as they're done here," she shares, her demeanour relaxed. "How are things with you and James?" she casually asks.

"We're fine, thanks."

"We missed you at the gala in Paris last week."

"Yes, I had an important case this week I needed to prep for."

The tone of her next question catches me off guard slightly, and there's a hint of concern in her voice that immediately makes me wary. "Oh right, so things are okay between you and James, then?"

"Yes, why do you ask?" I reply, my tone carefully neutral.

"Well, it's just after that article came out, I just wondered, wanted to make sure you were all right."

"What article?" My heart skips a beat, and I can feel the first tendrils of anxiety curling around me.

"About James and Mel." The mention of an article about James and Melinda sends a jolt of apprehension through me. My brows knit together in confusion.

"Oh, you haven't seen it? I'm so sorry, I thought you would know." Her apologetic tone does little to ease my growing apprehension.

"Know what?"

"Melinda was at the gala last week. It came out yesterday, I think, a picture of the two of them, together. They looked... close." Her words land like a punch to the gut, a wave of hurt and confusion washing over me. James hadn't mentioned seeing Melinda at the gala. I attempt to remain stoic despite the turmoil now brewing within me. What does she mean, 'they looked close'?

"Oh, yes, James did mention something about seeing her. I'd forgotten. There's an article online, you say?"

"Yes, but I'm sure it's nothing." As much as I want to brush off Amanda's dismissive words, they linger, heavy and unsettling.

"Did they look close?" The question tumbles out before I can stop it, and I instantly regret it. Her hesitation before answering only fuels the anxiety gnawing at me. It's like she's playing some sort of strategic game, carefully considering her next move, and I can't help but feel like a pawn on the board. Despite knowing better, the doubt has already taken root, and it's not going anywhere easily.

"Um... yes, for a while, it looked like they were...

reminiscing." Her response lands like a blow, her words confirming my worst fears. The image of James and Melinda together, seemingly lost in reminiscence, sends a surge of pain through me. I nod silently, trying to keep my composure while my mind races with a whirlwind of emotions, questions.

Amanda stands and places a hand on my shoulder. "Looks like they are wrapping up down there. I'm going to get myself ready to go home. Nice to see you, Nikki. See you again soon, and don't worry, I'm sure it was nothing." She smiles but it doesn't reach her eyes.

"Bye, Amanda."

When she's out of view, I instinctively reach for my phone, but then I remember the strict no-phone policy on set. I'm left alone with my spiralling thoughts.

Half an hour later, James finally makes his way over to me, looking happy but tired.

"Hey, babe." He greets me with a warm smile, oblivious to the storm brewing inside me. "I'm done here for today. What did you think?"

As he sits down beside me, I'm torn between the desire to confront him about the article and the fear of what his response might be. I force a smile. "That was a lot of work for what seems like a very small scene!"

James laughs. "That was a retake – we needed to tweak some things now we are near the end of filming. Ready to go home? It's been a long day!"

"Yeah," I say weakly.

"Come on, then. Let's go get my stuff and get out of here."

Forty-One

The article:

A LOVE REKINDLED?

James Keller spotted embracing ex-wife, Melinda. Could they be rekindling their romance?

James Keller was in Paris at the weekend attending the Eve awards and was spotted embracing ex-wife Melinda Stratford. The couple, who divorced eight years ago, haven't been seen together in public since their split. James has recently made headlines with new British girlfriend Nikki Harper, but Nikki was noticeably absent as the former couple looked close. Could this be the start of an old flame reigniting? A love triangle?

As I read the words, the world seems to tilt slightly on its axis. James and Melinda, spotted together in Paris, their embrace captured for all to see. The image burns into my mind's eye. James, dressed casually, his back turned to the camera, enveloped in an embrace with his ex-wife, Melinda. Her slender frame, her dark hair cascading down her back, so similar to mine, clad in a sleek black jumpsuit with a gold belt.

The first picture shows them locked in an intimate embrace, Melinda's chin resting on James's shoulder, her eyes closed in what looks like contentment. Her fingers pressed into his back, a seemingly silent declaration of affection. Though James's face is turned away, the intimacy of the moment is undeniable, a stark reminder of the bond they once shared.

In the second image, they stand facing each other, hands clasped on each other's shoulders, smiles lighting up their faces. But it's the inclusion of the smaller picture that sends a chill down my spine. It's me – alone, looking sombre. I recognise the moment immediately – it was taken as we left the restaurant in New York. James was right beside me, his hand intertwined with mine. Yet, they've airbrushed him out, creating a narrative of loneliness and unhappiness, as if I'm rushing away from something unseen. It's a manipulation, a twisted representation that couldn't be further from reality.

But despite the distortion, the undeniable truth of James's embrace with his ex-wife remains. The painful reality of their connection is captured in those images.

As I sit on the sofa in James's trailer, my thoughts whirl like a tempest, consumed by the image and article before me. I scrutinise the picture, studying every detail. Do I truly believe the picture? Not really. But James's silence about seeing Melinda adds a troubling layer to the situation. His omission leaves a void, a silence that speaks volumes. Just then, James emerges from the bedroom, changed and ready to go, interrupting my thoughts.

"I'm tired. You ready to go home?"

I slide my phone across the counter, the article glaring up at him from the screen.

"Why didn't you tell me you met Melinda?" I keep my tone calm, but inside I'm angry and hurt. James picks up the phone, his eyes briefly skimming the article before he lets out a dismissive sigh. His reaction stings as he hands me back my phone, not bothering to read the article. I look at him, expecting an answer.

"For fuck's sake! I didn't tell you because I've been really busy and there's nothing to tell." His agitation annoys me as he zips up his bag.

"Really? You bump into your ex-wife that you've not seen in years, have what looks like a 'moment' with her, get photographed, and don't even bother to give me a heads-up?" I retort. My frustration rises, matching his.

"As far as I know, there was no media there!" His voice grows sharper.

"So, you thought I wouldn't find out?" I counter, my voice trembling with suppressed anger.

"No, I told you, there's nothing to tell. I saw her, I said hi, and that is all there is to it," he snaps.

"Amanda seems to think there could be some truth in it. She said you two looked close."

"Amanda is talking bullshit!" he snaps again.

"Is she?" I challenge him, meeting his gaze as his dark eyes bore into me. "I wouldn't have questioned it if you'd have told me about it in the first place, instead of letting me find out like this!" I say, pointing to the phone. "Have you slept with Amanda?" I blurt out.

"*What?*" he almost yells at me. "No!"

"She said you two had a *fling* once!"

"Like I said, she's talking bullshit," he snaps. His shoulders drop; he looks tired.

"Look, I'm sorry I didn't tell you. I'm just tired, I want to go home." With a heavy sigh, he gathers his things and heads for the car, leaving me to stew in my anger and frustration. Reluctantly, I follow suit. I'm pissed off. Sean locks up and begins the drive home. The silence in the car is deafening, a stark contrast to our usual chatter and intimacy. James retreats into his phone, while I stare out the window. *Poor Sean*, I think.

"Hey, Sean?" I break the silence. "I need to get something from town. Would you drop me off and pick me up in about an hour?"

"Sure," he confirms. James looks at me, slightly surprised that I'm detouring. "What do you need?" he asks in a softer tone.

"Just some bits and I'll get us dinner while I'm there." I meet his gaze, and for a moment, I see a flicker of vulnerability in his eyes.

"Okay, do you want me to wait for you?"

"No," I respond coldly, staying resolute in my decision to take some time apart to cool off. I can see he's no longer agitated; he looks tired and concerned. I am still cross, though, so he can be concerned for another hour at least. As Sean drops me off in town, I don't spare James a second glance, my silence speaking volumes as I exit the car. Instead, I focus my attention on Sean, offering him a brief nod of appreciation before stepping out into the bustling streets.

I'm still anonymous; I'm only recognised when I'm

with him, so I wander freely around some clothes shops for a while, browsing aimlessly, my attention divided between James and the racks of clothes in front of me. Eventually, I decide to seek refuge in a nearby coffee shop, craving the familiar comfort of a warm drink and the solace of a quiet corner. I dial Lizzie's number, the familiar ringtone echoing in my ear as I wait for her to answer. As soon as her voice fills the line, a sense of relief washes over me.

"Hi, darling! How's things?" She answers joyfully.

"Hey, Lizzie." I sigh. "Have you got time for a chat?"

"Sure, what's up?" Her joyful demeanour shifts to one of concern.

"He bumped into his ex-wife last week at some event in Paris," I start, careful not to mention his name just in case someone is within earshot. "He didn't tell me that he'd seen her. I only found out because Amanda told me. There's an article online – she thought I'd already seen it."

"What article?"

"Search his name and his ex's name," I tell her. The line goes quiet while she searches.

"Oh! I've found it," she says at last, her voice filled with a mix of disbelief and concern. As she reads through the article, I brace myself for her reaction. "Okay, well, that's not so bad. You know these people will turn the most innocent thing into something it's not just to get a story. He's big money for them, right?" Her words serve as a reminder that media sensationalism often distorts the truth for the sake of a story.

"Right. But he didn't tell me he'd bumped into her; it happened a week ago and he's been with me every night since."

"Have you asked him why?"

"Not directly," I admit, a pang of guilt tugging at my conscience. "But I confronted him about it earlier, and we just had our first fight over it. He brushed it off, said there was nothing to tell. He said he's been too busy, didn't think anything of it. He has been busy this week, long hours on set, but still…"

"Maybe there wasn't anything to tell," she suggests, siding with him. "Listen, he's so into you. You don't really think he'd do anything, do you? Because I don't."

"No." I sigh, but then I remember Amanda's words. "Amanda was there last week. She saw them. She said they looked close, like they were having a moment."

"And you believe her over him? Amanda? The most disingenuous person you've met, you said?"

"Good point. Oh, I don't know, I do believe him, but I'm annoyed that he didn't tell me," I say, the hurt still fresh in my heart.

"As you should be," Lizzie agrees, her voice firm yet empathetic, "but honestly, I really don't think you've anything to worry about. Where is he now?"

"Home. I was on set with him this afternoon when I found out. I confronted him when he'd finished filming for the day, we had a fight, and I asked Sean to drop me in town so I could cool off."

"Good idea," Lizzie acknowledges. "So what now, go home and have great makeup sex?"

I chuckle weakly at her suggestion, the tension between James and me still unresolved. "I think he's as annoyed with me for not trusting him as I am with him for not telling me."

"Well, go home, tell him you trust him, but you're hurt he didn't tell you about it, and take it from there," she advises. "He'll be fine and hopefully apologetic."

"Sound advice as always," I reply gratefully.

"Always," Lizzie responds warmly. "Now go home and good luck, love you!"

"Thanks, love you too."

I feel better having spoken to Lizzie. I wonder if James has a confidant in times of turmoil. Mark crosses my mind briefly, a trusted friend who can offer a different perspective on situations. I pop into the food hall and grab a luxury Thai green curry for our dinner, quick and easy, and call Sean.

Ten minutes later I'm in the car with Sean again, saying nothing as usual, staring out of the window. "Nikki?" I look up, startled. Did he just speak to me, voluntarily?

"It's not true," he says calmly and glancing at me in the rear-view mirror.

"What isn't true?"

"What's written online, and what Amanda said." Ah, James has confided in Sean. "I was there last week, I saw it all. I don't know what James and Mel said to each other, but it wasn't what it's been made out to be. I have privileged access to him, don't forget; I see everything." He sounds genuinely concerned and I feel a sense of relief wash over me.

"Hmm, you do, don't you," I acknowledge, and in that very moment, I decide that I really like Sean. James was spot on with him; he's honest and loyal.

As I walk into the kitchen, James is sitting on the sofa in silence staring into his drink; he looks up at me as I walk over to the fridge to put the contents of dinner inside.

"Are you okay?" he asks softly, his voice breaking through the silence that hangs between us. "Did you get everything you need?"

"Yes," I say, more abruptly than I intended. As he approaches me, the tension between us intense, I can't help but notice the subtle details – the way his dark jeans cling to his frame, the faint scent of spiced wine lingering in the air, the warmth of his gaze as it meets mine. In that moment, all the doubts and insecurities melt away, replaced by a fierce longing for closeness.

"I'm sorry I snapped at you and I'm sorry I didn't tell you." His voice carries a genuine tone of remorse. "I've been so busy this week, it genuinely slipped my mind, and I promise you that what's written is not true, nor is what Amanda said." He reaches out, his touch sending a shiver down my spine as he gently brushes a stray strand of hair from my face.

"I know," I reply, my voice softened by the warmth of his apology.

"I had no idea she was going to be there, I was caught completely off guard, and yes, it was nice to see her after all this time, but there's definitely nothing there anymore. I love you. You mean way too much to me. I wouldn't do anything to jeopardise what we have. We chatted for about five minutes, that's all. I told her all about you. She's happy for us. She's also happily married – we've both moved on," he explains earnestly.

"I was really hurt that I had to find out from someone else rather than you," I admit.

"I know, and I'm sorry. I should have told you."

"I'm sorry too," I respond, feeling the tension between

us slowly dissipate as he wraps his arms around me. I relax into his embrace.

"You don't believe what was written, do you?"

"No, I don't. I don't think I ever did; I was just hurt that I found out through Amanda and then she said you looked close. It snowballed for me," I confess.

"I'm really pissed at her for that."

"Don't be, not worth it. No damage done, right?"

"I hope not. You know things like this are going to happen; we have to come up with a coping strategy."

"I need to learn to cope with it, you mean, but you've got to be completely transparent with me, rule number one."

"Deal, lesson learnt. Friends again?"

"More than friends."

"I love you so much."

"I love you too." He pulls me close, pressing a tender kiss to the top of my head, before letting out a deep sigh.

"While we are talking, there's something else you should know."

I pull away from him slightly and look him in the eye, wondering what else.

"I've never slept with Amanda. Years back, we went out for dinner a couple of times. We were both single, but nothing happened with her, I promise you, but…" He pauses, thinking of his next sentence. "She did make a pass at me recently," he reveals. I take a step back and release my hold, my mind racing with questions.

"What do you mean by 'a pass'?"

"She tried to kiss me. She was pretty drunk."

"Where? When?" I press.

"Remember the London premiere? The after-party?"

"That was ages ago!" I exclaim, trying to comprehend the timeline of events.

"I know. I'm sorry. You were at the bar with Suzanne. She came over to me and said she wanted a private word about the film we're working on now, so I went out into the hallway beside the lobby with her."

"Then what happened?"

"She said she really enjoyed working with me, she thought we worked well together, made a good team." He pauses. I just stare at him, waiting for the next instalment. "Then she tried to kiss me."

"Did you kiss her?"

"No! I told her it's not what I want. I'm with you and I'm happy with you. I promise I didn't kiss her," James reassures me.

"And you didn't do anything to make her think you would be interested?" I ask, needing to understand the full extent of the situation.

"No," James asserts firmly, his gaze unwavering. "Listen, I just think she was a bit drunk and emotional. I may be wrong, but I think she and Martin may be having some issues," James offers, his explanation tinged with empathy.

"And that makes it okay?" I retort, my frustration bubbling to the surface again.

"No, of course not, but I genuinely think she was just having a moment. Honestly, babe, you have nothing to worry about." He pulls me close again and I sink into his embrace.

"I know, but there's something about her that I struggle

to get on with. Has anything happened since? Has she said anything about it, tried anything again?"

"No, and I've just let it go. I'm still working with her on this film, and her husband is the director."

"And you're the producer," I remind him.

"Yes, but we are close to finishing. I just want the job done with no interruptions."

"Okay," I concede, a sense of unease lingering in the air.

"Nik, I need you to trust me and let me deal with it," he pleads with me.

"Okay."

"Promise?" James implores, his gaze searching mine for reassurance.

"I promise, providing she doesn't try anything again or try to antagonise me again." My resolve is firm.

"I don't think she will," he reassures me.

"And you promise to tell me if she does?"

"I promise."

The next night, James and I do a little PR, as we venture out for dinner in Soho, enjoying a much-needed date night. He poses for a couple of selfies, our smiles genuine, and I get my first public kiss!

Forty-Two

Over the following weeks, we adapted well to cohabiting. I love coming home and seeing his belongings around, his jumper on the kitchen chair, his shoes in the cupboard, his toothbrush next to mine. He is still working long days in the London studio, but filming is due to finish very soon and the postproduction will start, the release date being late January. In between his work and my work, we host dinner parties, quite a few, with various people, but Lizzie and Duncan, Mark and Julia are our firm favourites. I love it that we all get on so well together – so well, in fact, we agreed to all go on an 'adult-only' holiday to Barbados after the release of the film.

We travelled with his sister Louise and her family to New York to celebrate Thanksgiving with his parents and his other sister, Dianne, and we agreed we would spend Christmas with my family at my parents' house.

Christmas comes around quickly; we've been living

together for almost three months with no hiccups, no arguments, and no outside noise; it's been lovely. Work has kept me busy; filming has finished, meaning James has been around a fair amount, with not too much travel.

It's Christmas Eve's eve and I'm in bed when James's phone rings beside me. Rebecca. It's 10pm here, so 5pm for her, assuming she's in New York now.

"James?" I call out to him in the bathroom. "Rebecca's calling."

"Okay, just coming," comes a reply.

I answer the phone. "Hi, Rebecca, it's Nikki. James is just coming."

"Hi, Nikki, how are you?"

"Good thanks. He's here, I'll pass you over. Have a great Christmas!"

"Happy holidays to you too," she replies.

James sits on the side of the bed and takes the phone from me; he leans forwards, resting his elbows on his thighs. I lie back and watch him closely. I'm not listening to a word he says. I can't take my eyes off him, sitting there in his briefs. Despite being in the UK now, his skin is still golden. His hair is dark and damp from the shower; his lats are wide and defined. I've never felt so much physical attraction to anyone. He takes my breath away; my body aches for him. Sex with my ex was just something I did; sex with James is something I want, really want. I love feeling that closeness with him.

"Okay." James sighs. "Thanks for letting me know. Have a great Christmas, speak soon." He hangs up the phone, places it on the bedside table and lies down next to me.

"All okay?" I ask, snuggling into him.

"She's letting me know about an article that came out today."

Not again, I think. "What article?"

"A Hollywood online one."

I give him a questioning look. "A US trash mag?"

"That's the one." He gives a half laugh. "Nothing major. Articles come out about me all the time, but she's on high alert after the last incident. She knows I'm pissed because, a, I didn't know Mel was going to be at that event in Paris, and, b, she didn't see the article afterwards. She dropped the ball and thinks I might fire her."

"Will you?"

"I might if something like that happens again. Anyway, apparently a close source has told them I'm unhappy about being in the UK. I can't even be bothered to read it."

"Oh. Are you unhappy?"

He looks at me like this is the stupidest question ever asked.

"Babe," he says, planting a kiss on my lips, "I'm the happiest I've ever been. I'm at the top of my career and I intend to stay there but more importantly I have you to share it with. I love coming home knowing you're there. I'm very happy." He kisses me again.

"So, who is the source, then, or have they just made that up for drama? It was probably Amanda," I say flippantly.

He shrugs. "That thought did cross my mind, probably not though."

"She wouldn't, would she?" I think for a moment. Maybe she would.

"Listen, Allison and Rebecca have contacts. They are going to check it out. Let's not worry about it, okay?"

"I'm not worried!" I say nonchalantly. "So, are you going to join me under the covers and give me my Christmas present or are you just going to lay there and tease me?"

Forty-Three

Christmas Eve and James has been working from home today. I spent the morning clearing some work emails, so I can relax over the break, and wrapping gifts for Lizzie's girls, Louise's children and gifts for Mark, Julia and their two as we are seeing them tonight. We have a rule in my parents' house that the adults don't buy for each other; we only buy for the girls. Mum and Dad buy for each other. Lizzie and Duncan buy for each other, and while I was single, I jumped in with Mum and Dad. This year, though, I'm no longer a third wheel. I have my own partner to buy for, but what the hell do you get someone who has everything, or if they don't, they have access to it? I've spent weeks thinking about it, and all I could come up with was cuff links! He says he doesn't want anything, but what he really means is he wants something I can't afford, like a helicopter.

We've both used the gym today, so we wouldn't feel bad indulging over the festive period. I gave up my high street gym soon after it became public knowledge that I was dating him. I found that people would stare. I'd hear whispering on the gym floor. Instead, I took Julia's advice and joined her private members' gym. I still use it unless I'm working out with James. I love working up a sweat with him, a different kind of sweat. We both lift weights and run; we are quite competitive with each other and like to spur each other on.

Later that evening, Nigel drops us at Mark and Julia's house for the evening. Mark opens the door wearing his best Christmas jumper.

"Ho ho ho!" he says playfully. It's a red knit with a fallen snowman on skis holding a beer and flashing lights; the slogan reads 'ON THE PISTE'. Jules then appears at the door; she's also wearing a Christmas jumper, also in red with white writing that reads 'UP TO SNOW GOOD!'

"Oh, you two are just perfect for each other! I feel underdressed!" I laugh as we go inside.

"Don't be silly. You look gorgeous as always, very chic," Jules compliments me. I'm wearing a brown animal print long floaty skirt with a tight black ribbed turtleneck and knee-high black boots with killer heels. James is in black jeans tonight, with a light grey V-neck sweater and a light purple shirt underneath.

Their entrance hall boasts the most beautiful real tree, standing an enormous twelve foot tall and tastefully decorated in gold and red.

"Oh, that is absolutely gorgeous!" I say, admiring the tree and breathing in the pine smell.

"Thanks," replies Jules. "Nightmare to decorate!"

"Did you do it?"

"This year, yes, but next year we are getting the professionals in again, aren't we, darling?" She gives Mark a stern look. I smile.

"We decided not to decorate this year as we are not going to be there much," I say, hopeful that next year we will go all out, in our own home.

"Fair enough. Anyway, come on in, guys!" Jules leads us through to the kitchen where Mark gets out the beer and wine. There's a Christmassy spiced aroma in the air from the lit candles on the island and another smaller tree in the far corner, again beautifully decorated in pinks and silver. Their two children, Ava and Thomas, come running into the kitchen, waving toy swords and pretending to battle each other.

"James? Can I be in one of your movies? *Pow!*" shouts Thomas. They are in their pyjamas ready for bed, but they are wired! Very noisy, charging around like Duracell bunnies on speed.

"They will not go to bed!" Jules states, with a look of exhaustion on her face and taking a big gulp of wine.

"Have they been like this all day?" I ask.

"Pretty much!" Mark replies. "It might be a long night!"

"Oh dear!" I reply sympathetically. "Perhaps James can read them a story?" I give him a playful nudge, expecting him to come up with an excuse not to.

"Sure I can!" he says. Jules and I look at each other wide-eyed.

"Thomas? Ava?" He raises his voice above their noise. They stop what they're doing and look at him. He's very commanding; I feel a little thrill go through me. "Why

293

don't we go upstairs, and I will read you both a really exciting story!" Thomas is immediately keen, but Ava needs a little more persuasion.

"And I'll tell you the story of how I once pranked my parents by changing all the clocks in the house."

"Okay," Ava succumbs.

"Good girl!" They say good night to all of us and James takes them upstairs. Peace reigns! Half an hour and he's back, looking pleased with himself.

"Are they asleep?" Jules asks him eagerly.

"Ava is. Thomas not quite but he's settled at least. I said you'd pop up and say good night."

"I will. You are my knight in shining armour. I thought they'd never calm down. I love this time of year, and I love to see the joy on their little faces, but fuck me, it's hard work!" We laugh.

"They're good kids!" he says.

"Right, mate, now we can get on with our evening, hopefully. We have decided what we are ordering." Mark hands James the local Indian takeaway menu to choose his dish. "What are Duncan and Lizzie up to tonight?" he asks me as James flicks through the menu.

"Same as you, I suspect, battling to get the kids to bed!"

He laughs. "Probably. Shame they couldn't come over, but we'll see them at New Year's. Are you with them tomorrow?"

"Yeah, we're spending tomorrow with them and my parents. At least if their girls stay up tonight, they should go to bed early tomorrow – they'll be so exhausted!"

"You hope they do!" he teases me.

Once James has decided, Mark places our food order,

and we settle on the sofa in the kitchen. I glance outside. The patio lights are on, and I'm reminded of my first time here, when James asked me if I wanted to officially date him, and now we're living together. I look at him now, smiling, laughing, enjoying time with his friends, enjoying time with me, and my heart feels full.

Fifty minutes later and our food arrives from the best Indian takeaway in Richmond. It smells delicious, the spicy aroma mixed with coconut, and a nice bottle of wine, or two, maybe three, oh, and the shots!

Forty-Four

Christmas morning. We wake early. I roll over and snuggle James; he puts his arm around me. "Merry Christmas, baby," he says, placing a kiss on my head.

"Merry Christmas!" I give him only a peck this morning – a heavy night on the alcohol and I'm not as fresh as I'd like to be. "Ouch!" I say, groggily lifting my head from the pillow to accommodate his arm.

"Ooh, bad head?"

"Yep."

"We drank a fair amount last night, or should I say, you drank a fair amount!"

"You didn't do too badly yourself! Those two are a bad influence!" James laughs at me. We left their house at about 1am, got home and got a bit frisky with each other.

"Hmm, tequila!" he reminds me. Ooh tequila – I feel slightly sick – a few games of Yahtzee, and truth or dare. Oh my God, truth or dare! I remember now and I wish

296

I didn't. I cringe at the memory. We played quite a few rounds. I chose dare for the first round: read out the last text you sent. That was easy; it was to my mum. Allow another player to blindfold me and feed me an item from the fridge. Mark got that one and I got a cucumber slice. Finally, gargle water until my next turn. James chose dare once and he had to give a one-minute foot rub to Mark. Now the truth questions. I learnt that Jules once stole some sweets from her friends' parents' shop; I learnt that Mark dined and dashed in his teens; and I learnt that James had a crush on one of his teachers.

"James?" It's Julia's turn to ask him. "Do you ever watch your own movies when you're alone?"

"No, not for entertainment purposes anyway."

"So, you do, then?" Mark laughs.

"No, I'm way too critical of them," he protests.

"Nikki, do you watch his movies when you're alone?" Julia asks me the same question. I try my best not to look sheepish. The truth is yes, on occasions I have done; I love to see him on the screen.

"Um…" I hesitate. "Err yeah I have done." I screw up my face in embarrassment. Julia and Mark high-five each other.

"Do you?" asks James teasingly.

"Sometimes, when you're away," I admit. "I miss you, plus I like them. I'm not going to stop watching them just because you're in them."

"Ahhh!" says Julia. "That's sweet!"

The more we drank, the more risqué the questions got. I learnt that Julia's favourite sex position was reverse cowgirl and they learnt that I had performed a rusty trombone! James did his best to keep a straight face when I answered that, but I think they knew.

"Nikki, truth or dare?" Mark asks.

"Truth!" I challenge him.

"Okay." He relaxes back on the sofa like he's going to enjoy this. "Do you…" he starts slowly then gathers speed, "want to marry James and have lots of babies with him?" He's trying to make me squirm; he looks me straight in the eye to see if I flinch. I don't. I'm a lawyer! A drunk one! Jules sits up straighter, keen to know the answer, and James relaxes back with his drink, like nothing fazes him, and just waits for my answer. I let them wait for a few moments before I finally shout, "Yes!" A little too enthusiastically. I raise my shot glass up and clink it with Mark's! It didn't bother me last night, being so bold. It didn't appear to bother James either – he laughed at my reaction – but now in the cold light of day, I feel more than a little embarrassed!

"Poor Nigel, we dragged him out so late!" I say, trying to wipe the image of me being overzealous from my mind!

"Don't worry, he's well looked after," James reassures me. "So, truth or dare, that was funny."

"Hmm," I murmur, hoping he says no more. He pauses, thoughtfully.

"It got me thinking."

Oh shit, here we go, ground swallow me up. "Oh yeah? What about?"

"We're happy living together, right? I know I am, are you?"

"I am, I'm very happy."

"So, I was thinking, why don't we make it more

permanent, and look at buying somewhere to live, here in the UK, outside of London?"

"Why? Can you no longer afford the rent?" I tease.

"I don't *want* to afford the rent, but seriously, why don't we?"

"You really want to?"

"I absolutely do, and not just for financial reasons!" he jests.

"I'd love to!" I kiss him, on the lips; what a wonderful Christmas gift. At this precise moment I'm not sure what excites me more, living somewhere of our own or just house shopping!

"Let's do it, then. Start shopping for us." He holds me tightly. "What time are we due at your parents?"

"At 1pm. They are playing a few holes of golf whilst dinner is cooking."

"Okay," he says softly as I turn on my side and he spoons me. "I love you," he says.

"I love you too." We drift back to sleep for another hour.

Several hours later, we are all thoroughly stuffed after a glorious Christmas lunch, courtesy of Mum and Dad. To fend off the inevitable food coma, we bundled up and took a brisk walk through the fields behind my parents' house, and James managed to go unnoticed.

Back at the house after we'd blown away the cobwebs, Lizzie's girls were doing their best to wait patiently for their gifts. I say 'patiently', but they were practically glued to the tree, fingering every gift, trying to guess what was in it, holding them up, shaking them, trying to sneak a peek under the paper. At long last, Lizzie and Duncan decide to put them out of their misery. What followed was a whirlwind of torn wrapping paper and discarded packaging, as Mum frantically tried to collect the debris in a black sack. With presents out of the way, we settled into a game of charades. James, unsurprisingly, was a natural. It was girls versus boys, and I was teamed up with Lizzie and Mum – who, bless them, were about as useful as chocolate teapots. Needless to say, the boys won. A typical family Christmas, full of love and laughter.

James and I had exchanged gifts before we arrived at Mum and Dad's. He'd surprised me with a pair of exquisite diamond stud earrings and a beautifully hand-crafted wooden jewellery box, which hopefully means more to come. Oh, and did I mention a house? I did get him the cuff links in the end, eighteen-carat gold, engraved with the initials 'JN' on them. He seemed genuinely touched and promised to wear them at the premiere, and, with a little help from Allison, I managed to snag VIP tickets to a concert, a sold-out concert! I think he was pleased!

Upstairs, Duncan is valiantly trying to calm the girls down and get them to bed – I think he might be there some time – while we all settle down to watch what I consider to be the best Christmas movie ever – *Die Hard*. James, however, disagrees. He likes the film, but he thinks the best Christmas movie is *The Holiday*, which, coincidentally, happens to be Mum's favourite too, so he scored some serious brownie points with her. I suspect he might secretly prefer *Die Hard* but is trying to keep on Mum's good side. We'll just have to agree to disagree on this one.

My parents' lounge is spacious with its high ceiling and

warm oak panelling lining the walls. Large windows flood the room with natural light. There's plenty of sitting room and a square coffee table that looks like a giant footstool, its dark glass top giving it away. A magnificent fireplace holds a crackling log burner, and in the corner stands a real Christmas tree with warm white lights twinkling softly, adding to the room's cosy charm.

Dad stands from the chair and begins gathering glasses.

"Right, before we settle down to watch the film that screams Christmas at you, does anyone want a tipple?"

"Oh, good idea, Keith," Mum agrees. "I'll have a Baileys please, oh and can you bring in the sweet tub and a few nibbles?"

"I'll have another wine, please, Dad," I add, following suit.

"Me and Duncs will take another wine too, thanks," Lizzie chips in.

"James? Anything for you?" Dad asks.

"Yeah, but I'll come and give you a hand," James replies, getting up from the sofa.

"Oh good, we'll start house shopping!" Lizzie teases, her eyes sparkling.

"Go for it," James says with a grin.

"What's the budget?" she asks, utterly unabashed.

"There's no budget," James responds nonchalantly, prompting Lizzie's eyes to light up like a child in a candy shop. He smiles at us, then heads off to the kitchen with Dad. Mum remains in her chair, flicking through the *Radio Times*, while Lizzie and I resume our earlier house-hunting mission, this time with renewed enthusiasm.

"Found one!" Lizzie exclaims, waving her phone excitedly. "It's got a bloody helipad!"

"What?" I exclaim, leaning over to see. "Well, that's it, then – James will be sold! Let me have a look."

Lizzie hands me her phone, and I first check the location – close by, which is promising. Then, I glance at the price tag: £6,990,000 for a six-bedroom detached house. Wow! I scroll through the twenty-five photos, starting with a shot of the helipad, which features a large 'H' that looks big enough to be seen from space. It appears to be close to the house – imagine the noise! There's also a large pond with a charming wooden bridge, a long tree-lined drive, a beautifully manicured lawn, a cinema room, an indoor pool with black tiles (which gives the water an unsettlingly dark appearance), a gym, and a tennis court. It's undeniably stunning, but with its modern and somewhat clinical vibe, I'm not entirely sure I love it. I add it to the favourites and continue the search.

A few more beautiful homes catch my eye, but none of them feel quite right. We need land, we need privacy. Then, one listing stands out: price on application. The one below it is £9 million, so this is likely more. But, as James said, there's no budget. The location is also nearby, rural but with a train station close. Oh my God! It's gorgeous! The first photo shows a front entrance that features a tower with a spiral roof, giving it a slightly gothic, church-like appearance. The red brick and stone building stretches out in an L-shape from the tower. According to the listing, it's in an Italianate style. Without even looking at the other pictures, I'm in love. All ten thousand square feet of it, along with the ten acres of grounds.

"This one," I say to Lizzie.

At that moment, Dad pokes his head around the door. "Mandy, love, can we borrow you in the kitchen?"

Mum doesn't look up from her magazine. "Why?"

"Oh, we just need your help with something."

Mum raises an eyebrow, as if the request is terribly inconvenient, sighs a heavy sigh, and gets up to follow Dad out of the room.

"Oh wow!" Lizzie exclaims, scooting closer to me as we scroll through the pictures together. "The kitchen has *three* islands! Who needs three?"

"I do!" I laugh, admiring the circular island in the centre and the two curved ones in mahogany. There's also a breakfast table and a cosy seating area – just in the kitchen! The stairs, oh, the stairs! A grand staircase at the end of a long, wide entrance hall, complete with its own fireplace, sweeps dramatically up to a galleried landing.

"Oh my God! That master bedroom! And two en suite bathrooms, each with their own dressing room! Shit me, it's huge!"

"Isn't it gorgeous?" I exclaim.

"It certainly is!" Lizzie agrees. She reads the summary out loud. "The main house is ten thousand square feet, comprising three reception rooms, a playroom, a sunroom, a beauty room, a cinema room, a games room, six bedrooms, seven bathrooms, and a leisure suite with an indoor pool, jacuzzi, sauna, and gym. There are also offices and garaging, plus a three-bed flat and a two-bed flat. Oh my God! Do you need all that?"

"Maybe." I smile mischievously.

"That pool is gorgeous! I think I'll be moving in with

303

you!" Lizzie says, half joking, half serious. The decor is quite dark, with grey walls and shades of beige and brown. I absolutely love it!

"There's no helipad, though, but look at the grounds." I swoon, zooming in on the pictures. "Oh, and those gates! Look at them!" The gates, situated at the end of a long tree-lined driveway, are big black iron gates with the letters 'HH' in gold. The house is called Hartland Hall.

"Oh, I just love it!" I declare.

"Now you just need to convince James… Oh, speak of the devil." The door opens, and Mum walks back in, whispering something to Dad with a bowl of sweets in one hand and a bowl of nuts in the other, which she places on the coffee table. Dad follows with a bottle of champagne and some glasses.

"Champs?" Lizzie asks with a grin.

"Yes, it's Christmas Day, so why not?" Dad replies, smiling joyfully at her. Even Mum is smiling! Lizzie and I exchange glances, sensing that something is up. The door opens again, and James and Duncan enter, carrying glasses.

"Are they down?" Lizzie asks Duncan.

"Yep, both out like lights!"

"Good." She moves to sit on the sofa opposite with him. James comes and sits next to me as Dad expertly pops the champagne cork.

"Well done," James compliments him as he fills our glasses and raises a toast.

"It's wonderful to have all three of my girls here, along with my granddaughters. I feel very lucky, and seeing my two girls looking so happy warms my heart."

"Is he pissed?" Lizzie whispers, laughing. I stifle a giggle.

"No, Lizzie, I am not! Just happy, that's all. I've had a wonderful day with wonderful people."

"He's definitely pissed!" I say, laughing, as James nudges me.

Finally, we let Dad finish his toast. "Merry Christmas, everyone!"

"Merry Christmas, Dad!"

"Merry Christmas!" James hands me my glass and wraps an arm around me. "Did you find anything?" he asks.

"Two potentials," I reply.

"One of them has a helipad!" Lizzie calls out from across the room.

"Oh, sold then!" James laughs. "Show me later." He pulls a soft, warm blanket over us and we snuggle down to watch what I still insist is the best Christmas movie ever: *Die Hard*.

Late the next morning, after a leisurely breakfast, James and I say our goodbyes and head out to spend the day with his sister Louise and her family – much like we did yesterday, with more food, more booze, and plenty of laughter.

"Uncle James! Uncle James!" The two older kids come hurtling towards him, arms wide open, their excitement infectious. To them, he's like Father Christmas, and he certainly didn't disappoint this time.

James had gone all out and had their gifts delivered to the house, ready for them – an all-singing, all-dancing baby bouncer for the little one, an electric Porsche for the middle child, and a massive ten-foot trampoline for the older two to share. The looks on their faces were priceless, pure joy radiating from them. Rob and James rolled up their sleeves and spent the next two hours outside, assembling the trampoline while the kids buzzed around them, too excited to wait.

Later, as we all sat around the table, sipping on drinks and chatting, we shared our news. "We're looking to buy a place here in the UK, somewhere closer to you," he says with a smile.

Louise's eyes lit up, her face breaking into a wide grin. "That's fantastic! You don't know how happy that makes me!" She was absolutely thrilled, and I could tell that, for her, this news was the best gift James could have given.

Forty-Five

New Year's Eve

*a*s James finishes shaving in the bathroom, I stand in front of the mirror, trying to decide on a dress for the evening. My wardrobe is strewn with options, but I'm finding it hard to settle on the right one.

"Oh, I forgot to mention – Sean has a date tonight," James says casually, glancing at me in the mirror.

"Sean? Really?" My curiosity piques instantly. Who does he speak to enough to get a date with? "Who's the lucky girl?"

"Yep, he's taking her to The Ivy for dinner," James continues, a mischievous glint in his eye. "And then they're coming here to see in the new year."

"Very sweet of you to get him that table," I say, arching an eyebrow. "Or should I say, very sweet of Allison to use your name to get him that table."

James chuckles, not bothering to deny it. "Either way, he's sorted for the evening."

"So, who is she? Is she coming here too?" I press, eager for more details.

James grins at me, clearly enjoying this little game. "Yep, but you'll have to wait and see."

"Ooh, how exciting!" I exclaim, already speculating as to who it could be.

His tone shifts to a more serious note. "Speaking of exciting things, we haven't had a chance to discuss the two properties we saw yesterday."

We'd visited two stunning properties the day before – Hartland Hall, which is vacant as the family have moved abroad, and the helipad property. Both were gorgeous, but we hadn't had time to discuss our thoughts on them properly.

"I think I know the answer, but did you like either of them?" James asks, watching me closely.

"I did," I reply, slipping into my underwear, my voice tinged with excitement.

"Let me guess, the very expensive one without the helipad?" he teases.

"Correct," I admit with a grin. "The other one was lovely, and I'd be more than happy there, but if I'm honest, my heart is with Hartland Hall."

"That's good," he says, stepping out of the bathroom to sit on the bed facing me. "I preferred that one too."

"You did? Even without the helipad?" I look at him in surprise, trying to read his expression.

"Yes, I mean, let's be honest, we could always put one in, or just land somewhere in the massive grounds!" He laughs, clearly unbothered by the absence of a helipad. "It's got everything we want. I liked the feel of it the moment we walked in, and the location is perfect. I can see us living there."

"The price tag isn't so great," I murmur, feeling a bit guilty over the £13.5 million cost. I know James is incredibly wealthy, but I can't help but feel the enormity of the sum.

"Let me worry about that," he says dismissively. "So, do you want it?" he asks, as if he's offering to buy me a new dress, not an estate worth millions.

"Are you serious?" I question, not daring to believe it.

"I am if you are," he replies with a grin.

"Holy shit, yes! Really?" I finally allow myself to smile, the excitement bubbling up inside me.

"Really. Leave it with me," he says, getting up to kiss me lightly on the lips before heading to his wardrobe.

"What does that mean?" I ask, my mind still reeling.

"Exactly what I said – leave it with me. If the lady wants it, then the lady shall have it."

I throw my arms around him, kissing him all over his face. It feels like a dream. Where we live now is impressive, but this… this is something else entirely.

With a newfound spring in my step, I finally settle on my dress for the evening. It's a night for black tie, so James and I are pulling out all the stops. I opt for a full-length black dress that clings in all the right places. The single sleeve is elegant, and the high slit adds just the right amount of allure. Black sequins catch the light with every step I take, and I sweep my hair into an updo, leaving a few loose strands to frame my face and highlight the stud earrings he gave me for Christmas. My perfume – a soft, floral scent – complements his spiced cologne perfectly. I keep my makeup subtle, except for my lips, which I paint in a bold, Marilyn Monroe red.

For his part, he's dressed in a classic black jacket with satin lapels, a crisp white dress shirt with double cuffs, and the gold cufflinks I gave him for Christmas. His hair is freshly cut and styled with a slight spike; it's edgy, and I like it. As he applies his cologne – a rich, old spice aroma that's unmistakably him – I feel irresistibly drawn to him. He looks devastatingly handsome, and I can't help but feel like the luckiest woman in the world.

We've kept the guest list intimate, just sixteen of us. Our closest friends, Mark and Jules, along with Lizzie and Duncan, who are staying over for the night. My parents are watching the girls, giving us a rare chance to celebrate without interruption. Claire and Richard, Ivy and Tyrone, Suzanne and her husband Mitchel, Sean and his mystery date, and finally Amanda and Martin round out the group. I'm not thrilled about Amanda and Martin – Amanda, actually – but James insisted, and I've resolved to be the perfect hostess regardless. Louise and Robert were invited too, but they had other plans.

As the catering team finishes up, the first guests arrive – Lizzie and Duncan. I show them to their room to get changed, giving me a moment to breathe before the rest of the guests begin to trickle in, all looking spectacular in their formal wear. Tyrone arrives wearing a deep red velvet jacket that stands out beautifully against his black trousers and white dress shirt. He's a striking figure – tall, with a shaven head, deep brown skin, and a smile that could light up any room. Linking arms with Ivy, I whisper to her as we walk into the lounge.

"He's hot!"

"I know!" She swoons.

The last guests to arrive are Amanda and Martin, fashionably late, of course. Martin looks every bit the gentleman in a white dinner jacket that complements his salt-and-pepper hair perfectly. Amanda, meanwhile, is wearing a white fitted off-the-shoulder dress that bears a striking resemblance to the one I wore to the premiere. The scent of her perfume is potent, hitting me like a wave the moment she steps into the room – it's the kind of fragrance that sends a shock to your senses, much like a strong red wine. But I must admit, she looks good. We all do.

"Hey." Lizzie sidles up to me as I'm pouring myself another drink.

"Hi, want a top-up?" I ask, offering the bottle.

"Go on then," she says, holding out her glass.

"Oh, I haven't told you yet, have I?"

"Told me what?" She raises an eyebrow, intrigued.

"James and I looked at those two houses – you know, the ones we found on Christmas Day?"

"Blimey, you two don't hang about, do you?" She takes a swig of her drink, clearly impressed.

"No, we don't. It's one of the things I love about him – he's decisive, just like me. Anyway, we've chosen."

"Ooh, which one?" she asks, leaning in.

"The big one!" I can't help but grin like a Cheshire cat.

"Oh my, so not the one with the helipad?"

"Nope, the other one. We both preferred it. You just have to see it, Lizzie – it's even better than the pictures!"

"And the pictures were amazing! So, what's next? Do you make an offer?"

"I guess so. James just said to leave it to him."

"Wow! Well, fingers crossed you get it. Knowing James, you will."

"I hope so, I really love it," I say, my excitement bubbling over. We clink our glasses and head back to join the others.

The next couple of hours are great fun. Everyone is in high spirits, indulging in food, drink, and the kind of light-hearted games that bring out the best in people – Heads Up!, charades, a bit of dancing, and plenty of conversation. It's the perfect way to ring in the new year. But despite the festive atmosphere, a small cloud lingers over my mood: Amanda.

I can't help but notice her behaviour; subtle though it is, her flirting with James hasn't escaped my attention. Each time she's near him, her hand finds its way to his arm or shoulder – a fleeting touch, just enough to remind him she's there, and to make it clear that she's interested. James seems either completely oblivious to her advances or he's choosing to ignore them, which I suppose I should find reassuring. But it doesn't stop the unease from creeping in.

Maybe it's the alcohol – Amanda's had more than her fair share, and perhaps it's making her bolder than usual. Maybe I'm overthinking things, letting my imagination run wild. That said, she's barely exchanged more than a few words with Martin since they walked in. I can't shake the feeling that there's more to her actions than just a bit of New Year's Eve exuberance.

It's 11pm, and the door buzzes. James heads out to answer it. "Who's that?" I ask, following behind.

"The moment of truth," he replies, then I remember: Sean was coming over, with a date. He opens the door and Sean walks in with a smile on his face, which stops me dead in my tracks. Before I can greet him, James says, "Hey Sean, come on in. Allison! Good to see you!"

Allison?

James greets her warmly, even planting a kiss on her cheek. I quickly recover, stepping forwards to welcome them both with a smile and a kiss on the cheek, though the gesture feels a bit awkward given the circumstances. "Hi! How was your dinner?" I ask, trying to mask my surprise.

She looks good, she's smiling, and her mousey hair has been blow-dried with a slight wave, which softens her face. She's wearing a nice black dress, quite formal still, with kitten heels; she even looks like she's wearing a bit of makeup. She looks… feminine, and happy!

"It was wonderful," Allison replies, her smile still in place, her eyes sparkling in a way I've never seen before.

"Yes, it was very good, thanks for organising it for us, James," Sean adds, looking just as happy.

"My pleasure," James replies smoothly. "The least I can do given how well you two look after me. Come on in, you know everyone here. Can I get you both a drink? We've got a bottle of champs open if you want some?"

"I will have a glass if I may?" Allison responds.

"Can I have a beer to start with?" Sean asks, offering his arm to Allison as they make their way into the lounge. I can't help but feel a rush of warmth as I watch them together – they're sweet, unexpectedly so.

I follow James into the kitchen to fetch their drinks, still processing this unexpected turn of events. "James?" I whisper, even though it's just the two of us. "Sean and Allison?"

"I know!" he whispers back, looking just as amused as I am. "He confided in me some time ago that there was someone he liked. I had my suspicions it was her, but I think, given their jobs, he was cautious."

"As he should be," I say, the lawyer in me kicking in.

"No lawyering me now!" James teases me. "Do I need to draw up new contracts for them both now that they're potentially entering a carnal relationship?" He winks at me, clearly enjoying the situation.

"You might want to consider it!"

I laugh.

Forty-Six

It's a quarter to midnight, and the party is in full swing. The music pulses through the room, mingling with the hum of lively chatter. I look around for James, but there's no sign of him, so I slip out of the room into the hall and towards the kitchen to get the champagne for the New Year's toast. The kitchen door is slightly ajar, and I freeze as I hear a familiar voice. Amanda. Her tone is unmistakable, though shriller than usual, thanks to the drinks she's had.

I pause, my hand hovering above the door handle. Something makes me hesitate, like an instinctive warning that tells me not to barge in. There's a small gap in the door, just enough for me to peer through. The kitchen is dimly lit, with only the glow from the island lights casting shadows. James is by the fridge, reaching in for the bottles of champagne, and Amanda is right there beside him.

"Here, let me take that," I hear her say, her voice syrupy sweet.

"Thanks," James replies.

Suddenly, Lizzie appears behind me, making me jump.

"What are you—" she starts, but I quickly hush her, pressing a finger to my lips.

"Shh! Listen," I whisper. She leans in closer, her ear to the door as we both strain to hear.

"I'm glad we've got a moment alone," Amanda says, placing the champagne bottle on the island with deliberate slowness. "I've been trying to get you by yourself all evening."

"Oh yeah? What's up?" he replies, not seeming to notice her subtle advance, but I do. My heart clenches as I watch her move closer to him, her hand sliding across the countertop. He places the third bottle on the counter, turning towards her, but she's already too close – far too close for my liking.

"You know I like you, James. I mean, really like you," Amanda purrs, her fingers trailing down the front of his shirt. My breath catches in my throat as I turn to Lizzie, whose eyes are wide with disbelief.

"Go in!" Lizzie mouths urgently, pointing at the door. I shake my head, feeling a knot of guilt twist in my stomach, but I can't move. I need to see how this unfolds.

"Amanda," James begins, his tone serious, but she silences him with a finger to his lips.

"I know you're with Nikki, but I can't help it. I'm really attracted to you. I want you." She leans in, clearly aiming for a kiss. My heart pounds in my chest, dread curling in my gut as I watch. For a split second, James doesn't pull away. Instead, he lets her kiss him, a fleeting moment that feels like an eternity, but just as quickly, relief washes over me as he stops her, gently removing her hand.

"No, Amanda, stop," he says, stepping back. "This isn't going to happen. You're a beautiful woman," he says, his voice steady, "but I love Nikki. I'm in love with Nikki. And I have the utmost respect for Martin. This isn't going to happen – not with you, not with anyone."

He steps back again, putting further distance between them. From my angle, I can't see her face, but I imagine the sting of rejection is written all over it.

"I'm sorry, Amanda," James adds softly. "I don't want to hurt you."

Amanda hesitates, then tries one last time, taking a step towards him, her voice dropping to a sultry whisper. "Are you sure I can't tempt you?"

"Very sure," James replies, without a flicker of doubt. "Please, would you bring a bottle through with you?"

With that, he turns away, heading for the door. Lizzie and I scramble back into the lounge, our hearts racing as we rejoin the others, trying to act as though nothing has happened.

A few moments later and I feel James's hand rest on my back. "Hi, darling," I say, a wave of relief washing over me.

"Hi," he replies.

"Everything okay?" I ask, searching his face.

"Yep, everything is fine," he says, pressing a kiss to the side of my head. I follow his gaze as Amanda re-enters the lounge, a practised smile on her lips as she saunters over to join Ivy, Tyrone, Claire, and Richard. Martin still nowhere in sight. James turns to Mark, and together they begin organising the glasses for the New Year's toast. Lizzie tugs me aside, concern etched on her face. "Are you okay?" she asks quietly.

I let out a sigh. "Yeah… I knew it, though, I just knew she had a thing for him. I see women throwing themselves at him all the time, but they're just fans. She's different, she's relentless."

Suzanne strolls over, catching the tail end of our conversation. "Hey, who is relentless?" she asks. "You all right, Nikki?"

"Yeah," I reply, though my voice lacks conviction.

"What's up?" she presses. I hesitate for a moment, then decide to confide in her. "Amanda just tried to kiss James in the kitchen."

Suzanne's expression barely changes, as if she's not surprised. "What did he do?" she asks, calm as ever.

"He kissed her back. Only for a second, but still…"

Suzanne's eyes widen slightly, though she quickly masks her surprise. "What happened after?"

"He pulled away," I say, trying to keep my composure. "He told her to stop, that it wasn't going to happen," I add, the memory of his firm rejection a small comfort. "But… that moment – it was like everything slowed down, and I couldn't believe what I was seeing."

"Babe, he firmly shut her down!" Lizzie reassures me. "You know he's madly in love with you. You'd have to be blind not to see that!"

"Yeah, I know… but it's still not easy to witness."

"I agree with Lizzie," Suzanne adds, her eyes darting around to ensure no one else is listening. She lowers her voice. "But I have to tell you, it's not the first time she's tried it on with him."

"What?" I turn to her, my eyes wide with shock. "What do you mean?"

"I overheard her at the premiere, the one you were at."

I breathe a sigh of relief. "Oh, yes… James told me about that. He told me he refused her then, too. Did he?"

"He did, yes. He made it clear he wasn't interested, but it seems she didn't get the message."

"And it seems that when she drinks, she's all over him," I mutter.

"Watch her," Suzanne warns me. "I like Amanda, but I wouldn't trust her." Just then, James taps his glass, drawing everyone's attention.

"Guys! It's nearly midnight. Should we head out to the terrace to see the new year in?"

"Jolly good idea!"

"Yes, let's go!"

"Definitely!"

We put on our coats and go out onto the terrace to join the men. It's a nice, large, private space where we can hear Big Ben ring in the new year. The skies above are clear, the stars are twinkling, and though it's chilly, at least it's not raining! The London Eye shines bright blue, ready for the spectacular fireworks. We huddle together, glasses poised, when Mark suddenly asks, "Hang on, where's Martin?"

Just then, the door opens, and out walks Martin. "Sorry, just had to take a call," he says, shooting a brief look at his wife, who doesn't seem to notice the disgruntled expression on his face.

"No worries," James responds quickly, clearing his throat. "Hey, before the new year rings in, I just want to say thank you to all of you, our friends, for joining us tonight. I hope the new year brings you everything you wish for!"

"Hear, hear!" comes the cheerful response.

"*Ten! Nine! Eight! Seven! Six! Five! Four! Three! Two! One! Happy new year!*"

Big Ben chimes, ringing in the new year as fireworks burst into the sky. I throw my arms around James.

"Happy new year, baby!" I whisper, kissing him deeply.

"Happy new year! I love you so much!" he says, holding me tight and lifting me off the floor. We break apart as fireworks explode overhead and we all exchange New Year's kisses and hugs. Out of the corner of my eye, I see Amanda take a step towards James, her eyes locked on him. My heart skips, and before I can react, she's there. She throws her arms around his neck and – oh my God – she plants a full-on lingering kiss on his lips, right in front of everyone. My stomach flips, my blood boils. She doesn't care that I'm standing right here; she doesn't seem to care that her husband, Martin, is watching with a look of disbelief on his face. James is frozen, a look of shock on his face. His hands awkwardly out in front of him as he tries to step back, but Amanda has him locked in her grip. The nerve of her! My head pounds, my vision blurs with fury.

"*Amanda?*" I shout, my voice loud enough to snap everyone's attention. All eyes are on me, then on her. I step forwards, my voice low and threatening. "Get your hands off James. Now!"

She steps back, slowly, her smirk unfazed as she wraps herself in her pristine white coat. She gives a little laugh, almost a cruel, sarcastic laugh, and I can feel my pulse racing.

"I've had enough!" I can barely contain the fire in my voice. "I heard you tonight, in the kitchen with James. He said no, Amanda. No. And not for the first time either. Take the bloody hint."

James steps towards me, concerned, but I hold my hand out to stop him. I'm not done. My eyes burn into Amanda, who is still wearing that infuriating smirk. "I don't know what your game is, but it ends here. Now."

Martin steps forwards, quiet but firm. The rest of the group is rooted to the spot, frozen in silence, with the sky still lighting up above us.

"What did you say?" Martin's voice is steady but with a calm that cuts through the tension like a knife. He looks at me, and I feel a pang of sympathy for him.

"I'm sorry, Martin," I say softly, "but I saw Amanda try to kiss James tonight. In the kitchen, just before we came out here."

Amanda's face shifts, and she jumps to life, her voice shrill. "I did not!" she snaps. "*He* tried to kiss *me*!" She points at James, accusingly.

James lets out a short, incredulous laugh. "Amanda, you know that's not true."

Martin doesn't flinch. He's eerily calm. "You're lying, Amanda. I know that's not what happened." His voice is cold. "I heard you. I was in the next room, finishing a call. I heard everything." Lizzie shoots me a wide-eyed look, and I glance back, unsure how this will unfold.

Amanda flounders, her composure cracking. "It's not what you think, Martin," she stammers, trying to touch him, but he pushes her hand away.

"What was it, then?" His eyes are hard as he glares at her, then looks back at me. "You said it wasn't the first time?"

James moves closer to me, his voice steady. "She tried to kiss me at the London premiere," he admits. "I didn't say anything because I thought she was just drunk and emotional."

"It's true," Suzanne chimes in unexpectedly. "I saw it. I heard everything." James looks at her, surprised. "I was coming out of the bathroom when it happened." Martin stands expressionless, absorbing it all. My rage has softened, but my heart races. I glance at James, who looks quiet, pensive. I can't tell if he's angry – if so, with whom? Me or Amanda?

Then Amanda's voice, bitter and sharp, cuts through. "How's Mel?"

James blinks. "What?"

"You know, Mel? Your ex-wife? The one you looked 'close' to at the gala." Her voice drips with venom.

James looks baffled. "Why are you bringing that up? What are you talking about?"

But it hits me like a sledgehammer. Amanda's smirk, her taunting, and suddenly it all falls into place. "Did you set that up?" I ask, my voice calm but laced with suspicion. "Did you arrange for Mel to be there that night?"

Amanda shoots me a slanted smile. I can feel the anger rising again.

"You did," I whisper, shocked. "Did you leak the photos too?"

She shrugs. "What does it matter if I did? The fact is it happened. They were close. The pictures prove it!"

"It matters to me!" I shout, anger rising in me again.

"It matters to me too," James says, his voice hardening. "Did you do that, Amanda? Did you set it up?"

For a moment, there's a flicker of something in her eyes – hurt, maybe – but she quickly masks it with anger.

"You humiliated me!" she suddenly screams, champagne spilling from her glass as she points at him.

"When? When?" James shouts back, clearly at the end of his rope. She glares at him. "You're kidding! For saying no to you at the premiere?"

Martin holds up a hand, his voice colder than ever. "I've heard enough! Amanda, I'm leaving," he says to her.

"Okay," she replies quietly, like she knows she's lost the fight.

"No, I mean I'm leaving you; you can come home with me tonight but tomorrow you pack your things and get out; I've also had enough!" Everyone looks stunned; we weren't expecting that. I certainly didn't want that to happen. I just wanted her to back off James. James holds out a hand to Martin. He accepts.

"I'm sorry, Martin," he says to him.

"Don't worry about it, James. I'm sorry too. Thanks for a nice evening, up until that point." He glares at his wife, ex-wife now maybe. Martin gives me a hug and I apologise to him again, then he leaves with Amanda in tow. Poor guy must be very hurt and embarrassed. James walks them both to the door, while we all stand on the terrace, not speaking, wondering what the hell just happened, the fireworks still exploding around us.

"Are you okay, Nik?" Jules breaks the silence.

"Yeah, I'm okay, poor Martin, though!"

"Yeah, to be fair, though, he didn't seem that surprised that she'd done that," Mark observes.

"No, he didn't."

The chat resumes among us, mostly about Martin and Amanda, but life starts to come back to the party. For a while, I thought I'd ruined everyone's night. Then James walks back out onto the terrace. I don't know what he's thinking. Is he going to be fuming at me for the chaos I just caused? I step towards him.

"Hey," I say. "Are you okay?"

"Yeah," he says with a heavy breath. He moves towards me and to my relief puts his arms around me. "That was intense."

"I'm so sorry."

"It's not your fault," he reassures me.

"I've been watching her all night, trying to flirt with you, then I heard you in the kitchen with her. I'm sorry I eavesdropped. Then when she kissed you just now, I saw red, I couldn't let it go. She's pissed me off from the moment I met her. Have I made things difficult?"

"No, no, you haven't, it's fine. I'm glad you called her out." He kisses my head and whispers in my ear, "It was quite a turn-on. Martin is cool with us. Don't worry about it, not our problem. Let's enjoy the rest of our night."

"Okay." I smile at him. He kisses me again and then suggests we all head back inside to the warm to continue our frivolities.

It's another couple of hours before people start to leave. The place is an absolute mess, which means a good party was had by all, minus the little hiccup in the middle. Lizzie and Duncan head to bed, as do James and I. We are so exhausted we snuggle and crash – no competition with Liz and Duncs tonight!

Forty-Seven

The first few weeks of the new year are a whirlwind, and true to his word, James secures the house for us, and we move in shortly after we return from our holiday. I'm absolutely over the moon – our dream place. Promotion for the new film flies into overdrive, with James caught up in endless press conferences and interviews. It feels like every day there's a new headline, a new photo op, a new event. As much as I love seeing him in his element, I can tell it's exhausting for him.

Work for me has ramped up too, and I'm spending more time in the office than I expected. The long hours are tiring, but in the back of my mind, there's a beacon of hope – Barbados.

The movie premiere in London kicks off in grand fashion, and this time, I'm walking the red carpet with James. Martin joins us, but I can't help but notice Amanda is keeping her distance, subtly but deliberately. It's the first time I've seen her since that chaotic New Year's Eve, and

I'm relieved she's not causing any drama. When it's time for the cast group photo, Amanda stands far away from James, as if she knows better now. I hear Martin didn't throw her out as he'd threatened. Instead, he's given her another chance, but from what I can gather, she's on a very short leash.

After London, the premiere tour heads to Europe – Paris, to be exact. I have to skip that one, as I've run out of holiday leave. I choose to save my time for the Stateside premieres. Plus, I wanted to turn those into a bit of a vacation for us, sorry, holiday not vacation!

The LA and New York premieres were unforgettable. By the time we hit New York, which happened to be on Valentine's Day, I was finally feeling comfortable on the red carpet. I've even got my own glam squad now – something I never thought I'd say!

Between the two premieres, James turned forty-one, and we marked the occasion by visiting his parents and heading out for a swanky dinner in New York with some of the cast. Martin was there, but Amanda, unsurprisingly, was 'otherwise engaged'.

For his birthday, I went all out and got him an Omega Seamaster watch – almost as expensive as the one he bought me. My recent bonus made it possible, and I knew he deserved something special. But I also wanted to make him something more personal, so I put together a photo album/scrapbook of our first year together – filled with photos, clippings, and memories, all good ones, of course, and I left space at the back so we can continue adding to it. It's a gift from the heart, and when I gave it to him, the smile on his face said it all.

Barbados

The Coral Bay penthouse is nothing short of breathtaking with floor-to-ceiling windows offering a view that looks like it's straight out of a postcard – the turquoise ocean stretching out endlessly. It's just past lunchtime when we arrive, and the others won't be here until later this afternoon, giving us a few precious hours to settle in, just the two of us.

Sean and Allison flew in with us, still technically working but blurring the lines between business and pleasure. They're sharing a room now, which is sweet to see. We leave them to check into their room over in the Pearl wing, and the concierge meets us with a tray of tropical cocktails. "Welcome to Coral Bay," he says with a warm smile before guiding us to a private elevator that whisks us up to our suite.

As the beautiful white double-height doors swing open, they reveal an expansive covered terrace, where the warm island breeze sweeps over the light beige marble floors, and breathtaking views of the ocean. On the far side of the terrace is a private pool, with sun loungers, and in the middle, under cover, sits a dining table for ten, surrounded by a relaxed seating area and a fully stocked bar – our social hub for the week ahead. The decor is sleek and minimalist, with an air of sophistication, elegance, and serenity. The concierge walks us through the suite, pointing out the details before leaving us alone to soak it all in.

"Wow, these views are amazing," James says, stepping out onto the veranda next to the pool. The heat of the day mists over us. "What do you think?" he asks, slipping his arm around my waist.

"I think we're never leaving." I laugh, savouring a sip of my cocktail.

Below us, the hotel pool sprawls out, with luxury loungers dotted with dark red umbrellas. The view stretches beyond the hotel's pristine boundaries to the white sandy beach and the wide expanse of blue ocean, shimmering under the sun.

"Let's go claim the best bedroom!" James winks, taking my hand as we wander through the suite.

Each room is stunning, but the master bedroom takes my breath away. A huge four-poster bed sits grandly in the centre, draped in fine linens. There's a cream-coloured sofa, a spacious dressing area, and a spectacular marble bathroom that feels like a spa in itself. The pièce de résistance? A private terrace with two sun loungers overlooking the ocean.

"This is perfect," James says, flopping onto the bed and patting the space beside him. "Come join me. What time are the others due to arrive?"

"They land at two thirty, right? So, probably around three thirty," I reply, sitting down next to him.

He looks at me mischievously. "That gives us about two hours."

"For what?" I ask, though the playful glint in his eyes tells me everything.

He grins, eyes twinkling. "To familiarise ourselves – with that bath through there and this bed." That Hollywood love mist has definitely followed us to Barbados!

I run us a nice bubble bath while we unpack our suitcases. Hanging on the back of the bathroom door are two white towelling robes. I undress, slip into one and sit on the edge of the bath, gently swishing the water to even out the temperature.

When the water is just right, with a generous layer of bubbles, I slide off the robe and hang it back on the door. Grabbing two fluffy towels from under the sink, I place them at the top of the bath, ready for later. I call out to James, "The bath's ready!"

Dipping my toe in first, I sink into the water, letting it flow over me. It feels heavenly. James comes in with a glass of fizz and places it on the edge of the bath beside me.

"Thanks." I smile, watching as he starts to undress. He pulls off his fitted white T-shirt, revealing those perfectly toned back muscles that taper into a 'V'. Then, with a slow ease, he unbuttons his jeans and slides them off, tossing them casually onto a basket in the corner. Off come his boxers, revealing his muscular frame; he's been working out hard and it shows. His legs are powerful, his body an artwork in motion. When he turns to face me, I can't help but grin – a broad, unapologetic smile. His defined chest, his strong shoulders, the way his body moves with effortless confidence – it's hard to believe this gorgeous man is all mine.

He steps into the bath, at the opposite end, sliding down into the water until he's comfortable. I playfully run my foot up his chest, tracing his muscles beneath the warm water. This is the life. Even now, almost a year on, I'm still pinching myself. That night when I was stood up could have turned out so differently. Fate intervened, and here I am – sharing a luxurious bubble bath with James Keller, the man of my dreams, and, quite possibly, the man of many others' dreams too.

The other four arrive later in the afternoon and settle into their rooms before we all head down to the hotel's open-air fine-dining restaurant overlooking the white sandy beach of Barbados. The dress code is 'elegantly casual', so us ladies dress up and the boys pull out their smart suits, looking effortlessly dashing. The food is exquisite, a perfect blend of French and Mediterranean. Allison and Sean join us as well, even though they're technically still working; James is trying to ensure they don't have to work too much.

Allison, I must say, looks completely transformed in her elegant mid-length navy-blue dress with lace trim, arms modestly covered as always, and black open-toe kitten heels. Even her nails are painted. She seems to have a regular hairdresser now too as her hair is coloured a nice caramel colour and sits just on her shoulders with soft bangs. She's a world away from the frumpy Allison in that dull, shapeless suit and flat shoes I first met at the premiere. And she smiles more now, too. Amazing what some good sex can do!

The next four days are fantastic; we have so much fun. We spend our time lounging by the pool and frolicking on the beach. We hire jet skis and paddleboards, zipping across the turquoise waters. One afternoon, we take a catamaran out and sail over the stunning sea, snorkelling over the coral reefs and spotting leatherback turtles. James, of course, draws attention wherever we go. Fellow holidaymakers approach him for pictures, and while Mark gets his fair share of recognition, it's James most people gravitate towards. Mark takes it all in his stride, joking and laughing with everyone.

Forty-Eight

It's the penultimate night of our vacation, holiday! Date night! While the guys are out enjoying a round of golf on the picturesque grounds, the three of us girls opted for a peaceful afternoon at the spa. Allison chose to unwind in her own way, catching up on emails and finishing her holiday read, meaning we can let our guards down a little and talk more freely. After indulging in massages and treating myself to a lovely coral nail polish, we recline on the sun loungers, basking in the warmth of the fading sun while leisurely sipping on wine.

"So, where are you guys going for date night?" I ask.

"Mark and I are going to one of the hotel's restaurants, you know, the same one we had dinner in on the first night. I thought the food was exquisite!"

"It really was." I nod in agreement. "What about you, Liz, where is Duncan whisking you off to?"

"We are venturing off-site!" Lizzie says with excitement. "There's a little local restaurant that has good reviews about a mile down the road, so we thought we'd give it a try."

"Sounds good. While you're out, keep an eye out for a lively club or a spot with live music. I'm in the mood for some dancing tomorrow night. It's our last night tomorrow, and I feel like letting loose! James won't mind being spotted!"

Lizzie grins. "Too late for that!"

I laugh. "Oh no, what have you seen now?"

I'm so used to this now; I noticed a long-lens camera hiding behind the stacked sunbeds on the beach the other day. The public beaches here in Barbados offer little protection from prying eyes. Liz retrieves her phone, quickly finding the article and shares it with me.

James Keller vacations in Barbados!

Jet skis, paddle boards and volleyball. James Keller has been spotted on the beach in Barbados looking relaxed as he vacations with his girlfriend, Nikki Harper. They have been joined by long-term pal Mark Layton and his wife, Julia, and another couple.

The article continues with the usual of what we are wearing, noting how happy and relaxed we look. It's a kind article and the pictures are flattering. One shot captures James stealing a kiss with me on my sunbed – thank goodness my stomach looks toned in my black bikini! There's another one of us sitting on a jet ski and another shot of James, Mark, and Duncan joining in a lively game of beach volleyball with some locals. James looks particularly dashing in his dark blue swim shorts – I might just make it my phone's wallpaper!

"Hmm," I murmur, handing the phone back to Lizzie with a dismissive wave. "We are definitely going out dancing tomorrow, then!"

Jules, ever curious, leans in. "So, what's James got planned for tonight? Where is he taking you?"

"He's keeping it tightly under wraps," I reply with a hint of excitement. "He insists it's a surprise and that I'll love it. Do you think Mark knows?"

"If he does, he hasn't said anything to me," Jules muses, soaking in the sun's warmth. "Hmm… I wonder if there's a surprise in store," she adds with a knowing smile.

"Like what?" I ask, completely oblivious to her insinuation.

"Maybe a gift?" she suggests, exchanging a glance with Lizzie, and the penny drops.

"No… you don't think… do you?"

"Perhaps," Jules nods thoughtfully. "You two have been together a year now."

"Not quite but nearly."

"Even so, has he been acting strange lately?"

"No more than usual," I quip. "No, I don't think he will," I add, trying to sound casual, but suddenly, my nerves are getting the better of me.

"You never know," Jules teases. "And remember what I said early on? I think you two will end up married."

"I'll be sure to keep you posted when and if that happens!" I smile teasingly at her. As I recline, my mind races and my stomach flutters with anticipation. He wouldn't propose tonight… would he? There have been no signs, but what if? He did take a confidential meeting earlier today. Oh my…! I start to fidget.

"I'm not going to think about it!" I blurt out, feeling panic rise. "I can't. I won't relax, and he'll wonder what's wrong with me, and then I'll have to explain to him that you two put that thought in my head. It will be embarrassing and awkward and I'll be a mess; nope, not thinking about it!" I take a breath as they laugh at my mild panic attack.

"Chill out, darling!" exclaims Lizzie, passing me my drink. "What time are you going out?"

"I'm to be ready by 6:30."

"It's 5pm, love. You'd better get your skates on!"

We make our way back up to the suite. It seems the boys are still out, most likely enjoying a beer at the country club.

"I'll go and take a shower. Would you two lovely ladies be my glam squad in the absence of mine? He said to dress up."

"Sure, give us a shout when you're ready," says Jules as I head off to my bedroom.

After a refreshing shower, I pamper myself with scented moisturiser and carefully select a black lace thong and a matching strapless bra. Wrapped in my bathrobe, I call the girls to assist with hair and makeup. Minutes later, as Lizzie and I sift through my wardrobe and Jules lays out makeup options, James strolls into the room…

"Hi, babe." He greets me with a kiss before saying hi to the other two.

"You're back! You guys have fun?" Jules asks him.

"Oh yeah, it was great. And I won!" James announces cheerfully before excusing himself to freshen up in the bathroom.

Lizzie straightens my hair and sweeps it elegantly back from my face, while Jules adds a touch of drama to my eyes with a bold winged eyeliner and dark shadow, finished by a striking red lipstick. Since using a glam squad, I've been much more adventurous with my makeup! I love this classic look, and I wear it well, even if I do say so myself. Gazing at my reflection in the mirror, I can't help but feel fabulous.

As James emerges from the bathroom, wearing only a white towel wrapped around his waist, his clean-shaven face and damp hair eliciting a smile from my friends, I'm reminded of the first time I saw him in a similar state, back at my apartment after our exhilarating skydiving adventure.

"Don't worry! I'll change in the other room. I'll be out of your way in a minute," James assures with a smile as he grabs his clothes and leaves us to it. I put some more deodorant on.

As I prepare myself, the nerves kick in, prompting a bout of laughter from the girls. "I don't think I've been this nervous since our first, second, and third date!" I jest, spraying on some insect repellent and quickly masking it with a mist of perfume. Lizzie hands me my dress – a fitted black strapless number that falls just below the knee, exuding classic elegance. She zips up the back as I put on the diamond stud earrings James gifted me, along with a delicate diamond necklace and my trusty Rolex watch.

Completing the look, I slip into a pair of sparkling heels.

"You look amazing!" Lizzie compliments, sinking back onto the bed.

"Absolutely, Hollywood glam all the way!" adds Julia, echoing the sentiment.

"Thanks, girls. I've got butterflies!" I confess, rubbing my stomach nervously.

"Oh, I love that feeling! Just remember, it's just James; you know you'll have fun with him. Go with the flow, whatever happens!" Jules winks at me, sending my stomach into another flurry of excitement.

"Right, I'd better get myself ready for my own date with the hubby," Lizzie announces, rising from the bed.

"Same here. Have a fantastic time! Maybe we'll catch up later, depending on when we all get back," says Jules.

"Thanks, girls. Wish me luck," I reply with a smile.

"You don't need it!" they both declare, blowing me a kiss before departing.

Forty-Nine

At 6:25pm, I give myself one final glance in the mirror before grabbing a black sparkly cardigan to ward off the evening chill, along with a gold clutch. I am ready. Stepping out onto the main terrace, I find James seated on the sofa, patiently waiting for me. He stands when he sees me and smiles widely, to which I respond with an equally beaming grin, feeling like the luckiest person alive. He's wearing a dark navy-blue suit with the tie I bought him and a white shirt. I melt when I see him; my heart flips, as does my stomach, again.

"Hi, baby," I say, approaching him. He is wearing my favourite spicy scent again that never fails to captivate me. He places his hands on my waist and plants a kiss on my lips.

"Hi, gorgeous. You look beautiful. Are you ready?" he asks, his deep eyes gleaming.

"Yep. Are you going to tell me where we are going yet?"

"No." He flashes that trademark white smile and takes hold of my hand.

We walk into the lobby of the hotel hand in hand, looking very glamorous. A few hotel guests who are milling around pause and stare as we walk through. In the corner of my eye, I catch sight of someone discreetly snapping a picture with their phone, but I couldn't care less at this moment.

"Hi, Sean," I say joyfully.

"Nikki." he responds, in his usual monotone manner.

Sean escorts us out to the front where a car is waiting for us, and opens the door. James and I settle into the plush backseat while Sean takes his place in the front beside our driver. We drive about fifteen minutes down the road, over a bridge leading to a quiet marina. Boats. He's taking me on a boat! Which one, though? We pull up and exit the car, making our way along a long path past some beautiful yachts to a gate with manned security, who open the gate and let us pass through. As we round the corner, I see the biggest and most impressive yacht yet. Its sleek white exterior gleams and the darkened windows give it a mysterious, sophisticated look. It must stretch at least two hundred feet, with three impressive decks. The name written in italics on the side reads *Boracic*, which immediately brings a smile to my face.

"*Boracic*?" I laugh softly. "As in skint?"

James grins, clearly pleased with the playful irony. "I thought you'd appreciate the humour."

"Are we going on this?" I ask, my excitement barely contained.

"Yes, dinner on this tonight!" replies James looking pleased.

"Wow!" I breathe, taking his hand as we walk up the

gangway. The deck feels solid underfoot, but I still tread carefully, glancing around at the yacht's sheer size and luxury.

As we step aboard, we're greeted by the captain, who hands us a glass of champagne each. "Welcome aboard," he says warmly. Five other crew members, including the chef, are lined up beside him, all in crisp uniforms.

The captain gives us a quick safety briefing, and then leads us upstairs to an expansive lounge area.

"James, this is incredible," I say. My eyes widen as I take in my surroundings, a blend of modern luxury and timeless elegance. Plush, cream-coloured sofas, panoramic windows, offering breathtaking views of the ocean, and soft lighting illuminating the space.

Through tinted glass doors I catch a glimpse of the outside deck, partially sheltered from the deck above. Sean gives us a discreet nod and heads off to speak with the crew, ensuring everything is perfect for our evening. James leads me outside, where a man sits playing a piano and a lady with tumbling blonde hair, looking like a mermaid, is playing a harp, together creating the most beautiful melody. A gorgeous dining table set for two awaits us, complete with candles and a vase of fresh flowers. Along the edge of the bow, a bench with rich purple velvet cushions beckons, alongside a tempting jacuzzi.

I look around in awe. "This isn't yours, is it?" I ask, half-seriously, because with him, anything is possible.

He slips an arm around my waist. "Well," he says, with a playful glint in his eye, "up until a few hours ago, it belonged to Jacob Hyde. Now? It belongs to us."

I blink at him, speechless. "You're joking."

He just grins. "Signed the papers today. Surprise! I've borrowed Jacob's crew for tonight, though."

I laugh in disbelief. "You mean *the* Jacob Hyde – tech giant, billionaire tycoon Jacob Hyde?"

"That's the one," he confirms, clearly bemused by my reaction. "We met a while back and got along. When the opportunity came up, I made a call, and here we are."

I shake my head, still trying to absorb it all. "This is... incredible," I say, turning to take in the luxurious surroundings, the soft glow of the sunset casting everything in warm light.

He watches me with a smile. "I had a feeling you'd like it."

"So, this was what your top-secret meeting was about today, then?" I tease, trying to sound casual as I trace my fingers along the edge of the beautifully set table. The boat is incredible – beyond anything I'd imagined. But there's a tiny flicker of something I can't ignore, a feeling I'm almost embarrassed to admit. Part of me had let my mind wander in a different direction, wondering if tonight might be about something else. Something involving a small box and an entirely different kind of surprise.

James smiles, looking pleased as punch, with that warm, steady gaze of his. "Yes, it took a little longer than planned, but it was worth it," he says. He's so proud, so certain I'll be thrilled by the grand gesture. And I am – who wouldn't be? It's breathtaking, luxurious, and wildly romantic.

He studies my face for a moment with that familiar twinkle in his eyes, perhaps noticing my conflicting emotions but not saying anything. "I wanted tonight to be perfect," he says softly, his arm warm around me.

"It is, it really is," I say with a smile, feeling a bit more settled. "Where are you planning to keep it?"

"Here for now. But come summer, maybe I'll move it to the Med… Spain, perhaps?"

"Hmm, Spain sounds lovely."

We stand for a while, soaking up the beauty of the island. It's peaceful, with just the sound of the sea gently lapping below us; the lights on the island are starting to glow as the sun sets. The water below takes on a deeper, almost eerie darkness. I hear the engines hum as the water below us starts to swill.

"Are we going somewhere?" I ask.

"Only up the coast and back, just a couple of hours." He raises his glass in a toast and clinks mine. "Cheers, baby, happy vacation!"

"Happy *holiday*," I reply, playfully bantering with him. James raises his eyebrows at me; I respond with a sarcastic smile.

"Okay, you win," he concedes, smiling back at me. "Have you had a good time?"

"I've had the best time," I say, wrapping my arm around his back and cuddling into him. "It's been nice having company too, fun."

"It has. We're lucky to have some really good friends."

I can hear the crew below us radioing to each other as we glide away from the dock and out of the marina. We stand side by side, gazing out over the horizon, the lights of the island getting brighter as darkness starts to fall. The warm glow of the circular ceiling light above the dining table and a faint light from behind the tinted glass of the cabin doors adds to the romantic atmosphere. I still feel nervous, excited.

The yacht sails smoothly through the calm waters as James leads me to the bow where the view of the coastline is breathtaking. We take a seat on the bench, and I notice the musicians start to sing their own rendition of Harry Styles' 'Adore You'.

"Sweet song," I remark.

"It is. By the way, I've ordered food for us; I hope you don't mind?"

"No, I don't mind. What did you order?"

"Beef Wellington," he reveals with a mischievous smile. "Just for fun!"

"Beef Wellington? You mean a posh beef Wellington that's cooked properly?" I laugh as I remember our first time cooking together.

"Hey, we cooked it well that night! We made a great team. We *make* a good team."

"We do." I smile warmly at him.

He puts his arm around me, and I settle into his warmth. We soak up the atmosphere, and listen to the music for a while, enjoying just being together in this idyllic setting, free from stress, no pressure, and no cameras. A crew member interrupts to let us know that dinner will be served shortly. James courteously pulls out a chair for me and drapes his suit jacket over his chair before taking his seat at the elegantly set table with a pristine white tablecloth, fine silverware, and colourful fresh flowers.

Our first course is served: a delectable free-range

poached egg with asparagus, peas, crispy shallots, a Béarnaise sauce, drizzled with a truffle dressing. It's delicious; of course it is. We have a Michelin-starred chef on board with us!

"I really love that you've done this for me tonight. It's a perfect way to spend date night. Did the boys tell you what they're up to tonight?"

"Oh, they did. But I kept them guessing about our plans."

"So… they have no idea you've bought a super yacht?" I ask, raising my eyebrows.

He just shakes his head and grins. "Not a clue."

"I think they'll be quite jealous when they find out. I asked Lizzie to keep an eye out for a bar with live music or a decent club while they're out tonight. I want something upbeat tomorrow for our last night, put my dancing skills to good use!"

"Sounds good. Sean might have a fit, though." He laughs, and I envision the reaction of our ever-watchful friend in a nightclub.

As the first course is cleared away and they inform us of the next one, James pours us each a glass of champagne. The conversation flows as easily as the fizz.

James raises his glass. "To us. To good food, good company, and unforgettable nights."

"To us," I echo, clinking my glass against his.

"So," he begins, "how are things going with the new client you just landed?" He smiles at me.

I take a sip of my drink, contemplating the question. "It's coming along well. The team's been really pumped about it. Lots of late nights, I'm sure, but it'll be worth it."

James nods. "That's good to hear – not about the late nights, obviously. I knew you'd nail it."

"John is pleased."

"As he should be. That's a lot of money you've just brought in. Another promotion on the cards?"

"Huh, I doubt that, but hopefully a nice bonus!" I wink at him over the rim of my glass.

This time the chef personally brings out our beef Wellington, presenting it with a flourish. The aroma is mouthwatering, and I can't help but be impressed by the attention to detail.

"This looks amazing," I say, picking up my knife and fork.

"Only the best for you," James replies.

The beef is perfectly pink, encased in a golden puff pastry, and served with a side of creamy mashed potatoes and steamed vegetables. We take our first bites, savouring the flavours. "Mmm, this is incredible," I say, closing my eyes in appreciation, letting the taste linger. "Almost as good as the one we made!" I tease.

"Mmm, yep, this Michelin-star chef has nothing on us!" he says. He pauses as his gaze meets mine. "You know that I think you're stunningly beautiful."

I laugh, feeling a blush rise to my cheeks. "Flattery will get you everywhere, Mr Movie Star."

He looks at me with a glint in his eye. "I hope so," he says.

The conversation drifts effortlessly as we talk about plans for the new house, the cars and the helicopter he's eyeing up! We discuss his work plans for the next few months. He's going to South Africa not long after we get back, to scout out filming locations, so house preparations will be down to me, which I'm looking forward to.

As we finish our meal and the crew clears our plates, the musicians wrap up their song and start to leave. "Oh, they're leaving?" I ask him, glancing over at the retreating musicians. "Where are they going? Will they be back?"

"Yes, they've done their stint. They'll probably have some food with the crew," he informs me with a gentle smile. "I know we don't get much time alone together, out, so I thought you'd appreciate the privacy. I've organised the playlist from here on in."

"You have?"

"I have," he says, grinning at me, and at that precise moment, the surround speakers begin to play a song that I recognise instantly! Darren Hayes, 'So Beautiful'. Norway, the song we danced to in that secluded restaurant.

"Dance with me," he asks, rising from his seat and extending his hand towards me. I take it, allowing him to pull me close. No rhumba tonight, just a slow, intimate dance, cheek to cheek. Karl didn't do romance, not with me, and I never wanted him to either, but with James, I crave it.

We move in sync, our bodies pressing together. I close my eyes as our cheeks brush against each other's, his fingers tracing light patterns on my back. A familiar feeling starts to stir within: desire. He leans in, kissing me softly at first, then with a deep, hungry kiss. We part and I whisper into his ear. "You know," I say, running my fingers over the nape of his neck, "I could get used to nights like this, just you and me… alone."

His eyes darken slightly as he looks at me, a spark of

understanding passing between us, a spark of desire as his hand slides down to caress my bum.

"How well do you know this yacht?" I ask, my voice low and inviting.

"Not that well, but given we just bought it, maybe we should explore it."

"Hmm, I'd like that. Do we have time?" I ask.

"I reckon so," he says, taking my hand and leading me back inside.

A crew member, standing behind the bar, looks up as we enter. "We will be back in a few moments. Please do not disturb us," James commands, taking me through the lounge and down a spiral staircase. "Oh, hold off on dessert until we're back, please," he calls back.

I giggle as we rush down the stairs, not knowing which way to turn.

"This way," he says, pulling me along a corridor. He opens a door on the left and peeks inside. "Nope," he says, as we move along to the next one.

"Won't we get caught?" I whisper, feeling nervous and excited at the same time.

"No, they will leave us to do whatever it is we are doing," he reassures me.

"But they'll know what we're doing!" I state, feeling a slight embarrassment wash over me.

"Maybe," he says, turning and smiling at me. "In here," he says, opening a door.

It's dark in the room, with only the light from the hallway illuminating a cosy bedroom. A guest room that we are about to mess up. The door clicks shut, leaving me standing in darkness, my heart rate increasing. Within moments, he cups my face in his hands and kisses me. I wrap my arms around his neck as he pushes me back against the wall, slides his hand up my thigh, lifting my dress to reveal my knickers. His kisses trail down my neck as his fingers explore under the material. I close my eyes, lean my head back and groan with pleasure, as endorphins surge through me. I fumble with his belt, unhook his trousers, slide the zip down and reach inside. The feel of him in my hand only adds to my arousal. I tug at his trousers as his lips return to mine. He takes control, pulling them down along with his shorts. He lifts my leg up and moves my panties to one side as he enters me, both of us letting out a gasp.

He thrusts against me, pressing me against the wall, his movements restricting mine, heightening my desire. My eyes adjust to the darkness. "Bed," I gasp between breaths.

"Hold on," he whispers, gripping my bum and lifting me off the floor. He turns and takes two steps towards the bed, and we collapse in a heap, trying to stifle our laughter, our pleasure. He pulls my panties off, lifts his shirt, and resumes with urgency, pushing until there's no space left between us. I lift my hips, feeling him rub against me, a quiet moan escaping my lips.

"Shhh," he murmurs, but I can't help it. The sensation is overwhelming. I'm so close. I grasp his bum, pulling him even closer, if that's possible, desperate for the release.

"Don't stop!" I instruct, lifting my knees. "Don't stop." He smiles and thrusts rhythmically until I reach a sweet orgasm, my body trembling with pleasure.

Still feeling the sensation, I push him off me, turning

him over. Kneeling on the floor, I take him in my mouth, treating him to the same rhythmic thrusts he gave me. It doesn't take long before he's breathing hard, warning, "I'm close," his head lifting to watch me. I don't care. Never before have I let a man do *that* in my mouth. He lifts his hips, pushing and holding my head down. "Agh!" he cries, breathing hard as he finishes, his body shaking. I'm left with no choice but to accept his gift and swallow, feeling a rush of satisfaction as he collapses, spent.

He sits up and looks at me, a smile tugging at his mouth. "You okay?" he asks.

"Mmm hmm" is all I can manage as I climb up from the floor and dress myself again. I sit next to him on the bed as he pulls up his trousers.

"Just for the record," he starts, "you instigated that. That was not part of my plan for tonight. Well, maybe later it was, but not right now, here."

"You didn't want to?" I ask playfully.

"Of course I did," he says, briefly kissing my lips. "You're awesome, and I love you." He stands, smoothing himself out, and offers me a hand. "Dessert?" he asks, laughing.

We return to the deck, with a look of post-coitus smugness, to enjoy our dessert of a mini cheesecake and an espresso while taking in the romantic ambiance of the yacht, the lights of Barbados twinkling in the distance and the smell of the fresh sea air. I find it very relaxing, and I'm treated to a diverse array of music, adding to the magic of the evening.

The yacht has turned. James pours us another glass of champagne, and we retreat to the bench under the stars, the breeze still warm.

"I must use the bathroom – back in a moment. Try not to fall overboard," he jokes as he stands and heads inside. It's so peaceful; I sit back on the bench, staring out into the distance, almost in a trance. I'm lost in the tranquillity until a familiar deep voice breaks my thoughts. I can't quite make out what is being said but the voice is very deep and familiar. I listen intently… then the song kicks in – oh my God, Barry White, 'Just the Way You Are'. I smile to myself and listen to the song.

As James returns, I notice he's donned his suit jacket again; he looks handsome, with an air of elegance and sophistication. He takes a seat next to me and looks curiously at me smiling at him.

"What's up?" he asks.

"Barry White?" I give him a questioning look.

"Yeah, what's wrong with Barry?"

"Nothing. I'm excited to hear what treat you have for me next?"

"You'll have to wait and see!" he teases. "You know I feel extremely lucky to be here with you."

"Me too," I reply and lean in to kiss him. As our lips meet, the intro to the next song plays, and I instantly recognise it. It gives me goosebumps – Van Morrison, 'Someone Like You'.

"Oh, I love this song," I say to him.

"Good, I'm glad," he says, then he seems to get distracted by something in the distance behind me and his eyes dart out to sea. "What's that?" he says, squinting.

I follow his gaze. "What?" I enquire.

"Over there, in the distance, can you see that?" he asks, pointing behind me. I twist my body to try to catch a

349

glimpse of whatever has caught his eye, but I see nothing. It's just dark.

"I've no idea what you're talking about," I begin to say, turning myself back to face him. "I can't see…"

My words trail off. He's no longer seated next to me. Instead, he's down on one knee, holding open a box that contains the most exquisite ring I've ever seen – a yellow diamond flanked by two glistening white diamonds. My hand flies to my mouth in shock as I realise what's happening.

James looks up at me, his expression serious yet nervous. "Nikki, I love you so much, will you marry me?"

I know my answer. I've known it for a long time. But in this moment, overwhelmed by emotion, I find myself unable to speak. My heart pounds in my chest, and all I can do is nod, tears of joy welling up in my eyes.

"Will you?" he repeats, his expression growing anxious.

I take a deep breath, steadying myself, and finally find my voice. "Yes!" I practically squeal, unable to contain my excitement. "Yes, I'd love to marry you!"

Relief floods James's face, and he sits beside me once more. Without hesitation, I throw my arms around him, overcome with joy. I bloody hope he's got hold of that ring. "Yes, yes, yes, a thousand times, yes!" I exclaim, my heart overflowing with love and happiness.

Fifty

I n the car on the way back to the hotel, I text Lizzie and Julia to see where they are. Jules is back in the suite, having a drink with Mark, and Lizzie and Duncan have just pulled up at the hotel. I tell them to wait up and we will join them for a drink.

James squeezes my hand one last time before letting go, expertly concealing the ring as he wraps his arm casually around my shoulder. I tuck my arm under his suit jacket.

"Ready?" he asks, smiling warmly.

I nod, feeling excited. "Let's do this."

We discussed earlier who we were going to tell right away – our close friends here, of course, but we'd be swearing them to secrecy. No magazine exclusives or social media announcements, just an intimate, private moment for now. James had spoken to my parents about it on Christmas Day, and according to him, Dad had trouble containing his excitement, which explains his odd behaviour that night.

As we step through the door, the room is filled with the hum of laughter and lively chatter. James throws on his best poker face, honing his acting skills and greeting everyone with a mischievous "Evening, y'all."

Jules looks up, her eyes sparkling with curiosity. "Hey, you two! How was your night?"

"Hi," says Duncan. "Where'd you go?"

James smirks, relishing the moment. "We went for a little cruise, dinner on a very fancy yacht."

I jump in, knowing the name-drop will stir up the room. "Not just any yacht – Jacob Hyde's yacht."

Duncan's eyes widen; he nearly chokes on his drink. "No way! Jacob Hyde's yacht? Seriously?"

"Well…" James starts, his smirk widening as I suppress a grin. "It's not exactly his yacht anymore." The room falls silent, all eyes on us with anticipation.

James glances around before saying, "We have a bit of news." I see Lizzie's eyes gleam with excitement.

"I bought the yacht!" he declares, grinning.

"What?" Jules and Duncan shout in unison.

"Yep, signed the deal today. We celebrated with dinner on board tonight." I glance at Liz, noticing her smile has wavered just slightly, a flicker of concern in her eyes. Maybe she's worried this wasn't exactly my dream. James catches my look and squeezes my shoulder, reassuring. "Nikki had no idea."

"Wow!" Mark exclaims, raising his glass. "Nice one, mate."

"Thanks, buddy, oh, and I asked Nik to marry me and she said yes," he announces casually.

For a heartbeat, there's silence. Then the girls leap

up from their seats with shrieks of excitement, grabbing my hand to examine the ring. "Whoa!" they exclaim. "Congratulations!"

Duncan stands up and shakes James's hand firmly before pulling him into a hug. "Welcome to the family, mate! My new brother-in-law!"

"Thanks, buddy," James replies with a genuine smile.

Mark claps James on the shoulder, pulling him into a man hug. "I knew it! I'm so pleased for you both, really."

"Cheers, we're over the moon," James says, before pulling me in close again.

We get a drink and fill them in on our evening. I tell them all about the proposal and James gives them the details of the ring, to my surprise and theirs. The centre stone is a radiant-cut yellow diamond, just over five carats. It's got near perfect clarity. The white diamonds either side are one carat each, and the band is eighteen-carat white gold.

I stare at him, suddenly understanding the weight of the rock on my hand. "In other words, it's expensive," I murmur, not daring to ask how expensive. The room bursts into laughter, and Jules shoots me a wink.

"It's worth it," James says softly, leaning in to kiss me on the forehead. "You're worth it."

"Show me again. It's beautiful," declares Julia, having another look.

Lizzie nods, barely able to take her eyes off it. "It really is. You're one lucky girl, Nikki."

"I'm not going to wear it for a while, though. This is the last time you'll see it until we're married," I admit, feeling a bit sad about it. As much as I want to show it off to the world and let everyone know that James Keller is officially off the market, I understand the need for secrecy.

"Why?" Lizzie asks, sounding a bit shocked.

Mark answers for me before I can. "Media. I imagine they don't want it in the press yet."

"Exactly," I confirm with a nod. "We just want to keep things private, no big announcements."

James stands and tops up my glass. "That's right, no one else is to know about it. We want it to be our moment, not a media spectacle," he says quite firmly.

"Can I get the first exclusive interview with you, then?" Mark asks cheekily.

James laughs, giving him a playful nudge. "Maybe, if it stays a secret until after the wedding."

"So… when is the wedding?" asks Lizzie.

"Don't know yet. Soon, though – next few months – but it will be just a quiet and intimate affair. No magazine deals. We don't want a media circus," I tell them.

"Yep, the sooner the better," says James.

"Well, I think it's great news, and of course we will keep it a secret, won't we, Mark?" Duncan looks at Mark in jest. James knows Mark well enough, and even though he is media, he trusts him, and I reckon James will do that exclusive with him.

Duncan raises his glass, grinning at us. "To James and Nikki! May you enjoy a long and happy marriage – congratulations!"

"James and Nikki!" they all echo.

Fifty-One

Four months later

It's finally our wedding day. Thanks to our amazing family, friends, and a few signed confidentiality agreements, we've managed to keep it all a secret – no media frenzy, no unwanted attention, just us and the people who matter most.

A stunning white marquee now stands in the grounds of our home, and as I watch from an upstairs window, I can see people are busy working away, setting up tables, flowers, and decorations. There's a chef preparing food for the wedding breakfast, and a live band setting up.

James's parents, his sister Dianne, her husband, and their son flew in from the States a few days ago and have been staying with us. The house has been bustling with activity for the last week.

We moved into the new house just over three months ago and it already feels like home. Apart from his South

Africa trip, James has been around quite a lot, which is nice because this house is quite a lot larger than I'm used to, like ten thousand square feet bigger! He's been busy setting up his business in one of the offices we have here. I have my own office for when I work from home. Sean, Nigel, and Allison have their own office as well. The house is big but busy, so I set the rule up early that no staff or co-workers, other than our housekeeper, are allowed in the main house unless invited, and no one is allowed upstairs except me and James. They are often in the house anyway but at least this way it minimises the chances of me bumping into Sean while I'm wearing not a lot. I'm not sure who that would be more embarrassing for!

The wedding itself is an intimate affair – just our immediate family plus our closest friends, twenty-three of us in total for the ceremony. We have another hundred or so people coming to a reception being held at our house later who think they are coming for a housewarming party. They have no idea that by that time we will be married! The thought makes me smile as I watch the preparations below. In just a few hours, I'll be walking down the aisle.

It's 3:30pm and I'm lounging on the sofa in my bedroom, sipping champagne with Lizzie and Julia, who has grown to feel more like a sister over the last year. The ceremony is at 5pm. I have an hour before I need to leave. My glam squad have outdone themselves today; my makeup is soft and natural, and my hair is styled half up, half down, flowing over my shoulders. Instead of a veil or tiara, I've chosen a pretty pearl headband to add some sparkle and glamour.

Half an hour passes, and Mum arrives. She knocks gently on the bedroom door and lets herself in.

"Hi, darling. How are you feeling?" she asks, coming to stand next to me in front of the dressing mirror, wearing a light pink skirt suit and matching hat. "Your hair looks very pretty that way." She smiles.

"Thanks, Mum. I'm feeling good, probably the champagne." I laugh, taking another sip. "How's James?"

"Pacing up and down." She smiles, accepting a glass of fizz from Lizzie. "I think he's more nervous than he's letting on. He does look very handsome."

"We'd better be going," says Lizzie, glancing at her watch. "Has Duncan got the girls ready?"

"Yes, all the children are ready – they look very sweet!"

Lizzie and Jules hug me, wishing me luck, before leaving for the registry office, leaving me alone with Mum.

"James and Mark are on their way to the venue, your dad is downstairs waiting for you, so shall we get you in this dress?"

My dress has been waiting in my dressing room for a week, hanging in its protective cover; James hasn't been allowed in there – thankfully, he has his own dressing room. It's an ivory, strapless gown, fitted down to just below my knees before fanning out into a small train. The lace detailing is exquisite. I step into it carefully, and Mum helps lift it over my hips. The material is heavy, but it feels luxurious. She fastens the buttons using a crochet hook, working diligently.

"You might need help getting out of this later," She chuckles. "I hope James knows how to use a crochet needle!"

I sit on my bed as she helps me with my shoes, closed-toe kitten heels, perfectly matching the colour of the dress. Standing up, I smooth out the fabric.

"Oh, you look absolutely beautiful," Mum says, stepping back to admire me. "Shall we go downstairs and get your dad? I think he's more nervous than James!"

I nod, taking a deep breath. It's almost time.

As I very carefully walk down the sweeping staircase, I see my dad is pacing the hallway below, looking very dapper in his suit; he freezes when he sees me.

"Wow, what an angel you are!" he says, taking my hand, a tear welling in his eye. "James is an incredibly lucky man!"

"Thanks, Dad," I say, leaning to kiss his cheek. My heart is beginning to pound. "I think I'm ready."

He smiles warmly, squeezing my hand as he escorts me outside. Waiting by the car is Nigel, standing tall and composed. There's no horse-drawn carriage, no classic wedding car – just my own sleek, dark-windowed Range Rover. It feels perfectly understated, just like we wanted.

"Nikki, you look absolutely beautiful," says Nigel, helping me into the back of the car. With my parents beside me, we drive off.

The registry office is nestled away in a quiet village a few miles away, far from prying eyes, one of the reasons we chose it. As we pull up, Nigel steps out and opens the door for Mum, who heads inside to let them know we have arrived, giving me and Dad a few moments together.

"He's a good man that James," he starts. "I know when I first met him, I was a little star-struck."

"Only a little?" I tease, raising an eyebrow.

"Okay, a lot star-struck," he admits with a grin, "but I've got to know the man behind the big screen and he's really lovely, Nikki; you're very well suited."

"I know," I say, a rush of emotion welling up inside me. "I still think back to the night I met him; it feels so surreal to think that I'm now marrying him."

"Well, I'm glad you did meet him. He's a fellow car enthusiast – what more could I ask for? And that track day? The whole place to ourselves? Unforgettable! I can get my car fix through him." He winks at me. "Oh and not forgetting the helicopter!"

I laugh, rolling my eyes. "Seriously!"

He chuckles before his expression turns serious. "Seriously, though, I hope he knows he's a very lucky man. Now come on, let's not keep him waiting."

Nigel opens the car door for us and Dad helps me out. We make our way inside and suddenly I'm standing at the double doors, my heart racing, knowing that in half an hour, I'll be Mrs Keller. The nerves hit me all at once, my palms beginning to sweat.

As the doors open, I see James standing there, looking more handsome than ever in his classic black-tie attire. His famous smile, the one that makes my heart flutter every time, is beaming as he waits for me at the end of the aisle.

Fifty-Two

an hour later, we all arrive back at the house in a convoy of cars, still riding the high of the day. As we pull up, the staff are waiting to greet us, handing each of us a glass of champagne. The ceremony itself had been perfect – short, sweet, and intimate, lasting just thirty minutes, including the signing. James had written his own vows, and I'm certain they even managed to melt my mum, who'd been misty-eyed the entire time.

Nikki,

You are beautiful to me every day, but today, you've taken my breath away.

I know life with me may not always be easy, but I want to share every moment – good and bad – with you by my side on this crazy ride.

I promise to love you in every moment, whether we're near or far, to laugh with you, cry with you, and always make you feel cherished, and I will dance with you, even when the music is over.

From the night we met, I knew you were special, and today, I feel lucky to call you mine. Let's take on the world together and have an adventure.

As the first of the guests start to arrive at the house, James and I make a quick retreat upstairs, slipping away before we are spotted. Our staff for the evening greet them warmly, offering a glass of champagne before ushering them into the grounds.

"So, Mrs Keller, how about consummating the marriage now?" James teases, his hands trailing playfully over my dress.

I laugh, shaking my head. "Absolutely not! We don't have time, and good luck getting this dress over my hips!"

He grins, undeterred. "I can try, can't I?" He leans in for a kiss instead, satisfied for now. "You look stunning, Mrs Keller," he says, handing me a glass of champagne as we settle onto the sofa.

"I love being Mrs Keller," I say with a contented sigh, leaning into his arms. Mrs Keller, Mrs James Keller – it sounds perfect.

Before long, James gets a text from Mark: all the guests have arrived and are happily corralled in the garden, waiting for us. It's time. We exchange a glance and head downstairs, still in our wedding attire, to the hallway just outside the double doors leading to the garden. The moment we're announced, we'll lead everyone into the walled garden, where the marquee awaits.

I'd sneaked a peek earlier – it's magical. The ceiling is draped in black fabric, studded with fairy lights like stars, two chandeliers hanging elegantly from the peaks. Ten white-clothed dining tables, each adorned with vibrant, colourful floral centrepieces, fill the space. The band's already set up next to a sleek black-and-white chequered dance floor, and the bar is fully stocked, with even more inside.

Nearby, four-foot-tall LED letters spell out 'MR & MRS' – yes, it's cheesy, but I adore it.

We can hear the buzz of conversation from outside. Someone asks, "Have you seen them yet?"

James and I share a smile as he quickly messages Mark, letting him know we're in position. Then, the sound of silverware tapping against crystal rings out, and they fall silent.

"Ladies and gentlemen," Mark begins. "Welcome. James and Nikki wanted me to pass on their apologies. Unfortunately, you've all been brought here tonight under false pretences." There's a ripple of murmurs from the guests. "For reasons that will soon become clear, this is not the housewarming party you thought it was. No – this is actually a *wedding*!"

Gasps fill the air.

"And now," Mark continues with a grin, "may I introduce you to the new Mr and Mrs Keller!"

Mark throws open the doors and we step outside together. The moment feels surreal, like time slows as everyone stares at us – some in shock, hands covering their mouths, others beaming in surprise.

Then, applause erupts. As we move forwards towards our guests, the warm sound of congratulations fills the air. My dad catches my eye, grinning ear to ear, and I'm swept up in hugs, air kisses and handshakes.

Among the crowd, I spot Ivy, standing still, her

expression unreadable. Guilt washes over me as I approach her, head lowered.

"How the fuck did you keep this from me?" she hisses, her tone sharp.

I brace myself, but then she breaks into a huge smile. "You can't usually keep anything from me!" She pulls me into a hug, laughing. "I'm so happy for you! Annoyed – but happy." She steps back, holding me at arm's length to look at my dress. "You look absolutely stunning! I love this on you."

She lowers her voice, raising an eyebrow. "You're not, you know…?" She glances down, eyes flicking to my stomach.

"No!" I laugh, shaking my head. "Definitely not!"

"Thank God! So, where's the rock?" she asks. I lift my hand, showing her my engagement ring now joined by a diamond wedding band.

"Holy shit, that's gorgeous!" She gasps. "You are one lucky lady – no, wait, he's the lucky one!" She pulls me in for another tight hug.

"I'm so sorry I didn't tell you," I say, guilt tugging at me again. "We wanted to keep it quiet, out of the media. The fewer people who knew, the better."

"Fair enough," she replies, her tone softening. "I'm just impressed – and slightly terrified – that you managed to keep this from me!" she teases.

The night was just perfect! The wedding breakfast was a hit, and the cake was nothing short of a masterpiece. Three tiers of indulgence: vanilla sponge, chocolate sponge and red velvet, beautifully decorated with white icing and cascading blue and ivory roses.

The band kept the energy high, getting everyone up to dance. Everyone was in good spirits. For our first dance, well, there was only one choice: 'So Beautiful'. My dance teacher, who had been giving us lessons for weeks, looked on with pride. And, as it turns out, James, with all his other talents, is a natural dancer too!

Fifty-Three

For the two days following the wedding, we kept a low profile. James's family was still with us, although they'd be heading back to the States the next day. We were all lounging together in the living room, preparing to watch *The Mark Layton Show!* Mark hadn't managed to secure an exclusive interview with James – the timing just didn't quite work out – but he was given the honour of being the first to announce our wedding publicly, on his show. We'd asked all our guests to stay tight-lipped until the announcement aired.

Mark's show always includes a news segment, and tonight he looks particularly sharp in his grey suit, sitting confidently behind his desk. He glances at the camera with that familiar cheeky grin.

"Ladies and gentlemen, for the final piece of tonight's news, I have a very special announcement, and I'm afraid it may break a few hearts." He pauses for dramatic effect. "I can confirm," he pauses again, letting the tension build, "that James Keller married Nikki Harper this weekend!" As he says the words, a wedding photo of James and me flashes up on the screen behind him. The audience erupts into applause and cheers, the camera sweeping across rows of surprised, wide-eyed faces.

"Yes, it's true!" Mark continues, beaming. "Many hearts will be in tatters tonight, because the stunning Nikki is officially off the market!" The crowd let out a mix of boos, laughter, and whistles.

"It was a small, intimate affair, just family. But I had the absolute honour and privilege of being the best man," Mark adds, as another picture appears – him and James side by side, looking sharp in their wedding suits. More cheers erupt.

"I scrub up well, don't I?" Mark teases. "Anyway, from all of us here, huge congratulations to James and Nikki on their marriage! We wish them a lifetime of love and happiness." The audience claps and cheers again, rising to their feet this time. Mark waits for the noise to settle before turning back to the camera with a softer tone. "And from me personally – James, Nikki – I love you both."

He blows a kiss towards the camera; I can't help it but I find myself welling up and blowing him one back, much to James's amusement. He laughs, shaking his head as his phone starts to buzz – the news has officially broken. The camera pans around again and the audience is on their feet, cheering!

The next morning, Sean walks into the kitchen, his expression unreadable. "There's press outside," he states flatly.

"What?" I look up from my phone, feeling a twinge of anxiety.

"Yep, about fifteen of them at the gate," he confirms, taking a seat at the table across from me. James, meanwhile, is calmly making coffee, unfazed by the news.

"We're supposed to leave in just over an hour, James," I say, my voice rising with a hint of panic. He doesn't seem bothered in the slightest, pouring coffee like it's just another day.

"Coffee, Sean?" James asks, offering him a cup. Sean nods. "It's hardly a surprise. Are they at the other entrance too or just the main gate?"

"I'll check." Sean heads over to one of the kitchen cupboards where we keep the CCTV monitor. After checking the feed, he nods. "Nope, just the main gate."

"Good. We can leave from the other side," I suggest hopefully.

"Or…" James says, handing us our coffees, "we could wander down there, say hi, confirm what they want, and maybe they'll leave?"

Sean's face wrinkles in disapproval, and I can't say I blame him.

"Where's Allison?" James asks.

"In the office," Sean replies.

"Call her in," James instructs. Sean dials her number, and a few minutes later, Allison arrives, rubbing her temples at James's plan.

"Let's just do it," she finally says, sighing. "Then we can get on with the day. Sean, make sure you have a gate fob."

After finishing our coffees, we make ourselves presentable and head out on foot down the long, tree-lined drive. The house is hidden from view, so it's not until we round a bend that the press spot us.

"Congratulations, James and Nikki!" a few of them shout as we approach. There are about fifteen reporters, their cars parked along the grass verge. Cameras are instantly raised in our direction.

They're from various magazines and news outlets, all eager for a shot of us and a glimpse of my ring. We smile politely, offering them a few pictures but avoiding any questions about our honeymoon in Bali.

At the back of the group, I notice two young girls, teenagers by the look of them, one holding a phone high, the other with a poster of James from *Driver's Fury*, clearly not part of the press. They're hanging back shyly, hoping for something but too nervous to ask. James spots them and calls them forwards.

"Do you want me to sign that?" he asks, gesturing towards the poster.

"Yes, please," one of the girls says, her voice barely above a whisper as she hands it to him. Sean hands him a pen as he asks for their names and signs the poster with a smile. The braver of the two then musters the courage to ask, "Can we get a picture with you, please?"

"Of course," James replies warmly. Their eyes light up as Sean opens the gates slightly to let them in, holding back the rest of the crowd. James puts his arms around both girls, and I snap a few pictures with their phones. They look absolutely thrilled. Before they leave, they ask for a picture with both of us, and we happily oblige. Sean then gently escorts them out, both girls grinning from ear to ear. As the gates close behind them, we thank the reporters and head back up the drive.

"That wasn't so bad, was it?" James says with a smug

grin. "Hopefully, they'll leave us alone now, and we can get on with our day – and our honeymoon!" He squeezes my hand, excitement sounding in his voice.

Sure enough, by the time we're ready to leave for our flight, the press has gone.

Fifty-Four

Five years later…

J step out of the green room, escorted down the corridor towards the studio. My heart pounds with a mix of excitement and nerves. I'm shown to my seat in the front row of a two-hundred-strong audience, nestled among other guests and their entourages. The lights are still bright, and the warm-up guy is pacing back and forth at the front, working the crowd, making sure everyone's energy stays high.

On set, Russell Knight, the chat show host, sits in his chair, poised and ready for the cameras to roll. His show is a well-oiled machine, and tonight feels no different, yet I can't help but feel the electric buzz in the air.

"Quiet in the audience, please!" a voice shouts from somewhere to my right, and I glance up just in time to see the 'QUIET PLEASE' sign illuminate above my head.

"Cameras rolling!" another voice announces, followed by "Three, two…"

The title music kicks in, echoing through the studio as Russell straightens in his chair, a smile playing on his lips, ready for the next segment. The lights dim over the audience, leaving us in near darkness except for the faint glow of a couple of overhead spotlights.

"Welcome back," Russell begins, and the audience bursts into applause, following the cue above their heads.

"So, my next guest is one of Hollywood's greats. He's been in the business for over three decades, starred in countless blockbuster movies, and shows no sign of slowing down. Ladies and gentlemen, I give you the one, the only – Mr *James Keller*!"

The crowd doesn't need another prompt. They're on their feet, cheering, clapping, and whistling. The doors at the back of the stage swing open, and there he is, looking as sharp as ever in a dark grey suit with an open white shirt. His hair – still as it was when I first met him – is short, dark, and perfectly neat. He's just as strikingly handsome as ever. Judging by the roar from the audience behind me, everyone agrees – he's still *hot*.

James does what he always does, standing for a moment, looking humble as he acknowledges the crowd with his signature white smile. He waves at them, his charm undeniable, and then makes his way over to Russell, greeting him with a warm handshake. The audience, still erupting with cheers, slowly begins to calm as James unbuttons his suit jacket and takes a seat opposite Russell. Russell, ever the pro, sits back and lets the audience soak in the moment.

Finally, the 'QUIET PLEASE' sign flashes, and the chatter dies down. Russell leans forwards, grinning. "I feel like we shouldn't even ask questions. We should just sit here and admire you for a bit," he quips. The audience laughs, as does James. They exchange a few pleasantries, talking about James's impressive film career over the past three decades, before turning to his latest project.

"So, the long-awaited movie comes out in two weeks, *Driver's Fury: Showdown*," Russell says, and the audience erupts again.

"We've been waiting *five years* for this! Five years!" Russell exclaims. "I've seen it – watched it last week," he adds with a knowing nod. James smiles, acknowledging the praise. "I'm not just saying this because you're sitting here, but I loved it. I was a fan of the first two, and without spoiling anything, this film ties up a few loose ends… well, almost," he teases. "So, will there be a fourth?"

James plays it cool. "Well… maybe, maybe not."

They chat about the film's production, especially some of the high-octane scenes like the one where the car rolls four times. A clip plays on the screen behind them, and I can't help but cringe. I was there, watching it happen, with James inside.

As the interview winds down, Russell, like many before him, tries to pry into James's personal life. After all this time, I still find it fascinating how people react to him – fans wanting just a moment with him, an autograph, a photo. He's magnetic, drawing everyone in.

"So, James," Russell says, turning to him, "we know you're quite private, but you live in the UK now, right? With your lovely wife, Nikki." The camera pans to me, and I give a small smile and wave. "There she is," Russell adds, beaming.

"Yeah, that's right. I love it here. It's not as intense as the States."

"Can you pop down to the local shop? Do you even go to the shop?" Russell asks, clearly amused.

James grins. "Err… yeah, I've been known to go."

Once, I think, *just once.*

"And," Russell continues, turning to me again, "do you mind if we share the story of how you two met?" I smile and give a little nod. Russell looks back at James. "I hear you met Nikki on a night out in London, in a restaurant?"

"Yep," James says, smiling.

"Just a random night, you both happened to be dining in the same place?"

James nods. "Yep, that's right."

Russell grins. "So, tell us. She was meant to be meeting someone for a date, but he didn't show?" The audience boos dramatically. "And you, ever the gentleman, swooped in and asked her to have dinner with you instead?"

James laughs. "That's right. Lucky for me, he didn't show. I saw her sitting at the bar, and I don't know… I just felt I had to talk to her."

"Love at first sight?"

"Something like that," James says, "though I'd only seen the back of her at that point!"

Russell chuckles. "What if she'd been with someone? A boyfriend, husband… or girlfriend?"

James shrugs, laughing. "I wasn't thinking that far ahead! But no one came, so I introduced myself and said hi."

"And she was still a mystery to you at that point?"

James shakes his head. "I overheard her telling the

bartender she'd been stood up. So, I told her the guy didn't know what he was missing and bought her a drink."

The audience swoons audibly.

"Then I said goodbye and went back to my table, kicking myself for not inviting her to join me."

James continues, "So, I was dining with Mark and Julia Layton that night. I told them I was going to invite this young lady I'd just met to join us for dinner."

Russell laughs. "As you do."

"They thought I was mad. But I ignored them, went back to Nikki, and asked if she'd like to join us. She said yes. And well… the rest is history."

The audience bursts into applause.

"So, we've actually got a picture of you both from that very night," Russell says, smiling. James looks surprised. A photo appears on the screen – a candid shot of the two of us, James's arm around me. The audience gasps at the sweetness of it.

"You'd only known each other a couple of hours when that was taken?" Russell asks.

James nods, still smiling. "That's right."

"You look like you've known each other forever."

Russell flashes a grin as he turns his attention to me. "Nikki, what's it like being married to James?"

Without missing a beat, I shout up at him, "Amazing!" And it truly has been – five years of excitement, adventure, and love. Of course, we've had our ups and downs, because who hasn't? But the experiences we've shared have been nothing short of extraordinary. We've travelled the globe, met fascinating people, and created memories I'll cherish forever.

We're still living in the house we bought just before our wedding, though now we have a few extra homes dotted around. There's the apartment in New York, the charming cottage in Wales, a house in the South of France, and, of course, one in Beverly Hills. James even got himself a helicopter, which now lives in our garden. My dad is completely obsessed with it – last time he went to meet his old mates in London, he arrived by helicopter!

When James bought his new toy, he got me one too – a gorgeous black Steinway grand piano that takes pride of place in our lounge. And not long after we got married, I fell pregnant with our first baby, a beautiful girl named Evelyn. Soon after, we welcomed our second daughter, Adele. My parents were over the moon, and life became even more of a whirlwind. With two little ones in tow, I decided to change careers and became a consultant, which allowed me to choose projects and spend more time with James and the girls. As life got busier, we hired a nanny. Allison, bless her, handled the interviews. If they passed her test, we knew they were perfect, and she is amazing.

Speaking of Allison, she and Sean tied the knot and now live in one of the properties on our grounds. They're both still working with us, and I couldn't be happier. I'm rather fond of those two. Rebecca is still James's agent, and the lovely Nigel is still by our side, though we've added two new security team members to the mix. Our little entourage is growing!

As for Martin, he divorced Amanda and remarried someone he met on a film project – Samantha, a brilliant film editor, who, I must say, is lovely and doesn't flirt with my husband! Amanda has kept a low profile, living in LA somewhere. We haven't heard from her in a while. Claire and Richard are still around, with Claire continuing her lawyer work, and we catch up whenever we can.

Ivy, my dear Ivy, married her Prince Charming, the handsome Tyrone, and they had a baby boy, called Umar. I couldn't bear to part with her when I changed careers, so she came with me. She's my rock, and somehow, she and Allison get along like a dream!

Life is good – really good. Oh, and as for the mile-high club? I'm now a fully-fledged member!

James chuckles as he continues, "It's funny, I remember telling Nikki early on, before we were really in the public eye, that some people would adore her because they like me, some wouldn't like her because they like me, and others wouldn't like her simply because they don't like me."

"Oh, so that's two out of three people who might not be too keen on her!" Russell laughs. "But I think she's quite well-liked. You both are. And I hear it's your wedding anniversary today?"

"Yes, it is, five years," James confirms with a grin.

"Today? And you're here?" Russell looks impressed.

"I am, but she's here too," James says, looking over at me with a smile.

"Well, congratulations to both of you on five years of marriage!" Russell reaches out to shake James's hand. "Any romantic plans for after the show?"

James smiles mysteriously. "I have some plans, but I'll keep the details under wraps."

"And your daughters?" Russell asks. "You keep them out of the limelight, right?"

"Yes, we want them to have as normal an upbringing as possible," James says. "My eldest kind of gets what I do, but they're still too young really. They've seen a few trailers and snippets, but that's about it."

"Do you think either of them might follow in your footsteps?"

"You never know," James replies with a shrug.

"Well, it's been a pleasure having you on the show," Russell says warmly. "Before you go, we've got a little something for you, or should we say, your wife."

As Russell gestures, a runner appears with a stunning bouquet of fresh flowers. James accepts them with a smile and a handshake, then walks over to me, hands me the bouquet with a tender kiss, and returns to his seat. The audience erupts in applause once again.

"Ah, that's lovely," Russell remarks. "Congratulations once more, and good luck with the release of the new film! Everyone, go and see *Driver's Fury: Showdown* – it's brilliant! Mr James Keller, everyone!"

The title music plays, and Russell and James stand, shaking hands and exchanging thanks.

"And *cut*! That's a wrap, everyone! Thank you!"

Even as filming ends, the audience's cheers continue. Russell and James make their way through the crowd, with Russell coming over to congratulate me on our anniversary while James engages with the audience. Sean keeps an eye on things as James works the room, greeting fans with charm. After about twenty minutes of mingling, James finally comes to get me, and we head backstage to the green room.

When we're ready to leave, Nigel is waiting by the car.

"So, where are we going?" I ask eagerly as Nigel drives us through central London.

"Wait and see, Mrs Keller," James replies with a wink, kissing my hand. "But I can tell you we're staying in the Hyde Park suite tonight." My eyes light up – apart from home, it's my favourite place to stay with him, full of wonderful memories.

Before long, we pull up outside a restaurant in Mayfair. Sean opens the car door and escorts us inside, though not before James takes a moment to pose for a few photos with fans. The maître d' leads us to our table, passing the pianist playing a beautiful black grand piano. To my delight, we're back at the same restaurant, and the same table where it all began – where I was stood up, and my life changed forever, for the better.

Our best friends, Mark and Julia, are already seated at the table, waiting for us with a bottle of champagne, and we are joined by two other very special people, Lizzie and Duncan.

"Happy anniversary, baby. I love you so much." James kisses my lips.

"Happy anniversary, darling. I love you too," I reply.

About the Author

E Chapman lives in leafy Surrey with her husband, two young children, a dog and two cats. Whilst working in finance, E Chapman found a love for writing and penned her debut novel, *Stood Up*. In her spare time, when she isn't writing, E. Chapman enjoys ballroom dancing.

Acknowledgements

To my friends, Fiona C, Sarah B and Sarah W – the fiercest cheerleaders a girl could ask for. Thank you for believing in me and pushing me.

For Mum – who endured every plot update, doubt, and creative crisis with endless patience. Thank you.

For my daughter, age 10 – keeper of secrets and expert winker. And for my son, age 7, and my husband – surprise! I wrote a book.